Second Lives

Leon Archer

ISBN 978-1-63525-747-2 (Paperback)
ISBN 978-1-63525-748-9 (Digital)

Christian Faith Publishing, Inc.
296 Chestnut Street
Meadville, PA 16335
www.christianfaithpublishing.com

Printed in the United States of America

1

THE ALUMNI BANQUET

Sitting alone in his car at the far corner of the school parking lot, Roland left the rented vehicle running for the comfort of the air-conditioning. It was a sultry afternoon, too hot to have the windows down; and even though the huge coppery sun was now sinking lower into the gauzy haze of the west, it still felt like a sauna outside on the blacktop. Off to his right stood a large unfamiliar brick-faced building that housed the gymnasium. He only knew that was what it was because of the large GYMNASIUM emblazoned above the doors. It had been erected years after he had graduated.

It stood where there had once been a playground plus an adjacent area of scattered trees, scrub brush, and sumac. That overgrown land was not part of the school grounds; it belonged to Old Mr. Ridgeway. They were not supposed to go there, so of course, it became sacred ground for him and his friends, and they would sneak away to wander there during recess if the teachers didn't catch them. It was where he and his childhood friends engaged in mock pirate sword fights like they had seen on the silver screen, only using maple saplings and sumac branches for swords, and it was where he got his first kiss (as a fourth grader) from a girl named Mary.

He turned the engine off and stepped outside. The heat clutched at him immediately. There was no breeze, and the air was still stifling; sweat quickly began to pop out on his forehead. He walked over to a wooden bench at the edge of the parking lot and sat down. Closing his eyes, he tried to visualize what it had been like during all those years when he had been a student at the Bradley Central School. For a moment he thought, *Man, I feel like a Plains Indian seeking a vision in a sweat lodge.*

At first there was nothing but the penetrating heat and the shrill sound of cicadas singing. He attempted to peer into the past, seeking that which was but could not be changed, finding not visions but rather a dark blankness, no sign posts, no touchstones, nothing to guide his quest. It wasn't until in his mind's eye, he began to focus on his present location that an image actually appeared, but it was the gymnasium. He was stuck in the present, desperately seeking the past, hoping to better understand the present and see a path into an uncertain future.

He stopped trying to intentionally capture the past or force it into focus. It wasn't working. The thoughts and amorphous intentions that still gripped his mind and had brought him back to Bradley were interfering. He shivered in the heat. Letting go—at least for the moment—of the angst that he had allowed to permeate his thinking, he felt a pleasant growing release. He relaxed as the image of the gymnasium disappeared and the huge blacktop parking lot reverted to a playground and the forbidden sacred grove.

Visions beyond his control, without apparent rhyme or reason, now appeared and dissolved in irregular succession. A narrow gravel driveway appeared leading from school street to the small rectangular staff parking lot next to the school. Swings on the playground came into view, where he had once tried to swing so high that he could loop over the pipe above. Sherry Miller watched him as he attempted the impossible, and when he accepted defeat and came back to earth, she laughed at him.

Laughter faded into a vision of the library. He loved to read, but he also whispered with his friends. The librarian sent him out for talking. Sherry Miller laughed. The scene faded and then became a classroom with everyone standing along the wall for a spelldown. He misspelled a word and sat down to the snickering of Sherry Miller, who had been standing next to him.

In the following scene, he was standing, blowing through the new harmonica he had gotten for his birthday from his Uncle Leon. Sherry noticed and asked if he could play it.

"Sure," he answered and began to puff out some unconnected notes. Sherry laughed and walked away.

George Butler loomed up with him in the vision. They were talking about Sherry Miller, the prettiest girl in their class.

"Pig Latin," George was saying, "ouyay ovelay erryshay illermay, you love Sherry Miller. Do you get it?"

The vision faded into another, one of Sherry Miller looking right in his face saying, "Ouyay, ovelay, erryshay illermay," and she was laughing at him again.

The school cafeteria swam into view. He was a freshman walking toward his friends with a tray full of food when his foot hit something slippery and the tray and food went flying landing on the floor right next to Sherry Miller. He would have been embarrassed enough without her laughing.

Laughing. Laughing. He was jerked from the vision, hot and angry, to the sound of two women walking across the parking lot toward the school, laughing and talking as they went. He left the bench and climbed back into the car and started the engine. It felt sooo good as the air conditioner kicked in and the cool air massaged him, wicking away the moisture on his body.

I'll cool down a bit, he thought. *I can see, and I can think, and I can remember from in here. There's no sense in cooking.*

As he became more comfortable, he started observing more carefully and thinking more clearly.

So much had changed; very little looked familiar. It had been so long since he had left, and he had never once returned. His mother and father had moved to Florida to escape the frigid-lake effect of snow-filled winters, leaving little to draw him back. As he gazed around, he tried to tell himself that he wasn't really sure why he had come for the reunion. After all, he had missed what had been billed as "The Very Important Twenty-Fifth-Year Class Reunion" ten years before.

No, he thought, *I didn't miss it, I chose not to go. There's a difference. And I chose not to attend the thirtieth, and I'm not really sure why I'm bothering with this one—partly curiosity, I guess.*

Nervously tapping his fingers on the steering wheel, he knew it was more than curiosity that had brought him back to Bradley.

His class hadn't been all that large—fifty-seven students. Small towns with small centralized schools had a tendency to turn out good students, but not in big numbers, and Bradley Central could have served as the blueprint for all small schools. He had a couple of good friends in his class, but no one that he could ever claim as extremely close. He had never made waves—actually enjoyed school for the most part, did his homework, and managed As and Bs without much effort. He had never felt a need to excel in high school, leaving that to those who seemed to be more driven to do so.

He had enjoyed sports and had been on the varsity football and baseball teams. He hadn't been so hot at basketball and never tried to improve because basketball just didn't appeal to him, but he could hit a baseball or a softball farther than anyone else in the school. He had been a reasonably good outfielder with an uncanny ability to throw a one-bounce strike to home plate from just about anywhere in the outfield, much to the surprise and discomfort of quite a number of runners.

The thing he liked doing most was fishing. His mind had been focused on bullhead season, trout season, pike season, bass season, and in the winter, ice fishing season. He was never happier than when he had a fishing rod in his hands. A momentary smile crossed his face as he thought of those days when life was so simple, so long ago.

As he watched and reminisced, people were arriving and then disappearing into the side door of the school. Out of nowhere, he began to feel a growing sense of melancholy instead of expectation. He saw people of all ages, some in their teens and some that were quite elderly. The alumni banquet would be attended by graduates from many classes—not just his—while the reunion the next day would bring together only his classmates and some spouses for a picnic and reminiscing.

How different the school looks now, he mused, observing how numerous building projects had added here or subtracted there. Still, for someone who had attended when the building was much smaller, the original basic square structure could be perceived—even after it had been wrapped in the added wings and alcoves.

I don't really want to do this, he thought.

Just as he was thinking about putting the car in gear and leaving it all behind, he happened to recognize one of his old friends walking toward the entrance, perhaps his best friend. They had spent many wonderful hours fishing and hunting together, and suddenly, it seemed like only yesterday. The weight began to melt off his shoulders as he drew a deep, healing breath. Some of the uneasy feelings faded. He hadn't seen Bob since high school, and it would be worth the evening if for no other reason than to have the chance to talk with him.

Still, he knew there was another reason why he was in that parking lot outside the school, and it had little to do with old friends or the reunion and banquet. It had lured him from across the years and across the country, and now it was the cause of a tumult inside his head and his chest. There was no denying it; he knew he was here because of Sherry Miller. For some time now, whenever he looked at a woman, Sherry's face had come unexpectedly into his mind. That might not have been unusual if it had not been for the fact that Sherry had the distinction of being one of the very few people that he really didn't like. Yet she had the power to bring him three thousand miles to an alumni banquet and class reunion, and he was having a difficult time dealing with that.

Realizing it would be foolish to turn back now, he stepped out of the car and made his way to the side door, which appeared to be the proper entrance for the evening.

Walking through the door and down the brightly lit corridor, he moved to the sound of people's voices. As he arrived outside the school cafeteria where the dinner was to be held, the first people from his class that he saw were Adele Mapleton and Margie Terkoski, wearing name tags that identified them as Adele Mapleton Marley and Marge Terkoski Knowlton. The still-petite Adele was wearing a diamond that dwarfed her dainty ring finger, while the now-plump Margie wore no ring at all—although there was a noticeable, light-colored indentation where a wedding ring had probably rested for most of the past thirty-five years. They were the kind of things that he had begun noticing recently.

Adele smiled and said, "Hi, Ron, we are sure glad you could make it. It's been a long, long time. A lot of the class is here." Reaching out, she handed him a name tag.

He glanced at the tag, which had his high school graduation photo on it. It startled him for just a moment because the picture looked so much like his son, Bryce.

"Thanks, Adele," he replied, surprised that she would have remembered his high school nickname.

It took him back to those high school days of yore. He had been called Ron by a few of his friends, though his name was Roland. He had preferred Ron, but over the ensuing years, the apparently more impressive Roland had become his only handle. His class had voted him *most likely to have ten kids and live in the Bradley countryside down near the creek.* He didn't know which idiot on the yearbook staff had come up with that prediction, but it had been so wide of the mark that it was off the map.

Instead of remaining in Bradley, Roland had gone to college, partly because it was the thing to do and partly just to get away from his hometown. Entering college as a liberal arts major, he changed to business at the end of his freshman year. That change was one of the best decisions he had ever made.

He had never been very suave when it came to the ladies in high school. While he had lusted after several pretty Bradley girls, his social graces had been far from perfect, and getting dates sometimes proved frustrating. Then he had what he thought was the fantastic good fortune of landing a date with Sherry Miller, the most beautiful creature in Bradley. Asking her out was one of the few times that he did something on a dare that worked out well—or so it seemed at the time.

Sherry had a great figure and long blond hair that shimmered in the sun. With her looks, she could have been mistaken for a star in one of the surfing or beach party movies that were sweeping the nation. Every boy in school was smitten by her, but most of them just worshipped her from afar and talked about her whenever they got together in their raunchy all-male groups. It was in the locker room before a baseball game that one of the guys called Roland on a whimsical brag about being able to get a date with any girl he wanted and dared him to ask Sherry for a date. She was so beautiful that Roland was overawed at the prospect of even asking for a date with her, but he was trapped by the male code of the dare. Finally, mustering up his courage, he had done the impossible and asked her for a date; and unbelievably, she had accepted.

Spending nearly every cent he had to his name, he had taken Sherry out for dinner and a movie. Feeling incredibly awkward, thanks to his lack of experience with girls, when he talked, it was mostly about familiar things—himself and fishing. After the movie, a six-mile ride back to Bradley on a Greyhound bus, and a short walk to Sherry's home—he went for broke and bravely suggested a good night kiss. She had laughed at him.

"Thanks for a nice evening, Roland, but I don't make it a habit of kissing anyone on a first date."

That might not have been so bad except afterward, Sherry told all her friends about turning him down and about what a loser she thought he was. He didn't know about anything but fishing. After that, it seemed like everywhere he turned, someone was snickering. Even the guys had razzed him. Now thirty-five years later, he could still feel the sting, and he knew it had something—maybe even everything—to do with his being in Bradley for the reunion.

Perhaps the memory of being turned down for a kiss could have been easily forgotten, but being fingered as a loser by Sherry had left such an unbelievably sour taste in his mouth that all the intervening good years could not erase it from his mind—even though it had hibernated for many years only to be awakened by the latest reunion invitation. It made no sense to harbor such a thing, and in his better self, he knew it. It was a curse that he had to find a way to lay to rest, but he had never been able to find a resolution to the resentment that still dogged him after all the years. That was why after pondering the reunion invitation, he had told himself that the only cure lay in Bradley, and it was time to set things right and get Sherry Miller out of his head.

2

Roland's Life
After Bradley

Following graduation, he enrolled in the University of Pennsylvania. Possibly because of his high school social life, or lack thereof, he had poured himself into his university studies while other guys wasted themselves carousing and making out with every coed that fell under their spell. Whatever the reason, it led to a rewarding 4.0 GPA, but he wanted to switch his major to business at the close of his freshman year. He had been extremely fortunate to find entrance into the Wharton School of Business at the university, where he rapidly developed a rock-solid grasp of finances that often astounded his professors. Leaving the university four years later with an MBA and a load of debt, he was ready to discover whatever the world had to offer.

He had not picked up a girlfriend in college, so other than college bills, he had no new baggage when he left. He had headed for the West Coast, drinking in the countryside and sights that he had never seen before. As fate would have it, the first place he paused for more than a day after graduation was in Mavis, and the rest became history.

He had his sights set on Seattle or Portland. He had never been to the West Coast, but it held a mystique for him, and businesses were springing up and growing like weeds. There were some old, well-established giants like Boeing, but he was thinking about new start-up companies where he might have a chance to distinguish himself and grow with them.

Being financially strapped, he had been willing to temporarily interrupt his westward migration when he saw the "Help Wanted" ad for an accountant. He interviewed for the job, and even though they made it a point to tell him that he was way overeducated for the position, they also had an immediate need for someone, and he was hired on the spot. Fortunately for him and his employer, he liked the work and the people he worked with, and above all, he was very good at what he did.

Mavis had been a sleepy Great Lakes city surrounded by vast expanses of forests. It had retained a small-town feel even as it had grown over the years into a decent-sized bustling city, but changes had been coming to the whole area south of Superior, and Mavis was feeling the effects as well. Industries and jobs were closing or leaving the area. Even though the city was feeling some stress, Roland felt comfortable there, but he never intended to stay in Mavis for long. The West Coast remained his destination, and he made no attempt to hide the fact that he planned to move on after a year or so. His boss, recognizing a good thing when he saw it, had given him a good raise and was able to persuade him to stay for at least a second year. It was then that the next life-changing event came about.

How he got involved in that first political campaign always remained a little fuzzy in his mind. He had worked in Mavis as an accountant for a little more than a year when somehow he had been hoisted onto the minority ticket by some of his politically minded friends to fill a spot, most likely open because it was a losing slot and no one else wanted it. It was a lark for those who persuaded him to run, but once committed, Roland quickly decided he would at least try to make a real effort and mount a reasonable campaign. While his friends mostly lost interest once he had made the ballot, he set to examining the workings and projects of the current administration.

The mayor running for reelection was an odds-on favorite. Most people seemed to have a favorable opinion of the man, while almost no one even knew who Roland was. Being unlikely to garner even 5 percent of the vote, his political career probably would have begun and ended in one anonymous campaign if it hadn't been for a new revelation: the mayor had lost a considerable sum of money gambling at an Indian casino, but more importantly, his bankroll had come from the city coffers. It had started small but rapidly got out of hand as the mayor tried ever more frantically to break even. When everything hit the fan, the casino was close to half a million ahead.

Even then, the election might not have dropped into Roland's lap, but incredibly, as the investigation of the current mayor was in full swing, the next likely official the mayor's party picked to fill his shoes and his slot on the ticket was soon discovered during the investigation to have had his hands in the city's pockets as well. The details were still being disclosed, and being so close to the election, there was still a chance that the latest scoundrel might win just the same. Roland campaigned the last few weeks on a platform of honesty and integrity and put forward some plausible, concrete ideas about how the city could begin to recoup some of its losses. People listened, liked what they heard, and when election day came, just barely more than half of those voting decided to give him a chance.

After being sworn in, he had worked assiduously to repair the city's financial foundation without laying the burden on the taxpayers. He spent countless hours assisting the city council in the task while tightening controls and making sure no embezzler would ever find it so easy to dip into city funds again. But even more importantly, he laid out a vision for reviving the city and bringing new tourism to the area. He had managed to gain the ear of the CEOs of a few companies, and they were each leaning toward opening branches in Mavis. He did so well that after his first two-year term, he was swept back into office by a landslide for two more years.

Early in his second term, he had begun working closely with US Senator Thornton, finding ways to win some grants to help bring his vision and wide-ranging concepts to fruition. The future was looking bright for Mavis and for Roland.

He worked well with the city council and seldom found himself at odds with them. He also considered John Crawford, the county chairman, a personal friend as well as being very important to the city. They found each other easy to work with, and Roland usually spent several hours each week in John's office. It was not a difficult thing because for reasons of economy, the city and the county shared the same office building. The arrangement paid great dividends to Roland, John, the county, the city council, and most importantly, the citizens of Mavis and the surrounding area.

One of the reasons he often gravitated to John's office had little to do with the city's or the county's business. John's secretary was young, very attractive, and single. He found her easy on the eyes and her voice pleasing to the ears, and every time he was near her desk, his heart beat so loudly that he thought she must certainly hear it. For her part, she was always pleasant but never seemed to be anything more than businesslike in any conversation she had with him.

It seems that Betty, without trying, was able to flip the switch that had been turned off years before by Sherry Miller. When he finally admitted to himself that he had to get to know her better, it took him several weeks trying to come up with a plan that would ensure she would accept an invitation to dinner and not pass it off with a laugh. His infatuation with her was so strong that it could crowd out other thoughts and duties, which led to an embarrassing situation for him.

He had found it increasingly difficult to keep his mind on city business. Thinking of her was consuming him, and he needed to really get to know her better. She might have a boyfriend. She might not have any interest in him at all. She might pass his approach off with a laugh, but he had to know. He finally decided the best approach was just to do it and let the cards fall where they might. Though he was now a man of at least modest means, good reputation, and comfortable position, he still was apprehensive when he put everything else out of his mind and approached Betty at her desk, asking her if she would like to join him for dinner that evening.

She gave him such a strange look, which in his heart he was already preparing himself to be rejected, and he almost answered, "Well, thanks anyway," before she replied, "Why, I'd be honored, Mr. Mayor."

It would have been hard to describe his feelings at that moment. Perhaps it could be said that he was elated, relieved, scared, and in love all at the same millisecond. Walt Disney would have called it "twitterpated." He felt like his feet were no longer touching the ground, and for a moment, he stared at her with a foolish grin on his face. He wondered if she could, indeed, hear his heart pounding. When he started breathing again, he set a time to pick her up but then nearly forgot to ask for her address and if the time would be convenient. Once again her eyes indicated that she found the encounter still a bit strange, but she was smiling nonetheless.

As he left for his office, his mind was racing on ahead. Where would he take her? Should he get her flowers? Or would that be presumptive or overkill? What should he wear?

Oh, good grief, he thought. *What if I'm wearing a suit and she is dressed casual, or if I dress casual and she is dressed up? She probably thinks I'm an oaf. No wonder she looked so puzzled.*

He would call her as soon as he was back in his office. He didn't want any loose ends or any awkward moments because somehow, he knew deep down in his soul that he was going to marry Betty. He felt a desire for her that made his chest feel like it would explode at any moment.

"Roland, are you okay? Roland?"

He was jerked back out of his reverie by the voice and found he had been navigating city hall without consciously seeing anyone or anything, like a lake boat in the fog.

"Sorry, Ralph, I was lost in thought there for a minute."

It was his secretary, Ralph Lutz.

"Thinking about tonight, eh? That's good."

"Wait a minute, Ralph, you know about tonight? I didn't realize the news could possibly travel quite that fast."

He noticed that Ralph also gave him a puzzled look. "Are you sure you are okay, boss? We've been working on tonight's meeting for weeks now. Of course, I know."

His head nearly exploded. "Oh, the meeting, yes. I'm fine, everything is fine. We are all set, right?" he fumbled.

"Ah, yeah. Well, anyway, we know there will be some very influential people there—including, of course, the governor and Senator Thornton. I have a final confirmation from them. Business and banking is going to be even better represented than we had hoped. It looks like everyone is thinking about hopping on the bandwagon, but you never know. You will need a majority of them in your corner if the whole revitalization project is going to gel, especially the governor and Thornton. They are the key. I'm sure you'll be at your best tonight. You have a real way with words. Well, I've got a few minor details I need to finish taking care of," he said as he started to walk away.

"Yeah, I've got some details to take care of too," Roland mumbled, his shoulders sagging.

How could he have possibly forgotten the revitalization meeting was tonight even for a moment? It was impossible! No wonder Betty had looked so puzzled. Yes, he had everything prepared and the plans were all settled, but how could something so big and important go completely out of his head? Talk about awkward, here it was in spades. Then as utter despair fell cold and gray around him, from somewhere— perhaps from his guardian angel—the only solution came to him.

He hurried to his office and dialed her number.

"Hi. Betty? This is Roland Holtz. Look, I was so pleased that you accepted my invitation that I left out some very important details. You must be aware that I have a meeting with the Revitalization Committee and Senator Thornton. It's more of a social affair where we can all pat each other on the back, while the real feelings, questions, and concerns of all parties can be shared off the record prior to the actual business meetings. We won't make any overt big pitches, and we won't conduct any actual business on the surface. It gives us a chance to chew on things a bit and know where people stand and meet some of the movers and shakers that are never part of our official meetings but have a lot to do with how everything will turn out. It's all on the up and up, and even the press will be there to keep us honest."

He paused for a moment before continuing, "I'm afraid I didn't make myself very clear when I asked you, but what I'd like is for you to attend everything with me. There is nothing wrong with a secretary at the meeting. After all, Ralph will be there too. Though it's an informal meeting, it will still be a semiformal occasion, so dress for it. I'll pick you up at six thirty instead of six o'clock. There will be shrimp cocktail and lots of finger foods followed by a prime rib dinner. I hope all that will be okay with you."

He listened to her favorable reply, and once again, he was floating in air. *What a woman*, he thought.

That evening, Betty looked stunning. She took his breath away, and his heart had begun pounding once again when she came to the door. Later, he felt like a prince as he introduced her to friends and associates she might not know, as well as Governor Swenson and Senator Thornton. She was demure, smiling, unobtrusive, yet nearly always nearby. Her eyes were twinkling, but she seemed to be more interested in the people and the gala surroundings than in the mundane give-and-take. He had no idea that all that time, she was cataloging everything that people around him were saying, missing nothing of import—be it words, expressions, body language, or feigned support. In days to come, she would be more valuable to him than he could even begin to comprehend at that moment.

Later that evening, she consented to a quiet drink at Michael's Bistro to just relax and visit.

She had broken the ice when she said to him, "Mr. Mayor, you forgot you had that meeting tonight when you first asked me to dinner, didn't you?" Her eyes were dancing, and a disarming smile played across her face.

For just a moment, he was tempted to deny it, bluff his way through it, but then admitted, "Yes, I was like a schoolboy. I have been wanting to ask you out for some time, and today asking you out to dinner had been crowding everything else out of my mind. I know it may not seem probable or even possible, but as dumb as it seems, that's the truth."

She looked intently into his eyes, smiled, and said, "I like you, Mr. Holtz, you didn't try to weasel your way out of that. You appear to be an honest politician, a rare commodity these days, unfortunately."

"Well, you've got it partly right, Betty, and as long as we aren't in the office or on official business, call me Roland, not Mayor or

Mr. Holtz. But I have to confess, I was desperately looking for a way to explain my faux pas when I called you to straighten out the date information. I was fudging it. I said I left out some details, but apparently, you saw right through my attempt to not appear the fool. But more to the point, the truth is, I'm no politician, honest or otherwise. I can do the job well enough, but as hard as I work at it, and as much as I like seeing things work out, my heart isn't really in it. I don't intend to continue on as mayor, even if the revitalization deal is a resounding success, and I'm confident it will be."

She protested, "Roland, you are the one making this all work, and everyone will expect that you will direct the project from the mayor's office. Don't you think you have to consider the people as well as yourself?"

He took a small sip from his drink and replied, "I'm not going to leave before my term is up, but I am reasonably sure that by then, everything will be in place. I'm hardly indispensable. There's no doubt that the whole project will be great for all the area around Mavis and the lakeshore, but the council and a new mayor will be able to steer it from there. Once the deal is done and everything is firmly on track, I plan to announce that I'm not going to run for a third term. I'm not exactly sure what I'm going to do." He continued, "But if I am going to be completely honest, I first have to be true to myself."

He went on to tell her how he had been planning on going to the West Coast in search of a position with a good business before he had become sidetracked in Mavis. He shared about some of the companies he had thought might be ones he could fit in with. He made it clear that it had never been his intention to find a career in politics, nor to settle down in the Midwest. It had just sort of started happening, and if he didn't escape now, he wasn't sure he could ever do it; and that thought had unsettled him, left him feeling trapped.

She said, "Roland, you know the people here really, genuinely like you, and I'm sure they expect you will be around for some time. You have all kinds of support for the project, but without you and without some careful choices and wise shepherding, it could still fall apart before it ever gets firmly established. There are people out there and in our midst that see this whole thing as an opportunity to advance and enrich themselves, and they are only onboard for what's in it for them. Fortunately, the majority of the people whom you have enticed with your vision are mainly in it for the people, their constituents, but every one of them still has their own agenda and their own hang-ups and their own concerns or questions."

He nodded in agreement. "I know there are some loose ends still, but I was hoping that most concerns could at least be identified by tonight's meeting so we could start addressing them before we started to hammer things out. I know I learned a lot tonight."

She continued to probe, "What's in this for you if you are not going to run for mayor again?" she asked.

"I don't know, I guess the great feeling of accomplishment that comes with a big job well done. I didn't go into this with the idea that I was going to personally profit from it. I just wanted to make things better for the citizens of Mavis, and I wanted to put some of my business ideas into practice. I know that when I got the two colleges and the county hospital interested in joining in with business leaders to meet local needs and spur employment while at the same time allowing those entities to develop their own local branch offerings—I was on a high. And when I got the new businesses to locate here, especially the plastics manufacturing facility, it took me three days to come back down to earth. You know those things already being in place helped anchor the whole plan. It provided some concrete examples of what we could do if we really wanted to put our minds and our money to work."

"So you are going to leave with nothing other than your suitcase and a good feeling when this is all over? Is that what you are telling me?" she asked.

"Betty, the things I will take away from this have nothing to do with where Mavis will go from here, and they won't cost the people or the government a single red cent. I admit that I have made a number of invaluable friendships and contacts that may prove very useful in the future, but that just happened as a natural course of events, it was never my purpose," he said.

He further admitted to her that he had already received a couple of offers of employment from out of the blue in recent weeks that might prove rather lucrative and that one of them had really appealed to him. He indicated that he hadn't made any decisions or commitments yet. However, if the revitalization proposal became reality, he was going to have to make a choice. But he had already decided his choices wouldn't include the mayor's office.

He eventually came back to the present situation by reviewing the progress and current status of the revitalization proposal, not exactly what one should do on a date, but he couldn't help himself. He told her that he felt like everything was ready to fall into place and that it seemed there were few, if any, reservations among the stakeholders.

After his rendition, she stared, contemplating her nearly empty glass. "I believe I'd like a second drink, would you like another?"

He picked up his half-full glass and swirled the liquid around before replying, "I'm not much on drinking. I almost never have more than one glass of anything, even beer or wine, but this Tom Collins has gotten pretty warm, so yes, I could go for one more," and he motioned to the waiter.

Once she had the cold glass in her hands, she looked around the nearly empty restaurant. She took a couple of small sips, looking at him thoughtfully, and her eyes narrowed as she said, "May I offer you some insights from tonight's meeting?"

It was well over an hour later when the owner came to their table and told them he was sorry but he was going to be closing soon. Looking around, they could see chairs on tables that should have been an early hint, and there were no other patrons left in the restaurant. Roland left a sizeable tip on the table. He figured it came to peanuts for what he had received during the last hour. He might have learned a lot at the meeting, but it had become worth infinitely more thanks to Betty.

3

THE MAYOR'S LADY

Monday morning, Mr. Crawford came to Betty's desk and told her that the mayor wanted to see her in his office. Looking at her, he shrugged his shoulders, indicating he had no idea why the mayor wanted to see her. His secretary ushered her directly in when she arrived, closing the door behind her as he left them together.

"Betty, have a seat," he began. "First of all, I want to tell you, I had a marvelous time Friday night, much better than I ever would have had without you, but I spent the rest of the weekend thinking about what you shared with me. With your ability to see beyond the surface of what's happening and what is being said, you are wasting your talents where you are. I intend to get together with the council and explore the possibility of creating a temporary position of special adviser to the mayor's office. I would also like to suggest to them that you be hired to fill the position. I sincerely believe your insight and your ability to read between the lines could be invaluable to me and to Mavis during the months ahead. But before I do anything, I'd like to get together over dinner and explore the possibilities. What do you say?"

"I say this is a sneaky way to ask for a second date, but if the council agrees to such a position, and if I accept, what would my duties be exactly?" she asked. "You know people are going to talk about this?"

"Why should they?"

"I take it you haven't seen the Sunday paper?" she asked more than stated. "We made the front page."

She handed him the paper, and there was his picture with Senator Thornton and Governor Swenson, with Betty near Roland's side. The caption in bold letters was, "THE MAYOR'S LADY?"

"Let me answer you this way, Roland. If you truly do not intend to run again, I am willing to come onboard for the rest of your term, should the council decide it would like me for the job. However, if you have any idea that you might be talked into running again, I won't spoil your chances by taking any position you might offer and possibly leaving you open to gossip, but I can help you either way."

Shortly thereafter, the position of special adviser to the mayor was approved. Over the ensuing six months, the actual start of the revitalization project became a reality, and it ended up being funded well beyond what had been expected. Even in the first stages, it was apparent to everyone that the project would far outstrip the promises that had been made for it. Senator Thornton and Governor Swenson took as much credit as they could for the positive changes that were taking place, but everyone knew that Roland was the inspiration and the driving force behind it all. No one but Roland was aware how much Betty had influenced the final outcome.

Betty, as special adviser, was always at his side and played a huge, unsung part behind the scenes, warning of rough spots and noticing who needed to be stroked, while he reaped the credit for the smooth meshing of all aspects of the project. He was praised by the press, the people, and government officials. There were rumors of a serious move underway to have him run for a seat in the US House of representatives.

In the midst of all the well-orchestrated uproar and gratifying changes swirling about Mavis in a rapidly growing crescendo of construction, jobs, and national recognition, he finally got to what had become uppermost in his mind. One evening, after a full day in the office, he and Betty were having dinner at the restaurant where they had eaten numerous times since that first night.

"Betty, I am convinced that I could not have brought the city to where it stands today without your help. You have been indispensable to me and to the entire project. I appreciate you more than you might realize, even though I have told you time after time how I feel about the practical effects of your insight and judgment. At this point, I have only one question remaining."

"What's that?"

"Will you marry me?"

She looked at him quietly for some moments before she replied, "I have expected this question might be coming perhaps ever since our first date. I have never met anyone quite like you before, and I really like you, but please don't make me give you an answer right now."

It was not the response he had been anticipating, but he was not ready to let it go at that.

"I know that wasn't the most romantic proposal in the world, but I have fallen in love with you, and it has nothing to do with politics, business, or jobs. I would like nothing more than to spend the rest of my life with you. Please don't think about it too long, because if you do, I think I will bust."

"Roland, you are the kindest, most honest, most open person I have ever known, and I'm not saying no, but there are some things you should know about me. We've never talked about ourselves, our past, or our personal lives. We need to do that. At least, I need to do that."

At first, he was tempted to pooh-pooh her answer and tell her he couldn't care less about the past, but he knew her well enough to realize she was dead serious, and making light of it would absolutely be the worst thing he could possibly do.

Instead, he said, "Betty, we deserve a vacation. Do you ski?"

They spent three days at the lodge, skiing a little and sitting a lot in front of the fireplace cuddled up on the couch. It was all on the up and up; they each stayed in their own room. Two days of small talk and simply enjoying one another's company passed quickly. On the third day, she let out a huge sigh and took both of his hands in hers as they sat once again on the couch with no one else around.

Looking into his eyes, she began, "Roland, I've been enjoying this time together so much that I have put off getting to what I really need to talk about. Please don't comment and don't interrupt what I'm saying. I need to get it all out at once, and I need to do it now, or I may never be able to do it."

She brushed away a tear and began, "When I was sixteen, I was raped by an older boy. I don't want to go into all the details, but I tried to fight him off, and I just couldn't stop him. He was apologetic afterward, saying he loved me and he was sorry he got carried away. He took me back to my home and dropped me off. I was so ashamed I could hardly bear it. I didn't tell my mother. I avoided the boy at school, but I began to notice his friends were looking at me and sometimes smirking. One of my friends finally asked me if it was true what the boys were saying, that Charlie and I had had sex. I might better have said yes and let it go at that, but instead, I told her he had raped me. Suddenly, for whatever perverse reason, even my girlfriends began to steer clear of me. It was like I had leprosy."

She brushed away another tear. "Honestly, Roland, I didn't know what to do. I even thought about killing myself. I didn't think things could get any worse, until I found out I was pregnant. There was no way I was going to be able to keep that a secret, so I told my mother the whole story. It was the hardest thing I have ever had to do, but she hugged me and told me it wasn't my fault and tried to assure me that she and my father would take care of it and everything was going to be okay.

"I was terrified that my father might kill the boy for what he had done, but I was terrified even more by what my father might think about me. I couldn't even bear to be in the room with them when he came home and Mother told him what had happened. I hid in my room in my bed while they talked.

"After a while, there was a soft knock on my door, and my father came in and sat down on the edge of my bed. I sat up. I was so frightened. I didn't know what he was going to do, but when I looked at him, he was crying. He took me in his arms, and we both cried. It's the only time I ever saw my father cry. He told me the same thing Mother had: it would be okay."

Her tears were flowing freely now, and her voice started to crack. She paused to take a long, deep, quivering breath before continuing, "I don't know what my father said or did after that evening, but the parents of the boy actually came to our house and apologized for their son and asked me—us—to try to forgive him. I never have. I don't think I ever will."

Then, for an instant, her eyes were steely and angry, but sadness quickly replaced the hard look.

"There weren't places to get a legal abortion, and my parents wouldn't have allowed it anyway. I ended up that summer staying with my Aunt Sue, and my little girl was born early that fall. My mother had suggested before she was born that they could legally adopt her, but when the time came, I felt like I couldn't bear seeing her every day and being reminded about the whole affair. I know Mother was horribly disappointed, but she understood.

"I named her Melissa before I gave her up for adoption. The boy's parents had also expressed an interest in adopting my child or at least being allowed some connections to her as she grew up, but they didn't know when she was born. I gave her up without letting them know. They never saw their grandchild, and I know it hurt them. I wanted to hurt them, and I wanted to hurt their son. It was the last bit of retribution that I could get, but in the end, I think I turned out worse than they did. I have never seen my little girl since the day she was born, and I have wondered about her every day since. My father left for Yankee Station shortly after that.

"When my father's A6 was shot down over Vietnam in early December, we waited to hear if he had been captured or if he was dead. The year 1970 turned out to be the most horrible year of my life, not just because of giving up my daughter that fall, but my mother became extremely ill the week before Christmas after finally learning my father had been declared killed in action. For some time I felt like there was a connection somehow between my father's death, my mother's illness, and my giving up Melissa—like I was being punished by God. I swore right then that I would never let any other man take advantage of me and that I would make my mother proud of me and also my father, no matter where he was.

"I want you to know that you are the first man, other than my father, that I have trusted since I was raped. I had never been out on a date since then up to the night you took me out to the meeting for our first date. I said yes to going out to dinner with you partly because I wanted to see how you would squirm out of it—although, I admit, I thought you were pretty good-looking. Since then I have seen something in you that made me start to think about life again. I am very grateful for that, but I'm not sure I'm ready for marriage yet. Please be patient with me."

She bent over and kissed him softly on the forehead. He responded by lifting her right hand and kissing it before making any comment.

Then he said, "I don't blame you for the bitterness you have had or the things you did because of it. I am almost overwhelmed that you trusted me, but I am extremely grateful that you did. With your permission, I am going to continue to wine and dine you during the months ahead as we finish our duties in Mavis. I cannot imagine anyone else in my life other than you, and I'm going to do my best to get you to say yes, no matter how long it takes."

After that weekend, their conversation turned more often to sharing about the places they would like to visit and the things they would like to do and what was really important to them. Haltingly at first but steadily, she fell more in love with Roland and secretly began to wish they had more time for themselves. And just as steadily but not so slowly, she began desiring a man in her life and all that entailed. Not just any man, she knew only Roland would do. Her body quivered when he held her, and she wanted more, so much more. What a boy had once forcibly taken from her, she yearned to give freely to Roland. She knew she was in love, and she desired him with her whole being. But something continued to hold her back, and she kept her feelings under wraps by working even harder and thinking about the city's needs instead of her own.

They worked well together, watching his vision for Mavis come to pass, but more and more, the machinations of politics began to stalk the city as the successes of the revitalization project grew one upon another. His local party was gearing up for another Holtz landslide, while some were looking to bigger things for Roland. It seemed others were making plans for him, totally unaware that he was making plans of his own.

One evening, as they were finishing a quiet dinner at their favorite restaurant following a busy day at the office, almost in a whisper, he began sharing about the direction things were going politically.

Shaking his head, he said, "Betty, I am getting a lot of pressure to run for Congress. Even Senator Thornton . . ." She put her hand on his and a cautionary finger to her lips.

She quickly looked around the restaurant. It was a slow Monday night, and there were only a few people near them, and none of them seemed to have any interest in what they might be saying.

She whispered, "Let's get our bill and go to my place and talk about this. There might be hungry ears here."

The waiter came to their table and asked if they had enjoyed the meal and if they would like the dessert menu.

"The meal was excellent, as usual," Roland said, "but we are going to pass on dessert tonight. Would you bring the bill please?"

In the security of Betty's living room, he enumerated the benefits and the future of running for Congress.

He started where he had left off at the restaurant, "Senator Thornton believes I am a shoo-in for a seat in the House, and he is pushing me to run. The senator also told me in confidence that he is planning to retire in four more years at the end of his term and that he would do everything in his power to see I took his place in the Senate when that time came. As far as the House, the party seems to be in agreement with him, and I know it's an honor that they want me, but even if I knew I would definitely become a senator in good time, I'm not at all sure it's where I want to go."

He went over all the pluses that becoming a member of the House and then a senator could bring, all the while knowing in his heart it was not what he wanted. She listened patiently until he asked her how she would feel if he turned down an almost sure thing.

Finally getting her chance, she began with a disclaimer, "Roland, I appreciate you asking me, but in the end, this is a decision you have to make for yourself. However, since you did ask me how I would feel if you turned down this opportunity, I'll tell you.

"I have been aware of the pressure that you have been getting. In fact, two people even came to me, hoping I could somehow encourage you to toss your hat into the ring. I know you well enough to know that you are not going to allow anyone to persuade you to do something you don't feel is right, and I certainly wasn't going to try. The one thing I hadn't been sure of was whether your determination to get out of politics would change when you began considering the prestige of the position and what you might do for our state and the country from it."

She paused for a moment, studying his face, and then continued, "If I am reading you correctly, you really *don't* want to stay in politics just like you told me, but the fact that you just said you weren't sure if it's where you want to go indicates to me that you still haven't completely given up the idea, even though I'd like to think you have. However, if you do accept the challenge, I'm sure you will be elected, and I will do everything I can to see that it happens."

Again she observed his face for the effect of her words before continuing, "So how do I feel? If you turn down this opportunity, I'll think you are crazy. Such a chance may never come again. But on the other hand, I have been watching you struggle with this decision, and to be completely candid, I believe you should follow your heart. Personally, I have had enough of politics, and I've been hoping you had had enough as well."

He breathed a lot easier after she intimated that she had believed for some time that his heart wasn't in it and she had told him that, for what it was worth, neither was hers. There was dismay from other quarters when he announced that he was not going to run again for mayor, even though many consoled themselves, believing they would be voting for him for the US House of Representatives.

Later there was utter, stunned disbelief when true to his word to Betty, he announced he was not going to run for Congress. He thanked the people profusely for their trust and support but told them he was ready to go back to private life. The only one who was not filled with dismay and disbelief was Betty, and that was when she said yes.

4

NEW LIFE TOGETHER

It had hardly been a storybook courtship. She had struggled with painful memories, and even after discretely sharing her past with Roland and feeling the woman inside her coming to life again, there were times when panic threatened to overwhelm her. Once she said yes, she had felt a release from the tension that had been gripping her, and from that moment on, their relationship blossomed and deepened into something new and very special.

In the end, they both knew what they wanted, and they both believed they had found it. A week after leaving office, they were married, and he believed he was happier than any man has a right to expect to be. Betty, for her part, knew the love of her life was truly in her arms and in her heart, 'til death do them part, and all the loathsome scars of having been raped were fading into nothingness. A year later their son, Bryce, was born, and two years after Bryce, Melissa arrived, named in memory of the girl Betty would never see again.

During that time, they had made two moves, and Roland had discovered he was in his element. Their third move found him taking over as CEO of a struggling business, which soon would be the fastest growing company in Houston, Texas. He had made it a principle to keep business separate from the rest of his life, but once the children were both in preschool, he asked Betty to join him at work, and in good time, she was officially brought onboard as a personal secretary to the CEO.

She sat in on meetings, both in-house and with clients, observing, saying nothing. It was through her sixth sense and keen observations that she proved the most valuable, as had been the case in Mavis. They were a perfect pair at work and with their family.

They took family vacations on Whidbey Island in Puget Sound. Betty's mother still lived in Oak Harbor, where she had stayed after her husband was lost over Vietnam. It had been the home of his squadron. Betty introduced him to crabbing for the big, tasty Dungeness crabs and trolling for Chinook and silver salmon. He bought a boat that he left in Oak Harbor just for such occasions. They even bought a piece of property where they could build a house in the future.

Betty had said, "I wouldn't mind living right here now, but it is a long commute between Whidbey and Houston. Maybe we could look for a company in Seattle."

It seemed life could not get any better.

The twelve years flowing from the time they spent that first evening in the bistro talking became the most wonderful, most fulfilling years that either of them had ever known. Betty used to say that it was like Camelot, only ten times better. By the time Bryce was five, they had begun to take their children to church each Sunday. They both believed in the value of good morals, and church seemed a natural avenue to help build them in their children. Roland always tried to maintain a low profile in the congregation, but it was difficult. They gave generously and attended faithfully, but over time, something always seemed to be missing.

One evening, after the children were in bed, Betty sat down by her husband and asked, "How do you feel about our church? I mean, why are we there?"

He looked a bit puzzled as he put down his book. "You know, it's strange that you should ask that because I've been asking myself the same question. We go every Sunday, and I'm sure some of our offering helps people in need, but I don't feel like I'm getting a whole lot from the sermons."

She continued, "I'll leave it up to you, but I think maybe we might want to check out some other churches. There are a couple closer to us than where we have been going. Maybe we should check them out first."

Leaving as quietly and gracefully as they could, for a while they floated from church to church, visiting for a few weeks in some and getting out as quickly as they could from others. At times they went for a short period without attending any church at all. They discussed returning to the first church they had been in but decided that was not an acceptable solution.

Critiquing churches became a Monday night ritual for them, made somewhat difficult because they weren't completely sure what they were looking for. They talked about size of churches and congregations, the pastors' preaching, programs, and whether it was where they ought to be.

It was by chance that they discovered the church that they were to eventually call home.

Betty was getting her hair done one Monday morning when the hairdresser casually mentioned that she had been very busy lately because her church was having a missions dinner Wednesday evening and that she was in charge of it. As they chatted, she told Betty the dinner was going to be quite a gala affair.

Intrigued, she asked, "What exactly is a missions dinner, and why are you having it?"

The stylist was a wealth of information. Once Betty had gotten her started, she fairly gushed with general information about her church and missions, the missionaries that would be there, and with specific information about the dinner. Then, almost as an afterthought, she offered hopefully, "If you would like to come to the dinner, I think I could get you in. I have planned for a few extra people, and there should be a few more tickets."

"Is it open to children?" she asked.

"Heavens, yes," the stylist said. "How many of you might come in total?"

"There would be four of us, my husband and me and our two children," she said, holding up four fingers.

Then she shared the frustration they had been feeling about finding the right church. For the rest of the session, that and the dinner remained the topic of their conversation. When Betty left, she assured the woman that if there were still tickets, she would see her Wednesday evening at the dinner. She gave the woman her phone number and asked her to call as soon as she knew they could get in.

Once she got home, she called Roland at their office.

"I've just been getting an earful about the Bentwood Christian and Missionary Alliance Church. I think we may be going there for dinner this coming Wednesday. I think it might be the church we have been looking for."

"What do you mean you think we may be going?" he asked.

"Well, it depends on whether they have any room left or not, but I wanted to make sure you didn't make any other commitments for Wednesday night, just in case."

That Wednesday evening, they pulled into the parking lot and surveyed the church. It was attractive, fairly good-sized, but nowhere near as large as their first church. Bryce and Melissa were interested in the other children that were playing outside or walking in with their parents. They were both curious about missionaries, and Roland had to admit that he was interested in seeing them and hearing about what they did.

Several men and women greeted them as they walked in. One lady walked up and greeted them with a big, warm smile.

"Good evening. I don't think I have met you before. My name is Nellie."

Roland introduced himself and Betty and their two children, explaining that they were visitors and had never been there before. Nellie led them over to a table that had church literature on it.

"Here is a brochure that will answer a lot of questions you might have about the church and our programs," she explained as she handed them the neat packet of materials.

While they stood there talking, Nellie reached out and corralled a young couple passing by.

"Hi, Bob, This is Roland and Betty Holtz. Would you give them a tour of the church and show them where dinner is going to be," she said, even as she was surveying the next visitor in her personal mission field.

As it turned out, the couple that Nellie had introduced to them were parents of a boy and girl about the ages of their own children. Joy and Bob Harmon were longtime members of the church and very outgoing. They offered to guide them around and show them the church facilities if they were interested.

The Harmon's youngsters were badgering their parents to let them take Bryce and Melissa to their classroom to see the missionary decorations that they had helped to make. Bob looked at him and asked if it would be okay with them.

"Sure," he answered.

The children headed out with Bryce and Melissa in tow to show them their classroom and the missionary project they were working on.

"They'll be okay," Bob said. "They'll meet us in the fellowship hall before dinner starts. You'll stay for the program after dinner, won't you?"

Betty looked at Roland, and he said, "Sure, we are going to stay. Where is the missionary from?"

"We actually have two missionaries. One is from Irian Jaya, and the other is from Gabon. John Cutts, the missionary from Irian Jaya, will be our speaker tonight. You will like him. He's unusual on the mission field because he flies an ultralight. His mother is Gracie Cutts. She and her husband, Bill, were missionaries who worked in Irian Jaya on a Bible for the Moni People in their own language. She is a wonderful person and an incredible speaker. They wrote a book, *Weak Thing in Moni Land.* You might want to read it after you hear their son tonight."

The dinner and the missionaries were the main topics the children talked about for the next few days, and when he asked if they would like to go to church Sunday at the Christian and Missionary Alliance Church and hear the other missionary, they shouted, "*Yes!*" and it was seconded by Betty.

Soon afterward, he bought the book about the Cutts and read a chapter every night to the kids until it was finished. Every week became a new adventure for the family. Later on, as the children grew older, they loved the youth group on Wednesday evenings, and Roland and Betty enjoyed the small group meeting that gathered at the Harmon's home on Thursday night. Weeks turned into months, and months into years, as they studied the gospel and asked lots of questions. On Sundays they listened to the pastor preach messages that almost invariably seemed to be aimed directly at them. More than once they heard a salvation message, something that they had never been confronted with in other churches they had attended.

One day Betty came in the front door and sat down beside him in their living room and said, "Honey, I've got something to tell you."

"Don't tell me you're pregnant," he half joked.

"No, something even better than that. I've accepted Jesus Christ as my Lord and Savior."

It took Roland a few seconds to digest the information.

"What do you mean exactly?" he asked.

"Well, I admitted that I was a sinner. I told God I was sorry and asked him to forgive me for all my sins and allow me into heaven."

"Betty, you are the kindest, most loving, honest person I have ever known. I wouldn't call you a sinner. God certainly wouldn't keep you out of heaven."

"But remember last Sunday. The pastor said that we have all sinned. I know, we've heard all that before, but I was talking with Joy today. I asked her about it, and she explained it all to me. Now it makes perfect sense, and I know I've been forgiven.

"I never forgave the Jones family for what their son did to me, and I guess in my heart I have never stopped hating them, even though I thought it was gone after we were married, but it was still lurking in the background. Today I forgave them, and now it's like a huge weight has been lifted from my heart. I actually feel sorry for Mr. and Mrs. Jones and for what I did to them when my first Melissa was born. They were good people. What happened wasn't their fault. I feel like I am suddenly really alive. I am going to look them up, tell them I'm sorry, and ask them to forgive me. It's wonderful, dear. You need to accept Christ as well."

That was Monday. On Tuesday Betty sat down with Bryce and Melissa right after dinner and explained to them about Christ's sacrifice and why they needed to accept him. They had some questions, and Roland, listening from the den, had some questions of his own. He followed the conversation and could feel the urgency in her voice. Then he felt his heart jump when first Melissa and then Bryce prayed for God to forgive them and for Christ to come into their lives. Before long, the three of them marched into the room and informed him it was his turn.

"Okay, guys, I tell you what. On Sunday I'll talk to Pastor Bob. I would like to be real clear on what we are doing here."

"Oh, Daddy, don't wait," Melissa pleaded. "What if something happened to you before Sunday, where would you go?"

"Now, don't you worry, nothing is going to happen to me between now and Sunday." But even as he spoke the words, a disquieting sensation of unreasonable foreboding seemed to settle around him. "After all, what can happen in three days?"

Thursday morning he found it impossible to shake the uneasy feeling that had gripped him since Tuesday, and he spent his few free moments during the day thinking about how easily the rest of his family had made their decisions. As strange as it seemed, he knew they were right, but he was struggling with the suddenness of it all. He believed the Bible was God's Word, and he tried to follow the Ten Commandments as closely as he could. He supported the church and gave to the poor, very liberally. He believed Jesus was God's son. He believed that Jesus died on Calvary for the sins of man. Why was it so hard for him to personally do what appeared to be so easy for his family?

That night when the time came for prayer and praise during the small group meeting, Joy beamed as Betty started by sharing with the group that she and the children had accepted Christ as their Lord and Savior that week. Everyone was so excited, and she was asked to share more about how it had happened. He was quietly relieved that in the exuberance over the event, no one thought to ask about him.

His mind was still racing later that evening as he tried to go to sleep. He lay beside Betty, gazing at her as she slept peacefully. She seemed even more beautiful to him than the day he had married her. She had never steered him wrong in anything. He had always listened to her wisdom and advice, which was part of the reason for his success. He knew she was right now.

When he finally drifted off to sleep, he was thinking, *I need to talk with Betty about this tomorrow. I can't wait until Sunday.*

When he woke in the morning, she was already up and off with the children to school. He knew she wouldn't be in the office that day. There was nothing that required her attention, but beyond that, Fridays were normally her own special day, and work seldom impinged on them. Once he arrived at work, he wished she had been there to sort of act as a guide in this spiritual leap of faith. He didn't know what to say. So in his office, sitting quietly at his desk, he just simply asked God to forgive him for his sins and come into his heart as he had for his wife and children.

He wondered at first if he had done it wrong. He didn't really feel any different. He couldn't detect the Lord's presence, but he knew he wanted more than anything else to share with his family the step he had taken.

But that day, in an instant, a drunken driver at four forty-five on Friday afternoon took away the love of his life and their beautiful daughter, Melissa. If it had not been for Bryce, meaningful life would have ended for Roland at four forty-five as well. Instead, as he sat beside a motionless Betty in the hospital room, holding her cold hand. Tears streaming down his face, he recounted to unhearing ears how much he loved her. He promised she would be proud of Bryce, though he knew she had always been proud of their children. When he left the hospital that night, he felt his business days were over, and the agony of his life without Betty and Melissa was just beginning. It would also become a life without church.

He had ignored God's offer for so long, and now just when he had finally come to the point that he personally asked Christ to come into his life, God had ripped his wife and daughter away from him, senselessly destroyed them. God hadn't embraced him. He had slapped him down. His wonderful Betty and his precious Melissa had accepted Christ's forgiveness, and God allowed a drunk to crush the life out of their bodies. What kind of a God would do that?

The funeral was difficult for him. He was glad that Amanda had flown down from Oak Harbor. Bryce needed her, and he needed her as well. No matter what she might have been feeling inside, his mother-in-law was a tower of strength for all of them.

The pastor had come to visit Roland after the funeral and tried to comfort him, but everything fell on deaf ears and a broken heart. The Harmons and other members of the small group did their best to help him through the dark days, but he wasn't looking for help, and he refused to be consoled.

In the months that followed, Bryce had asked to go to church numerous times, but Roland always told him emphatically, "No, we are not going to church," or "Forget about church."

He was not aware that his son prayed for him faithfully every day, but Bryce was reading his Bible and had a tremendous burden for his father.

As soon as it could be accomplished, Roland resigned from his position as CEO. He was given a generous severance payment and some stock options that later became very lucrative. Sometimes he did consulting work for his former company, but though the directors were amazed at what he was able to do for them just as a consultant, he never felt he was as effective as during the days when his adviser had been by his side. For some time, occasional offers of employment would come from large businesses. He had no interest in them.

Most of his time was spent with Bryce. Bryce had become the one constant that made life bearable, and sometimes he would share those offers with him. At first his son asked him why he didn't take one of the jobs.

"Dad, you could make millions of dollars in a few years with these guys," he would exclaim.

He always answered the same way. "Why?" he would ask. "I have all the money I need, all we need, why should I give up my time with you to make more? You are more important to me than all the money all the companies in the world could offer me. Always remember, there is no value in money for money's sake."

When Bryce was fifteen, he and Roland moved to Seattle. Betty had loved Seattle and the sea from the days when her father was stationed at the Naval Air Station on Whidbey Island. Her mother still lived in Oak Harbor. That was the last place she had seen her father before he flew his A6 to his carrier assignment and left for Yankee Station off North Vietnam.

They had vacationed in the city numerous times and usually spent holidays on the island at her mother's home. They had even planned to retire on the island and had a place picked out. So when Bryce told his father that he had a desire to move to the Seattle area, Roland was pleased, as he had been thinking about Seattle for several days before that. It was an eventful move for both of them.

Bryce had inherited his mother's insight and judgment, and like his father, he was as sharp as a tack when it came to finance. With a minimum of help from his father, he already had put together a portfolio that most investors would drool over. Physically, he was tall, well built, and handsome.

It was also shortly after moving to Seattle that Roland had finally given in to his son's renewed requests to go to church. At first Roland almost never attended himself, but Bryce became a popular member of the youth group. He roped his father into being a chaperone for some of the youth activities, and through that he had found new friends and started to join his son for church many Sundays, but his real attitude toward God and religion was still influenced by the loss of his wife and daughter.

They had been very close since the accident, but now their relationship deepened and broadened as Bryce matured. He was always asking his father questions about his family origins and background. Roland had never spent any time looking for information about his and Betty's ancestors, but it became a passion for Bryce and his father. Twice, for a few weeks during summer vacations, they traveled east and visited cemeteries and county archives in search of information about their ancestors and locating their final resting places.

They discovered that one of Betty's ancestors had fought and been wounded in the Battle of Sackett's Harbor in the War of 1812. He had survived, and long after the war, he had been buried in a Lowville, New York, cemetery in the 1840s. They had located his gravestone, and Bryce had made a rubbing of the inscription. The two of them spent many hours doing genealogy searches, reveling in the information they found. Roland told him all the stories that he had ever heard about his family and about himself. So they checked out Roland's family next and found many interesting things—most of all that one of his ancestors had come over on the Mayflower.

Some of Bryce's favorite stories were those Roland told him about Mavis and his days as mayor. As he grew up, Bryce thought about public service, and he thought about college. He and Roland often discussed which schools had the strongest business programs, but he was caught off guard when Bryce—then beginning his junior year in high school—came home one afternoon and asked him if he thought it would be possible to get an appointment to Annapolis.

It must be in the genes, thought Roland.

He had not forgotten that Betty's father had been a naval officer. He had been shot down on a mission over Vietnam. His body had never been recovered, but a picture of a teenage Betty standing proudly beside a handsome naval aviator, her father, rested in a place of honor on his desk, as well as a large picture of her father beside his A6.

It was not difficult for a man with Roland's background and connections to get an appointment for his son, especially since Bryce was a straight A student as well as an accomplished athlete.

Bryce received his appointment to Annapolis. When summer came, Bryce was ready to go, even though he still had some time before he had to report. He and Roland went fishing on the sound for halibut and put out some crab traps for the always tasty Dungeness. It was always more fun to catch the fish and crabs than to purchase them at Pike's Market. While they fished and relaxed, they discussed what the future might hold for each of them. Bryce wasn't sure if he wanted to make a career in the Navy, but he thought it was a possibility, and Roland was equally unsure if he would want to get back into business while Bryce was away. He would certainly have a lot of time on his hands then.

"Why would you do it, Dad?" Bryce would reply to his father's talking about reentering the business world. Then smiling, he would say, "We already have all the money we really need."

5

AFTER ANNAPOLIS

Remembering his son's jibe after he had departed, Roland tried being idle, but it was more difficult than working. It just was not in his nature, and finally, a company made him an offer he couldn't refuse. It wasn't the money. Other offers had been more lucrative, but he felt there was almost unlimited opportunity to lead the company to greater profits while at the same time truly improving the lot of mankind. He believed that, done correctly, with careful planning, people across the globe would reap wonderful benefits as the company grew and expanded. It was a chance to make a for-profit company more profitable while at the same time being almost philanthropic. He was up to the challenge, and long before Bryce had graduated Annapolis, his father had already taken the company well beyond what had been expected of him.

However, he eventually came to the point where his position was no longer a challenge. He couldn't explain it, but once again, he had to move on. The direction and tone that he had brought to the organization would continue if future management was wise and didn't become greedy, but his heart was no longer in it. For some time an ache had been growing; he was so lonesome. For the first time he began to think about the possibility of getting married again, but he just couldn't convert the thoughts into actively looking for women he might like to date.

He decided to sell his home overlooking Alki Beach and move out of Seattle. He had been thinking about moving to Snoqualmie where he would be a little farther from the ocean than he liked, but people there were not overly likely to know who he was if he kept his head down. Maybe there, away from the city, he could begin looking for the right woman.

Price was not a concern for him, but the home he ended up buying was considerably less than the selling price of his Alki home. He bought something that was not huge, but it was still way more than he really needed. He hired someone to clean every other week, and he found a yard care crew to keep the outside looking neat. He thought about a cook, but since Bryce had left, he usually went out to eat, and when he did not, he cooked something simple on the grill. He had a veranda with a grill and a wonderful view of the mountains. He often spent the late afternoon sitting on the veranda, thinking, as he enjoyed a medium rare steak and a cup of coffee.

It was on one of his last visits to see Bryce before he went on active duty when his son said matter-of-factly but gently, "You know, Dad, it's high time you quit blaming God for Mom's and Missy's death."

He had never expressed such a thought to Bryce, but he knew instantly that his son was right. He had blamed God when he wasn't blaming himself. Maybe if he had accepted Christ when his family had begged him to that night, things would have been different. He didn't know. He stared at his son but had no answer for him.

Bryce continued, "Dad, it's time you let God know you're sorry. It's time you ask him to forgive you. He will, you know. You've done everything Mom would have wanted you to do, but that Sunday never came. You turned your back on God because you thought he'd turned his back on you, on us. You don't know it Dad, but I've been praying for you literally every day since Mom and Missy died. I know you will accept Christ. I don't know when, but please be sure to let me know when you do."

Roland wanted to tell his son right then that he had accepted him just before his mother's death, but he couldn't bring himself to admit that he was right. He had been blaming God for their deaths. But instead, he said only, "I'll think about it, son."

Once Bryce was assigned and on duty, Roland returned to Snoqualmie. With a great deal of time on his hands, he began learning to play the bagpipes, something he had always wanted to do. He also started taking painting lessons, and he began to write science fiction. It was a page or two at first, but soon he would turn out several pages at a sitting. Earlier he had purchased a bigger boat for himself and Bryce, and now he would go up to Oak Harbor and take Amanda fishing or crabbing if she would go. Sometimes he would just sit on the boat and paint the time away, but most importantly, he thought about what his son had said. As sort of a peace offering to God and for Bryce's sake, he started regularly attending church.

And it transpired that slowly, this millionaire many times over found some solace, refuge, and purpose in giving to missions and digging into God's Word. He served on boards of several organizations that provided needed services and food both in the United States and abroad. He took time out to fish and travel. He visited Bryce when it was possible and was warmed by the belief that his son had made the right decision. He couldn't help thinking how handsome Bryce was in his uniform and how proud Betty would have been of him, of how proud his grandfather would have been of him. His grandmother was elated.

When the weather was decent, he would drive to the harbor in Seattle just to ride a ferry to some other location on the sound. It didn't really matter where. The longer the trip, the better, because it was the ride and not the destination that he was interested in. He had his own boat, but riding the ferries was one of his favorite things to do when he just wanted time to think and remember. The time on the ocean was always soothing. Sometimes he would drive to Mukilteo and take the ferry over to Whidbey Island to visit his mother-in-law, who still lived in Oak Harbor, where he kept his boat at the marina. Other days he would take one of his two boats out for a day of fishing or crabbing. Waiting while the pots soaked, attracting crabs, gave him plenty of time to think, even paint.

He found himself frequenting the same restaurants, especially for breakfast. He seldom cooked, and often breakfast would find him in a restaurant overlooking the sea, eating a couple of eggs over easy and wheat toast. The servers got to recognize him even though they didn't know who he was. He always left a more-than-generous tip.

Sometimes they would note a faraway look on his face as he sipped his coffee, but they had no clue about the turmoil he was experiencing.

It was one morning on the ferry to Bainbridge, while absentmindedly looking out the window at the choppy water and the blue sky, when he remembered that evening when his wife and children had marched into the room and informed him he needed to accept the Lord. Tears suddenly welled up in his eyes and began to run down his cheeks. He wiped them away, not caring if anyone saw him. How he wished he could have gone back to that Wednesday evening in the den. What a fool he had been. He took a few deep breaths and wiped his eyes once more. He knew what he had to do.

He didn't spend much time in Bainbridge before boarding the next ferry for the return to Seattle. After landing, he drove to the Alliance Church that he had been attending. He walked inside and asked the secretary if he could see the pastor. Over the next half hour, he poured out all the pain, the anger, and the sorrow that had engulfed him whenever he had a free unguarded moment. For a long time the pastor never said a word. He knew a soul was emptying itself of all the baggage with which Satan had labored to enslave him. He knew that when the vessel was finally empty, it could be filled to overflowing with God's grace.

Finally, Roland sobbed, "What can I do, Pastor? I accepted Christ once, but I immediately turned my back on him. I've been so bitter, so angry. Can he forgive me for that? Will he take me back? I'm so lonely, and in spite of everything I do, I still feel horribly empty."

The pastor was quiet for a moment and then softly said, "Roland, do you remember about the night before Christ was crucified? Peter, just a few hours before, had said he would die for Jesus but then turned around and denied Christ three times. Jesus forgave Peter and used him mightily thereafter. Peter had known Christ better and longer than you knew him, yet even after Christ predicted Peter would do it. He still denied him three times. Can Christ forgive you? Certainly, if he forgave Peter, he can forgive you. The Bible tells us that heaven rejoices when a sinner returns to the fold. It sounds to me like they have been waiting a long time for you. It will probably be one big celebration. He's waiting for you with arms wide open,

Roland, just like any father would wait for his son. I believe you are ready. I know he is. Let's pray, and you can tell him you're sorry and ask for his forgiveness."

He left the pastor's office a new man, and the first thing he did was call Bryce.

"You asked me to call you and let you know when I stopped blaming God and asked him to forgive me. I just did it."

There was a silence for a moment, and then he heard Bryce say in a soft voice obviously choked with emotion, "I love you, Dad. You have made me very happy, and I know Mom and Melissa are happy right now as well. I can't stay on the phone. I really do have to go, but I'll call you tonight, and we'll talk."

And that night they talked and talked and talked, and Roland discovered that somehow, the ache was finally gone.

The next day he called Amanda and told her what he had done. She had been praying for him for years, and she was overjoyed to hear his news. "Praise the Lord!" she said. "Have you told Bryce?"

"Yes, we had a long talk last night. I'll stop up and see you in a few days, and we can talk."

He continued to do all the things he had been doing before, but now he did them with a new purpose, not as a way to ease his pain or to try to be a good person but just to say thank you to God. Everything had changed, yet he still felt there was something more. There was a spot not even God seemed to be able to heal. He was weary of living alone, and he prayed that God would provide the right woman in his time.

It was shortly after that watershed event that the invitation to his high school class's thirty-fifth-year reunion came in the mail. He had never answered any of the other reunion notices he had received over the years, but for some reason, he felt strangely drawn to go to this one.

The invitation sat on his desk for three days before he wrote a check for the alumni banquet and class reunion and filled out the form confirming he was coming. Later, as he dropped it in the mailbox, he had a strange feeling that Sherry might be there, and he wanted to see her, but he had no idea what he would say or do when he saw her. He had never forgiven her, and he wasn't sure he wanted to. Still she had been almost constantly on his mind since he had received the invitation. In truth he wasn't sure exactly what he wanted; it had been a long time since he had felt so conflicted.

6

SHERRY MILLER

The e-mail had read, "Roland Holtz is coming to the alumni banquet and our class reunion! Are you coming? If you both come, everyone will want to be there. It will be the best reunion ever! I sure hope you will come—PLEASE!"

She didn't immediately click the return arrow to send her pat answer, for suddenly, her head was spinning, and she needed time to think. Delores always asked her to come to class reunions or special events at Bradley, but she almost always claimed she was too busy to attend. However, Roland's name popping up out of the past was strangely unsettling. It had brought an instant flash back to a single incident in her high school days, unleashing a cascade of memories and emotions. She actually still had the snail mail invitation that had come a couple of weeks before. She was in the habit of sending a return donation to the alumni scholarship fund, but she had never had any intention of going to this one; she wasn't much on reunions.

She had received the e-mail from Delores, who had been able to almost single-handedly maintain a friendship with her ever since graduation, sending cards and notes, pictures of her family, and tidbits about their classmates. Once PCs had brought about e-mail, she gave Delores her personal e-mail address, cautioning her not to share it with anyone else. Delores was one of a very tiny circle of people outside of her business with direct personal access to her. All others had to contact her through Robynsworld.com.

Delores was special. She had been a confidant in high school and beyond, and she had never once betrayed her trust. Over the intervening years since school, she had never asked Sherry for anything—no favors, no products, no money—nothing, being content just to be her friend. It was so refreshing. Sherry always opened her e-mails before she read any others—even those from her own daughter, although those were a close second. Delores was something she had precious little of: a true friend who loved her for herself, not for what she had.

She smiled as she thought about her hiring Delores's daughter after graduation to work for Robyn's World. Delores had not asked her to do it; it had been Sherry's own idea to offer her a job. Originally, it was a way she had found to say "thank you" to Delores, but it had turned out to be an excellent move all around. She had been a very conscientious worker, and her supervisors had early on recognized her efforts in even the most menial of tasks.

Sherry had sent her to college, paying all her expenses, with the agreement that in return, she would work each summer at Robyn's World and that she would become a regular employee for a minimum of four years after her graduation. That four years had stretched into a stellar seventeen-year career at the company, where she was now the youngest member of Sherry's senior staff—a position that she had earned many times over. Sherry often told Delores that she had raised a marvelous daughter and how much she appreciated her.

If Delores had a fault in Sherry's eyes, it was her eternal, but sometimes annoying, desire to see her become a Christian. In high school she had constantly invited her to go to the youth group with her, but she never had come. She told Sherry numerous times about Jesus and that she needed to accept him as her personal Lord and Savior. Over all the years since their graduation, two things had been constant: Delores's friendship and her desire to share her faith.

She mused, *How many times has Delores said, "Sherry, you need the Lord to make your life complete?" I wonder what complete is? I thought my life would be complete when I married Hughie. I thought it was complete when Marcy was born. I lived for her. She was wonderful, but it always seemed like I still needed more. I worked hard and sacrificed to start Robyn's World and make it a success, and it has succeeded beyond my wildest dreams. After Hughie's death, Marcy and the business consumed my life, and I told myself I had arrived, like I was finally complete, but I feel haunted by an unreasoning insecurity that never goes away.*

In the world's view, Sherry had it all. She was rich, famous, and still good-looking. She owned and managed a multimillion dollar business that continued to grow, but she knew she was not as happy as Delores. Sherry was alone in the midst of her empire. She could surround herself with people anytime she wished, but inevitably, that was when she felt the most alone. After all these years, she still missed Hughie, and she had never been able to shake the guilt she felt about his death. He had hardly been God's gift to women, but he had loved her, and that compensated for any shortcomings he might have had.

Truth was, there was now no shortage of men who would have jumped at the chance to marry her and share her kingdom, and several had already indicated they would like to fill that role. The problem was that she could never get past the feeling that it was her business and money that appealed to the potential suitors rather than simply her. But more importantly, none of them struck her as someone who could be a soul mate, someone who might finally fill the void she was feeling in her life, and she was far from being desperate.

Of course, there was Geoffrey. He was the closest thing she had to a realistic matrimonial prospect. They were always at the same shows, and they had spent weekends in Paris, Rome, London, and other places that stir the imagination of lovers the world over, but they were not lovers. She liked Geoffrey very much. He was thoughtful, kind, considerate of others, and it was obvious that he cared for her. She could have had him in the blink of an eye. He was always the perfect gentleman, and he was not without considerable means, but the more she tried to think of him as a husband, the more she parried his efforts to move their relationship to a new level.

She had begun to question whether she might not be looking for too much, but it always came down to the same thing. There was no magic between them, no spark. She knew marriage to him would never relieve the ache she felt when nights were cold and long.

She shifted gears and thought for a moment about Roland. She couldn't picture him from high school; although she remembered that she had gone out on a date with him once. She had actually kind of liked him, but Hughie had been furious with her and threatened to beat Roland up if she went out with him again. She protected herself, and Roland too, by belittling him to her friends. She had always felt bad about that part because other than being a bit boring, he had seemed to be kind and considerate. If it hadn't been for Hughie, she would have given him another look. She had even wondered a couple of times over the years what her life might have been like if she had married him instead of Hughie, but she had burned those bridges behind her so many years before when she made fun of him with her friends. There was no going back at this late date.

Of course, she knew who Roland was and what a force he had been in the financial world. But for the last few years, he had been flying under the radar. She had no idea what he was doing at present. She was fairly sure that he wasn't married because she had seen an article a couple of years earlier on the ten most eligible men in the country, and he was one of those featured. It had raised her spirits and warmed her to read about him back then; she couldn't help it. She thought that it would be interesting to compare lives, if nothing else, and maybe she could even apologize for the actions of a foolish high school girl so long ago.

She was not one to go to reunions. She had only been to one, and that was shortly after her daughter had been born and well before her business had suddenly lit up the world of cosmetics. After that, there was no time for such things, and Delores's personal urgings to attend each ensuing one had always resulted in only a polite excuse and a thank-you. But this one was different. Something within her was stirring, and she felt herself inexplicably excited by Delores's message.

Sherry looked at the e-mail and hit *Reply*.

She wrote, "Delores, as usual, the business requires most of my time, and it is very difficult for me to get away even for a day. I'm sure you must realize that [she smiled as she finished her message], but on the other hand, to blazes with all that. Let's make it a reunion to remember—I'm in! Love, Sherry."

She paused for a moment to think about what she was doing and then hit *Send*. It was done! She was committed.

Smiling, she thought, *I'd like to see her face when she reads this.*

Then in moments, a panic attack began as she started having second thoughts.

This is all pretty foolish. I'm going to feel dumb and out of place at this reunion. Probably, the others will feel as awkward as I will, and even if Roland does come, I would be crazy to even think that there could be any possible connection between us. He probably doesn't even remember me. I certainly didn't do anything to encourage him back then. He might be one of the ten most eligible men in the country, but that doesn't mean he is looking, and even if he is, nothing says he might be the one for me. Oh, crap! What am I doing?

She was ready to e-mail Delores and tell her that she had not checked her calendar before her last e-mail and she had forgotten she did have an important overseas meeting on the reunion date. It would be impossible for her not to attend the fashion meeting as the cost to the business could be enormous. She would tell her that she would have to bow out of coming to the reunion as much as she really wanted to be there. But before she could lie to her friend, a new e-mail arrived from Delores.

Clicking on "Second Thoughts," she read a prophetic message:

"Sherry, I am so excited that you are coming. I am equally sure that at some point, second thoughts or an important meeting will rear their ugly head, and you will be tempted to back out. Do NOT DO IT! At all costs, you must come. I cannot explain why, but I am confident that the Lord is in your decision to come. Give him a chance this one time. Psalms 46:10. Love, Delores."

She was strangely shaken, almost overwhelmed, that Delores seemed to be reading her mind, and the message was the final decisive nudge she needed. She wrote the date on her calendar and sent a memo to her personal secretary to clear that date completely and enter the reunion, including two days before and two days after the event.

Then she replied to the e-mail, "I promise I will be there. I am curious to see why your Lord wants me to attend. Sherry." And she clicked *Send*.

Still uneasy, she could not get her mind back on business, and after several fits and starts, she finally decided that she had to get out of the office. There was nothing really pressing that afternoon, and she needed some time to think and reflect on what she was doing. Calling her secretary in, she confirmed that the reunion and extra days had been put on the calendar and also confirmed that there was nothing that needed her attention before the following day. Then she went home.

The first thing she did after she came in the door was make a cup of coffee. After taking a few sips, she went to the library to find her old yearbook. It was lying by itself where it had been untouched for years except when it was being dusted off by the cleaning lady. She took it down, surprised at all the memories that flooded into her head the moment it was in her hands. She carried it into the living room and put it down gently on the stand by her favorite chair. She just looked at it, still sipping her coffee, trying to get her head around what was happening. She turned and went back to kitchen for more coffee even though her cup was still half full. She wasn't quite ready to begin this journey, as the pages from her past, and perhaps to her future, sat waiting for her by her chair.

After pouring a second cup of coffee, she returned and settled down in the easy chair with her Bradley High School Yearbook, leafing through it until she got to the senior section. She took a good look at Roland's senior picture for the first time in thirty years. There was no signature with it, no comments, no funny sayings for her benefit. She had almost forgotten that he had actually been a good-looking guy, or it had just not made an impression on her in high school. She read his profile, chuckling at how far off from reality it was. Of course, hers was no different, predicting she would be an airline stewardess before getting her big break in Hollywood.

Studying his picture, she could not help thinking, *What a beautiful smile.*

She tried to remember what he was like in high school, but nothing much came to her. Of course, she remembered her one date with him and that he certainly wasn't a ladies' man back then. She suddenly realized that the only thing she really knew about him back in high school was that he liked to fish.

She thought, *I never found out anything about him. I just wasn't interested enough, what with Hughie and all, and besides, I was just a kid.*

It was not surprising that she knew more about his adult life than of that from the years they were in the same class. She knew today's Roland was rich, but that was of little consequence (*so am I*). She knew he was a widower (*I'm a widow*), single (*me too*), with a grown son (*I have a grown daughter*), and that for the most part, he avoided the limelight (*not me, I like it*). But still he was more of an enigma rather than a known quantity.

She felt a little guilty at first because her mind couldn't help being haunted by poor, doting Geoffrey even as she thought about Roland.

I wonder if he has someone special in his life. Maybe he had no interest in finding someone new.

But still, wasn't she interested in a new love, a new life partner, a new hope, a new beginning? So why not think the same could be true of him, but even as she fantasized, the practical Sherry began to shove her way to the front of the bus.

The practical Sherry told her, *Geoffrey is really interested in you, and he would do just about anything for you. Just because Roland is coming to the reunion does not indicate he would have the slightest interest in you, and it is ludicrous to think such a thing. There was nothing between you in high school, why should there be anything now when the only thing you really knew about him in school was that he liked fishing? Give me a break.*

All that evening, the practical Sherry and the romantic Sherry dueled until finally they were both exhausted and sleep temporarily ended the contest.

MOTHER AND DAUGHTER

The days after found Sherry struggling to keep her mind on the requirements of the business. She had always been a very hands-on person when it came to work. Even when Robyn's World had muscled its way into prominence and become the barometer for beauty products and then jewelry and fashions, she exercised her personal control, often much to the discomfort of her executive staff. She *was* Robyn's World, period.

But she was aware something had been changing for some time even though she tried desperately to deny it. As big as it was, and as lucrative as it was, and as much as she involved herself in its operation, Robyn's World no longer completely satisfied her nor fulfilled her. She told herself it did, but she knew she was lying. At one point, she had stepped back and looked at her life, and what she saw left her with more questions than answers. She had power, money, and fame; but when she tried to look into the future, she felt a chill because it materialized as bleak, cold, and lonely.

As she sat behind her desk, looking at her life, it occurred to her that her daughter was now no longer calling her, pleading for her to take a break and spend a week or two with her. She had long before stopped coming to visit because her mother was always preoccupied with the business or on the phone at all hours, having precious little time for the daughter she said she loved.

Sherry could not find a release from the feelings that were disturbing her ordered world until finally, she called a Friday afternoon meeting of the senior staff and surprised them with an announcement.

"I am going to be taking a two-week vacation starting Monday. If there are any decisions in your respective departments that must be made before I return, you have my authority to make them. I don't foresee any crucial, earth-shattering problems arising, and I will not be accepting any calls or e-mails from anyone, including from any of you." Her staff appeared stunned as she continued, "I have complete confidence in you. If everything goes well in my absence, and I am sure it will, there will be a bonus for each of you. Myron will be your go-to person. If necessary, keep him informed of what you are doing, and if you do feel you absolutely have to discuss an item, he will be your sounding board. And Myron, make sure you work closely with my secretary, and keep her in the loop."

There were a few questions, and she gave them some insights and a couple of assignments. After which, she dismissed them, but she had her secretary remain behind.

"Gwen," she said, "I want you to know that I might take longer than two weeks, but there is nothing wrong with me, no health problem or anything like that, so don't be concerned. I saw that look in your eyes. No one, not even Myron, knows this business better than you do, but it was important for me to put him in charge. Ride herd on him, but do it with a light touch. When I get back, I'd like your assessment of how he did and how he worked with the others and with you. It will be important to me. Now, I have a phone call to make. I don't want to be disturbed."

When Gwen was gone, she sat down at her desk and looked at the phone. It was an old-style push-button phone with a handheld receiver that rested over the top. She preferred it to her new cell phone. She was almost afraid to make the call. It had been a long time. Taking a deep breath, she dialed her daughter's number.

She heard the answering machine pick up and her daughter's voice saying, "Hello, this is Marcy. I'm not available to come to the phone right now, but if you will leave a short message and your number after the beep, I'll get back to you as soon as possible."

Sherry fumbled for a moment before starting. In all her years of business, she had never become comfortable speaking to machines.

"Marcy, this is Mom. I'd like to talk to you. Call my cell phone when you get . . ."

That was as far as she got before she heard Marcy's voice, "Mom, is that really you? I just got out of the shower, and I heard your voice. Is there something wrong?"

"No, there's nothing wrong. Can't I call my daughter without something being wrong?" she asked.

Marcy sounded cautious and suspicious as she replied, "Well, Mother, when was the last time you called me? What is going on if there is nothing wrong? I can't believe you just called to pass the time of day. You aren't calling to try and persuade me to take a position at Robyn's World again, are you?"

"No," she said. "I've given up on that. I wanted to know if you would still like me to come and visit you and if this would be a good time to do it. I'm taking a vacation for a few days, and I would really like to see you."

"Oh my gosh, Mother," she gasped. "Are you serious? I can't wait to see you. When will you be arriving?"

"I know it is crazy, but I would like to come tomorrow morning, if that's not too soon for you. If that doesn't work for you, just tell me what would be best. Can you get a little time off next week?"

"Look, Mom," Marcy said, "I've got a lot of vacation time built up, and I know I can get the time off, but tell me, you aren't going to spend all your time here on the phone and doing e-mails, are you? I don't need to take a vacation for that."

Sherry confessed, "It will be hard, but I've already made my decision on that—no e-mails, no phone calls, and nothing about the business. I can do it if you can."

"Done," said Marcy. "I am pumped, Mom. Thanks for calling. Even though you are coming tomorrow, it will be hard to wait for you. Just e-mail me your flight schedule. I love you, Mom."

"I'll call you with the flight information. I love you too. Have a great day."

She couldn't believe how good she felt. Here she was ready to turn the reins of the business over to the staff. Yes, they were more than competent, and granted, it wasn't for very long, but she had never even considered doing that before. She was cutting herself off from any contact, and she was going to spend some quality time with her daughter. The idea of total time with Marcy gave her pause, not just because of being cut off from her business, but because she began to realize how little she knew about Marcy's life over the last four or five years.

"I have wasted a lot of time when all the while I thought I was making great use of it, but I'm going to start making up for that. Marcy and I have a lot of catching up to do," she told herself.

After Gwen had made reservations for a one-way first class flight to Seattle, Sherry left the office with mixed emotions. As she thought about actually cutting off all contact with her business, it became intensely evident to her that Robyn's World had consumed her life and that it still held her in its thrall. It occurred to her that all the years that she thought she was controlling Robyn's World, she had been allowing it to control her instead. It would not be wide of the mark to say she was terrified as she thought about the days ahead. Neither the disconnect with the business nor the reconnect with her daughter was going to be easy for her.

Over the years, she had always planned ahead and knew just what she was going to say and do at every meeting, at every show, and in every situation that could be foreseen. She usually had a pretty good idea of what to expect from the people she was meeting with, and she could be in control, but her time with Marcy was going to be unscripted.

Sherry only knew she wanted desperately to see her daughter. She wanted to hug her and tell her how much she regretted not being a better mother and ask for forgiveness. She hoped that it was not too late to become a real part of Marcy's life once again, and if that were possible, she would never let herself lose that connection. There was so much she wanted to say, but it was going to have to be basically unplanned, ad lib, and from the heart.

The flight was right on time, and when Sherry reached the baggage area, Marcy was there waiting for her. She looked so beautiful. For a moment, Sherry's mind went back to the business as she thought that all her models should look like her daughter. Marcy threw her arms around her mother and gave her a kiss and a long hug.

"I can hardly believe it, Mom, you are actually here. How was your flight?"

They exchanged pleasantries about the flight, and neither one of them said anything about Robyn's World. Sherry had two bags, which showed up in the first batch to come down the belt to the carousel. They each grabbed one and wheeled away to the parking garage.

Once again Marcy said, "I can hardly believe you are here. I'm so pleased, you can't know how much this means to me. I had sort of lost hope of your ever coming here to see me again, but here you are."

Sherry stopped and took her hand, looking directly into her eyes. "I'm sorry, Marcy, that I have been so foolish. I realize I lost sight of what should have been most important in my life. I am years too late, and I can't get them back, but I will never let anything come between us again. That's a promise."

Marcy looked carefully at her and then laughingly asked, "Okay, who are you, and what have you done with my mother?"

They both laughed before Marcy softly asked, "Are you sure you are okay? You aren't sick?"

"Do I have to be sick to visit my daughter? No, I actually feel like I am the healthiest I have been in years."

"Did you really mean it, Mother? No cell phones, no e-mails, no business interference?" Marcy asked.

"I sure did," said Sherry. "I'm carrying my cell phone, but only for emergencies. It's turned off, and I left my laptop at home. It took me a long time to appreciate that I had turned you off or tuned you out whenever you came for a visit. I don't blame you for not coming to see me lately. I was pretty poor company. I was a full-time pro at business, but you paid the price for it, and for that I am truly sorry. I am hoping you can forgive me and we can get a fresh start."

She paused for a moment, trying to keep her composure before actually sobbing, "I love you, Marcy." And then they alternated between crying and laughing all the way to the car.

When they were leaving the parking garage, Marcy said, "So how is business going these days?"

Immediately, she thought, *I'm an idiot. I didn't want to talk about her business, and it falls right out of my mouth.*

She was relieved but amazed when Sherry answered, "Fine, but I'm not here to talk about business. The business can speak for itself. I am here to talk about you, me, and us."

Soon after they left the airport parking lot, Marcy began to point out places of interest in the distance, spending her time being a tour guide rather than probing for the reasons her mother had come to see her. As they crossed Lake Washington and approached Mercer Island, where Sherry had offered to buy her a home, she could not resist making a comparison of it to the location she had chosen instead, and she ended by claiming, "Pretty soon you'll see why I prefer to live where I am rather than on Mercer."

It was about a fifty-minute drive from SeaTac airport to Marcy's home in Snoqualmie, but the time passed quickly, and soon they were pulling into Marcy's driveway. Yes, it was true. Marcy could have lived anywhere, even on Mercer Island if she had wished. Sherry would have bought her a wonderful home on the lake if she had wanted it. She had offered to do so when Marcy moved to the West Coast, but Marcy had insisted she wanted to be nearer to the mountains, and she had fallen in love with the Snoqualmie area.

When they pulled into the driveway, Sherry had to admit that the view composed an exceptional panorama, and she began to understand why Marcy loved the northwest. Of course, the mountains couldn't compare to the Alps for size, but they were spectacular in their own way. The Alps were almost sterile and foreboding, while the mountains around Snoqualmie seemed alive and inviting.

After taking Sherry's luggage to the guest bedroom, they moved to the kitchen where Marcy started a pot of coffee. She put a small plate of cookies on the table and sat down across from her mother.

For a moment, the only sound was the coffee machine puffing and gurgling.

Then Marcy opened the real conversation.

"You are not ill, so what is going on with you? Don't get me wrong. I am very, very pleased that you have come. You have no idea how happy I am that you have come, but I have asked you so many times without any success, and now here you are all on your own. You say you want to get a fresh start, and I'm okay with that, but what's up, really?"

"Marcy, I'm scared."

"Oh, no," said Marcy, "there really is something wrong with you. Do you have cancer or what?"

"No, no, honey, I'm fine. I'm not scared about my health. I'm scared about what I've become and what lies ahead for me. I can't explain it, I just feel it. My life has been Robyn's World for so long that I'm not sure if the real me still exists, or if Robyn's World is all I am. A few days ago, I took a long hard look at my life and realized that Robyn's World had squeezed everything else out of my life, including you, and I'd let it happen. I don't want to die with it that way, and the only way I can see to prevent that is to take back my life. That's what I'm trying to do."

"Wow. That's pretty heavy stuff, Mom. What brought that all on anyway?"

"It's kind of a long story, and it may sound crazy, but it has all come to a head in the last few weeks," Sherry said, and then she proceeded to tell Marcy the thoughts she had been having about living single and about possibly getting married and the dearth of prospects that appealed to her.

"Geoffrey is about as close to being someone that I would marry as anyone has come, but I just can't see myself married to him. He's a decent person, and I think he cares for me in a way, but I fear being married to him would be almost like being married to Robyn's World. Marcy, I don't want just anyone. I want someone that really loves me and, for lack of a better term, turns me on.

"A few weeks ago, I got an e-mail from my old friend Delores. You've met her. She asked me to come to the thirty-fifth reunion of our high school class, and she mentioned that Roland Holtz would be there."

"*The* Roland Holtz?" Marcy asked.

"Yes, *the* Roland Holtz," Sherry mimicked. "He was in my class at Bradley. He was actually quite a handsome young man, but he was a little rough around the edges. I think time has changed him, just like it has me, and as foolish as it sounds, I'd like to get to know him again, and who knows, maybe he might feel the same way."

"Mom, you never told me you went to school with Roland Holtz. That's amazing! So are you saying you think he could be Mr. Right?"

"Well, I'm not sure if it's what I think that matters," Sherry said, and then she went on to relate the story of her date with Roland and the fallout from that, including Hughie's threat and her solution. That changed the tone and the direction of their conversation.

Marcy used the mention of Hughie as an opportunity to broach a subject that had long left her with more questions than answers.

"Mom, do you realize that since I was a little girl, you have told me almost nothing about my father? I have a few pictures, and I know he loved motorcycles, and I know he died in a motorcycle accident before I was two, but that's really about it. Tell me about my father. I'd really like to know more about him."

So out of respect for the husband of her youth, Sherry went about painting a perhaps overly domestic picture of Hughie as she knew him from the time they met until the day he died, and Marcy listened, captivated.

"I met your father when I was a junior in high school. He had graduated the year before while I was still a sophomore, but I had been aware of him. It would have been hard not to have been. He stood out from the rest of the guys, and I guess I was infatuated by the way he dressed. He looked for all the world like James Dean in his denim pants, white shirt, denim jacket, and engineer boots, and he certainly was a rebel. He actually owned his own motorcycle, wore a Harley motorcycle cap over his long, slicked-back hair, and smoked Camel cigarettes. He was everything that my parents loathed, but I couldn't take my eyes off him," said Sherry as she began her story.

"At times some of us during lunch period would go to the Snackery, a little diner not far from the school, where we could get away from cafeteria food and buy a burger, fries, and a cherry coke. Hughie stopped in there fairly regularly, and before long, he learned from someone that I had a crush on him. One noon hour, he came into the Snackery and sat down next to me. I could hardly breathe. I felt like I was going to melt."

She stopped for a minute to collect her thoughts and memories. Then Sherry smiled and continued, "Hughie offered me a ride back to school that day on his motorcycle, and I was scared and thrilled at the same time. I know that it was stupid of me, but I just couldn't help myself. After that, Hughie would often give me a ride to and from the Snackery, and all my friends were so impressed that this older guy was interested in me.

"He asked me to let him pick me up and take me to school in the morning, but I knew my parents would have a fit if they learned about Hughie, so I told him no. Eventually, of course, my parents found out all that was going on. It's hard to keep things secret in a small town. However, when it came time for my junior prom, I went with Hughie. I packed my dress in a bag, and when Hughie arrived at our house, I climbed onto his bike behind him. My parents were flabbergasted, but there wasn't much they could do at that point.

"After that, the battle lines were drawn between my parents and Hughie and me. Your grandmother and grandfather threatened me, and they threatened Hughie. They begged me to tell him I wanted to break it off. They tried to buy Hughie off, and they tried to figure a way they could get the law to do something. They told me over and over that Hughie would never amount to anything and that I was just throwing my life away if I didn't get rid of him. The more they tried to get us apart, the more I was determined that we would always be together.

"They wanted me to date other boys, and that's why, when he asked me, I agreed to go out on a date with Roland. They were a lot more excited about it than I was, but I really wasn't interested in anyone other than Hughie. Roland seemed so immature. Compared to him, he was just a kid."

"But, Mom," she interjected, "tell me what my father was like. Was he rough, tender, thoughtful, smart? What was it about him other than his motorcycle that made you marry him?"

Sherry got down to a little more personal level.

"Hughie was not what one would call a scholar, but even before he had graduated high school, he was known as an excellent mechanic, especially when it came to bikes. I don't think I ever saw him when he didn't have a little grease under his fingernails, but I didn't mind that. He acted tough, but he was always considerate of me and treated me like I was the world's finest gold. When he held me and when he kissed me, I felt like there was an electric current running through my body."

"Did he ever get fresh, Mom, you know," Marcy was blushing as she asked the big question, "you know, did he try to get you to have sex with him?"

"Maybe it's hard to believe, honey, but he never got out of line. He kept his hands to home, and he never brought the subject up. I had sort of hoped he would ask so I could tell him I wasn't that kind of girl, but it's probably a good thing he didn't because I think I might have gone all the way with him if he had asked. That would have been terrible because it would have validated everything my parents thought about Hughie, about us. They had their own plans for me, and they didn't include your father.

"It was at Christmas during my senior year that Hughie gave me a ring and asked me to marry him. He had been hinting for some time, so it wasn't a complete surprise to me. I said yes, but we had to wait until after I graduated. There was no such thing as a married girl in high school back in my time, and it would have been a huge mistake, especially if I had gotten pregnant.

"So we waited until after I had graduated. I was still too young to get married without my parent's permission, and they made a point of telling me so. One morning I met him at the Snackery, and we took off on your father's motorcycle and headed south until we hit a state where we could get married. Then we kept on going all the way to Georgia.

"It wasn't until after you were born that my parents found out where we were. They moved down to live near us and bought the house where we lived with them after your father's accident and before we moved to New York City.

"Your grandfather and grandmother still didn't approve of Hughie when they moved to Georgia even though we were married and had you. They were pretty insensitive, and even though your father tried to be accepted by them for our sake, they drove him to distraction. They weren't the least bit reticent in suggesting how Hughie could better himself. They probably were trying to be helpful in their own way, but all they accomplished was to make your father feel like he wasn't much of a husband and father.

"Hughie always liked to have a beer or two at the end of the day, but once your father started drinking more than he should, they became even more critical. Hughie wanted to move away, but I thought we could work our way through things and that my mother and father would change their attitude. I begged your father to stay where we were, but things didn't get better. I believe my parents' attitude was the reason for your father's drinking."

Sherry had always believed that their irritating efforts to remold Hughie into a son-in-law that they could approve of played a large part in the accident that claimed his life. They, on the other hand, saw his demise only as an unavoidable result of his life choices and foolhardiness. She had never forgiven her parents, but for the sake of Marcy, she had managed to coexist with them until Robyn's World took off and she and Marcy moved to New York City. After that, her only concessions were Christmas and birthdays and finally, Marcy's graduation, but her ambivalence never lessened. Even though she knew Marcy should get to know her grandparents, it never bothered her that her parents grieved over being kept at much more than arm's length from their only grandchild. As far as she was concerned, her parents had never done anything for them except cause them grief, and they were going to pay for it.

After her mother's slightly slanted rendition of Hughie's life and the revelation of the original friction between her grandparents and her father before he and Sherry were married, Marcy had compiled a picture of a loving father who struggled to provide for his family and grandparents who were at best aloof, distant, and uncaring.

Marcy asked questions to fill in sketchy spots, aware that there was probably a lot more to the story than she was being told, but at least the conversation had begun to answer some questions she had always had about her grandparents and why they seldom went to see them and they had almost never come to see her and her mother either.

Sherry had not expected to be dealing with this topic and was uncomfortable with it. Hoping to relieve the tension she was starting to feel, she suggested, "Marcy, why don't we take a break and go for a ride? I'd love to see some of the countryside. We can talk about your father later, and maybe I can be more specific when I have had a little time to think and remember. He was an interesting man, really, and I did love him dearly, and you would have loved him too if he had lived."

"Okay," Marcy replied, "we can take a ride, do you have any place in mind?"

"No, not really, Marcy," Sherry said. "I thought maybe I might like to go to Whidbey Island. You took me there once right after you first moved out here. We were near a place called Anacortes, I think, but I can't remember the name of the town where we were. It was a quaint little place that had several antique shops and a little bakery that had fantastic focaccia bread."

"I know," said Marcy, "it was La Conner."

"Yes, I think that's it. It's not too far to go, is it?" she asked.

"No, Mother, we can be there in a couple of hours. We can go to Mukilteo and take the ferry over to Whidbey and then go the length of the island, or we can run up Route 5 and take Route 20 across to where we turn off. It's about the same time either way. Actually, probably the best thing would be to go one way and come back the other. That way you would get to see more."

Sherry avoided conversation about family on their drive, asking questions about the sights along the way. Once they arrived at La Conner, she was able to let down her guard.

"Let's go into that shop," she said to Marcy, pointing to the large antique shop. "I don't know why, but I always enjoy looking at the antiques. Maybe they will have a good piece of carnival glass. I still collect it when I find a really choice piece."

So they stopped at several antique shops, without finding any decent carnival glass.

"I don't think it is as common out here as it is back east, Mother," Marcy commented. "Why don't we go on down to the bakery where you got the bread the last time we were here? If I remember right, it's the Calico Kitchen."

The bread was just as good as Sherry had remembered it. She savored a couple of slices and then bought a loaf to take with them. They moved down the street and bought ice cream. The scoops on the cones were large and were a perfect finish for their impromptu lunch.

Walking back to their car afterward, Marcy said, "It's been quite awhile since I've been here. I'm glad you asked to come."

They left La Conner and soon were heading south toward Deception Pass and Whidbey Island. Reaching the far side of the bridge over the pass, Marcy said, "I'm going to stop here, Mother," as they pulled into the parking lot. "It's a beautiful view on such a nice day."

As they stood on the bridge, watching the fast ocean current far below, Sherry had to admit the view was beautiful and breathtaking. She actually loved the ocean, though she seldom spent much time near or on it. She began looking forward to the ferry ride across to Mukilteo before their drive back to Snoqualmie.

"It's getting kind of late, Mother, and this has to have already been a long day for you. I think we should get started back. It will be dark before we get home even if we leave now. We could stop at Ivars and get some clam chowder and a cup of coffee when we get to Mukilteo. How does that sound?" she asked.

"You're the driver," Sherry answered. "I go where you go."

When the ferry docked, they drove off, parked nearby, and went into Ivars. Sherry remembered the chowder from years before, and it was just as tasty as she had remembered. They ate the delicious soup and crackers as they sat in the car. Marcy was right. It had been a long day, and now as she finished the last of the creamy repast, Sherry felt weariness creep over her. As Marcy started out on the final stage of the day's journey, she drifted off to sleep, and the next thing she knew, Marcy was gently shaking her.

"Time to wake up, Mother," she said. "We're home."

It seemed to Sherry like they had just left Mukilteo. She slept well that night, but the next morning after breakfast, Marcy returned to their conversation.

She had been an intelligent child, and even while she was quite young, she had been able to see that her mother never acted very friendly toward her grandparents. She had always felt torn between wanting to be closer to her grandparents and not wanting to upset her mother. It was almost as if her mother didn't even want to recognize their presence. Their home always seemed to grow colder when her grandmother and grandfather came. As she grew older, it seemed like her mother always had important meetings in Europe when birthdays rolled around, which ruled out getting together with her grandparents.

"Mom, didn't Grandma and Grandpa like us?" Marcy asked. "They almost never came to see us. I hardly knew them, and when we went to visit them, they always looked so sad even when they were smiling at me. Were they mad at me? Why didn't they love me? I loved them even if they didn't love me. Maybe they just didn't know how much I wanted a grandma and grandpa around." A tear slid down her cheek as she continued, "I cried when we went to Grandma's funeral, but I didn't see you cry. Mom, what was the reason we never got along? Was it me, or was it that they could never get over the fact you left them for my father? I have wondered about that so much, and my heart has ached over it so many times. I'm sorry I'm crying, but it almost destroyed my life before I realized I had to let it go, but I still can't help wondering why things were the way they were."

Sherry almost choked because of her daughter's words as they cut into her soul more deeply than she would ever have thought possible. She tried to speak, but nothing came out at first. She stopped, took a deep breath, and then another, before she attempted to sooth her daughter's pain.

"Marcy, your grandparents loved you very much." Now where could she go? She told the truth. "You weren't the reason they didn't come to see us, I was." Then she lied, "I was so busy with the business that I always gave them the impression that they shouldn't come." Then another truth, "They would have come if I had asked them, but let's talk about it later, it's complicated."

"Mom, it may be complicated, but I think it's high time we talked about it. I think it is time we went to Grandpa and set things right. It's time we told him we love him. Even after all the things he and Grandma might have done or not done, you must still have some love for them in you. I don't think things can ever be right if we don't go to see him. I've been thinking about it ever since Grandma died. And now I feel so bad that we didn't do it before then, we've got to do it now."

Sherry recoiled at the suggestion. "Marcy, I can't talk about that right now. It hurts too much, and I didn't come here to hurt. Please just give me a day or two more, and we will discuss it, but I am not up to it right now."

Marcy reluctantly agreed to wait, and the following days were filled with mother-daughter things and talk about Roland Holtz and the upcoming banquet and reunion, but the answer to her quest to their relationship with her grandfather never resurfaced. And with that, she became even more determined to do something about her grandfather, even if she had to do it alone.

8

THE BANQUET

Roland's reverie had ended as he walked into the large room and scanned the gathering. There were alumni from many different years, some even from the most recent class now graduating.

At first he thought, *Who are these people?*

But on taking a second look around, he saw his old friend Bob Cummings again. They had often fished together, and he had been the catcher on the varsity baseball team. And there was Don Love, as notably heavyset now as he had been incredibly thin in high school. As he continued to recognize some of his classmates scattered among the crowd, it dawned on him that the years had been hard on some and yet rested lightly on others. He didn't know what he had expected, but what he was looking at sure wasn't it.

Then at the far side of the room, standing near a table covered with finger foods arranged around a large cake, he saw Sherry Miller talking with two other people. Suddenly, he acknowledged to himself why he had come. Somehow he was going to repay the indignity he had suffered at her hands. One way or another, if it were possible, he was going to walk away from her with a laugh, letting her know what a mistake she had made that night so long ago. He wasn't in any rush to make his way over to her. He allowed himself to actually enjoy renewing acquaintances of people who had been his classmates forty years before, most of whom he had never laid eyes on since graduation.

Because he had always tried to maintain a low profile, he thought some might have no idea that he was a millionaire many times over, but really, he knew that was a forlorn hope. If anyone had not known about him before, once it was made known that "he" was coming to the reunion, everyone learned who he was. Roland could sense the awkwardness of it all. How he wished he could have had Betty standing there with him at that moment, but he did his best to set his classmates at ease, speaking first and shaking their hand.

He was relieved when Bob showed up to say hello. "Hi, Ron, it's great to see you again. From what I hear, you've done pretty well for yourself."

"Bob," he replied, "you haven't changed much since we graduated. What have you been doing? Have you always lived in Bradley since then?"

Bob laughed and replied, "Hell, no, I became a union carpenter, but jobs were scarcer than I liked, so I moved away. Ended up in South Carolina, got married, and raised a family. I moved back here about two years ago after my wife died. My kids were spread out all over the country, so I came back here to retire and do some fishing. The trout fishing sucks, though, it's not like when we were kids."

"Hey, Roland, see Sherry Miller over there?" he said, nodding his head in her direction. "I think I might like to get married again if I could talk her into it. Isn't she something? She looks like she has hardly changed a bit."

Sherry had seen him the moment he walked through the door. How handsome he was! She didn't remember him being quite so good-looking when they had been students, yet he didn't look all that much different. Just now, he had a presence about him, noticeable even at a distance. He certainly looked pretty good for a fifty-three-year-old. Without looking directly at him for more than a few moments, she observed him scanning the room.

I wonder if he's looking for me, she thought. *Probably not. It's absurd for me to think he might be. I wonder if he remembers me or even wants to remember me?*

There were only three things in her life that she had grown to question: one, that she had ever ignored her parents; two, that she had been foolish enough to have married Hughie; and three, that she had laughed at Roland instead of closing her eyes and kissing him on their first and only date.

How different things might have been, she thought wistfully.

None of those things had seemed the wrong thing to do at the time, but the ensuing years had become replete with second thoughts.

She had been down this road in her mind many times before. As much as that period in her life tormented her, she always came to the same eventual conclusion: it was no one's fault but her own, and given the choice of changing it and never knowing Marcy, or living it all over again and having her, the answer was always the same. She would have married Hughie. She always ended up feeling guilty because she had also gradually come to see her parents' side of the equation with more empathy, but she had been too proud and stubborn to tell them. In her thoughts of the past, there seemed to be no path that would have solved all the problems, and once again she put what-ifs and might-have-beens out of her mind.

She went about mingling with the rest of the class, trying to move closer—without looking like she was trying—to the group that had started to form around Roland, just as classmates had around her at times. She was not going to overplay her hand. She wasn't even all that sure she had been dealt one to play with. He might not even remember that night at her house.

That might not be all bad, she thought.

A couple of times she believed she had caught him looking directly at her as he spoke to others, like Bob. Each time his gaze slowly shifted away, but she was becoming more confident that sooner or later, he would make his way to her, and then, who knows?

He was aware that she had been watching him, and he was careful not to abruptly break eye contact when she met his gaze. He simply, slowly turned his attention to someone else, not giving her any indication that he desperately wanted to say hello. He was still in the process of working his way in her direction when everyone was asked to be seated.

The dinner started, and they had ended up at opposite ends of one of the long tables. There was a buffet line featuring roast turkey, stuffing, ham, candied yams, cabbage salad, mashed potatoes and gravy, ziti, squash, pickles, and of course, cranberry sauce. It was Thanksgiving in June. The food was actually very good, but Roland's mind wasn't on the meal.

As people finished their dinner, the huge cake was cut and distributed. The MC introduced the evening's speaker while alumni and their guests were enjoying the cake. The speaker, a member of the fifty-year class, rambled on about renewing old friendships, sharing life's experiences, and remembering days gone by as everyone listened politely.

A special recognition was given to members of the alumni of twenty-fifth-year class and the alumni of the fiftieth-year class, and one representative from each took a turn to reminisce at length about school day experiences at Bradley High. There was a lot of laughter over good times remembered. After that, the school superintendent was called on to speak.

He came to the podium, took out a few notes, and began, "First I want to ask the kitchen staff to please come out."

When the small group had assembled near the door to the kitchen, he said, "Let's give them a hand for a great meal. Thank you so much."

Turning his attention back to the alumni, he continued, "I also want to thank you all for coming tonight. I am impressed by how many have come, as well as how far some of you have traveled to be here with us for this occasion. Jeff Martin, class of 1989, came the farthest, all the way from Manila in the Philippines.

"I have only been the superintendent of your school for a few years, but ever since the day I began, I have marveled at the quality of Bradley's alumni. Graduates of Bradley have contributed to our country and our society in many, many ways. They have become inventors, educators, artists, doctors, lawyers, military personnel, nurses, businessmen and women, writers, broadcasters, and the list goes on and on. Some of those graduates have elected to remain here in Bradley and raise families in our community. They are our community's backbone, our bright future. But it really doesn't matter whether a graduate is employed in some distant corner of the world, like Jeff Martin, or lives right next door. Bradley is proud of every one of her alumni near and far. But I want to take just a minute to recognize four of the alumni who are here tonight who have had extraordinary careers."

He paused for a moment and checked his notes before continuing, "As I call your name, would you please stand and be recognized. Sherry Miller Williamson, owner and CEO of Robyn's World, one of the world's premier cosmetics companies." There was a round of applause as she stood.

"General Russell Bliven, US Army." Another round of applause as the general saluted.

"Dr. Mildred Johnson, renowned for her cutting-edge cancer research." Again applause.

"And last but not least, Roland Holtz, former mayor of Mavis, a Midwestern city, and former CEO of several of the largest companies in the world."

Applause rang out once again, and the four settled back into their seats.

The superintendent continued, "I can't think of anyplace else I would rather be this night than in the company of so many fine people. It is an honor to be Bradley's superintendent, and thank you all once again for coming."

After a last round of applause, there was a benediction, and finally, mercifully, it was over. Some groups gathered for pictures; some continued to chat; while others quietly dispersed, preparing to head for their cars.

Roland was reeling in surprise. He had no idea that Sherry had become not just a businesswoman but a very famous, wealthy, and respected one at that. Apparently, it wasn't just her good looks that had been attracting people to her that evening. He was not really up on women's fashion, but it was obvious that Robyn's World was a household name with women. He made a note to check it out online that night.

He couldn't say that it had been a wonderful evening, because in many ways, it hadn't. Oh, he had enjoyed meeting some of his old friends, and it had brought back some pleasant memories, but he was still too filled with the idea of getting even. Well, not exactly getting even, just letting her know what an opportunity she had passed up so long ago. It was all so out of character for him that he should have been self-aware of the fact. But he couldn't let go of the old pain and embarrassment he had endured because of her, and having reared its ugly head, it crowded out his better self. Also, for the first time in a very long time, he didn't have a plan, a clear understanding of where he was going next—especially since learning that Sherry had hardly suffered from not knowing him better.

Suddenly, it didn't matter, because from behind and to the side of him came a pleasant, "Hello, Roland," and as he turned to face her, she continued, "I didn't get a chance to talk with you before dinner, but I didn't want to let you get away without at least saying hello. You have done extremely well for yourself since we graduated."

"Hello, Sherry," he said. "You haven't done badly yourself. I saw you earlier, but I got tied up with so many others that I didn't get a chance to get over to see you before dinner. How have you been?" He wasn't expecting anything more than a polite answer, so he was not quite prepared for the response.

"I've been making my own way for some time now. You probably remember my boyfriend, Hughie. We got married right after graduation. He seemed like the answer to everything for me back then. I hate to admit it, but I was pretty naive and stuck on myself back in school, and I thought my parents were right out of the Stone Age. Hughie was my ticket out, but we weren't ready for the struggles we ran into. The best thing that came out of all that chaos was my daughter, Marcy. She's grown and off on her own now, but she's still my little girl."

For a moment, he thought of Melissa. She would have been grown and off on her own too had she lived. "I had a daughter," he heard himself saying, "but she was killed in a car accident along with her mother."

"Oh, I'm so sorry, Roland. I can't begin to imagine how horrible that must have been for you."

This wasn't going the way he wanted. He was feeling adrift. He needed time to think about the situation, and since Sherry didn't appear to be vulnerable, how would he repay her for her mistreatment of him so long ago?

He bailed out, "Look, Sherry, I flew in from Seattle today, and I'm staying for the reunion tomorrow. Will you be there?"

"I plan to be."

"Okay, I have to leave and make some calls before it gets too late, but the reunion will give us a chance to talk. I'm looking forward to it."

"Sounds like a plan, Roland, I'll see you there. Have a good night."

He watched as she walked away. She was graceful. She was actually still very beautiful even up close. No wonder every boy in the class had thought she was the living end. She certainly had aged better than many of his other classmates.

After a few more good-byes to old "friends," he walked out into the parking lot. There was no sign of Sherry. Mildly disappointed, he walked up to his rental car and opened the door, looking around once more before getting in and starting the vehicle. He wasn't really tired. It was only seven o'clock back home in Seattle.

Arriving back at the inn, he went to his room and turned on the TV. Flipping through the channels, he found nothing very interesting, so he took out his Bible and began reading. He had been in Romans, so he continued in chapter 12, and some of the verses left him a bit uncomfortable.

> Recompense to no man evil for evil. Provide things honest in the sight of all men. If it be possible, as much as lieth in you, live peaceably with all men. Dearly beloved, avenge not yourselves, but rather give place unto wrath; for it is written, Vengeance is mine; I will repay saith the lord.

74

When he read those verses 17 through 19, he was convicted that what he had been planning to do was not only wrong, it would be like an affront to God. Sherry wasn't evil, and she wasn't his enemy, but he had been planning to treat her like she was. He had been looking for revenge, but at the same time, he was finding himself drawn to Sherry in a much different way. He had no idea what he was going to say to her in the morning.

He put the Bible to one side and got ready for bed. He was more than aware that 8:00 a.m. Eastern Standard Time next morning would be a tad early for him. He decided to put off looking up Robyn's World, but it took him some time to fall asleep, and even then his rest was fitful, and then he dreamed of Betty.

9

THE REUNION

The next day, the conversations at the reunion were mostly about high school memories, families, life experiences, and what was going on in peoples' lives at the present. Some classmates were able to fill in information they had about people who were not there for those who were wondering about them. Delores spent a great deal of her time talking with Sherry, so much so that Roland ended up spending much of his time with Bob talking about fishing, past and present. He had thought that maybe he might be bombarded with questions about his career and successes, but that was not the case. In some way, he even felt a little let down that it didn't happen, but he still found himself enjoying the small talk and pleasantries.

There was a catered buffet luncheon about one o'clock, and two hours or so after that, people began to drift away. Some had homes nearby, and others had a distance to travel. There were lots of good-byes and promises to get together again or to stay in touch. He felt a twinge of genuine sadness that it was nearly over, but he still wanted to spend some time with Sherry. He knew that she hadn't left, and he found her locked in another conversation with her friend Delores.

He walked over to where they were sitting.

"Hello, Delores," he said. "I see you and Sherry have had an awful lot to talk about. I was hoping I might get to talk with her for a few minutes before I have to head back to Seattle."

There was a little bit of hyperbole there, but Delores, bless her soul, took the hint.

"I have to get going anyway," she said. "I'll give you a call tomorrow, Sherry. Bye." A hug, and she was on her way.

Roland apologized for interrupting their conversation. She didn't seem to mind.

"I love Delores like a sister," she said, "but even sisters need some time apart. I'm sorry, I know you wanted to talk today, but it was really hard to get away."

"I understand. I got pretty involved a few times myself, but I have to admit, I enjoyed it. I didn't think I would before I came, but I did. What do you say we go to Gino's and I'll buy a pizza? We can talk there. The sidewalk café area would be perfect this evening. Leave your car in town, and you can ride with me."

Gino's was located in the next town, about six miles to the south. It didn't take long to get there. The restaurant sat right across the street from the town square, and a band was playing in the gazebo when they pulled up.

He said, "I'll be darned, this must be one of the few places in the world where a band still plays in a town park on a hot summer Saturday afternoon. They aren't half bad. Let's sit on a park bench for a little while. I'm not very hungry just now anyway. What about you?"

"Sounds fine to me," she said, and they sat down next to each other and listened to the music, each one wondering what the other was going to talk about.

Roland had learned a lot about women since his days in high school, so he let her do most of the talking, but he did start the conversation.

"So tell me about Robyn's World."

"What would you like to know? It's the fifth largest cosmetics and fashions company in the world. I am the sole owner. Robyn's World had $320 million in total sales, which generated a net profit of $24.8 million last year."

"No," he broke in, "I could find all that online. Tell me how you got started and when. And tell me about what you did after high school. What happened to Hughie?"

"I eloped with Hughie right after high school. We rode his motorcycle south, got married in Virginia and didn't stop until we got to Georgia. We rented a little apartment, and he got a job as a mechanic at the local garage. We didn't have much money, but for a while, we were very happy. Our daughter, Marcy, was born the first year we were married, and shortly after she was born, my parents discovered where we were and moved to be near us. I know they meant well, but it became a living hell for Hughie. Being around them always left him feeling somehow ashamed and inadequate, and he had a very difficult time dealing with that.

"I tried to help out by coming up with some homemade, organic beauty products that I sold at the local flea market. I would take Marcy with me, and I think she even helped draw in the people. Before long, I had customers waiting for me every weekend, and people were coming to our home during the week as well. That was both good and bad. We had some extra money, but making my products and then selling them on the weekends took up most of the free time Hughie and I could have had together. I wanted the money partly to get my parents off his back, but he resented my efforts to placate my folks. After a while, he started drinking, and he could be unpleasant when he had too much. I began feeling trapped by forces I couldn't deal with."

Neither of them was any longer aware of the music. It was as though they were all alone together. He continued to listen to what she was saying, making no comment, but his earlier attitude was softening as he could see by her face that she still felt the pain of those days.

Sherry went on, "My parents never really accepted Hughie. They found fault with all sorts of trivial things about him and weren't hesitant about letting him know it. They were constantly critical about how we lived and how little we had, especially money. I think if they had left us alone, we would have been okay, but they were just more than Hughie could handle. He began drinking way too much, way too often. One night after we had another argument about the time I was spending with my cosmetics, he went out and took off on his motorcycle. I had been too foolish to see that he was more interested in me than in any money I was making. He would often ride his bike to burn off steam and calm down, but that night he wrapped his bike around a tree.

"The police got me out of bed at two in the morning and gave me the news. I felt so guilty because of our argument, but I believed the truth was his motorcycle accident was really a direct result of my parents' interference in our lives, and I hated them for it."

"What did you do?" he asked.

"Well, what could I do? My husband was dead, he hadn't had any life insurance, I had a two-year-old child, and I didn't have enough money to make ends meet. I sold our home to pay for the funeral, and Marcy and I moved in with my mother and father. I didn't want to do it, but I couldn't see any other way out. It was really hard for me because I blamed them for Hughie's death, and they were still running him down even after he was buried. At first I tried to get them to stop putting him down, but they just couldn't seem to get over being miserable. It was terrible.

"I was determined to be on my own with Marcy just as soon as I could, and I worked hard to expand my production and build my sales. I have always thought that my misfortune had turned out to be a boon for my business. People heard about my story and my products and bought the cosmetics to help me out but then learned how good they were. It was still slow going, but before long, I had to find a facility to produce my products because the garage of my parents' home was too confining. I finally used the money I had left from selling our home and took out a loan to get a storefront with an adjoining area for production.

"My parents offered to put up the money to help pay for the storefront. They even offered to work in the store for me for free. They said they would help me all that they could, but I knew they were just trying to sooth their own consciences, and they didn't have enough free cash lying around to be able to help out a whole lot anyway. Besides, I didn't want to end up owing them anything. I didn't want to give them the satisfaction of thinking they could make up for their treatment of Hughie that way. I told them outright that I didn't want anything from them, and I meant it, but I did let them watch Marcy when I was working."

He saw a hard expression creep over her face and could hear the bitterness in her words. He was realizing that there was a sad, dark side in Sherry's life.

He ignored the implications and attempted to navigate around the shoals by asking, "Did you run everything yourself? It sounds like a pretty big order."

"Yes, for a while, I did everything. I worked as much as sixteen hours out of each day, seven days a week, but after a few months, I was totally worn out. I almost never got to spend any time with Marcy unless I took her to the shop with me. I realized that killing myself wasn't what I needed to do, and more importantly, Marcy needed more of my attention than I was giving her. At times she would just cry and hold on to me. I finally had to admit that I needed help, and I hired a young woman. She ran the shop for part of the day. Fortunately, she was a wonderful person and very dependable. She learned quickly and became a very dedicated worker and, eventually, a good friend. As a matter of fact, she continued to work for me for over twenty years."

Roland was impressed and asked, "So why did you call your shop Robyn's World?"

"I didn't at first. I called my shop Sherry's Natural Cosmetics, but that was sort of lame, and I knew it, but I just couldn't come up with something better. Then one day, Marcy was watching a robin in my parents' yard. I still lived with them [the hardness resurfaced for a moment], and she said, 'Mommy, there's a bird out there with your plants,' and I told her it was a robin and that he spent a lot of time out in our backyard because that was his world. For some reason, it clicked with me. I spent an awful lot of my time at the shop, so I changed the sign on my shop to Robyn's World and used a robin as my logo. And that's what it has been ever since."

"So why didn't you name it Sherry's World if that was where you spent your time?"

"I think, unconsciously, I saw the perky robin as a carefree creature in a world where he was happy. My world was a long ways from that. I guess I named it with hope in my heart, hope that someday I might be as happy as the robin in the backyard."

"So there must have been a tipping point where you went from a mom-and-pop status in a little store front to an international cosmetics phenomenon. That hardly seems possible. What happened there?" Roland probed.

"I felt that lack of capital was the one thing that was really holding me back. I knew I needed to produce more, and I needed to advertise my cosmetics outside of my local area if I were ever going to grow, but both of those things required money I didn't have. I had been able to keep the payments up on the loan I had taken out, but I just couldn't begin to amass what I needed to go forward.

"My business grew, but at the rate I was going, I knew I would never be anything but a small shop lost in a small Southern town. I put away every cent I could. I paid my parents a fair share of the food and utility costs, I wasn't asking for charity. But after that, it was business and savings."

"Obviously, something must have worked out for you," Roland said.

"Roland, I am still at a loss to explain it even today, but three things happened in the space of a few weeks that changed everything for me."

"What were they?" Roland asked. He found himself being drawn into the story.

"The first thing was amazing—no, it was almost unbelievable, like out of a fairy tale. Shortly after I opened the shop one morning, a very distinguished-looking gentleman came in and told me he had been asked to give me something. He handed me an envelope. 'Before you open this,' he said, 'please sit down.' After I was sitting, he said, 'I cannot supply you with any answers to the questions you might have when you open the envelope, but I can assure you this is no joke. It is real. A check for a great deal of money is in the envelope. The person who sent me with this does not wish to be identified and only asks two things: one, that you not try to find out who he or she is, and two, that you tell no one you were given the money or how much it was. Now you may open the envelope.' Inside was a one-line note that asked me to please accept the gift in memory of Hughie and watch what God will do. With the note, there was a certified check for two hundred thousand dollars made out to me. That doesn't sound like a lot today, but it was a considerable sum back then."

"Wow, you are right, that is almost unbelievable," he commented. "Go on."

"I figured that money gave me more than enough to get moving, but everything might still never have come together if it hadn't been for a small advertising agency that contacted me out of the blue and a rather mysterious woman that came to my shop. It turned out that the wife of the agency owner had been using my products, and she was convinced her husband's business and Robyn's World could be an unbeatable combination. She convinced Brian, her husband, of the same thing.

"It wasn't until years later that I learned, it didn't happen by chance, that a very distinguished-looking gentleman had come into the agency and put the idea into her head. He told her that he understood I was going to be in need of all the advertising help I could get, and if they wanted to hook their wagon to a rising star, they should not waste any time contacting me. He must have done a great selling job. As it turned out, they were a perfect match and are still our agent, and we have both done handsomely. There were a lot of ins and outs and ups and downs, but today's Robyn's World Incorporated is the direct result.

"I could never figure out who could have been my benefactor, nor why, other than the note saying it was in memory of Hughie. It might have been someone from his family that we didn't know about or maybe a friend that had struck it rich, but whoever it was, he or she did one more thing for me. A few days after receiving the check, and before the advertising agency came on the scene, another person came to my shop.

"She was the mysterious woman I mentioned. She had a foreign accent and told me that she had a great deal of experience in cosmetics and had felt that it was important to come and talk with me and see if she could be of any assistance to me. But first she wanted to see my products. Then she wanted to see my production area. She sniffed everything, rubbed items on her skin, and she had a ton of questions. You know, it's funny now, but when she was asking me all the questions, I panicked for just a moment, thinking maybe this woman was going to steal all my hard work and information for herself. But then I figured, what the hell, she won't get much, and I told her all she wanted to know. After the complete two-dollar tour, she appeared to be deep in thought. She sat down in one of the two chairs in my shop and motioned me to sit in the other.

"She told me that she was quite impressed by some of my items. 'You have done amazing things for someone with so little formal knowledge about cosmetics,' she told me. She asked me what my plans were for the future. I told her I wanted to expand, hopefully to become a major company, but I didn't know exactly how to go about it. I wasn't sure what I would need, and I had no idea how to develop a mass market.

"We spent a long time talking about my business and the cosmetics business in general, before she asked me if I had any idea how much it would cost me to even have a chance of doing what I wanted to do and what the odds were that I would be successful.

"I admitted to her that I didn't know how much it would cost but that I had a considerable amount on hand. She looked around my shop, rolled her eyes, nodded her head, and said, 'I'm sure you do.' I ignored it and told her I didn't care what the odds were. I was going to make it a success. The last thing she asked me that day was if I was interested in finding other investors and had I considered borrowing money to help in a start-up. I had not considered that yet but told her that if it was necessary, I would be willing to do it. That was about the end of our conversation that morning. I may have left some things out, but that's pretty much the gist of it. She said we would talk again."

Roland couldn't keep himself from asking, "So who was this woman? Where did she come from? Apparently, she was able to help you?"

"I can't tell you a lot about her. Her name was Consuelo. I never knew just where she came from, but she had a great deal of knowledge about the cosmetics business. She apparently had been at one of the various craft shows I continued to think I had to do even after I opened my shop, but it was before I got the money. She told me my products had caught her attention. She had taken one of my business cards at the craft show, and as it turned out, somehow it was an old one with my father's address and phone number on it. I hadn't been using them after opening my shop, but it had gotten mixed into my new ones that had the shop address and number. She had come looking for me and found my father. She didn't tell him what she wanted, but he gave her the address for my shop. He told me later that he had figured she wanted to buy something from me, so he just sent her along.

"Consuelo was able to help me a great deal. Not only did she have a great working knowledge of all aspects of cosmetics, but she also offered to invest up to two hundred thousand dollars of her own up front. Thanks to her, I was bold enough to work out an additional line of credit with the bank. Money was no longer an issue. We leased part of a vacant factory building and converted it into my first real cosmetics manufacturing facility. Consuelo knew what was required to start producing in bulk, and we installed the best equipment we could find. She was instrumental in locating several people who had experience working in the field, and I hired them all. It was very exciting, and things were happening so quickly it was hard for me to keep on top of everything.

"Between Consuelo's expertise and Brian's advertising campaign, it was only a little more than a year before we were able to place our line into two upscale chains, and orders began flowing in. The only problem was that it seemed like she wanted to take the reins and run the business. I felt I was losing control, and because I had the most invested and the most to lose, I wanted to make the decisions.

"I had her sit down with me for a review of what we had accomplished and to plan where we were going. I gave her a great deal of credit, and I shared how much I appreciated her work and her drive. I told her that I didn't think I could have gotten as far on my own as we had together, but it was high time to deal with the administrative structure of the business for both of our sakes. I suggested that she should have a formal position in the company that reflected her abilities. I wanted her to be the executive officer in charge of operations, and I wanted her to be the front person for Robyn's World. I reserved the position of owner and CEO to myself, but I wanted her to have a voice in every decision I made.

"It took some time, but we were able to work everything out to our mutual satisfaction and understanding, and we agreed that it was important that we get legal counsel to help us set things up and to incorporate the business. After that, there was never any question about who was in charge, and for a few years, I leaned very heavily on Consuelo's instincts and good advice. She got me out to the business shows in Europe, and I learned so much and met so many people in the trade. She coached me through everything, and she never let me down.

"You know, Roland, I could tell you a lot more, but it would just be business stuff, and I'm getting hungry for that pizza you offered."

He replied, "That sounds good to me, but there are a few questions I still have, so I hope you don't mind visiting as we eat."

He took her arm as they crossed the street, and he was surprised how natural it felt to do so.

It was late afternoon as they sat down at one of Gino's outside tables. It was not as hot and humid as it had been the night before. In fact, it was just about perfect. They both commented on how pleasant and relaxing it was. A car or two passed by occasionally, and a couple of boys walked by with fishing rods in their hands. The river ran through town less than a hundred yards away.

Roland said, "I know where they are headed. There's a great fishing hole right under the bridge around the corner and down the hill. I fished there many times when I was a boy."

They ordered a medium pepperoni pizza and a draft beer, and then Roland told her about one of his boyhood fishing adventures that took place a stone's throw away.

"I decided one Friday," he said, "to bring a fishing rod with me when I came here for the movies. I came a few hours before the show started so I could fish as long as I liked. I brought a few worms and a couple of raw hot dogs with me for bait, and I went down under the bridge to try my luck. I had expected to catch mostly chubs and fallfish, which I never kept, and because I was going to the movies later, I didn't bring anything along with me to put fish in anyway.

"As it turned out, I caught and released quite a few big fallfish on small pieces of the hotdogs as well as a couple of bullheads. I hated to throw the bullheads back because they were good eating, but back they went all the same. About the time I was out of hot dogs, the fallfish had figured out what was going on and had pretty much quit biting, so I switched to using the worms I had with me, and the first thing I caught was a nice rainbow about fourteen inches. It was even harder to throw that fish back, but back he went. I caught a couple more fallfish, and then I hooked into a really big fish. It fought like it weighed a ton. I had no idea what it might be as I tried to bring it in, until it rolled at the surface and I saw it was a huge black bass.

"I wanted that bass more than anything in the world right then. I was afraid it would break the line or throw the hook and be gone. After what seemed like forever, I got the fish coming my way, and finally, it was worn out, and I got it up to the cement wall I was standing on. It was the biggest smallmouth bass I had ever seen, and I had seen a lot of them. I had caught a couple that pushed four pounds before, but this one must have weighed seven pounds, if it weighed an ounce, and had to have been close to twenty-four inches long. They just didn't come that big.

"I took it off the hook and held it in my hands, amazed at what I had caught. I was in a quandary as what to do with it. I didn't want to throw it back, but I realized keeping it was going to be a messy affair. Then as I struggled with my choices, holding that magnificent fish, something told me to put it back in the water, to let it go, and I did. It was a great feeling to give that fish its freedom. I've never been sorry I did it, even though it might have been a New York State record. I'll never know. But I knew then and I know now, sometimes letting something go is just the right thing to do."

The meal came, and they began eating the pizza before he asked, "Tell me about your daughter. Did you say her name is Marcy? Is she married? Do you have any grandchildren?"

"She's not married, and I'm not sure she is even thinking about it. She's nearly thirty-five, so I guess my chances for grandchildren grow dimmer each and every day. She is such a beautiful young lady I would have thought someone would have snapped her up by now, but it hasn't happened. She lives in Snoqualmie, Washington, not too far from Seattle."

He could hardly believe his ears. "What a coincidence. I live in Snoqualmie too. How long has she lived there?"

"She has been there about ten years. I was just out to see her this past spring. I have always wanted her to come and work with me at Robyn's World, but she wanted to make it on her own. I bought her a house for her birthday when she moved out west. It was a gift, so she couldn't very well say no, but for the most part, she does her own thing and pays her own bills without any help from me."

They fell silent for a moment as they worked on the pizza. Roland glanced to the north up Main Street, looking at the protruding structure that once blinked and shimmered with a myriad of colored bulbs and neon lights, advertising the Kallet Movie Theater. The lights and the bulbs were gone now, and so was the ticket booth that sat underneath the large triangular flashing structure, which had protected patrons from the weather as they bought their tickets. It had been flanked by the heavy red metal double doors on both sides. But all that remained was a great gray, unattractive reminder that once there had been a magic palace in the center of town.

"Do you remember the movie theater, Sherry?"

A pleasant feeling enveloped her as she replied, "Yes, I remember it. I thought it was the most beautiful thing I had ever seen back when we were in school. I used to love just standing outside and watching the lights flashing, seeming to chase each other in endless waves around the marquee. It was absolutely stunning when the snow was falling. It has been closed for a long time. It looks so forlorn. It makes me sad just to look at it. I remember the smell of hot buttered popcorn and the leathery smell of the seats and the sticky floor underneath them. I remember the fuzzy red-flocked wallpaper that covered the walls of the curved staircases leading to the lounge and restrooms on the second floor."

He took a few more looks at the old theater as they ate their pizza. She was right. *Forlorn* was a good description for it, but it still held memories for him.

"You're right," he said. "It does look forlorn now, and it was a beautiful thing in its day. I used to come here on Friday nights and watch the Westerns. It was one of my favorite things to do."

She replied, "I used to come with my parents. They were into musicals, so I saw about every one that came along."

"Do you remember that I took you there on the only date we ever had?" Roland asked.

Her heart jumped. "Yes, I remember, Roland. I've thought about that a lot of times since we left Bradley."

"So have I," he replied quickly. "I remember taking you to dinner at Benny's and to the movie afterward. I remember how beautiful you looked under those lights as I was buying our tickets. I could hardly believe you were there with me on a date. I remember we held hands for a while as we watched the movie. When we did, my body felt like it was on fire. I don't think there was anything I wouldn't have done for you at that time if you had asked. I've thought about that night a lot of times, and I always wondered if I did something wrong or if maybe you just disliked going to and from the movies in a Greyhound bus with me because you had gone places with Hughie on his motorcycle."

Her countenance began to change as he worked his way up to the raw indignation that he had never been able to forget.

"I remember walking back to your house with you and asking for a good night kiss. You have no idea of how hard it was for me to do that, but I wasn't hurt when you said no, and I didn't mind the little laugh that went with the refusal all that much. It wasn't until the days that followed and everyone began treating me like I was some sort of freak, and I learned that you had told your friends I was a lousy date, and you would never go out with me again. That pretty much ruined the rest of my high school life. I was never able to get a date at school after that. I actually hated you for a few years, and I even steered clear of girls in college because of it."

He didn't give her time to comment before he completed what he had to say, "I thought when I met my Betty, I had finally been able to put all that behind me, but the fact is, I had just covered it up. When I got the invitation to the banquet and reunion, I came because I wanted to see you so you would realize what you had passed up that night. I wanted to make you regret what you said and did. I wanted to hurt you like you had hurt me, but that was wrong, and what's worse yet, I knew it.

"But here's the most important thing. I still don't like what you did, but I want you to know that I forgive you. You may not believe there is anything for me to forgive, but I suffered more than you might be able to imagine, and I have held you responsible for that for way too long. But thank God, that is over and done with. When I leave for Seattle tomorrow, I will finally be free of all that."

The smile was gone from Sherry's lips, and from the look on her face, he knew everything had changed. Now the genie was out of the bottle, and he realized that he had hurt her. As quickly as it had happened, he regretted telling her.

Lamely, he said, "I'm sorry that I have probably messed up a good time and a great pizza dinner, but I had to get that off my chest. Let's finish our pizza, and I'll take you back to your car."

She wasn't willing to let it go.

"Roland, I am sorry too, sorry that I hurt you. I apologize for that, but it was not my intention. Hughie saw me that night, and he knew I had been out with you. He was angry, and he told me he was going to beat you up badly enough that you would never even look at me again. He wasn't just talking, he meant it. It was bad, but I told him there was nothing to the whole thing. I told him I was just fooling around and it wouldn't happen again. It took me awhile to get him settled down, but finally, he made me promise I wouldn't have anything to do with you and that I would make sure you stayed away from me.

"I should have just gone to you and explained, but I took the easy way out and told my friends that you weren't much of a catch. I told them I had no interest in you because you were so boring.

I probably said other things too, I don't really remember. I knew Hughie would get a report from someone about what I said, and I knew the word would get around, but it didn't occur to me how hurtful it would turn out to be for you. I wanted to keep you from getting beaten up, and I wanted to keep him from doing something stupid and getting in trouble. Looking back, I guess I was the only one who did something stupid. I really am sorry."

Up until the point when he had unburdened himself, she had enjoyed the time with him. He had seemed truly interested in her story. He was so handsome and so impressive that she really didn't want it to all end this way. She decided to test the waters.

"Do you think we could start over and forget about those things we can't change?"

Here was his chance, but he foolishly replied, "I don't know."

"I'd like to get to know you better, Roland, but maybe this is not the time or the place to talk about that." She was not going to go any farther than that.

There was an awkward silence. The two of them sat there, not knowing what else to say as they allowed one last chance at real honesty between them to slip away. Neither was able to tell the other about their true feelings.

She ended the short impasse, saying, "I think I've had enough pizza. It's probably time we leave." Reaching into her purse, she said, "But before we go, would you mind giving me one of your business cards? You never know when Robyn's World might need some advice. Here's mine," handing it to him.

He took it and put it in his wallet, at the same time taking out one of his own for her.

As she looked at his card, she thought, *You were right. You were full of hurt, and you don't know it, but you accomplished your purpose for coming even if you no longer wanted to. I do realize how much I lost, not thirty-five years ago, but right now. You are so real, so honest. You are all the things missing in most of the men I know.*

She had hoped he might actually be the prince charming of fairy tale fame that she had been waiting for, but it turned out he didn't seem to be searching for a princess.

She had even dared to hope that perhaps he might actually be the unknown reason for what Delores had written, "The Lord is in your decision to come. Give him a chance this one time."

Well, she thought, *I gave God a chance, but he didn't appear to be any more interested in me than Roland was. Delores was no prophet.*

For a short time—as they had listened to the band, talked, and then shared a pizza—a long-suppressed joy and hope had started to well up in her spirit, but it had been crushed, and a great sadness was washing over her as she stood up. When he offered his arm as they crossed the street, she ignored it.

It was a quiet ride back to Bradley. He pulled up behind her car and got out to open her door, but she had already gotten out before he had the chance.

"Thanks for the pizza," she said. Moving closer to him, she said, "I owe you something." Standing on her tiptoes, she planted a quick kiss on his lips and murmured, "That's for thirty-five years ago," and then she turned and started walking to her car.

As she unlocked her car door and opened it, she noticed he was still standing, watching her. It didn't matter.

"Good-bye, Roland," she said softly just before getting into her car.

He watched her drive away until the taillights disappeared as she drove over the little ridge at the north end of town. He certainly hadn't expected that his return to Bradley and the reunion would turn out quite this way.

I could have just let it go, forgot about it, he thought. *I didn't have to say anything about why I came back for the reunion. I blew it big-time. I screwed up my mulligan. All I had to do was agree that maybe we could start out fresh, but no, I couldn't even do that.*

He was still thinking about her on his flight back to Seattle the next morning.

10
RETURN TO ROBYN'S WORLD

Sherry walked into the suite, glancing around at the staff and other workers, nodding her head at the ones who looked her way as she passed.

Gwen stood up and said, "Welcome back. How was the reunion?"

"It was interesting," she replied. "Would you come into my office in about ten minutes please, and bring me up to speed. It feels like I've been away forever."

She had determined that she was going to throw herself back into her work and forget about Roland. As she walked into her office and closed the door, she was immersed in what had been her life for so long. It felt good to be back where she was in control. She settled down in the big chair behind her desk to get comfortable.

She called Gwen on the intercom, "Gwen, please have someone bring me a cup of coffee. You know how I take it."

Minutes later, Gwen came in with her pad and a cup of coffee. "I was already fixing it for you. No sense in someone else bring it in when I was coming anyway. Where would you like to start?"

"Well, are there any items that require my immediate personal attention?"

"Not at the moment," Gwen replied.

"Do I have any meetings scheduled for the next month besides the one in France?"

"Yes," Gwen replied, and she began to read a list starting with the most immediate and supplying the pertinent information.

She tried to focus on the business at hand. She wanted to shut everything else out and become the same person that she had been before the reunion, but Gwen's words quickly faded out of her hearing as her mind wandered to thoughts of Roland.

I wonder what he is doing today. I wonder if he has thought of me at all. It's hard to believe how everything seems to have changed somehow. I have not felt this way about any man since Hughie.

"Is there something wrong?" Gwen's words sounded concerned. "You looked like you were not even here."

"I'm sorry, Gwen. My mind doesn't seem to want to stay on task. Would you mind writing up a summary for me? I can't concentrate right now. Just get it to me as soon as you are finished so I can work with it."

"I can do that," she said. "It won't take me too long. I have most of it saved already. I can have it for you shortly."

"That would be great. Thank you."

After Gwen left, she took his card out of her purse and propped it up on her desk. She opened her e-mail and checked to see if possibly he had e-mailed her, but she was disappointed. She thought about e-mailing him, but she didn't know what to say. She couldn't tell him that she had a wonderful time; that would be foolish. She couldn't just say hello. She definitely didn't want to replow the ground they had covered at the pizza shop, but she wanted to make another contact with him.

I guess I'll wait for a while, she thought. *There's no sense in being impatient.*

She looked at the e-mails. There was one from Marcy, two from Delores, and one from Geoffrey. She opened Marcy's first; she wasn't ready to face Delores.

"Mother, we never really talked about Grandma and Grandfather. I told you we should go to visit him, but you sort of blew that off. If you don't want to go with me, that's okay, but if you don't, I'm going to go on my own. It's a piece of my life I need to get settled. I have been thinking about it since you were here, but I didn't want to do it without telling you. I really enjoyed the time we spent together. Thanks so much for coming. Love, Marcy."

That was not what she had wanted to hear. It didn't brighten her day, but she wouldn't try to stand between Marcy and her grandfather.

Maybe sometimes I'm just too stubborn for my own good, she thought. *But I can't start rethinking my whole life right now.*

She would answer Marcy later. Next she opened the first e-mail from Delores.

"Sherry, wasn't it great to see everyone again? I apologize for monopolizing so much of your time, but I couldn't help myself. I see you so seldom. Isn't that Roland a hunk? I could hardly believe how great he looked. You got to spend some time with him, right? He sure seemed nice. Bob said he hasn't changed a bit except he didn't want to go fishing. Roland told him he would take a rain check. Just the same, Bob said he didn't think he would ever come back to Bradley again. He saw him in the morning before he left, and he said he had acted like he couldn't wait to be on his way and acted kind of down too. Do you think it is possible to have his kind of money and be sad? Keep in touch. Delores."

She thought about the question. She was terribly blue herself, but she wasn't hurting for lack of money. She tried to tap into her feelings.

Why do I feel the way I do right now?

It wasn't as easy for her to diagnose as someone might imagine. She didn't realize it, but there were long-standing multiple walls of denial and blame now hampering her search, and now she was paying the price for building them. She had some choices to make, but she wasn't ready to admit she was the builder and that the walls played a huge role in why she felt the way she did, possibly because she wasn't able to connect the dots of her life and comprehend the hidden picture.

"What do I have to do to be happy?" she asked herself. "I have always thought it was building a great business, having money, being my own boss, and being respected by other people in the trade. And those things have satisfied me for so long. Is it possible to have my kind of money and be sad? Obviously, it is. What do I have to do to get out of this funk? What do I have to do to be happy?"

She opened the other e-mail from Delores.

"Sorry, I almost forgot to tell you. I'm still praying for you, you know, and you still need the Lord. He wants to be your heavenly Father. Remember, it's never too late to forgive or ask to be forgiven. I love you. Delores."

I know she means well, she thought, *but it does get a little old. I would have been a lot better off if I had just gone to youth group with her and let it go at that, but that was her thing, not mine. I've done okay on my own, and even if there is a God, he isn't interested in me any more than I am in him.*

She sighed as she opened the last e-mail. It was a "welcome back" from Geoffrey. She made a mental note that soon, she had to make up her mind what she was going to do about him. It didn't improve her state of mind.

But poor, insistent Geoffrey could wait. Right now she needed to deal with her daughter. She didn't want to damage the tender shoot of their new relationship, but she really didn't want to go with her either. She was very uncomfortable with having been put on the spot, but she had sense enough to know that she should not try to dissuade her daughter. Marcy was just as headstrong as her mother.

Hitting the *Return* button, she began to write, "Marcy, your grandfather and I have had a strained relationship since before you were born. I told you about some of that. I don't know if it would be good for him or for me to see each other right now, but if you feel you need to go, by all means do it. Love you, Mother."

There, she had said it. Marcy was free to do as she wished with her blessing.

She sat back in her chair and let her mind wander. So much had happened in the past few months. It had been an emotional roller coaster, and the ride seemed to be still continuing, but now it was plunging dangerously. She was no longer in control of her world, even in her own office. She had been thrilled when she saw Roland, then swept to unexpectedly great heights from a simple outing for pizza, only to quickly careen and fall. She had been drawing closer to her daughter, but now she had set out in a new direction, one that she didn't want to follow. Geoffrey was pressuring her, and Robyn's

World was swallowing her. And then there was her father. Sherry was beginning to experience more than sadness; it was a jumble of guilt and despair.

She needed some point to start putting the pieces into some sort of order.

Let's start with Roland, she thought. *I would like to get to know him better, but he hasn't made any attempt to contact me. What are my options? I can continue to wait, or I can send him an e-mail. Likelihood of success in either case—minimal. If he should get back to me, where do I go from there? Follow his lead or wing it? Why is this so hard? Maybe I need to be impatient. I need to get some closure on this, one way or another. I need to know if I should forget about him and move on. What's the worst he could say, "I'm not interested"?*

Turning back to the keyboard, she typed in Roland's address. She thought about the subject line.

What do I put in there? Wait, I don't have to give anything away here.

She typed, "Thanks for being honest." Moving onto the message, she wrote, "I was sort of hoping you might not remember our first date and the fallout, which was pretty stupid, but I appreciated your forgiving me. I reacted badly to what you told me, but at the time, I believed you probably had seen the last of me that you ever wanted to see once you had spoken your mind. I gave you my business card because my hope was that we might be able to get together again sometime in spite of the past."

She read her message several times before adding, "I'm sitting in my office, but I can't get any work done because I just can't stop thinking about you. How crazy is that?"

She had mixed emotions about sending the e-mail but then sent it just the way it was.

She moved on to another piece of the puzzle as she thought, *How about Geoffrey? Do I want him or not? Honestly, no. Then let him know that, but do it gently. He may be hurt, but he won't be devastated. Okay, that was easy. I'll do it later.*

Why am I suddenly not excited about the business? she thought. *I can't let it go on cruise control. Someone has to be in control—me. But does it have to be me? It's not fun anymore, but it's my life's work. I was right when I told Marcy my life was becoming Robyn's World. It's going to devour me if I don't do something to stop it. Maybe it already has.*

That night she got a reply from Roland.

"Sherry, I am sorry that I gave you the impression that I wanted nothing more to do with you. Once I got everything off my chest, I have to admit I was a bit confused by the results. You aren't any crazier than I am because you have been much on my mind since I got back home. I tell you what. The next time you are visiting your daughter, let me know you are coming, and we will spend some time together if you would like. After all, you will be right here where I live. In the meantime, I would enjoy hearing from you from time to time. Cheers, Roland."

She had to read the e-mail several times. She was thrilled to read that Roland had actually been thinking about her. True, he didn't sound like he was ready to rush into her arms, but the door was certainly open more than a crack. Still, she would wait a day or two before responding now that she knew Roland would be waiting for a reply.

Now the question was, how soon could she visit her daughter again, and what would she use as an excuse? She wasn't going to have to think about it long as the answer was already in the making.

11

IN THE HOSPITAL

"You've got company, Mr. Miller," the nurse said. "Someone is here to see you."

"Hi, Grandpa," she said as her grandfather turned to see who it was. "It's been a long time since I've seen you."

"Marcy? Marcy! Holy cow, you are a sight for sore eyes. It's so good to see you. Why are you here? Did someone call you?"

"I've just come to see how you are doing," Marcy replied. "I went to your apartment, and they told me you had been taken to the hospital four days ago. How are you feeling?"

"Well, to be honest, I've been a little under the weather, but I'm feeling better now just seeing you. I can hardly remember the last time I saw you. Just stand there a minute, and let me look at you. Why, you're all grown up. When did that happen?"

"It's been awhile, Grandpa, I'm thirty-three years old."

"Yes, I know," he said with a hint of sadness in his voice. "Where have the years gone? Is your mother here with you?"

"No, Grandpa, she was busy."

He nodded, again with a sad look, "Well, let me get out of this bed, and we can talk," he said as he sat up and slipped his legs out of bed. "We can go down to the solarium. It's nice and warm there."

"Is it okay for you to be up?"

"Sure, it is, they keep telling me I need to get up and move around. They'll be glad to see me doing it," he said as he stood up.

"My behind sticks out of this gown. If you would hand me my bath robe, so I won't accidentally flash anyone, I'll be ready."

As they walked down the hall, she held on to his arm. She had been alarmed by how frail he looked, but still he seemed fairly steady on his feet, and that reassured her. Soon they were at the solarium. It was well named, as the sun poured through the windows, warming body and soul alike. They settled down on the couch and just looked at each other.

Marcy asked softly, "What's wrong with you, Grandpa? What happened? Why are you in the hospital?"

"I don't think it's anything too serious. I was very dizzy, couldn't stand up, and everything just seemed to be swirling around me. I crawled to the door and pulled myself up enough to get it open. The Petersons down the hall heard me holler, and they called an ambulance, and here I am."

"Well, what did the doctor tell you?" Marcy asked.

"Not a lot. They are still running tests on me, but I am feeling a little better. I haven't been dizzy since the day after they brought me in. How did you hear that I was sick anyway?"

"I didn't hear, Grandpa. I came to see you because I wanted to talk about something with you. I didn't know there was anything wrong with you until the folks at your apartment building told me you were in the hospital. I was shocked."

"Well, I'm so glad you came. You have really made my day."

She looked around the room. There was no one else there with them. She put her arms around her grandfather and gave him a long hug.

"Grandpa, I think we have a lot of catching up to do, but I don't think you are up to it right now."

He smiled, shaking his head, and replied, "There's no time like the present. Who knows, I might not be here tomorrow, we'd better do it now. What do you want to talk about?"

"I hardly know where to begin, but I guess the first thing is to tell you how sorry I am that I didn't come a long time ago. I grew up hardly knowing you and Grandma, and lately, I've been feeling terrible about that.

"Mother came and visited me for a few days awhile ago, and I had a lot of questions for her that had been on my mind for a long time. She told me a lot about my father and how she thought you and Grandma felt about him. She really seemed uncomfortable talking about you and Grandma. I listened to her side of the story—as much as she was willing to share with me—and now I'd like to hear from you. Are you okay talking about this?"

He looked down and sighed. "Marcy, we need to talk about this somewhere else. I don't feel comfortable about getting into it here in this room. Let's check with the doctor and see if and when I might be going home. I'd prefer to talk about it there."

"Sure, I understand. When does your doctor stop by to see you? Has he been here yet?"

"He is usually on this floor between three and four. It won't be too long, so maybe we had better go back down to the room and wait there for him."

They walked slowly back to the room, and he climbed back into bed.

"I'm getting old, Marcy. I get pooped just walking that short distance. If you'll excuse me, I'm going to rest for just a minute."

In a few moments, he had dozed off. She sat in the only chair in the room and listened to him breathe.

Maybe it's a good thing Mom didn't come, she thought. *I think it will be better with just the two of us.*

She tried to remember the times she had spent with her grandparents, but she had only fleeting images.

And now it has come to this, she thought. *We have lost a lifetime because of misunderstandings, hurtful actions, and separation, and we will never be able to get it back. I should have been here ten years ago, there's no excuse. Instead, here I am, with Grandpa sick and maybe dying, and if we talk about Mom and my father, it will probably be hard on him.*

She sat with her thoughts, watching her grandfather sleeping, wishing she had decided to come years before while her grandmother was still alive. It was strange how she could grieve for people she had hardly gotten to know. She was so sad, but she knew that she was grieving as much for herself as she was for her grandparents.

A short time later, the doctor came in on his rounds. Marcy got out of the chair and introduced herself. He woke up at the sound of their voices.

"I see you've met my granddaughter, Doctor. She came all the way from the West Coast to see how I'm doing. I would like to put her name on those papers I filled out so you can tell her about my condition."

"I'll have the nurse take care of that for you right after I check you over. Have you been up today?"

"Yes, I have. Marcy walked down to the solarium and back with me earlier."

The doctor listened with his stethoscope before asking, "Have you been dizzy at all today, Mr. Miller?"

"No, I've been feeling a little better. A nurse walked with me whenever I had to get up, but I didn't need their help. Do you have any ideas about what's going on with me?"

"I think you may have been just run down. You were dehydrated when you came in. That's why we had you hooked up to the IVs for a while. You need to start eating and drinking more before we can send you home, but I'll have the results of all the blood tests tomorrow, and we can figure out what we are going to do with you."

She thanked the doctor and assured him that she would make sure he ate what he was supposed to. After the doctor left, the nurse came in with the forms, naming her as next of kin and as a person who could be given information on his condition.

"Are you going to be staying for a while?" he asked. "You can stay in my apartment. The guest room is ready. It doesn't get used much, but it's comfy. I've got the keys right here in the drawer." He opened the drawer and took out the keys, giving them to her.

"Thanks, Grandpa. I'll stay until after you've had your dinner, and then I'll take you up on the room."

"You said you spent some time with Sherry. Does she visit you often?" he asked.

"No, she hardly every comes to visit, but this time was right out of the blue. She didn't talk about the business at all, but I know it is going very well."

"How is she doing? Is she healthy? Is she happy?"

"I think she is healthy enough, and she looks good. Actually, she looks great, but I got the impression from what she said that she wasn't really very happy. I think she feels like life has sort of passed her by."

"Hhumph," he snorted, "she may have brought that on herself."

She ignored the comment. "She is thinking about getting married again. She is frightened of living out her life alone. I think that was why she came to see me. She felt we were way too far apart."

"We? You mean you and your mother?"

"Yes."

"Whom is she thinking about marrying? It's not likely it would be anybody I would know."

"She spoke about a couple of men, but I don't think she has anyone seriously lined up. She did mention an old high school friend that she was going to see at a class reunion, Roland Holtz. I haven't heard how that went."

"Well, anyone as pretty as your mother, and with all her money, shouldn't have much trouble in roping and branding the man of her choice."

"Do you know who Roland Holtz is? He is a very rich businessman. He's been the CEO of several companies. I don't think he will be very impressed by Mom's money."

"I thought you said he was a classmate of hers?"

"He was. He even took her out on a date once, according to Mom."

"Well, two rich people tied up in themselves and their money. They should be very happy together." Then his eyes lit up, and he shifted gears. "How about you? Do you have your sights set on a young man?"

"I haven't been looking real hard, but I've dated a couple of men that might be good prospects. I just haven't gotten all that close to anyone. I guess I'm kind of like Mom. She has some guys that are interested in her, but she says they just don't turn her on. I'm still looking for the guy that lights up my life. I don't want to end up with the wrong guy."

"That's wise, Marcy. Find someone who loves you and makes you feel special. You'll know when the right man comes along."

She wanted to change the conversation because she had something else on her mind. It was something that had just come to her. She wasn't sure if she should toss it out or not, but she decided to go with it.

"Grandpa, I'd like you to think about moving out to Washington to live with me. You don't have to make any decision right now, just think about it."

Her grandfather was surprised by the sudden offer, but he was pleased that she was interested enough in him to make it. He didn't know how he felt about it, but he said, "I will consider it. It's very generous of you to want to take me in. We can talk about it when I go home, but I am able to get along on my own still, you know."

Their conversation was interrupted at that point when dinner arrived. The nurse's assistant put the tray down and took the cover off the food.

It looks pretty good, Marcy thought.

He picked up his fork and poked at the food. "I'm not very hungry. Would you like some of this?"

"Grandpa, you aren't going to get out of here if you don't eat. The doctor said you needed to eat better, so get to it. It looks pretty tasty, and it smells good too. I want to see you up and out of here so we can talk."

He ate most of what they had brought, and he drank his coffee and juice.

"I feel like I'm stuffed," he commented. "I hope you are happy now."

"I am," she said.

He was sleeping when she left a short time later and drove back to his apartment. She wasn't sure what she would find when she got there. After all, he was a widower living by himself, but she figured she could do some cleaning for him. She was pleased and relieved when she walked in the door and switched on the lights. The room was immaculate.

She turned on more lights and moved around the apartment. The living room was sparsely furnished, containing a loveseat, a recliner, a small side table, and a television. The kitchen had a refrigerator, a small rectangular table with four chairs, and a four burner gas stove. There were a few kitchen items, such as, blender, toaster, and a small microwave on the counters. She checked the two bedrooms. Her grandfather's room was just as he had left it: the covers were pulled back, and a nightstand lay on its side where it had been tipped over. The guest room was just as her grandfather had claimed, ready for guests.

She looked for accessories. They were few, mostly framed photographs. She checked them out. One was of Sherry at graduation. She found two of herself as quite a young girl. She checked the refrigerator. There was very little in it: a quart of milk, a small jar of pickles, a small squeeze bottle of mustard, a few slices of sandwich meat, part of a dozen eggs, and a loaf of wheat bread. It seemed her grandfather had lived a frugal life with few frills.

She sat down in the recliner, continuing to look around the living room. Near the TV, there were several shelves partially filled with books. There was a small photo in a stand-up frame on one of the shelves. She got up and went over to look at it. It was her grandmother with a small child on her lap. It might have been her mother. There was a scrapbook of sorts underneath the picture. She picked it up and went back to the chair.

Opening the book, the first page had a newspaper clipping about her grandparents' wedding and a photograph of them. There were pictures of their parents, obviously taken at the reception. There was a birth announcement for Sherry Maureen Miller and a picture of the baby. As she turned the pages, she discovered her mother's report card for first grade and a picture of that class. She found more report cards, prize ribbons, newspaper articles, and nearly annual pictures of her mother in school. She had been a cheerleader and a volleyball player. Marcy had never known that. She gazed at the picture of her mother in her cheerleader uniform.

She really was a looker, she thought.

The next pictures had been taken after Sherry had married Marcy's father. One was of her with her mother and father. There were several pictures of her as an infant and as a child being held by her grandmother. There was her birth announcement.

There were more clippings. Some were about the local motorcycle shop, and one was a letter to the editor, praising the abilities of a new mechanic, Hughie Williamson. There was a picture of her dad. There was an ad for Sherry's Natural Cosmetics and another one for Robyn's World. There was a feature article about her mother and the new business she had brought to town.

After that, most of the pictures came from newspaper articles, although there was one taken at her graduation with her grandmother and grandfather. They looked so proud. There were lots of clippings from newspapers and magazines about Robyn's World and awards Sherry and her company had won. It seemed like her grandfather had cut out and collected everything that he could that had been written about her mother and her company. There were also a few clippings about herself.

It was obvious that her grandparents had cared about their daughter and their granddaughter. She became all the more anxious to talk with him. She was determined to do her best to see that he got out of the hospital and back home soon.

For two more days, she sat with her grandfather and encouraged him to eat and drink and to walk with her. His doctor was pleased with his progress and said he could go home the next day if she or someone could watch him for a few days.

Her grandfather said, "Well, Marcy, are you willing to spend a few days with me until I get back to my old self? We'll have time to have that talk you wanted."

She noticed he didn't mention going back to Washington with her.

"I'll stay as long as you need me with you."

The doctor said, "Ms. Williamson, would you come out to the desk, there are some papers I need to go over with you."

When she got to the desk, the doctor asked her to come into the office for a minute. When she went in, he shut the door before speaking, "Ms. Williamson, your grandfather is a very sick man."

"I thought you said he was just run down, dehydrated, and malnourished. Is he dying?"

"He isn't dying exactly, not right away anyway, if that's what you mean. I am convinced his dizziness and disorientation were caused by improper diet or just plain lack of food and drink, but there is something else we discovered when we did a complete blood count. We believe your grandfather has chronic lymphocytic leukemia. We would need to do additional tests to determine the stage of the disease and what sort of treatments might help him."

Marcy was confused, and she asked, "But didn't you say he could go home tomorrow if I could watch him for a few days?"

"Yes, and he can go home. If you can keep him eating, it would be the best thing we could do for him right now. He is quite run down, and he was somewhat depressed when he came in, but he has really perked up since you got here. Get him stronger, and then we can focus on his condition and decide on the best way to treat him.

"If left untreated for too long, the condition could easily lead to death. Without knowing what stage he is in, it is difficult to predict how long he might have, but because of the rebound we are seeing in him right now, I don't believe he is in imminent danger. However, he does need a thorough diagnostic workup soon."

"Doctor, I live near Seattle, Washington, and I cannot stay here indefinitely. I offered to take him home to live with me. Is there any reason why he shouldn't travel or why he couldn't get followed up out there and receive whatever treatment is needed?"

"Ms. Williamson, there's no reason as long as he feels like going. Personally, I think it would be the best thing in the world for him. He seems a different person with you around. If he goes with you, I can have all his information transferred to wherever you decide to take him for follow-up, and I can give you some suggestions for places in the Seattle area that have good results with treating this type of leukemia."

"That sounds fine to me. Have you told him about this?"

"No, not yet, but at some point, he needs to know."

"Could I be the one to tell him, Doctor?"

"Certainly. If he has any questions that you can't answer, just call me, and I'll have you both come in so I can explain everything in doctor talk," he said smiling.

When she walked back into the room, she said, "What would you like for your welcome home meal tomorrow? I'm a pretty good cook too, you know."

He thought for a moment before saying, "Am I really going home? If I am, I haven't had a nice lamb chop in years. If you wanted to get some lamb and fix it with fresh buttered carrots and real mashed potatoes, I'd feel like I'd died and gone to heaven."

"Well, let's not use that particular expression here in the hospital. How about you'd just feel special, because you are special, you know. If they discharge you, you won't be able to leave before eleven, so I'll have a chance to go to the market and pick up a few things before I pick you up and take you home. I'm pretty sure I can find some lamb chops."

She bought the lamb that evening along with five pounds of potatoes and a bunch of carrots. They would keep fine in the refrigerator until after she brought her grandfather home, and that night he could visit and watch her finish preparing dinner. She went to sleep that evening thrilled by the idea.

He was ready when she walked into his room.

"They told me I am going to be getting out but that I couldn't go until the doctor released me," he explained. "But I made them get my clothes so I could get dressed before you got here. I've been ready for about two hours. How do I look?"

"You look like my grandfather, and you also look a lot better than you did the first day I walked in here."

"You might think I'm crazy, but I believe if you hadn't come to see me, I might have died in here. I didn't feel like there was any reason to go on living, but your just being here has brought a joy to my heart. I had kind of lost hope of ever seeing you or your mother again. I could hardly believe my eyes when you came into my room. You don't have any idea of how good it made me feel right then."

They held hands and took a walk down to the solarium. She could sense that he was growing stronger and steadier. He had noticeably more color in his face, which had looked so pale when she first saw him. As they walked, she began to wonder what his life had been like since her grandmother had died and he was left alone. Those thoughts were disconcerting when she considered that she could have easily have made those years less lonesome, and so could her mother.

The doctor found them as they visited in the solarium.

"The nurse told me you were down here. Mr. Miller, you will be in good hands with your granddaughter, so I'm letting you go today. If you have any more dizziness, I want you to get back here, but I think we've got it under control."

The doctor shook his hand and left, and they headed back to his room. That night they feasted on medium rare lamb chops and celebrated his recovery and return home.

12

A TALE OF LOVE AND REGRET

He awoke to the smell of fresh coffee and bacon. It took him just a moment to remember that his granddaughter was there with him, and then he was getting out of bed and pulling on his robe. He walked into the kitchen as she turned away from the stove and smiled.

"You're up! I was just going to come and knock on your door. Breakfast is just about all ready. I made you a couple of eggs over easy. I think I remembered that you liked them that way. Have a seat."

He sat down, and she placed a plate with two strips of bacon and two eggs in front of him along with a smaller dish with two pieces of buttered toast. Then she put two cups of coffee on the table, before getting her own plate.

He waited for her to finish and sit down, and then he said, "Marcy, I have dreamed of having a morning like this ever since your grandmother died, but I never truly thought it would happen. Would you mind if I asked the Lord's blessing on this food?"

"Not at all, Grandpa."

"Lord, now I really know how much you love me. Thank you, Lord, for sending my granddaughter to me in my hour of need. Thank you for her love, and thank you for this food. Please bless it, Father, and bless the hands that prepared it. Amen."

"Amen," she repeated.

He picked up a crisp slice of bacon with his fingers and took a bite. Then he dipped a slice of toast into the egg yolk and took a bite of the dripping toast. He picked up the cup of coffee and sipped it carefully.

Putting his cup down, he said, "Marcy, this breakfast is perfect. I don't have bacon very often, but you got this batch just right. You can cook my breakfast anytime."

"I'm glad you like it. I think my favorite breakfast is bacon, eggs, and toast. You would make it for me when I was just a little girl. That's one thing I do remember."

"Yes, but I didn't have the chance to do it very often, not nearly as often as your grandmother and I would have liked. You were always off somewhere with your mother."

He finished every last bit of his breakfast and asked her if she would get him another cup of coffee. When she brought it to him, he sat with the mug cupped in his hands, watching her finish her breakfast. He drank the fragrant brew slowly, enjoying each swallow. He wanted to make the breakfast last as long as he could. He was almost afraid that he would suddenly awake and find it had all been a dream.

Finally, he picked up his plates and his cup and took them to the sink, and then he sat back down.

"You said you had some things you wanted to talk about. When you're ready, we can sit in the other room, and I'll try to help you see why things worked out the way they did if I can."

"Thanks, Grandpa. I'm not even sure what I want to ask or where to start. I'll probably wander around a lot, and maybe I won't make a lot of sense, but I need some answers about my childhood. Let's go ahead and sit in the other room, and I'll tell you what my mother told me. We can start from there."

Marcy watched her grandfather's face as she carefully related all that her mother had told her. She could see that her story pained him at times. Sometimes he would nod his head as if in agreement and other times shake it in disagreement or disbelief. He listened patiently without saying a word, even though she could see that he wanted to jump in at different times.

When she had finished telling her grandfather what her mother had told her, she said, "Grandpa, what's your side on all that?"

Instead of commenting, he asked, "Is there any coffee left? I could use another cup."

She got up and got him a new mug, filled it with coffee, and brought it to him.

"It's not very hot," she said, "but I can warm it up for you in the microwave if you like."

"No, this will be fine."

She sat back down, and her grandfather began, "Your mother was right. Martha and I were dead set against her relationship with Hughie. We tried to break them up, keep them apart. We thought your mother was making a big mistake, and we were only interested in her good, but it was like talking to the wind. The more we tried, the more she dug in her heels. We probably shouldn't have been, but we were completely taken by surprise when they took off and got married. That was probably the result of our first mistake. We should have welcomed Hughie to our home and tried to get to know him instead of trying to drive him away, but we didn't realize it then."

He took a few sips from his mug and continued, "Your mother wasn't exactly accurate about our moving to Georgia. We didn't discover where they were. She sent us a letter and told us about you and gave us the address where they were living. She wanted us to come down and give her some help taking care of you.

"We should have learned from our first experience, but we didn't. That was probably the greatest mistake we ever made. We probably could have straightened everything out. Your mother was right about how we treated Hughie after we moved. We thought he could do a lot better than being a mechanic in a bike shop, and foolishly, we didn't miss a chance to make our opinion known. I don't remember what all we said to him or to your mother—or to our friends, for that matter—but he quickly learned to avoid us, and he blamed your mother for our being there. They had some big arguments, and we were pretty likely the cause of most of them. But the worst fights were because he was not happy about how much time your mother spent on her cosmetics business, and that was a growing sore spot between them, especially when she started to earn a pretty decent amount each week. He really wanted her to quit, but your mother did not want to give up the money.

"Your mother has always blamed us for causing your father's drinking and his death. I know we were part of the problem, but I don't think your mother has ever been able to accept the fact that her business contributed to it as well. Did she tell you that they had a huge argument about money and her business the night your father had his accident? Your father had a temper, and sometimes he did foolish things when he was mad.

"From that day on, your mother began to treat us like we had leprosy. We were happy to open our home to the two of you, but it was plain to see that your mother really didn't like the arrangement. We cleaned out our garage so she could have more space for making her cosmetics, but she was looking for something bigger. When she bought the storefront, we offered money to help pay for it, but she refused our offer. We told her we would work in the shop for free to help her out, but she said she didn't want our help. Afterward she hired a woman to work in the shop. We felt bad about that, but all during that time, we had you with us, and that sort of took the edge off the hurt. It was wonderful to cuddle you and talk to you. Your grandmother was in her glory with you."

"Grandpa, did you and Grandma really love me?"

"What a strange question. Of course, we did. That's what I'm saying, Marcy. Your mother was absolutely correct when she said we loved you. Your grandmother and I loved you very much. We loved you more than anything else in this world. We loved your mother too, but she couldn't see it. The reason we saw so little of you after your mother moved to New York City was not because we didn't want to. It was because your mother always had a reason why she couldn't come to Georgia or why we couldn't visit you in New York. We saw you a few times at Christmas and on a couple of your birthdays, but it was very obvious that she wanted to keep us at more than arm's length. It broke your grandmother's heart, mine too, really. We tried reasoning with your mother, but she wasn't interested. It became almost like we didn't have a daughter or a granddaughter, but we never stopped loving either of you."

That rang true to her. Sherry had always had reasons why she couldn't visit her in Washington too.

While he paused to swallow a little more of his rapidly cooling coffee, she used the break to ask, "Grandpa, why are you living in this little apartment?"

"Well, it's what I can afford, and why would I need anything bigger? I'm the only one living in it."

"Grandpa, you didn't have much of anything in the refrigerator when I came. I had to buy bacon, butter, and some coffee just to make breakfast. You've always loved bacon, how come you didn't have any?"

"Well, my Social Security check isn't huge, and I have to keep within my budget for everything, including food, so I'm careful about what I buy."

"Why didn't you let Mom know you could use some financial help?" she asked. "She would have helped you. She's your daughter."

"I'm not at all sure that's true, Marcy. I hate to say this, but since you are honestly looking for answers and explanations, I will. The facts are, your mother went out of her way to make your grandmother and I pay every day of our lives for the way we had treated Hughie. She hurt us any way she could. In a way, I guess I don't blame her, but we tried our best to help her just the same. We gave her everything we had. We always hoped that if she became successful, there would come a day when she would forgive us. I'm still waiting, maybe we were wrong.

"I always thought we should let your mother know what we had done for her, but your grandmother wouldn't hear of it. So we never told her that we supplied the money that made it possible to build her new business. She doesn't know to this day, and don't you dare to ever mention it to her either, young lady. I'm only telling you because I want you to know how much we cared about you and your mother. I want you to know the truth, and I want you to know how much we regretted our treatment of your father. Don't ever think badly of your father either. He was a better man than we gave him credit for. If we could have only seen that. If we had only been satisfied with the fact that he loved your mother and she loved him, what a much better life we all would have had."

She was trying to take in what her grandfather was telling her. He looked so sad. She wondered what money he was talking about. This was something she had never heard about before.

"You gave Mother money for her business? She said you offered, but she wouldn't take your money or your help."

"That's true, but I worked out a way to do it so she never knew we were helping," he said.

And then he went on to explain how he and her grandmother had mortgaged everything they owned and sold everything they could as well as cleaning out their retirement account.

"By the time we were done, we had over two hundred thousand in cash. It was everything we had, but it was only money, and if it would help make up for the pain we had caused, we figured it was worth it."

He took great pleasure in describing for Marcy the people and methods they had employed to carry out their plan so her mother wouldn't refuse the money.

She was amazed, but she had heard enough. She no longer wanted to discuss the family relationships, not right then anyway. She had a plan of her own.

"Grandpa, you are going to come and live with me. The doctor said it would be the best thing for you. I'll see that you get a great breakfast every morning, and you'll love the mountains. What do you say to that?"

"I've been thinking about that since you mentioned it in the hospital. I was hoping you would ask again. I would very much like to live with you and finally get to know my grown-up granddaughter. Thanks for asking. I'd love to come."

They spent several days making arrangements for moving and packing his things. There wasn't much. Just about everything stayed with the apartment. What did not, they gave to the Petersons, who had gotten him to the hospital. Marcy made sure the scrapbook was packed. She wanted to spend some time back in Snoqualmie looking at it with her grandfather.

When they were on their way to the airport, he said, "You know, Marcy, I've never been on an airplane before."

"Well, you've got a treat coming, and this is just the first of many. I love you, Grandpa."

13

GRANDPA IS DYING

One morning, after she had her grandfather settled in for a few days, she sent an e-mail to her mother.

It read, "Mother, you need to come to Washington. There are three things you need to know. One, I brought Grandpa home to live with me. Two, he loves you very much. And three, Grandpa is dying. If you were telling me the truth and you want a new start with me and life, don't give me any excuses why you can't come, this is important. When will you be here? Love, Marcy."

It didn't bother her that her grandfather was not technically at death's door. It was worth being a bit devious because if there was any love left in her mother for her father, she was fairly sure hearing about his imminent death would bring it to the surface. It didn't matter what had taken place in the past; the present was much more important.

After she had sent the e-mail, she brought her grandfather a fresh cup of coffee out on the deck and sat down beside him.

"You know," he said, "your grandmother would have loved this place. She always wanted to stay somewhere near the mountains. Long before you were born, we had been thinking about taking a second honeymoon and going to France and Switzerland to spend a few days in Paris and go to see the Alps. Once you were born and we moved to Georgia, our plans sort of got put on hold.

"We never did get to travel, but if we could have come here before she got so sick, it would have been like a dream come true. She would have loved it. This is absolutely gorgeous, magnificent."

Marcy smiled and said, "Well, if you want to see the mountains, you wait 'til winter rolls around, and the view will be almost as good as the Alps."

"This ain't bad right here now, little girl. I feel the best I have in years. I've got a first-rate view of your mountains, with a breakfast when I get up that couldn't be beat in any high-class restaurant, and a beautiful girl that sees to my every need. But, hey, don't you ever have to go to work?"

"Sure, I do, but I'm working from home for a while. That's the nice thing about computers, e-mails, and cell phones. Sometimes I can get more done here than I can in the office. I've been getting a lot done while you take your nap in the afternoon.

"Today I want to go through your scrapbook with you and have you tell me about all the stuff. I have looked at some of it, but I stopped because I decided I'd rather do it with you, so I've waited. Would you like to do that?"

"I'd like that. You know, your grandmother and I would always watch for things about you or your mother to put in here. We used to get this book out and sit down and go through it together. It was the only way we could share your lives on a regular basis. It wasn't great, but it was better than nothing."

"It sounds like fun to me, Grandpa. I'm so glad the two of you put it together. But there is something else that I need to share with you, Grandpa. I have some information about the condition of your health. The doctor said to tell you when I thought you had gotten some of your strength back and you were eating well. I guess that time has come. Are you ready?"

"Do I have any choice?"

"Well, yes, you do. We don't have to talk about it today if you don't want to, but it would be better to do it sooner than later. You are doing pretty well now."

"Okay, I guess I'm as ready as I'll ever be. I take it that it's not good news?"

"Depends on how you look at it, Grandpa. The doctor told me your test showed that you were malnourished and dehydrated, and we have that under control. But the tests also showed that you have chronic lymphocytic leukemia. He also told me to tell you that it is not a death sentence, even though some do die from it. He told me we would need to get you in to see a doctor out here and find out what stage you are in. The one thing we can't do is do nothing. The good thing is that you have been getting stronger and putting on a little weight. The doctor said that would be a good thing. It indicates you are probably in an early stage."

"Well, Marcy, I know leukemia is not a good thing, but I've always thought it was more of a young person's disease."

"Obviously not, but I'll set up an appointment for you to see a specialist out here. Your doctor back East gave me some suggestions. I'll try to get you set up sometime in the next few weeks."

"It's okay. It is what it is. I'm not scared by it, and I'd just as soon find out where I'm at anyway."

That was that. It was easier than she had thought it might be. She would make some calls while he took his nap that afternoon.

After coffee and their conversation on the deck, they moved inside, and she put the scrapbook on the dining room table. Soon they became completely immersed in the intertwined lives of the Miller-Williamson family. One of the neatest things in the book were the handwritten comments that her grandfather or grandmother had added about her and her mother and how proud and pleased they were by the many successes.

It was several hours before they put it down when he said, "I'm kind of tired, Marcy. I'm going to take that nap now."

Then he went and sat in the big recliner, and in a few moments, he was asleep.

Marcy put a marker in where they left off before she closed the book. It had been an interesting experience. Now she needed to make some calls, but before she did, she wanted to check her e-mail. It had only been a few hours since she e-mailed her mother, but she decided she would check just the same. Her mother had a habit of checking her mail several times a day, so she might have already gotten back to her.

There it was! "My arrival." Her mother was coming. She clicked the message on and read, "I am at a loss to know why my father did not let me know he was ill. I will make arrangements to come out this week. I will let you know my arrival date as soon as I figure out my schedule and make my reservations. Let your grandfather know that I am coming. Love, Mom."

While Marcy was excited, her mother was not. Sherry dreaded even the thought of dealing with this situation, but she had felt she had to give Marcy an answer. Even as she did so, she remembered Roland's invitation to let him know when she was going to be visiting her daughter. She would see him first.

She made her own reservations at the Edgewater Hotel, booking a room overlooking the harbor. She did not want to go immediately to her daughter's home, and the Edgewater would be a very comfortable place to stay until she was ready. It would also be a good place to get together with Roland without taking a chance that Marcy might accidentally catch sight of her if she went to his home to see him.

She made her plane reservations next, flying direct, first class into SeaTac nonstop from Kennedy. She reserved a rental car for her stay, giving her some freedom of movement, making sure the vehicle had a GPS.

She usually had Gwen make all her reservations, but she decided to keep this trip to herself. She made the same arrangements with Gwen as she had with her reunion trip but told her it was a personal trip and that in this case, she would keep in touch during her absence.

That evening at home, she took a little more time composing her e-mail to Roland.

In the subject heading, she typed simply, "Coming to Seattle."

She thought about how she would explain why she would be staying in Seattle instead of at her daughter's home in Snoqualmie.

It seemed like a little white lie would work just fine, so she wrote, "Roland, I have some business to attend to in Seattle, so I will be staying at the Edgewater instead of at my daughter's home, but of course, I will be visiting her while I am there. My father has recently moved to Washington from back East and is staying with her. I would like to talk with you before I go to see my daughter if you are going to be free. We could meet in Seattle if it is convenient. Looking forward to it. Let me know, Sherry."

He was online and got her e-mail almost as soon as she had sent it. He hadn't expected to hear from her so quickly, but he was excited that he would be seeing her again. He didn't feel any need to be blasé about her message.

He quickly replied, "I will look forward to your arrival with great anticipation. I have nothing that cannot be rescheduled. How soon are you coming? Send me the details of your trip and stay, and I will work around them. Roland."

He was surprised by the depth of his own feelings. He actually tingled at the idea of seeing her again. Now, after all the years of his angst over the results of their first date had evaporated, he saw her in a new and exciting light. She could not come too soon, as far as he was concerned.

She had been pleased with his answer. It was obvious she had missed an opportunity with him that night at Gino's, but now she was getting a second chance. She wanted to explore his feelings further but thought it would be best to let that wait until she was actually with him.

She wrote back, "I will be in Washington Tuesday afternoon. I will call you after I am settled in at the Edgewater. Perhaps we can have dinner together."

His reply came a short time later. "Sounds like a plan. I'll be free."

Neither of them would have a long time to plan or think about what they were going to do or say when she got to Seattle, but she had a double dose because she had to consider not just him but her daughter and father as well. She was looking forward to the time with Roland; the other, not so much.

He, on the other hand, really had nothing to do that kept him from thinking about her. He sat at his desk and wondered what her business was in Seattle and how busy she would be. He thought she would probably be staying a few days with her daughter. Perhaps he would get the chance to meet her and her grandfather. He hadn't tried to find her daughter since he got back home, but it had been on his mind to do so. He just couldn't figure out a way to do it that wasn't awkward.

He moved to the living room, sat down in his recliner, and leaned back staring at the ceiling. He had a habit that when things were quiet and he was settled comfortably into his easy chair, he would think about Betty and the life they had together. He had loved her so much—and still loved her, at least the memory of her—but now the new thoughts of Sherry left him feeling guilty.

Staring at the ceiling, he whispered, "Betty, I still miss you with every breath I take, but it has been a long time now, and there are times when I am so lonely. Sometimes at night I reach out in bed to touch you, but you aren't there, no one is there. I long for the soft touch of a woman and a warm body to share my bed. You were more than my wife, Betty, you were my life. I hope you will be happy for me if I find someone to share the days I have left here on this earth. I'm going to be seeing Sherry on Tuesday. I just wanted to let you know."

He had no illusions about his wife, and he knew she was not present, but it had always brought him peace when he spoke to her as though she were. It still seemed natural somehow to share the special things in his life with Betty as he had while they were together.

Later, as he pulled the covers up around his neck, he thought about Sherry. He wondered what it would be like to share his bed with her. She was beautiful and had a youthful-looking body. He could imagine himself wrapping his arms around her, smelling her perfume and feeling the warmth of her body against his own. He finally drifted off to sleep, with a new hope in his heart.

She went to sleep that night after struggling with what lay ahead of her in Snoqualmie. She could hardly wait to see Roland, but that was overshadowed by the turmoil in her heart and mind over her father and Marcy. She wondered if she could share her feelings with Roland. Could he help her? She had told him some things about her difficult relationship with her father, and he might have some suggestions, but she knew that how things went at Marcy's would depend almost entirely on what she said and did. She wasn't sure how she felt now after all the years of enmity, but she knew she did not want to hurt her father any longer, now that he was dying. She had hurt so much when her mother died, but she had kept it to herself. What was it that Marcy had said? "I cried, but I didn't see you cry at Grandma's funeral."

I cried, she thought, *but I cried inside. I couldn't admit that I might have made a mistake shutting my parents out of my life. I wanted to hug Dad and tell him how sorry I was, but I just couldn't do it. They had ruined my life, but they never told me they were sorry for that.*

She finally had to quit thinking about it all. She thought instead about the good days with Hughie. Soon she was riding on a motorcycle, holding on to him without a care in the world.

14

THE DAY OF RECKONING

As she was checking in to the hotel, she heard a voice from behind her, "It's good to see you, Sherry."

She turned, and Roland was standing there, smiling.

"I decided to come and be here when you got here. I didn't want to sit around at home, waiting for you to call. I hope that's all right."

"Well, this is a surprise but a pleasant one. I don't mind at all. Let me get my key, and we will take a look at my room, that is, if you'd like to come up."

"I can hardly turn down that invitation. Besides, I've never stayed here, I'd like to see what the rooms are like. May I help you with your bags?"

"Thank you, but no, they are already on their way up."

As they got into the elevator, he said, "You are looking fantastic, much happier than the last time I saw you. I'm afraid I was responsible for that. I had been an angry fool because of you for so long, it was difficult for me to comprehend how much I wanted you right at that moment. Watching you drive away was one of the saddest things I've ever done in my life."

"Well," Sherry responded, "you can be pretty direct when you want to be. I guess it's safe for me to respond in kind. The main reason I went to the reunion was to see you again. I had become tired of living my life alone, and I wondered if you were still single and if there might be any future for us. When we parted that night,

I thought the chasm between us might be too wide, but perhaps I was wrong."

Their conversation was interrupted by the opening the elevator doors. He followed her out and asked what her room number was. Then he led the way down the hall to her room. She handed him her key, and he unlocked the door and opened it for her. Following her in, he closed the door behind himself. Her bags were sitting at the end of her bed.

"You should be very comfortable here," he said, walking to the windows. "You certainly have a wonderful view of the harbor."

She brushed against him as she moved to the window, thrilling to the unplanned touch.

"Yes," she said as she peered out, "it's almost a shame to have to move from here, but in a couple of days, I will need to go to my daughter's. In the meantime, let's enjoy it. Sit down, and let's catch up."

He sat down and watched her move slowly past him to sit on the bed. He waited for her to begin the conversation, enjoying just looking at her. She was looking back with a Mona Lisa smile. It was one of those rare times when everything was silent, suspended in time, words being momentarily superfluous, and neither of them was anxious to break the spell.

He had no way of knowing how much, at that moment, she wanted to pull him onto the bed with her. She yearned for ravenous kisses and the honesty of burning passion, but the foolish, impetuous thoughts passed as reason triumphed over impulse.

She reluctantly ended it when she said, shaking her head, "You know, Roland, I can't figure why you are still single. There must be thousands of women who would give anything to be Mrs. Roland Holtz. Why have you never remarried?"

"I could ask you the same thing. There must be thousands of men who would like to be your husband, but you have never remarried, have you?"

"No, I was too busy building Robyn's World to be bothered with a husband. I didn't have time. There were lots of men who tried to sweep me off my feet, but none who were able to compete for my love with my business. I never lacked escorts whatever function I was at, but they were nothing more than window-dressing. What's your excuse?"

"This may sound corny, but I was never able to get over my love for my first wife. Betty was the best thing that ever happened to me, and when she died, my world died with her. The only thing I had left was our son, Bryce, and I devoted myself to him. But he's in the Navy now, and he doesn't need me to watch over him."

"All these years," Roland continued, "I've kept my vows to Betty even though she was gone, but then with Bryce out of the house, I was so lonely I could hardly stand it. I had zero desire to go back to work. I took up music and art to help fill up my time, and yes, I still do some fishing, but as hard as I tried, nothing filled the emptiness I felt. In the end, I found my salvation, in more ways than one, in God and in being part of a church. That has made all the difference."

When she heard the "God" part, his stock tumbled, and she immediately thought of Delores. She was glad that she had resisted the foolish urge to pull him onto the bed and do her best to seduce him.

She thought, *How can anyone with the brains and common sense that he has possibly be taken in by the whole Jesus thing? What is wrong with people like Roland and Delores? I've never been like that, and I've done okay for myself.*

She said, "I'm happy for you. I really am. You've been able to put your old life behind you and make a new beginning. It was so sweet of you to be loyal to your wife for so long, but I think there comes a time in almost everyone's life when they need to forget the past and move on. I'm glad you were able to do it."

"I haven't forgotten the past. I just see it differently now. I probably will never stop loving Betty in a way, but now she is a wonderful memory, not someone to tie me down even if it were with bonds of gold and silk. I have been set free, and I feel it."

"That's rather poetic, you certainly have a way with words. I wish I had a wonderful memory like that."

"What about Hughie? You told me you loved him. Isn't he a sweet memory for you?"

"Yes, he is, but not in the way that your wife was, or I should say, is. He was more like a segment of my life that was there, and then it was gone. I can remember him, even weep for him, but my life has always gone on without a lot of thought about him. I guess I poured myself into Marcy much as you did with Bryce, but I was never encumbered by Hughie after he was gone."

He decided to take the conversation in a different direction as he asked, "What sort of business do you have here in Seattle?"

She had been prepared for the question. "I am going to be checking some of our outlets here. I want a firsthand look at how our products are being displayed and how they are represented by sales staff. I have people who do that, of course, but I thought it would be interesting to see things for myself as long as I was going to be in the area."

"I wouldn't think you would have time to see many places unless you are planning to be here for more than a few days."

"I only intend to do a small sampling. We have people who do this full-time all across the country, and I will no doubt be visiting some locations that have been checked by them. Mainly, I want to cross-reference what I see with the reports that get turned in by our people."

"Checking up on the help, eh? Do you do this sort of thing often?"

"Not really. Most of the time, I only see the information that comes from the senior managers of the different departments. They have their fingers on the pulse of Robyn's World. The business has grown way too large for me to personally get involved at the grassroots to any extent, but just the same, on occasion I like to get out on my own."

"I can understand," he said. "I used to visit every department when I was going to be taking charge of a business, before the employees knew who I was. I found it very useful to get a firsthand look at the various operations and the people carrying them out. When do you think you will be going to your daughter's? If it's okay with you, I'd like to meet her and your father too while you are here. Actually, I did meet him for just a few minutes before I took you out, but I don't remember anything about him. In any case, I would very much like to meet both of them."

"He probably wouldn't remember you either. I have to call them and make arrangements. I'm not sure if I will be staying with her or staying here and just visiting her and my father. I may be back and forth quite a bit."

"Well," he said, "I had hoped you would have a little free time, but you probably have a full schedule. If it is inconvenient for you to have me join you at some point at your daughter's home, I'll understand, but you said perhaps we could go out for dinner when you got here, so if you don't have anything planned for this evening, I'd like to take you out for dinner. I'll do better than pizza, and I promise no talk about our first date."

"I was hoping you would ask. I have nothing planned for the evening, and I'm not familiar with restaurants in the area. Marcy didn't know exactly when I was coming, so I'm free to kick up my heels a little this evening. Tomorrow will be soon enough to get down to business. The only thing I ask is that we have dinner early, maybe five o'clock. I don't do well with time differences. And what should I wear? I don't want to be overdressed."

"I am taking you to Canlis. I don't think you can overdress for dinner there. I am going to wear a suit, but I would think you could dress in whatever you feel comfortable with. Someone in your line of work should be able to handle that. I'll pick you up in the lobby at five o'clock. We won't be able to eat quite as early as you suggested. Canlis doesn't open for business until five thirty, but I can assure you it will be worth your time."

Later, after he left, she called her daughter. The phone rang several times before she answered.

"Hi, Marcy, this is Mom. I'm calling to let you know I will be at your house about eleven Friday morning. I rented a car, so you don't have to come and pick me up."

"You didn't have to do that, Mother, I'd be happy to pick you up."

"I know that, honey, but I wanted a car so I could get around on my own while I'm in Washington. I won't have any problem. I'm taking my GPS with me just in case the car doesn't have one, and if I run into any trouble, I can always call you. How is Father?"

"He's holding his own. I've told him you were coming. He is really looking forward to it, and so am I."

"Well, tell him it won't be long. I'll give you a call when I'm on my way from Seattle. I'll see you then. I've got things to do right now, but I'll be in touch. Bye."

Marcy didn't have to know she was already in Seattle.

She spent the rest of the afternoon relaxing and getting ready for their dinner date, thinking about Roland much of the time. It was obvious that he had more than a passing interest in her, but was he really what she was looking for? She needed to know more about him. She realized that she actually knew very little about him as a person. That would be her mission over the next few days.

One of the things she wanted to ask him about was his comment that God had been his salvation in more ways than one. She wasn't sure exactly how she would broach the subject, but she wanted to be sure she was not trying to hook up with a Jesus freak. While she didn't have anything against God or Jesus, or even against "Christians," she resented being beaten over the head by people who wanted to save her soul. Certainly, she didn't want to be married to one. If he was like Delores, she would prefer to just be good friends, not lovers.

She took her time getting ready for dinner. She was concerned she had not looked her best when Roland surprised her as she arrived at the hotel. She had gotten up early, and the flight from New York had not helped. She was determined to put a different face on things that evening.

She was pleased when he met her in the lobby with a, "Wow, do you look great!"

He took her hand and said, "I've got a limo out front. I decided I didn't want to drive tonight, and it looks like it was a good idea because I would never have been able to keep my eyes on the road."

"Well, thank you, Roland. You look pretty snazzy yourself. I was afraid I looked a little frazzled after my flight, so I made myself more presentable for tonight."

"You looked like a page out of a fashion magazine this morning, but you look like the cover on one now. Let's go so I can show you off."

As they sat in the limo on the way to the restaurant, he asked, "What is that perfume that you are wearing? It's really very nice."

"Thank you. It's called Conquest. It's new to our line, but already, it is becoming one of our most popular essences. I'm confident it will bump our sales up considerably this year."

"I'm sure if I should smell it in the future, I would immediately think of you. It makes a real connection."

"Then I hope you smell it often. What is this restaurant we are going to again?

"It's the Canlis. It is quite famous locally, and I would stack it up against any restaurant in the country, or Europe, for that matter. They have an interesting history. You wouldn't realize what a wonderful place it is, looking at it from the outside, but Canlis is gorgeous inside with a breathtaking view of Lake Union, and the food is fabulous. I'm sure you will like it."

When they arrived, it was obvious that the maître d' knew who he was, and he led them to a table for two with a grand view of the lake.

"I have to admit, I'm impressed, and I am seldom impressed by restaurants anymore. If the food is anywhere near as wonderful as the restaurant itself, I'll be even more impressed."

"Well, be prepared to be impressed because everything here is absolutely first class. I always have a hard time knowing what to order because every dish is outstanding, but I can suggest a couple for the uninitiated, if you would like."

She looked at the offerings in the menu. "I guess I may have to go with your suggestions because almost everything looks good to me."

"If you'd like the three-course meal, I'd recommend either the potato soup or the prawns for the first course. The soup has an enchanting flavor from the leeks and black truffles, but if you want something other than soup, they have the best prawns. Myself, I am going to have their oysters. This is one of the few places that I get them. Perhaps you are fond of oysters as well?"

"No, thanks, I think I will go with the soup. I have always enjoyed truffles in dishes. What do you recommend for our main course?"

"I was thinking we would have the filet mignon, but if you see something you would like to try instead, I'm sure it would be fine as well."

"I am going to go with the lamb. It is my favorite meat, and I've had it all over the world. If it is as good as you say the food is here, I'll know it."

"Good evening, sir, it's a pleasure to see you again," the waiter said as he came to their table. "Are you ready to order?"

Roland ordered their first and second courses and asked the waiter to suggest a wine to go with the meal. Before he left with their order, the waiter asked Roland, "Will you be wanting your usual dessert this evening, sir?"

"Yes, thank you. I ordered it ahead."

When they were alone again, he said, "We will have some time to talk. Canlis doesn't rush you or their food."

"What was all that about the dessert?"

"I am particularly fond of their Canlis soufflé, and it has to be ordered a half hour before it is served. The waiter has gotten to know what I like, and he makes sure I get it at just the right moment. I have to say, you look enchanting," he said. "That red dress looks like it was made for you."

"That's very perceptive of you. It actually was made for me. I have most of my clothes made for me by one of our fashion designers."

"They do a great job. No wonder Robyn's World is so successful."

"You know, at first, my company was successful because of me and what I did, but it has become way too big for that now. I have very little to do with the fashion division even though every part of the company eventually reports to me. At one time, it was heady and exciting, but today it is mostly work. I'm not saying I don't still enjoy parts of it, but really, I'm not sure where I go from here."

"What do you do for relaxation?"

"Mostly, I don't relax. I have always been a workaholic. I have already taken more time off this year than I have in the previous ten. I get nervous when I'm away from the office for too long."

"Don't you trust your staff and execs to keep things running smoothly while you're away?"

"Yes, I do, and there haven't been any problems while I've been away this year, but I still get nervous. I just can't help it."

"Maybe what you need is a good CEO to step in for you."

"Are you interested in the job, Roland?"

"No, no. I know next to nothing about the cosmetics and fashion industry." He laughed. "I don't think that would be a very good match. You might have a real reason to be nervous then. Besides, even if you were serious, I don't have any desire right now to be back behind a desk."

The waiter brought their wine and waited for them to sample it. "That's fine," said Roland, "a very good choice."

She sipped her wine. "This is a good wine, but I have to admit. I'm not a very good judge of wine. I'm just not much into wines."

"I'm sorry. You don't have to drink it. I should have asked before I ordered it. I'm not big on wines either, but this one will go well with beef or lamb. If you'd like something else, I can order it."

"No, it's fine, Roland," she said, taking another small sip. "It is growing on me."

When their meal arrived, he asked, "Do you mind if I say grace for us?"

She was caught off guard, but she couldn't say that she would rather he didn't, that would be in poor taste. She nodded her head and said, "Go ahead."

He prayed softly, "Lord, thank you for this meal. Thank you for bringing Sherry to Washington to share this meal and this evening with me. Bless this food, Lord. Amen."

"Do you always do that, Roland, even when you are out for dinner?"

"Yes, usually, I do. I even ask a blessing when I am at a business dinner. Some of my business acquaintances call me the pastor, but that doesn't bother me. In fact, a couple of times, I've been invited to give the invocation at large dinner functions."

"I have to admit, I am not used to it at dinners out in public, but thank you."

The meal was everything that he had said it would be. When it came time for dessert, she ordered the crème brûlée.

"I am going to pay the price for eating like this," she told him. "I will have to be careful tomorrow, or my clothes will start getting tight on me. I can't have that."

The desserts came, and even though she had moaned about the possible results of partaking of such things, she found the crème brûlée irresistible after one taste.

"You seem to enjoy that," he commented. "I like it as well, but I just have a difficult time ignoring this soufflé when I'm here. Would you like a taste of it?"

"Yes, I think I would. If it is so good that you can turn down this wonderful crème brûlée, it must be something special."

She took a spoonful of his dessert and slipped part of it into her mouth, rolling it around on her tongue and savoring the orange flavor.

"This is really very good," she said as she put the rest into her mouth. "Would you care for a bit of mine to see what you gave up?"

He paused for a moment before he accepted her offer. "Betty and I always ordered different desserts just so we could share them," he said. "Thanks for offering."

"No, I thank you, but if we should ever come here again, you will have to order something different because I will order that. Would you mind if I have just a little more?"

When she had finished savoring the shared soufflé, she said, "It is reminiscent of crêpes suzette without the flame. I enjoy them when I'm in Paris. It brings back memories for me."

"For me as well," he said, "pleasant ones."

The limo was outside when they had finished their dinner, and she happily slid close to him during the ride back to the hotel. And he, in response, had put his arm around her shoulder, drawing her even closer. Once again, she was experiencing feelings that had not been resurrected by anyone else for many years. She was actually sorry when the ride ended, but he extended the magic as he walked her back into the hotel holding her hand.

She had no reservations about inviting him up to her room, and he accepted the invitation without any feigned protests about the propriety of doing so. She had noticed how he had been looking at her that evening. She had been around enough men to not be surprised or embarrassed by surreptitious male glances, and now she was excited by thoughts of titillating him once he was in her room.

They both were experiencing the delectable excitement that comes to lovers tempting fate and defying scandal. As they walked down the hall to her room, he could feel desire growing in his heart and his body. It surprised him with its suddenness and its power.

Following her into the room, he thought how perfect her legs were, and then, lifting his gaze, he found his eyes irresistibly focusing on her hips beneath the red dress.

She turned toward him when she got to the end of the bed, and his eyes traveled up to where the cleavage of her enticing breasts disappeared into the deep *V* of her dress. He remembered catching himself looking at her breasts several times as they ate and especially as she had bent slightly over the table reaching out to share a dessert.

His involuntary thoughts and actions had an emotionally sobering effect on him, and his ardor melted away.

When she invited him to sit down, he said, "I'm sorry, Sherry, I know it's crazy, but I feel uncomfortable, almost guilty, about coming here with you tonight."

Surprised, she said, "But you were here with me this morning. Were you uncomfortable sitting here then?"

"No, but that was different. I didn't feel like I do tonight."

"And how is that?" she asked coyly, knowing how men seemed to feel and act when they were aroused.

He answered with a question. "Are you familiar with the story of David and Bathsheba?" he asked.

"Vaguely," she answered. "What's your point?"

"Well, David saw Bathsheba from his palace one afternoon when she was taking a bath on her roof, and he lusted for her. He was the king, and he could have just about any woman he wanted, but she was married to one of David's soldiers, and it was not lawful for him to have her. Even though it was unlawful and against God's Word and will, he took her anyway, and she became pregnant. Eventually, he caused her husband's death and brought her into his home. It was wrong, it was shameful, and God punished David for it."

"And your point is?"

"My point is that I find you very attractive and altogether too tempting for me to be here with you. I have to apologize for my thoughts because when we walked into this room, I was thinking things I should not have. I felt more like some kind of a sex-crazed schoolboy than myself. I haven't felt like that for many years."

"I said it this morning in the elevator, and I'll say it again, you are pretty direct. You certainly know how to make a girl blush, but you got my heart thumping too. I don't think we can always control our thoughts, but we should be able to control our actions—if we want to. I think we're okay."

"You are right, of course. I should have kept my thoughts to myself instead of embarrassing both of us."

"Don't be concerned. I'm more flattered than embarrassed, and you are every bit a gentleman. I know I can trust you. Besides, in all these years you've been single, you must have looked at a woman or two in that way, haven't you? Come on now, be honest."

"No, I haven't," he answered simply.

"Well, now I'm really impressed. That's quite a compliment you're giving me, you know. You make me feel like Helen of Troy in a way."

For a few moments, silence filled the room.

"For heaven's sake, Roland, sit down and quit fidgeting. You are making me nervous standing there. If you feel like you have to go, that's fine, but I'd much rather sit and talk with you. I promise I won't try to seduce you."

He sat.

She looked at him sitting in front of her. She could see the evening was quickly going downhill.

"You really do look uncomfortable. You know what, let's go down and have a nightcap, and we can visit in the lounge. How does that strike you?"

His faced brightened noticeably. "That sounds good to me, if you don't mind. I guess I'm a little old-fashioned."

They found a table off by themselves. He sipped his drink and then turned the glass around in his hand, looking at it.

"You know, I haven't had one of these since we were in high school."

"A drink?"

"No, a Tom Collins. I ordered it because I know what it is. I don't know the names of very many drinks. I know whiskey sour, mint julep, and fuzzy navel, but I don't like whiskey. I've never had a mint julep, and I have no idea what a fuzzy navel is, but it sounds gross."

"Do you like the Tom Collins?"

"It's okay. It's my fallback drink. I don't go into a bar very often. I always looked for the opportunity to cop a drink when I was in high school. It was something we guys thought was a big deal if we could get away with it, but after I graduated, it became unimportant to me, even in college."

"You know, you live a pretty Spartan lifestyle, no booze, no sex, and probably, no wild parties. Thank goodness, at least you like good food. What do you do with your life? What do you do for excitement?"

He swirled the drink in his glass. "I think I told you that I had taken up painting, and I am learning how to play the bagpipes, and I do some writing."

"But what do you do for excitement? I'm sorry, but all that stuff sounds rather boring to me."

"I spend time on my boat, and I fish for salmon and halibut. That can be pretty exciting at times."

"I've never done any fishing, so I'll have to take your word for it. Do you have a very large boat?"

"I have two boats. I have a twenty-four-foot Grady-White that I use for fishing and crabbing and a thirty-six-foot Bertram for real comfort on the water. I don't take the Bertram out too often. I feel like I need someone to go with me. I prefer to have at least a couple of other people onboard with me."

"Perhaps I could go out on your big boat with you sometime."

He became animated. "Hey, we could go out tomorrow if you would like to go. I know you have business to attend to, but if you could spare the time, we could go for a few hours in the afternoon. I would treat you to a crab dinner onboard if you like."

It was easy to see that she had perked his interest in a new way, and the earlier awkwardness in her room was forgotten.

"If I can work it out, when would we have to go?" she asked.

"Two o'clock would be best, but we could leave a little later if we have to. I'll work around your schedule."

She pretended to be thinking about her schedule before she replied. "I believe I can manage it. I can make it up the next day. I'll be in the lobby at two."

"That would be great. Two it is. You will want to bring a sweater. It can be cool on the water if there is any breeze."

They visited about the fishing and crabbing on the sound for a while, but she was feeling worn out after traveling and being out for dinner.

"Roland, it has been a wonderful evening, but I'm afraid I am going to have to say good night. The difference in time is getting to me. I need to get some rest, but I am looking forward to our trip tomorrow.

"I'm sorry again," he said. "You did tell me you wanted to go to dinner around five because you needed to turn in early, and here I have been keeping you up. I have enjoyed every minute of it, though."

"So have I, you needn't be sorry. I'll see you tomorrow." With that, she turned and disappeared into the lobby.

She was ready when he walked into the hotel the next afternoon. She hoped she was dressed properly for a cruise on the sound. Before he had gotten there, the theme song from *Gilligan's Island* had been rolling around in her mind for some weird reason.

When she told him about it, he laughed and said, "There are no desert islands within three hours of here that I know of, and I don't think we are likely to be caught in a storm. It's a beautiful day."

As they got into his car, he said, "By the way, my boat is the *Melissa*, not the *SS Minnow*."

"*Melissa*. That's a beautiful name. Why did you name the boat the *Melissa*?"

"It was in memory of my daughter. She died with her mother in a car accident when she was a child."

She paused for a moment. She could sense the conversation had turned painful for him. "I'm sorry, I didn't know about that."

"Hardly a day goes by that I don't think about them, but when I see the *Melissa*, I remember her face and the good times we all had as a family."

"What about your small boat, does it have a name?"

"Actually, it does. It's the *Que Sera Sera*."

"Is that your philosophy now, whatever will be, will be?"

"To some extent, it is. I have learned that there is little to be gained by worrying or getting angry over things, and life comes at us in ways we often don't expect. There are some things in our life that we can control to some extent and some things that we cannot, and much of wisdom is knowing the difference."

"You are amazing. You really are. I said you have a gift with words, and it seems you are a philosopher as well."

"Well, the boat's name came mostly from my experiences fishing and crabbing. You never know if you are going to catch salmon when you go fishing or crabs when you go crabbing. If you catch them, you catch them. All you can do is your best, and the rest is up to fate. Whatever will be, will be. The sooner one recognizes that, the happier one will be."

"So tell me, what are we going to be doing today?"

"Crabbing. Remember, I told you I would treat you to a crab dinner. There is nothing better than a freshly caught Dungeness crab. I brought the butter and a salad. If we don't catch anything, we will have a diet dinner, but I'm confident that won't be the case."

"What do we have to do?"

"Actually, all you will have to do is sit back and enjoy the ride. I put two pots out this morning with the *Melissa*, and when I pull them this afternoon, I think we will have crabs enough for dinner. I'll get them steamed up, and I'll even crack them for you."

"What are pots, Roland?"

"Traps. The crabs can get in them, but they have a hard time getting out. I put some fish heads and scraps in for bait. We only need two crabs for dinner, but if I get more, I'll take a couple back home with me."

"This sounds intriguing. I'm so glad you invited me to come. I've never done anything like this before. Where's the boat?"

"It's at the marina. We'll be there in a bit."

A half hour later, they were on the water, heading out to where he had his traps soaking. She was glad she had a sweater to counter the breeze. Small waves danced on the ocean as the *Melissa* parted them, throwing spray to each side. Once they arrived, he approached the first buoy and put the boat in neutral. As the boat glided next to the buoy, he caught it with his hook and pulled it into the boat and then began pulling the trap up from the ocean bottom forty feet below.

"Wow," she exclaimed as the trap was brought onboard. "You've got a lot more than two in there, that's for sure."

"Yes, I do. I hope we have a couple of keepers. There are quite a few females, but it looks like we might have three or four good ones."

"You mean, they aren't all good?"

"Well, they are good, but they are not all legal. I can only keep the males, and they have to be at least six and a quarter inches across the shell."

She had a question. "How can you tell the females from the males? They all look alike to me."

As he emptied the pot, he picked up a crab with his tongs and turned it on its back. "This one is a female." He explained, "Look at this flap. It's the tail, and on the females, it looks a little like the capitol building."

"Yeah," she said, "I can see that shape."

He tossed the crab over the side, followed by several that were too small before he turned one of the larger crabs onto its back with the tongs. "See the tail on this one, how it's much narrower and longer? This one is a male, and he is big enough to keep."

He dropped the crab into a bucket. He had two more male crabs that went into the bucket as well. All the rest joined their friends on the ocean floor. Moving on, the second trap was onboard shortly, and he dumped out the crabs and grabbed an especially large one.

"This is a really nice male. We'll keep him and one more, just in case two doesn't do it for dinner. I'll throw the rest back."

After hosing down the mess that the crab traps had made, Roland put a large pot of water on to boil in the galley.

"Bryce and I used to come out here a lot for crabs. He loved the ocean. I guess that's one of the reasons why he joined the Navy. I sure miss him. Would you like a bottle of water, juice, or a soda?" he asked. "I've got them all."

"Water would be fine for me."

He left and returned with a bottle of water. "You sit right where you are. I'm going to move the boat a little closer to shore and drop the anchor."

After the move, he joined her with a bottle of orange juice.

She commented, "This is so relaxing out here on the water. I think I can see why you like it. Do you come out often?"

"I can come just about anytime I want to if the weather is good, but I get tied up in other things at times, so I'm only out here once every two or three weeks, sometimes a little more often."

"What things tie you up? You said you painted, played the bagpipes, and did a little writing. That should leave you plenty of time to get out here."

"I'm sort of busy with church things and helping people. Once a month we go into the city with dinner for the homeless. I take a run up to Oak Harbor every once in a while to see my mother-in-law and spend some time with her. Actually, I usually keep both the *Melissa* and the *Que Sera Sera* in the Oak Harbor marina. Oh, yeah, and I do a lot of reading. I didn't mention that, did I?"

"Your mother-in-law is still living?"

"Oh, yes. I get up to see her fairly often. Sometimes I take her shopping, or we just go for a drive. She's a great person. She reminds me of Betty. I'm the only person she has other than Bryce. He was stationed for a while at Whidbey. She saw quite a bit of him while he was at the base. As a matter of fact, I'm going to see her tomorrow. I'm going to take her up one of the crabs I caught today. She likes them just as much as Bryce and I do. And speaking of crabs, the water is boiling. Excuse me for a few minutes, and I'll get dinner going."

She watched him walk into the galley. He was so different from the men she knew in her world. He was considerate, and she couldn't detect an ego. He was definitely handsome, and she enjoyed being around him, but church?

"They'll be a few minutes," he said when he returned. "You know, I was thinking, and I know you've got plenty to do, but would you like to ride up to Oak Harbor with me tomorrow when I take the crab up to Mom?"

"Could we go to La Conner also?" she asked.

"Sure, if you want to."

"When would you be going?"

"In the morning. I could pick you up at nine."

"Why don't you come earlier, say eight, and we could have breakfast at the hotel before we leave."

"It's a date," he said.

Once the crabs were done, he cleaned them and prepared the crab and took out the salad. He put a couple of folding chairs and a table out on the deck and spread a tablecloth over the top.

"Have a seat," he said, "and I'll bring you the best dish Washington has to offer."

The meal consisted of two plates of crab meat, each couched on a bed of fresh lettuce and attended by a small bowl of melted butter.

"I only brought one dressing for the salad, Thousand Island. I've always thought it went really well with crab. I hope you like it."

"This looks wonderful."

He said, "Let's thank the Lord for this food."

She felt her body tense, but she bowed her head as he prayed.

"Lord, thank you for this bounty of your ocean. Thank you for all that you have provided and for a friend to share it with. Now bless the food and this time we have together. Amen."

I guess I should have expected that after last night, Sherry thought as she began eating.

After a few forkfuls, she had to comment, "This crab is excellent. I don't think I have ever had any better. And the salad is just right, the dressing compliments the crab so well. You should have been a chef. How many other qualities do you have to surprise me with?"

"I have no idea. I guess you will just have to wait and see, but I'm glad you like the crab and the salad. I never order Dungeness in a restaurant. No matter how well they prepare it, I am always disappointed, because I compare it to this, and there is no comparison. Thank you so much for coming with me today. It is so much more enjoyable to share all this with a friend than it is to do it alone. I believe I'd use this boat a lot more often if you were out here to go with me."

"Maybe you might like to take my father sometime," she parried. "I think he would really enjoy being out on the ocean, and I know he would like the crab."

"If we could work it out, I'd be happy to do that. I would like to get to know him."

"When I get out to my daughter's, Roland, I'll make sure I get you over to meet him and Marcy. I'll be going out there day after tomorrow. I called Marcy and told her I'd be there Friday morning. She's pretty excited."

The afternoon passed quickly, and as they were pulling up to the dock at the marina, he said, "I'm sorry, I have been taking up so much of your time. Well, actually, I'm not sorry, because I've enjoyed it, but I feel bad because you probably haven't been able to get to very many stores. Are you sure you want to go tomorrow? We will be gone for most of the day."

"To tell you the truth, I have enjoyed our time together so much I could care less if I saw any more shops or not. It's not something I absolutely have to do. This really feels like a vacation, and I don't want to ruin it just to get to a store or two. So tomorrow's a date, and don't be late for breakfast."

Later, after he had dropped her off at the hotel, he thought about the next day. After breakfast, they should be able to make it to Oak Harbor by noon. He would call when he got home and let his mother-in-law know they were coming with some crab and that he would order a pizza when he got there. It would be good to see Amanda again. He hadn't been there for a couple of months. He wondered what she would think of Sherry.

That night he sat on his deck, thinking about Sherry and the past couple of days. It seemed so good to have a woman around, even if it was just for a few hours at a time. He really wanted to know where she was at spiritually, but he had felt uncomfortable about just coming out and asking her. As much as he was quickly coming to like her, he had a sense that she might not be on the same page when it came to belief. If their relationship was going to go anywhere, they needed to be of like minds. Otherwise, they might better just remain friends.

A possible solution came to him. Why not ask her to go to church next Sunday? See how she reacted to that. It might bring some clarity. At least it would give him a good opportunity to broach the subject of whether she was a Christian or not. He knew he had missed a chance when she had asked about saying grace, but he hadn't wanted to break the spell of the afternoon. Sunday would be soon enough.

He had things worked out in his mind by the time he crawled into bed. He would make it a point tomorrow to invite her to go to church with him. One way or another, he had to know where she stood. He couldn't help thinking how much he would enjoy having her beside him in his bed that night, but not for just a night. As much as he was excited by her, he had no interest in having a one-night stand.

He went to sleep, praying, "Lord, forgive me for any impure thoughts. You know my heart. I can't help thinking about Sherry, but I still want to be in the center of your will. I would rather be single than to be in a marriage that didn't honor you. Thank you for the great time I had today. Lord, I want to have a wife again. If it isn't to be Sherry, make that clear to me, but send someone that I can love and cherish. Do the same for Bryce, Lord, and keep him safe wherever he is tonight."

15

A SURPRISE FOR AMANDA

Roland awoke to the alarm going off. Slightly disoriented for a moment, thinking he was still praying, he quickly came to and turned off the alarm. He remembered he was up early so he could have breakfast with Sherry. He showered and dressed, humming as he did so. He completed his short mental list: crab out of the refrigerator, put in cooler with ice, put bottled water in cooler, put cooler in the car. He was ready, with plenty of time to spare as long as there were no holdups on the highway. He entered the hotel at ten minutes of eight and immediately caught sight of Sherry waiting for him.

"I knew you would be early, it seems to be your nature. I like that. I'm the same way, obviously. Let's go on in, there's a table ready for us."

After the waiter brought their coffee, she ordered eggs Benedict, and he ordered two eggs over easy, wheat toast, and bacon.

She smiled and said, "That's what my father had almost every morning for breakfast when I was a child. Once in a while, he might have oatmeal or French toast, but crisp bacon, eggs over easy, toast, and coffee was his mainstay."

"I'm looking forward to meeting him. Maybe we can get out to breakfast together once in a while as well as getting out in the boat."

"I'm sure he would like that. It's very nice of you to be willing to do it."

As she spoke, she was thinking this through. If her father became friends with Roland, it could well bring him closer; but at the same time, it might put her and her father into a closer relationship as well. She wasn't sure she was ready for that yet, but she could deal with that when the time came. If her father was as sick as it appeared he might be, it could be a moot point in any case.

Half an hour later, they were way north, and when they ended up at the Oak Harbor marina, she asked why they hadn't gone back to the marina where they started.

Roland explained, "We came up by boat because I left a car here at the marina when I took the *Melissa* down to Seattle, and I thought you would enjoy the boat trip up more than the drive we would have had. You will like Amanda. She is a real peach and sharp as a tack even at her age. I have asked her several times to come and live with me, but she says if I want her to live in my home, I'm going to have to move to somewhere around Oak Harbor. Lately, I've actually been thinking about it."

"Whidbey does have its charms," Sherry said. "Life is a little slower there, but it's a long ways from Seattle. I kind of like the city. I've lived in New York for so long I don't know if I could survive out in suburbia, let alone in a rural setting."

"I could, that's why I've been thinking about what Amanda said. They've got a very convenient marina in Oak Harbor where I usually keep my boat, and in just a few minutes, I can be fishing or crabbing. I don't need to be close to Seattle to be happy."

Once on the boat, they were barely underway when he said, "I always enjoy being on the water, whether on my boat or even on a ferry. I find it very soothing. Sometimes when things seem to be getting me down, I just get on a ferry and ride it. I always come back feeling better."

"What kinds of things get you down, Roland? You always seem pretty much up whenever I see you."

"I guess it's partly when I get to missing Betty after all these years. She was a touchstone for me. We were a great pair. But there were times, after Bryce went away, that I seemed to have lost my purpose in life. I tried working, and I tried not working. I traveled some, went out on my boat, painted, and wrote, but nothing seemed to help for very long. The ferry rides helped me to clear my head and relax, but they only had a temporary effect. I was really empty."

The ocean was calm and the ride smooth, so she stood up and put her hand on the back of his neck, massaging it and running her fingers through his hair. He responded to her touch by raising his shoulders and gently tilting his head back, still keeping his eyes on their course.

"It's been a long while since anyone has done that," he said.

"Do you want me to stop?" she asked.

"No. I didn't mean that. It feels wonderful. You can do that as long as you like, I won't complain. Betty used to rub my neck like that when we were driving. I would get a knot in my neck and shoulders, and her hands could take it away like magic. I liked it no matter whether I had a knot or not."

"Well, you keep your eyes on the water, and I'll massage your shoulders too."

She moved closer, getting behind him, and put both hands on his shoulders near his neck.

"I haven't done this in a long time either, but I think I remember how." She added softly, "There are a lot of other things I am remembering."

Eventually, her fingers grew tired, and she reluctantly ended the episode.

Snuggling close and leaning her head on his shoulder, she whispered, "I feel so good, Roland. It's hard to believe, but I can shut everything else out of my mind here with you. Thank you so much for asking me to come with you. I'm so glad I did."

Once the boat was secure in the slip, they drove the short distance to Amanda's home. He could sense Sherry's relaxed presence next to him in the car, and he was warmed by it, both physically and emotionally. She was so much like Betty in some of the things she did.

Her attention turned to the home when he turned into Amanda's driveway and turned off the engine.

"This is it?" she asked.

"Yes, it is, I'm surprised she wasn't outside when we arrived."

He got out of the car and came around to open her door.

"Thank you," said Sherry. "You are always the gentleman. They don't make many like you anymore."

Walking up to the door, he rang the bell. In a moment, the door opened, and a slender woman with a broad smile and silvery tinged hair stood looking at them.

"Come in," she said, "I've been expecting you."

Glancing around the house, she could see everything was tidy and neat, just like the outside. His mother-in-law was every bit as neat and proper as her home.

"Mother, this is my friend, Sherry Williamson, a high school classmate of mine. I asked her to come with me today. Sherry, this is Betty's mother, Amanda Anderson."

"I'm pleased to meet you, Mrs. Anderson," she said. "He has been telling me about you."

Amanda took her hand and said, "I'm pleased to meet you as well, and just call me Amanda. He hasn't told me a thing about you, so we will have to get acquainted." Looking at him, she smiled and said, "It's about time, son."

"Come into my living room, Sherry," Amanda said. "It's not much, but it's comfortable. Roland sees to it that I have everything I need, including very comfortable furniture. I try to tell him I can get along fine on my own, but he won't listen. He is a real prize, hang on to him."

He cleared his throat. "She is only my friend, don't get the cart before the horse. Now, Mother, if you would order your favorite pizza and have it delivered, I'll pay for it when it comes."

"It's already on the way. I ordered it just before you pulled into the driveway. I hope you like pepperoni and mushroom."

"You know, I do. Oh, by the way, I have something in the car for you. I'll go get it. Won't take a minute."

She turned her attention to Sherry. "So you were a classmate of Roland's. How long have you lived in the area?"

"I don't actually live in Washington. I live in New York City, but I'm out here to visit my daughter in Snoqualmie. I learned Roland was out here because I saw him at our class reunion in June. We had quite a conversation, and he asked me to let him know if I ever came out to see my daughter. He said perhaps we could get together. It's quite a coincidence that he lives in the same community as she does."

"Whatever brought you here, I'm pleased to see him with you. He has been lonely for way too long. He's a good man, and he deserves a good woman. His bringing you here today says a lot to me about you, even if he denies you are anything more than a friend."

"He and I haven't really talked about us, we've just been catching up from old times. I like him, but I don't know if we would really be a good combination or not. We've both been single a long time, and we are sort of set in our ways."

"Well, he's a good catch. He has lots of money. I suppose you know that."

"Yes, Mrs. Anderson. I know that."

"Know what, Sherry?" he asked as he came in the door with the bag of crab.

"That you have lots of money. Amanda was telling me you were well off."

"Mother, what are you up to? She isn't interested in how much money I have. She has plenty of her own. Sherry is the owner of Robyn's World, the cosmetics company."

Amanda raised her eyebrows, "Well, don't that beat all? I've used your stuff for years, but I never thought I'd meet the person who made them. I really like your skin cream. Look at my arms, no brown spots, no dry skin, and not too many wrinkles, thanks to you."

"Amanda, I just might have to use you in a testimonial advertising our skin cream, you look great."

She looked at him, "Son, I like the way this woman talks. You be good to her, you hear?"

"I will, Mother." He held out the bag, "Here are a couple of crabs that Sherry and I caught yesterday out on the big boat."

She smiled and said, "Thank you, thank you, both. They feel good and cold. I'll put them right in the refrigerator."

When she returned, she asked Sherry, "So how long are you going to be here in Washington?"

"I'm not sure. My father recently moved out here to stay with my daughter. He has some health problems he needs to deal with. He has an appointment with a specialist on Monday. So I'm going to be here for a while with them, but I don't know just how long that will be."

"Well, I'll pray for your father that everything will work out fine."

The pizza interrupted their conversation, but after the meal, Amanda said to her, "So tell me about your daughter. What does she do?"

"She's a designer, or planner, who works for a Seattle company, but I can't tell you exactly what she does for them. She doesn't talk a lot about her work. She's quite different from me. I always talk about my work, but I am learning it sometimes gets in the way of more important things."

"What's she like? Is she happy? Is she outgoing?"

"I think so." Taking a photo from her purse, she handed it to Amanda. "Here, this is a picture of her. She looks happy, doesn't she?"

"Why, she's gorgeous. She takes after you quite a bit. She looks so young. How old is she?"

"Let's see, she will be thirty-three in September. It hardly seems possible when I say it."

"I take it she's still single?"

"Yes. Sometimes I wonder if I will ever have grandchildren. She has had a few boyfriends, but apparently nothing too serious. She says all the men she knows act so immature, more like boys than men. I still keep hoping she will find the right man, but so far, he hasn't come along."

"Sherry, I know a man who is just bit younger than she is. He's handsome and single, and he'd make a great catch. Maybe we could get them together and see what happens."

"Mother," Roland interjected, "I can see where you are headed here." He explained to Sherry, "She is talking about Bryce. She thinks he's on his way to becoming a confirmed bachelor at twenty-five."

"He's right, dear. Bryce is a wonderful young man, and I don't say that just because he is my grandson, but he doesn't seem to be able to take the time from his career to find a suitable mate."

"I sort of know how that is," she replied.

He broke in, "Mother, I'm sorry, but we are going to have to leave. I told Sherry I would take her to La Conner before we head back to Seattle, and I don't want to be too late getting back."

"Okay. Sherry, you get him to bring you back up again when you have a little more time. Thanks for the crabs. I know I'll enjoy them."

She walked them to the door and then watched as they backed out of the driveway.

They look like such a nice couple, she thought as she watched them disappear.

Driving away, Sherry said, to him, "Why don't we forget about La Conner today? If we go there, by the time we drive back to Seattle, it will be getting late. I know I asked about going, but I'd rather get back to the hotel and get ready to go to my daughter's tomorrow."

"Whatever you wish. We can go another day if you would like. You know, Amanda seemed to take quite a liking to you."

"Maybe she's getting desperate. It sounded to me like she was trying to marry you off. Have you ever taken another woman up to meet her?"

"No, but she has told me a number of times that she has been praying that I would find a nice lady and settle down."

"Well, there you go. She probably thought her prayers have been answered. She really is a sweet lady. I enjoyed talking with her."

"I'm glad. She has been an important part of my life for quite a few years now."

He grew quiet as he drove down the side streets toward Route 20.

When he pulled onto the main road, he said, "Sherry, I've enjoyed the past few days immensely. I was wondering if you would like to go to church with me this coming Sunday."

"I don't know if I can. I don't know what Marcy and my father have planned."

"They could come too. Why don't you ask them if they'd like to go with us? It's a great church, and it's meant a lot to me over the last few years. I'm sure you would like it."

"I'm afraid I don't go to church very often. I never have."

His only response was a questioning, "Oh?"

She felt obligated to explain, "When we were in school, my friend Delores was all the time trying to get me to go to church or join their youth group, but I just wasn't interested. She has kept working on me unsuccessfully for over thirty years."

Pretty sure he already knew the answer, he asked, "So you aren't a Christian then?"

"Sure, I'm a Christian. I'm not a Muslim or a Buddhist or a member of some other religion."

He had never tried to lead anyone to the Lord before, but he had made up his mind that he would try to explain salvation to Sherry if she wasn't a Christian. In just a few months, he had gone from hating her to thinking she might be the one he could spend the rest of his life with, but above all, he was looking for a woman who loved the Lord.

He had his work cut out for him. During the rest of the ride home, he did his best to share Jesus with her, and by the time they arrived back at the hotel, she had pretty much decided he was not for her. She didn't make any commitment and had not given him much encouragement as he tried his best to open her eyes.

When they got to the hotel, she said, "You've given me a lot to think about, and I will definitely think on it. I'm not sure if I understood or believe everything you told me, but I'll think about it. Thank you for a lovely day. I'll call you from Marcy's later in the week."

On his drive back home, he spent a lot of time thinking and talking to the Lord.

"Lord, I don't think I did a very good job telling Sherry about you today. I'm sorry I'm not better at explaining your plan. She needs you, Lord. You know my heart, Lord, and you know I like her, but if she is not for me, I will understand. But, Lord, please bring her to the point where she would want to listen."

He didn't know if he would have another chance to influence Sherry, but he knew that he would see her again soon. He would have to be patient.

16

REALITY

Late in the morning, Sherry left the hotel for Snoqualmie. She was thinking about what Roland had said the day before. She had thought about it before she went to sleep too. He had been very insistent, much like Delores had always been. As much as she had come to like him, she was now convinced that probably, all he could ever be was a good friend in the manner of Delores. The thought did nothing to please or comfort her.

About twenty minutes from Snoqualmie, she called and let Marcy know that she was not far away. When she drove into the driveway, both Marcy and her father were standing outside, waiting for her.

He moved closer to her car as she got out.

"Hi, Sherry, it's good to see you. It's been quite a long time," he said as he reached out his arms to her.

Walking to meet her father, she gave him a perfunctory hug, but she winced involuntarily as his arms wrapped around her in a real embrace.

"Thank you so much for coming," he whispered in her ear.

She waited for his grasp to loosen and then stepped back and said, "Marcy told me you have been under the weather. How are you feeling?"

"I've been feeling better lately, but I still get tired pretty easy. I'm going to see the doctor on Monday. She made an appointment for me. I'll know a lot more after that."

She measured up her father. He was looking somewhat old and tired, but he wasn't as frail as she had been expecting. He had some color in his face, and there had been nothing wimpy about his embrace. He didn't look like a man at death's door.

Suddenly, she was horrified as she realized she had been disappointed that he looked so well, and guilt welled up in her, powerful and accusing.

The pain must have shown on her face because her father, misinterpreting her look, said, "Don't worry about me, I'm going to be fine. I don't want you to be sad because of me."

His voice had been full of genuine concern, and she surprised herself as she reached out and took his hand, "Let's go inside." She held his hand all the way to the door, only letting go so he could go through the doorway.

Once they were inside, Marcy asked, "Would either of you like a cup of coffee? It's still hot from breakfast."

As soon as they had their coffee, they moved out onto the deck to sit down, and Mr. Miller began to describe to her how Marcy had found him in the hospital.

"She had come to see me, but the folks where I lived told her I was in the hospital. I couldn't believe it when she came into my room. I began feeling better the moment I saw her. She had come all that way just to see me. She made me eat, and she made me walk, and she got the doctor to let me go home. She stayed with me, cooked for me, and then she invited me to come back here to live with her. So here I am. I'm so happy to be here, and now you are here too. God has been good to me. Every day is a new blessing."

What does God have to do with any of this? Sherry thought. *It was Marcy who brought you here, not God.*

She didn't voice her thoughts, and there had been such a personal disconnect between the two of them for so long that she really didn't know what to say to make conversation. Roland's desire to meet her father and Marcy popped into her head.

"There is someone here in Washington that I would like you to meet, Father. I think Marcy would probably like to meet him too. He actually lives right here in Snoqualmie. His name is Roland Holtz."

"Roland Holtz?" he repeated thoughtfully. "Oh, yes, are you thinking about marrying him?"

She shot Marcy a glance; she just shrugged in reply.

"Whatever makes you think that?" she asked.

"Well, Marcy told me you were thinking about getting married again, and she mentioned him as one of the men you had been considering. She said you had dated him in high school, but I could only remember Hughie."

"Well, let me set the record straight, Father. I did date him one time in high school, but that was it. The next time I met him after we graduated was at our thirty-fifth-year high school class reunion. That ended up not going really well. He had some unpleasant memories from school, and I was disappointed because of that. However, when I told him I was coming here to see you, he made arrangements to meet me in Seattle."

It was Marcy's turn to shoot a glance, and Sherry shrugged in return.

"He told me he would like to have the chance to meet you both. Would you be interested in meeting him tomorrow?"

"I sure would. What about you, Marcy?"

"Sure, I've been wanting to meet him ever since Mom told me about him."

"Then that's settled. I'll call him and make the arrangements. I'm sure he will come. He told me he could be free anytime."

The rest of the morning was filled with small talk about what each one had been doing recently. Sherry shared what was going on at Robyn's World, and Marcy explained that her job might be changing and she wasn't sure if she wanted to stay on or look for something new. A lot was said, but no one wanted to get to what was on all their minds, and that had nothing to do with Roland or jobs or business.

Marcy had made some sandwiches ahead for lunch, and as they sat down to eat, her grandfather asked if it would be okay if he asked the blessing. Marcy nodded, and he began, "Father, thank you for this food and for this beautiful day. Thank you for bringing my daughter here and for allowing us all to be together once again. Bless this food, Father, and please be with Sherry as she works things out in her life. Amen."

She had been sort of blindsided by her father's prayer, and she was beginning to feel like she was out of step. It had always been Delores, but then it was Roland, and now her father, and maybe Marcy, who knows.

After lunch, he excused himself for his afternoon nap, and Marcy and Sherry had a chance to talk.

"So exactly how is Father? You indicated he was dying, but that doesn't appear to be the case as I see it."

"He has been getting stronger every day since I found him in the hospital, but don't let that fool you. He is seriously ill, and like he said, we will know a lot more after Monday. He could go downhill as quickly as he has seemed to improve in the past few weeks. I do think your being here is going to be a plus for him, though."

She was ready to bring out her grandfather's scrapbook.

"Why don't you sit down at the table, Mother, I've got something I want to show you."

She retrieved the scrapbook and placed it on the table in front of her. "Open it up, I think you are going to be surprised."

Page by page, Sherry worked her way silently into the book. It was filled with baby pictures, school photos and school papers, report cards, and other memorabilia from her childhood. Then she arrived at those days when her time with Hughie had begun. She looked at Marcy momentarily and then started slowly turning the pages of her life once again, finding photos of her infant daughter and Hughie holding her. There was a photo of her mother and father holding a smiling baby in a lacy dress. Then, amazingly, there was a snapshot of Hughie at the garage standing by a motorcycle. There was a penciled-in note under it, "Marcy's daddy, the best man they've got." She read it twice. It was her mother's handwriting.

There was a picture of her and Hughie on his bike.

Who took that? she wondered, trying to remember. It looked like it had been taken in Bradley before they were married. There was a picture of the two of them at the senior dinner dance.

Where did they get that picture?

Then there were two copies of Hughie's obituary, one from the local Georgia paper and one from the *Bradley News*. There was a sympathy card that someone had sent them. It wasn't the printed verse that caught her eye but the handwritten note on the opposing page.

"Dear Jim and Martha, we are so sorry for your loss. We remember you had so many fears when Sherry and Hughie eloped, but it has been easy to see from your letters that he was growing on you and Martha as you got to know him. We pray that you will be able to comfort your daughter in these difficult times and help her raise that little girl you love so much. May God bless you all and give you peace. Dave and Melinda."

She couldn't remember her parents making much of an effort to get to know Hughie better in Georgia and certainly not in Bradley. She couldn't remember them saying anything nice about him either. Had she missed something in those days? Had Marcy made a difference in that relationship?

She moved on and gazed at long-forgotten ads and photos of her first shop. Every step of the construction of the first actual plant was pictured with the date of each photo. There were newspaper articles about Robyn's World and interviews that had been done by local and regional newspapers. Then one photo caught her eye.

She let out a gasp. It was the distinguished gentleman who had brought her the letter and check so many years ago. His photo had no information with it, no name, no date, no anything, just a picture. She quickly started to scan the next pages.

There were a few pictures of Marcy taken at an occasional Christmas gathering or birthday, but the record of her growth was spotty at best. Pictures taken at high school graduation and college graduation were the last ones of Marcy. There was more dealing with Robyn's World, especially articles from fashion magazines that extolled the great things about the new business and its products, but the meticulous recording ended about the time that her mother died. There were no other pictures of the man.

It was some time before Sherry finished the book. She had mostly looked at the pictures, not reading much from any of the articles, but long before she had finished, it dawned on her how much and how deeply her parents had felt a relationship with her and her daughter. The one scrapbook spoke volumes about the love her parents had for her and her daughter all through the years while she had taken out her relentless bitterness on them. The bitter separation over the years had eventually turned more into mere habit, but the results remained the same.

She looked at Marcy, but it was impossible to look her in the eyes. Her lips quivered, and her throat was so tight that at first she wasn't able to speak. She looked down at her hands resting on the closed book. Marcy remained silent.

When she had composed herself, she looked at her daughter once more and said, "Well, that was quite a journey down memory lane. I didn't realize Mom and Dad were that interested in our lives."

"Really, Mother?" Marcy let out a huge disappointed sigh. "Is that all you can say? Is that all that this book means to you? Every time I have looked through this scrapbook, I've felt cheated and I've felt ashamed. I can finally see I was a pawn being used to hurt Grandpa and Grandma, and I don't like it at all. I never quite comprehended it before, but I should have been able to see it. I know that you were really upset with them, but you were cruel. It wasn't right. No matter what they did, they didn't deserve what you did to them."

Stinging from the unexpected rebuke, Sherry immediately went on the defensive.

"My mother and father should have thought about the consequences before they destroyed my life. Your father might still be alive if it hadn't been for them. It may sound terrible, but I could not stand being around them any more than I had to. I didn't want to owe them anything, and I don't. I've made my own way, no thanks to them. I'm sorry if I hurt you in the process, but what's done is done."

Marcy was dismayed at her mother's response. "Mother, when you looked at this book, didn't you feel even a little bit sorry for what you did to your mother and father and to me? I watched you while you were looking at the scrapbook, and you were having a hard time not crying. Don't you think this might be a good time to admit that you were wrong and let it go? Grandpa and Grandma let it go a long time ago even though their hearts were broken."

Even as Marcy spoke, Sherry thought of the story Roland had told her about the big bass he had caught and released. He had said that sometimes, letting something go was just the right thing to do. And hadn't he let go of the anger that he had carried so long over her treatment of him after their date?

"Honey, I don't want to make your grandfather's life miserable, and I'm willing to be civil to him. I still don't feel I owe him anything, but maybe I can forgive him for your sake."

"Forgive him? For crying out loud, Mother, you are the one who should be asking for forgiveness, and you don't even know it. I'm going to tell you something that Grandpa told me not to. Grandpa and Grandma gave you everything they had to get Robyn's World started."

"What are you talking about? I never took anything from them. What did they ever give me besides pain?"

"They sold everything they could, withdrew the money they had in savings and retirement accounts, and mortgaged their home. They also borrowed all they could. They did all that for you. Where did you think the two hundred thousand dollars came from? Your fairy godmother?"

Sherry was startled. "How did you know I got two hundred thousand to use for the business? I must have told you the story about that money, didn't I? Did I tell you I had gotten a cashier's check for two hundred thousand dollars?"

"No, you didn't. Grandpa told me when he thought he was about to die, and he told me never to tell you. Didn't you ever wonder why Grandpa and Grandma seemed to be so poor, or maybe you just never took the time to notice while you were making all that money from the business that they had paid for. They spent twenty-five years working and going without in order to pay that money back, but they never complained, never said a word, even when Grandma got sick, they didn't ask you for help."

It was too much for Sherry to accept, and the inner turmoil she was experiencing announced itself with a sudden splitting headache, nausea, and a desire to be far away.

"Look, Marcy, I need time to think about all this, but I can't do it here. Tell Father I'll be back, but I have to go. I have to go now. I don't know if I can face him after what you have told me. I don't know if I can believe it either. I'm going to need some time."

"Where are you going to go?"

"I'll see about getting a hotel room in Seattle for the night," she said as she got up and headed for the door. "I'll call you. I won't be far away."

As soon as she was out of sight of Marcy's home, she stopped, got out Roland's card, and called him on her cell phone.

When she heard him answer, she said, "Roland, this is Sherry. I need to stop by and see you if that's okay. I don't have your home address. It's not on your card. Would you give it to me please? I'm just leaving Marcy's."

He gave her the address and added, "Look, I'm not home right now, but I can be there in about twenty minutes, just wait for me when you get there."

"Thanks, I'll be waiting. Bye."

She put the address into her GPS. It took a few more minutes to get there than the GPS had indicated, and he pulled into the driveway shortly after she did. Getting out of her car, she waited for him. She didn't know if he could do anything for her, but she knew she badly needed a friend.

After her call, he had thought that the situation was somewhat unusual. From what little he had learned about Sherry, he didn't think she was in the habit of doing anything on the spur of the moment. As he walked up to her, it was apparent that she was distraught and had been crying.

"Are you okay?" he asked.

Completely losing it, she began sobbing. Between sobs she got out, "Hold me, Roland."

He wrapped his arms around her as she buried her head into his shoulder, still sobbing. He could feel her shaking and tried to figure out what was going on.

"Did your father die?" he asked.

She sniffed and replied, "No."

He tried again, "I thought you were going to your daughter's today. Was there a problem? Is your father worse?"

She started sobbing again without answering. He was at a loss over what the crying was about, but he wanted to move out of the driveway.

He said, "Come on, let's go inside, and I'll find some Kleenex, and you can tell me what this is all about." He put his arm around her waist and gently urged her along to the house.

She had stopped sobbing by the time they were inside, and he quickly located the Kleenex, bringing the whole box to her.

"Here you are. Now wipe those beautiful eyes, and let's get to the bottom of this."

Wiping her eyes, she was aware of the makeup on the tissue. "I must look awful," she said. "My eyes can't be very beautiful right now."

He shrugged his shoulders and shook his head, "I'm more concerned about what has happened to you than what your makeup looks like. Is your father worse? Is that what has you so upset?" he asked.

She took a deep breath, dabbing at her eyes one more time, and said, "It's not Father, not really. I don't know where to begin. I feel like I'm the world's worst person. For the first time in my life, I really don't know what I'm going to do. I've made a mess out of my life, and I don't think there is any fixing to it. I can't go back and do everything over, and I can't act like there is nothing wrong. I am so ashamed. I will never be able to look my daughter or my father in the eye again."

"Whoa, whoa," he said, "hold on a minute, and tell me exactly what is going on. Did you have an argument with them?"

"No, it's not them. It's me, Roland. It looks like I have been so horribly wrong for so long, and now I still can't even bring myself to ask to be forgiven. I was so messed up that I thought it would be magnanimous of me if I forgave my father, when all the time I was the one who needed to be forgiven. I can't face my father. I have made his life miserable. I hurt my mother too, but she is dead, and I can never tell her I'm sorry. I can never take away her pain."

"Okay. I remember you told me that your relationship with your parents was a rocky one, but I guess I didn't realize the extent of the problem."

"It's more than just that, Roland. I've been a fool. My life for the last thirty years has been based on a false premise. I destroyed my whole family because of my pride and my pigheadedness. Now my father is dying, and my daughter thinks I'm terrible. No one could possibly know how terribly sorry I am right now."

Roland couldn't help himself, "There is someone who knows how sorry you are."

"No, Roland. I don't really think you could possibly understand how very bad I feel and how rotten I've been."

"I didn't mean me," Roland replied softly. "I meant God."

17
ROLAND, I DON'T BELIEVE IN GOD

"Roland, I didn't come here because I wanted to talk about God. I came here because I wanted to talk with someone who would listen to me, someone who would let me cry on their shoulder. I need someone who can help me set things right if it's possible."

"I can listen, and I don't mind your crying on my shoulder, but if you really want to set things right, you need to set things right with God first."

"Roland, I don't believe in God."

He sat down beside her.

"I know you don't. I realized that when we were coming back from Amanda's yesterday, but I had suspected it before that. I did my best to explain salvation to you, but I wasn't very good at it, and you weren't ready for it. The Bible claims people who don't believe are fools. Psalms 14:1 says, 'The fool hath said in his heart, there is no God.' The Bible also says, 'The fear of the Lord is the beginning of wisdom.' That's somewhere in Proverbs. Sherry, you need to know the Lord. I think that's where your answer is."

"Delores has told me I need to know the Lord more times than I can count."

"Delores is a good friend. She cares enough about you not to give up on you. You want your father to forgive you because you've acted like a fool and screwed up big-time, but you are having a

160

difficult time asking him to forgive you, so you came to me for help. But you don't need me. Your father loves you, and I think he will forgive you in a New York minute, all you have to do is give him the chance. After all, you are his child. It's like that with God. Once we know we need his forgiveness, all we have to do is ask for it. He is our heavenly Father, and we are his children. He loves us with a father's love, and his arms of forgiveness are always wide open."

She let that sink in before she replied, "Delores always said that I needed the Lord. I never asked her why. I thought God was for other people, bad people, you know, the sinners. Do you think I'm one of them?"

"Sherry, the Bible says in Romans 3:10, 'There is no one righteous, not even one,' and then in 3:23, it says, 'For all have sinned and fall short of the glory of God.' You see, you are absolutely right, you are one of them, we all are."

"You said that yesterday, but I couldn't accept that. I didn't think there was anything wrong with me, but that has all changed in just one day."

"The only thing that has changed is that you are able to see you were wrong. The question is, do you want to put things right?"

She started to cry, "Yes, I do."

"I don't mean just between you and your father. I mean, between you and God too."

"That's what I mean. What do I have to do?"

"Well, you've already started, and I have to tell you that I am excited for you. God asks us to admit we are sinners, and it sounds to me like you have already done that."

"I never thought I could do it, but I have. I really have sinned. I can understand it now."

"Then the rest is easy. He wants to be your Father. The real question has always been, Will you be his child? You need to tell Jesus you're sorry and actually ask him to forgive you for all your sins. God sent Jesus to be a sacrifice for us and our sin. Once we ask him for forgiveness and acknowledge him as Lord and savior, we are covered by his righteousness. At that very moment, our sins are gone. We become children of God. In First John 1:9, it says, 'If we confess our sins to him, he is faithful and just and will forgive us our sins and cleanse us from all wickedness.' You don't have to dredge up everything you've ever done wrong. He knows them all, and he will forgive them all if you want him to.

"Just talk to God. That's what praying is, talking to God. Tell him what you feel. Tell him you want to be forgiven. Tell him you believe in him and want to take him as your Lord and Savior. When you do, you will see everything in a whole different light."

Sherry was silent for a few moments as she collected her thoughts. She was at the brink of doing something she had never in her wildest dreams thought she would ever do, but here she was feeling somehow exhilarated by it all.

She started slowly, "God, I want to believe. I know that I am a sinner, and I have done a lot of things that I should not have. Please forgive me for all of them. I'm sorry for what I've done. I want to be your child. I do want you as my Lord and Savior, but, God, if you are really real, please prove it to me. Heal me and my family. Let my father and my daughter forgive me and love me again."

She looked at him and said, "I hope that was all right. Was it okay to ask for proof?"

"You were just being honest. There is no use in trying to fool him. God knows your heart. Let me read you something."

He got up and picked up a Bible from the bookshelf. Leafing through it, he found the page he was looking for and sat back down beside her. "Listen to this, from Psalms 139, King David is talking with God. 'Oh, Lord, you have searched me and know me! You know when I sit down and when I rise up; you discern my thoughts from afar. You search out my path and my lying down, and are acquainted with all my ways. Even before a word is on my tongue, behold, O Lord you know it altogether. Search me, O God, and know my heart! Try me and know my thoughts! And see if there be any grievous way in me, and lead me in the way everlasting!'"

Roland paused and looked up at Sherry.

"He's not going to hold your request against you. Even his disciple Thomas doubted, and Jesus came and took those doubts away. I believe he will do the same for you."

"I can hardly believe how much better I feel. But I know I need to go back right now and ask my father to forgive me. Would you go with me?"

"I am willing to go, but I think this is something you should do without me. I don't think I should be there at such an intimate moment. Remember, God will be right there with you. Trust him."

She stood up. "Then I'd better do it now while I still have the nerve. Pray for me that I can do it and that it will all work out."

As she was going out the door, he said, "I'll be praying, but if things go badly, come back here."

Marcy was surprised to see her mother when she answered the door.

"You decided to come back?' she asked.

"Yes, I did. When I left here, I went to Roland's and spent some time talking with him. Now I have a lot to talk with you and Father about, but first I need to confess something to you. I got into Seattle last Tuesday. I've been spending some time with Roland. It was something I needed to do."

"Oh?" Marcy said.

"I'll explain later. Is Father awake?"

"Yes. He's out on the deck. He was very disappointed when he found out you had left. Come on, he will be glad to see that you are back."

"Why don't you come out on the deck with me? I want to talk with you and Father."

"I'm back," she said as they walked out onto the deck.

He stood up, and she wrapped her arms around him and gave him a long hug.

He said, "My goodness, that was different! What has happened to you?"

"You go ahead and sit back down, Father. You too, Marcy. I've got some things to tell you, and I need to do it now."

When they were all seated, she began, "I have been a fool most of my life, but I didn't realize it until today. It took your scrapbook to open my eyes and Marcy's words to convict me. I couldn't handle it at first, so I went to see Roland, and he opened my eyes in other ways."

"I have been so selfish all my life. I always thought just about me. I came first, before you and Mother, before Hughie, and even before my own daughter. The only two things that became important in my life were Robyn's World and hurting you," she said, looking at her father.

"I have been so wicked. Father, I apologize for the way I treated you and Mother. There is not a strong-enough word to describe how I feel.

"You see, I made sure you never saw a lot of me or Marcy. I have always told myself that you were the ones primarily responsible for Hughie's death, and I never forgave you for it, when the fact is, I probably bear more responsibility for his death than anyone else. I am so very sorry for the heartache and pain I have caused. I am so very sorry for depriving Marcy of the joys of growing up knowing her grandparents."

Her father started to say something, but she raised her hand, stopping him, saying, "No, don't say anything. If I don't get this all out now, I may never be able to do it.

"Father, I am so embarrassed because you and mother sacrificed everything for me, and all I ever did was to despise you both in return. I never knew until today that you had anything at all to do with getting Robyn's World on its feet. I owe everything that I have to you, but I realized today that all I have is worth nothing compared to what I took away from you, Mom, and Marcy.

"I can't even begin to list every mean and despicable thing I did, and I can't take them back. I'd give everything I own if I could, but I can't. My heart is broken, and it's my own fault. I know I don't deserve it, but please forgive me for what I did to you and Marcy. Forgive me for blaming you for Hughie's death. Forgive me for being such a terrible daughter. Please."

She had made it through her confession and her plea for forgiveness without shedding a tear, but when she saw her father crying, she cried as well. She stooped to take him in her arms, and the two of them sobbed together, bittersweet tears of love.

When he had recovered enough to speak as they sat side by side, her father cleared his throat and said, "You have made me a very happy man. Of course, I forgive you. You have no idea how many times your mother and I prayed for you, that you would forgive us and come back to us, but it seemed like the more we prayed, the worse things got. I might have given up, but your mother said we needed to keep praying no matter what, and on the day she died, she made me promise I would keep praying, and I have.

"Your mother and I talked about this many times. We knew we had made a great mistake by not accepting Hughie just the way he was. We realized too late that if you saw something special, something worth having, in Hughie, we should have been able to as well. We should have realized it when we moved to Georgia, but we were still not happy that he had run off with you. Still, we tried to build a relationship with Hughie, but every time we started, we ended up somehow trying to change him. What we really needed to change was us, not him.

"I went to the garage a couple of times to see Hughie, not because I was interested in motorcycles but because I wanted to see what he did and find a way to praise him, to get to know him. Your husband had a wonderful understanding of engines and mechanics. His boss told me he was the best mechanic they ever had. I took a picture of him there at the garage. You probably saw it in the scrapbook.

"I thought maybe your mother and I were finally on the right track with him. The last time I saw him before he died, we had talked about his desire to own his own garage and bike dealership and about his girls. He wanted to provide so well for the two of you that you would never have to work. He really had a problem with you and your business. It made him feel inadequate somehow. He felt that you were working because you didn't think he was a good-enough provider.

"I never realized that he really had a goal. He wanted to do the very best he could for his family. He had a vision for your future. It was the first time that I felt really close to him. Thinking back, I think he could have been a wonderful son-in-law if we had had a little more time.

"I shared his dream with Martha that night, and we started to figure how we might be able to help him achieve it. I even went so far as to speak with the owner of the garage to see if he had ever considered selling. It turned out he wasn't interested, but your mother and I were willing to help Hughie financially in any way we could. I was so excited about it. We were both crushed when he died, but we had no inkling of the pain that was to come. All our lives were affected by his passing.

"I hope you can forgive us for taking so long to accept Hughie. We never meant any harm to him or you."

"I believe you," responded Sherry. "I could tell from your scrapbook that you never stopped loving me, no matter what I did. It was hard for me to handle that at first. How could you love me so?"

"It was easy. You were our daughter. How could we help but love you? Maybe it is explained best by the love chapter in the Bible. Your mother and I read it thousands of times. I learned part of it by heart. It says this, 'Love is patient, love is kind. It does not envy, it does not boast, it is not proud. It is not rude, it is not self-seeking, it is not easily angered, it keeps no record of wrongs. Love does not delight in evil but rejoices with the truth. It always protects, always trusts, always hopes, always perseveres. Love never fails.' Your mother and I survived on those verses, and today is a confirmation of the truth of those verses, because I love you with all that is within me."

"I love you too, Father. I love you more than any words can say."

Marcy had been watching this amazing transformation that was taking place in front of her eyes. A few hours before, she had wondered if anything would ever heal the breach between her mother and her grandfather, and now it seemed like she was watching a miracle.

Then Sherry turned to face her daughter, "I have done you a great disservice as well. I thought I was being a great mother, but I failed you. I have failed you miserably. The fact that you have turned out so well is a testimony to your strength of character and intelligence. I cannot take credit for any of it. As good as your life might be, it could have been immeasurably better if I had not taken you away from your grandparents. I hope you can forgive me for that."

"Mother, so many things about my life are finally making sense. I have had so many questions. I might never have known the truth if

I had not gone to see Grandpa. This is a wonderful day. If Grandpa can forgive you, I certainly can. I say we need to celebrate. This is a special day."

Mr. Miller chimed in, "This is the day that the Lord has made. Let us rejoice and be glad in it."

"I am rejoicing, Father, and I have one more thing to tell you. Thanks to Roland, I accepted Jesus Christ as my Lord and Savior today. I have been set free, and I feel like a new woman. This has to be the greatest day in my life. Do you two feel like celebrating with a dinner out?"

A few minutes later, she was on the phone.

"Roland, do you think you could get reservations for four at Canlis for tonight? . . . You do? Would you do it, please, and order the Canlis soufflé for me. We are celebrating . . . Yes, it went very well. Would you like to come over and join us? . . . Great! You have the address, right? . . . Okay, we will watch for you. Bye."

She announced, "You are going to love Canlis. They have wonderful food. Roland took me there for dinner one night, and I enjoyed it immensely. Do you have a suit or a sports coat, Father? You will need one, it's sort of a formal place."

"Wait a minute," she said, "there's someone else I need to call." She dialed the number and waited, listening to it ring. Then she said, "Delores, this is Sherry. I called to tell you that you don't have to pray for me anymore. I discovered I needed Jesus today, and I accepted him."

She listened for some time before she said, "Stop screaming already. I knew you would be surprised. I was too. Thank you for never giving up on me."

She was silent again for a few moments, until she said, "Okay, okay, I'll tell you all the details, but I can't do it right now. I am here with my dad and Marcy, but I promise I'll call you tomorrow and fill you in on all those questions. Oh, and before I go, the three of us are going out to dinner with Roland tonight. Maybe you shouldn't quit praying for me just yet. Talk to you tomorrow."

She turned back to her father, "You're a Christian too, aren't you?"

He smiled and said, "Yes, I've been a Christian for a long time, so was your mother. It helped us through some pretty hard times. Honestly, I feel like I am going to burst. I'm so happy."

She turned to her daughter next, "What about you? Are you a believer as well?"

"I've never thought about it. We never went to church, and no one has ever said anything to me about being a Christian before."

"Well, it's time you were thinking about it. You and I are going to have a lot to talk about tomorrow, and we'll all be going to church with Roland on Sunday."

"Mother, after all this, I think if there is such a thing as a miracle, then I do believe I have been witnessing one. I'll be ready to talk about it tomorrow."

Roland arrived soon after, and Sherry did the introductions, "Roland, this is my father, Jim Miller, and my daughter, Marcy Williamson. Dad, Marcy, this is Roland Holtz."

Her father shook Roland's hand and said, "I'm very pleased to meet you."

"The pleasure is all mine, Mr. Miller. I'm very glad to meet you both. Sherry and I have been getting reacquainted after thirty-five years, and I really wanted to meet you. We have reservations for 7:00 p.m., if that is okay with you all."

It was agreed that it was fine, and then Sherry said, "We are celebrating already, but I've told my daughter and my father what a wonderful restaurant Canlis is. It will be a great place for our quiet celebration dinner."

That afternoon, Roland enjoyed observing as the three of them celebrated becoming a family after years of being apart, but at the same time, he almost felt like he was intruding on something very special and personal. The thought crossed his mind that this might one day be his family as well, but there was nothing certain in that regard. Eventually, he noted the time and said they would need to leave for dinner in about an hour, so he was going to leave and let them get ready.

"I'll pick you up in an hour," he said.

That evening, Marcy and her grandfather were as impressed by the restaurant as Sherry had been a few days before when Roland had brought her there.

"It's sort of pricey," Mr. Miller said as he looked at the menu. "I'm not used to such a place."

"Order whatever you like, Father," Sherry said. "You don't have to worry about the price. I can afford it. From this day forward, you aren't going to have to think a second time about the price of anything, and you will never lack for anything if I can help it."

"Seeing as how you put it that way, I'll have the fillet mignon. I've always wanted to try it, but I never felt I should spend the money."

Waiting for their meal, Sherry said, "Roland, I almost forgot to tell you, we would all like to go to church with you on Sunday, if your invitation is still good."

"Of course, it is. I'd love to take you. I think you will like the people and the service. It will be the perfect finish for this week."

They were all in high spirits after the dinner as they headed for home. While their conversation centered a lot on the meal they had just eaten and the experience as a whole at first, it soon gravitated to Sherry's conversion and how the family was back together.

"It was so simple," she explained. "I could have done it years ago, but I was blinded by ignorance and my unreasoning desire for revenge. When I think about it now, I realize how petty and foolish I was. I gave up so much, and I was never really comforted by what I was doing. If I had only known thirty years ago how much better I could have felt, things would have been different. But thanks to God, all that is behind me, and for the first time in many years, I am truly happy."

"I know exactly what you mean," said Roland. "You blamed your father. I blamed God for my wife's death. You and I were both wrong, and it took way too many years for both of us to realize we were on a self-destructive course, even though we were both very successful in the eyes of the world."

Marcy was listening to every word, growing more interested all the time in the topic. She was happy for her mother, happy for her father, and happy for herself. She had plenty of questions, but she was content to hold them until the next morning. She knew what she was witnessing was real, but it was all so new to her that she had a hard time grasping everything that had taken place that day.

Arriving back at her home, she was sorry to see such a momentous day drawing to a close, even though it had gotten late.

As they got out and bid good night to one another, she couldn't help thinking, *He is a wonderful man. Mother is so lucky that he is interested in her. I think it is likely there will be wedding bells in the near future.*

As she crawled into bed, she was still thinking about all that had happened that day and how Roland had seemed like just a regular guy, not some self-important millionaire. Yes, he was a rich man, but one would never know it from his demeanor. He certainly was a lot different from any other man she had ever run across. Before she fell asleep, she had begun to think about the next day. She actually wanted to know more about what it meant to be a Christian.

She awoke early the next morning. No one else was stirring as she made her way to the kitchen and started the coffee. It only took a few minutes for the pot to fill up with the aromatic brew, and then she poured a steaming cup. She wrapped the hot mug in her hands, locking her fingers around it, feeling the warmth creep into her flesh.

Going back to her room, she put on a sweater and sat down. Sipping her coffee, she thought about Roland and her mother. She began imagining their wedding. It would be something to see. She was still picturing what the future must hold when she heard her mother's voice outside her door, "You up?"

"Yes, I'm up," she replied as she got up and went to the door.

"You must be cold-blooded to be wearing a sweater. It's a beautiful morning. I smelled the coffee, and I thought you would be in the kitchen, so I came out to join you in a cup."

"Great, let's go out to the table. You said yesterday that we would have a lot to talk about today."

Looking at Marcy across the table, she started, "You need to accept Christ and start living life as a Christian too. It's as simple as that." She amazed herself that she could be so bold and blunt.

"Mother, I have to admit I have seen some amazing things in the last few days—miracles, I guess—and I am interested in hearing about this accepting Christ thing, but I don't really see myself as needing to change. I believe in living a moral life. In fact, that might be why I am still single. I've never compromised what I believe just to hold on to some handsome guy who only has one thing on his mind. I don't go out drinking or use drugs. I support charities. I don't make a habit of lying. I don't cheat my boss with my time. When I work from home, I really do work. All in all, I think I'm a pretty good person. I think I already live a Christian life."

"Marcy, you may live an exemplary life, and I believe you do, but you will never come up to God's standards. I learned that yesterday. Let me try to explain it to you, but remember, I'm sort of new at this, you know."

Doing her best to explain the plan of salvation, she realized before getting too far into the conversation that she could use some help, and the only one she knew that could do that was Roland.

Stopping, she said, "Look, Marcy, we need to get some breakfast together and take care of Father, and then I'll call Roland and see if he can come over. He can explain this so much better than I can. I know what I want to say, but I have a hard time in putting it into the right words. I get it all scrambled up, and I certainly can't remember the Bible verses like he can. I don't even know them. That is, if that's okay with you that he is here with us. It wouldn't embarrass you, would it?"

"No, it wouldn't embarrass me. In fact, I'd like to hear how he explained what you have been telling me. I have some questions for him.

"Fair enough. Now let's get that breakfast going, I'm actually liking bacon and eggs."

Mr. Miller came into the kitchen while they were cooking. "Well, it's good to see the two of you working together on breakfast. The bacon and coffee smelled so good it woke me up."

Walking over to the coffee, he poured himself a cup and sat down at the kitchen table.

"I can't remember when I've felt better than I do right now. Do you know how much longer you will be here, Sherry? I know you probably want to get back to work, but I'm sure going to miss you when you go."

"I'm not sure exactly how long I'll be here, but don't you worry, I'll be here as long as you need me. I won't go until after we have you squared away. Besides, even when I go back to work, I can still be back out here almost at a moment's notice."

She turned her attention back to breakfast, dropping bread into the toaster as Marcy was dishing up the eggs and crispy bacon. Soon they were sitting at the table with him.

Their conversation worked around to getting Roland to come over.

"I have some questions for him," Marcy explained. "Mom has been telling me that I really need to become a Christian, but I don't know why it is so important. After all, I can't see where I am all that bad. I don't think God is going to send me to hell."

"Marcy," he said, "it isn't a question of good or bad, or whether you are better than someone else. God doesn't mark on a curve. Everyone fails, and getting 100 is impossible, and worse than that, no one passes the course without having a perfect score."

"Grandpa, it's not that I don't believe you and Mother are convinced about what you are telling me, but for me, I'm not convinced. I am willing to listen to what Roland has to say. In fact, I really am very interested, but I don't know if will make any difference."

After breakfast was over, Sherry called Roland, and he quickly agreed to join them. When he came in the house, he was carrying his Bible and a small notebook.

"Well, here I am. How can I help?"

Sherry answered before her daughter could speak, "I'd like you to share God's plan with Marcy the way you did with me. I can't explain salvation as well as you can. I tried, but I'm afraid I muddled it."

Marcy added, "I told Mom I don't have a problem with Christianity. I just don't see why I need to be saved. I really haven't done anything to be saved from as far as I can see."

"Wow! That's a great place to start from. Would you like me to show you why you are wrong and what you need to do about it? I don't want to pressure you in any way, but if you are really interested in hearing what the Bible has to say on the topic, I'll be more than happy to go through it with you."

"Honestly, if it was just about anyone else, I'd probably say no, but I'm willing to listen as long as you won't be offended by my being skeptical. Can we sit down while we talk?"

Once they were seated, he said, "I'd like to ask you a question before we start. Marcy, if you were to die today, do you know for sure that you would go to heaven?"

"Well, I think I would," she replied.

"Fair enough. One more question, just for the sake of discussion, imagine you were killed in a car accident today, and you suddenly found yourself standing just outside of heaven, and you were asked by the angel guarding the gate, 'Why do you deserve to be allowed to enter?' What would you tell him?"

She thought for a moment before she answered, "I'd tell him that I had always been kind, honest, and good; that I'd never stolen anything or killed anyone; and that I didn't swear. I hadn't done anything that should keep me out."

"I used to think that way too, Marcy, and so did countless millions before us when they died, but none of them were allowed in. The Bible tells us that God's standard for getting into heaven is perfection. I'm sure you've heard the saying, 'Nobody is perfect'? Well, it's true. The Bible, in Romans 3:10, says, 'There is none righteous, no not one.' And in Romans 3:23, we read, 'All have sinned and fall short of the Glory of God,' and if that isn't clear enough, in First John 1:8, it says, 'If we say we have no sin, we deceive ourselves, and the truth is not in us.' You have to understand, it only takes one sin to keep you out of heaven—one sin, no matter how insignificant it might seem, to keep you from meeting God's standard of perfection. It's recorded in Matthew 5:48, that Jesus himself said, 'Be perfect therefore as your Heavenly Father is perfect.'

"That leaves man with a problem he can't solve. We aren't perfect or righteous, and no one imperfect or unrighteous is allowed into heaven. God solved that problem for us when he sent his Son, Jesus, ultimately to die on the cross as a one-time, all-time sacrifice for our sins. Probably, the best known verse in the Bible is John 3:16. We see John 3:16 on billboards and signs at ball games, but we usually don't see the words to that verse. It simply says, 'For God so loved the world that he gave his one and only Son, that whoever believes in him shall not perish, but have eternal life.' That's it in a nutshell, Marcy.

"God's Son, Jesus, was a gift from God to us. That's called God's grace, and we receive it by faith, but if we don't accept the gift, it will do us absolutely no good. Ephesians 2:8 says, 'For it is by Grace you have been saved, through faith, and this is not from yourselves, it is the gift of God.' It's a gift Marcy, it's free. You don't have to earn it or pay for it, and none of us was ever good enough to deserve it."

As he opened his Bible, he continued, "I want to show you three more verses. The first is Acts 4:12. See right here, 'Salvation is found in no one else, for there is no other name under heaven given to mankind by which we must be saved.'"

Turning a few pages, he said, "The next verse records what Jesus told his disciples. John 14:6 says, 'I am the way, the truth, and the life. No one comes to the Father but by me.' And the last verse is Romans 10:9. 'If you confess with your mouth that Jesus is Lord and believe in your heart that God raised him from the dead, you will be saved.' When anyone does that, the Bible tells us our sins are washed away by his blood, and we are made whiter than snow. We get into heaven by his righteousness, not our own.

"When you accept Christ, something else wonderful happens. The Bible says in Second Corinthians 5:17, 'If anyone is in Christ, he has become a new person. The old life is gone; a new life is begun.' Doesn't your mother appear to be a different person?"

"Well, she has certainly changed a lot, that's for sure."

"Yes, she has, more than you know. Can I ask you a few more questions?"

'Sure."

"Do you believe in God, Marcy?"

"Of course, I believe in God."

"Do you believe you will go to heaven when you die?"

"I think I will," she replied.

"Do you want to *know* for sure that you would go to heaven if you should die?"

"Yes, I would like to be sure of that."

"Do you believe that Jesus is exactly who he said he is, the very Son of God?"

"I guess I always have believed that. I just never thought a lot about it."

"Is there any reason then why you shouldn't tell God you are sorry for your sins, even ones you can't remember, even if it's only one, and that you believe Jesus is his Son, and that you want to be forgiven? If you believe Jesus died for you to take away your sins and you want to accept his gift, he is offering it to you right now, is there any reason you should turn him down?"

"No, there isn't," she said softly, and the angels in heaven began to rejoice as Marcy invited Christ into her life.

It was a happy group of believers who went to church the next day. Roland could hardly wait to introduce the family to the pastor.

"Pastor, this is Jim Miller and his daughter, Sherry Williamson, and his granddaughter, Marcy Williamson. Sherry and I were classmates in high school. She and Marcy have both accepted Jesus Christ as their Savior in just the past couple of days. The Lord has been doing great things in their family."

"Well, praise the Lord. I'm so pleased to meet you both," the pastor said, shaking their hands, "and I'm delighted that you have found the Lord. I'm glad you are here with us today, and I'm sure you will find the people here are very friendly. Help yourself to some coffee. You have some time before the service starts. I'm sort of busy right now, of course, but I'd love to sit down and talk with both of you when I have a little more time. Perhaps we could get together some afternoon this week?"

Marcy spoke up, "I'd like that. I know what I did, but now I'd like to know where I go from here. What's my next step? Should I call your office to set up a time?"

"That would be excellent. I'll be expecting your call. I hope you enjoy today's service."

After he left them, Marcy said, "He does seem pretty busy, but I guess that's to be expected on a Sunday morning. I like him, though. I really do have some questions, and I'd like to see how I might fit in here."

Roland introduced them to several people around the coffee pot and in the foyer. No one knew Sherry was the owner of Robyn's World, and he didn't mention it, so she got a clear, unbiased impression of the people she met. They seemed very pleasant, and she knew that it was for herself, not for her business. She totally enjoyed the casual, friendly atmosphere. He took her hand when he was making introductions, but she didn't resist.

After the service, Marcy commented on how much she had enjoyed it, "I loved the songs and the group of singers. The pastor is a good speaker, and I understood what he was getting at in his speech."

"Technically, it's called a sermon or message, not a speech," he said. "But I agree, it was pretty good."

As they were leaving the parking lot, Roland asked, "Would you all like to come to my home for a little after-church snack? I make some crab dip that's fantastic, if I do say so myself, but it would only be an appetizer. I am hoping you would like to go out for dinner. I made reservations for us at Daniel's Broiler, Leschi. It's a beautiful place right on the shore of Lake Washington. The food is really first class. I think they have some of the best beef one can get. We have to be there at four thirty, so right now we've got a little time to snack and visit. Besides, Marcy and Jim haven't seen my place."

They all agreed that snacks sounded great and dinner at four thirty would be fine, and they were off for Roland's.

"This warm crab dip is absolutely the best. Where did you get the recipe?" Sherry asked. "I have to stop eating it, or I won't be able to eat any dinner."

"I actually came up with it on my own. I am a big fan of crab, and a little bit of Swiss cheese goes so well in it for flavor, but cream cheese is the biggest ingredient next to crab. I experimented with amounts and with this and that for seasonings. The one thing I have always found is when making anything with crab, when it comes to other ingredients, less is more. The crab has to hold sway over everything else. I want to taste the crab."

"I agree with Mom," Marcy chimed in. "This stuff is fantastic."

He had been wise enough not to make a very large batch of his dip, and when it was gone, they all agreed they could have eaten a few more crackers loaded with the marvelous crab appetizer.

"Would you like a tour of my home?" he asked. "I made sure it was shipshape before I left this morning."

"I would," said Marcy. "I'll bet this isn't your typical man cave."

And as they walked through his house, the others had to agree. One unusual aspect was his studio.

"These are your paintings?" Sherry asked.

"Yes. I know they aren't much, but I'm still learning. It's how I relax and take more time to see the world around me, to put things in perspective."

"I actually was thinking they were pretty good," she replied. "I wouldn't mind having a couple of original Roland Holtz oils hanging in my office."

He smiled.

They moved on from room to room, and all the while, both Sherry and Marcy were assimilating and cataloging those things that gave insight into just who Roland Holtz was. When they came to the den, they were greeted with the sight of wall-to-wall ducks.

"I collect very few things," he explained, "but I have a failing when it comes to duck decoys. I find it hard to resist adding one every once in a while. I don't know exactly how many I have, but the last time I counted them about a year ago, I had 127. Some have been done by relatively new carvers, and some are old Mason's and Steven's factory birds, but I have a fair number by Nathan Cobb, Elmer Crowell, Lee Dudley, and the Ward brothers, as well as a pretty fair smattering of other old carvers. I can enjoy myself spending an hour or two just holding decoys and admiring them, wishing I could have known all the men who carved them."

"Why do you find them so appealing?" Marcy asked.

"Each one of them has an untold story. I like to imagine what it might have been. I wonder what the carver was thinking as he formed them. What were the lakes and ponds they sat on, and did they ever break loose and get lost in heavy weather? Who were the hunters who might have bought them and hunted over them? But in the end, they remain marvelous, sometimes mysterious, pieces of American art."

"Well," Sherry said, "they are nice, but they hardly compare to artworks by the old masters. Paintings are not just beautiful, but they are an investment. Can the same be said about these decoys?"

"Actually, yes," he replied. "Beauty, of course, is in the eye of the beholder, but there are many collectors who find old decoys more beautiful than Rembrandts."

Picking up one bird that sat on a shelf by itself, he held it up and turned it around slowly. "Personally, I have little need for more investments, but to help answer your question, take a look at this decoy," he said, handing it to her. "What do you think that decoy might be worth?" he asked.

She said, "It appears to have some paint worn off, but I suppose it is more valuable than some of the others because it was sitting by itself and you picked it out. Would it be as much as a thousand or two?" she asked, thinking maybe that could be possible.

"Twelve years ago, Sherry, I paid eighteen thousand dollars for this decoy. I had it at a show last year and was offered ninety-five thousand dollars for it. I was only displaying part of my collection for other collectors to admire. I wasn't interested in selling it, but if I were, now it should bring even more than that at auction.

"I have a couple that are worth more than two hundred thousand each. I probably should keep them locked away, but they weren't meant to be kept out of sight. They were meant to be seen and admired. They are worth a great deal more to me here where I can see them than locked away in a vault."

"That is amazing," she said, looking at his collection with a new appreciation. "I would never have expected they had that kind of value."

Marcy commented, "If you don't mind my saying so, Mother, I think their real value probably lies more in the pleasure they give him, not in what they are worth in dollars."

"I like that," he said, "and you are right. I didn't buy them as an investment, even though I realize they have appreciated more rapidly than my stock portfolio. I take them to shows not to sell them but to share them with others who will appreciate them. I bought them because I feel good when I'm around them, but that's enough about decoys, let's move on."

By the time they had completed their guided tour, it was time to be leaving for the restaurant. When they got in the car, Sherry sat up front with Roland. She was thinking about what her father and daughter had said about Roland—what a catch he would be. There was no doubt he was handsome, and he acted more like a man in his early forties rather than early fifties, but what did they have in common? Could they be married and each live their own lives? Would they want to do that? Would she want to do that? Could he come around to seeing Robyn's World as she saw it? She suddenly found herself filled with doubt.

Dinner that afternoon was excellent and the view of Lake Washington and the marina just outside the restaurant was perfect, but Sherry, dealing with her thoughts and misgivings, could not enjoy it as much as the others did. Roland noticed she seemed to be lost in thought, appearing almost gloomy in unguarded moments, but he said nothing, feeling she might be concerned about her father's upcoming exam.

Later that evening, Roland sat in his den, holding and looking at a few of his decoys and thinking about what Marcy had said about them. It was so true. They were a source of pleasure, even wonder, and that was why he loved to display them while at the same time being so loathe to sell them. It pleased him that she could understand him in that way.

When he went to bed that night, he prayed, "Thank you, Lord, for Sherry and Marcy. I am so pleased that you drew them to yourself and used me to talk with them. I have asked you for someone to share my life, and I think Sherry might be that person. If it's your will, Lord, give me the right time and the right words to ask her. And, Lord, her father goes to the doctor tomorrow. Preserve his life. He has just gotten his family back. Would you please allow him time to enjoy them? If it be your will, Lord, touch him and take his disease away. And, Father, watch over Bryce wherever he may be and keep him safe."

He fell asleep while he was still praying.

The next morning, Marcy took her mother and her grandfather to the oncologist's office for his blood test and exams. After checking him over, the doctor spent some time explaining the disease and possible treatments. He had looked at Mr. Miller's records and the results of his earlier tests.

"Your records indicate that you were in stage 1 when the tests were originally done, but we will need to determine just how far and how fast the leukemia is progressing in order to determine the best treatment for you. Hopefully, you will still be in stage 1."

"What we are going to do today is run a new blood test and a new bone marrow test to compare with the earlier ones. It will be a couple of days until I have the final results. Then we can get moving on this. Do you have any questions?"

Sherry asked, "Can it be cured?"

"There have been some cases where it appears to have been cured," he replied, "but usually, we are more likely to be able to just manage it. Your father should have a good chance of living a reasonably normal life for quite some time, especially if this is still in stage 1."

"Do we need to schedule another appointment?"

"Not right now. I'll call you when I have the results from today's tests, and then we will set up an appropriate appointment for you. Right now your father is going to be prepared for taking a sample of his bone marrow. He won't feel much pain from the procedure, but he will probably be a little sore for a day or two."

On their way home, they were talking but avoiding the subject of his exam.

"You know, Father, Roland told me he would like to take you out on the sound to do some crabbing or some fishing if you'd like to go with him. He took me out crabbing last week, and we had fresh cooked crab right out on the water. It was the best I've ever had."

"That sounds like fun. I haven't been fishing for more years than I like to remember. I've never been crabbing, but if you enjoyed it, I'm sure I would. He seems like a very nice man, I really like him."

Sherry had thought about him a lot during the past few months and especially during the last week. She knew he was interested in her, and she was convinced that with very little encouragement, he would propose to her. But now, however improbably, she was no longer sure if that was what she wanted.

"I like him too," Sherry replied wistfully. "I met his mother-in-law in Oak Harbor, and she seemed very keen to move us closer together, but I'm not sure if we should be anything more than just good friends. We are really quite different people."

"Mother," Marcy chimed in, "I thought you were thinking you would like to marry him."

"I was thinking that, but like I have already told you, he has his world and I have mine, and I'm not sure we can put them together or find a middle ground that I'd be comfortable with."

"I don't understand, Mother. I would have thought, after all that took place last week, that you would be even more interested in him, not less. I really don't see the problem."

"The problem is, I have Robyn's World, and I can't just walk away from that. I thought I could, but I've realized I can't. Roland has made it plain he isn't interested in having a role in my business, and I can't let go of it. It's been my life for so long that I panic when I even think about not being there running it."

"But you told me you were afraid that your life was being taken over by Robyn's World and that you wanted to take your life back. You said you didn't want to die with it that way. Didn't you tell me you were afraid the real you no longer existed? You even said you were thinking about getting married again. What's happened to all that?"

"I felt alone when I said that, but I don't really feel alone anymore. I have you, and I have Father, and I've got a good friend in Roland. I have a real family again. I think that I am going to look for a good church when I get back East, and I'm sure I'll even make some new friends there. I'm going to expand my horizons. I don't intend to let Robyn's World consume me again, but at the same time, I can't let go of it. It's like I'm already married."

Sherry's father had been listening to the conversation, and he couldn't help joining in, "I think you're making a mistake. You are not likely to find another man like Roland. You had better think about it long and hard before you leave him here if he wants to marry you."

"He is a wonderful man, Father, and I have been thinking about what life together would be like for us, and that's exactly why I am going to put some space between us for a while. I'm not sure I could be the kind of wife he needs. I'm afraid he would find himself always competing with my business."

"Well, I still think you are making a mistake. Your business will not keep you warm on a cold night or scratch your back before you go to sleep. It won't share your joys when things are going great or your pains when things go bad."

Marcy, breaking back in, asked, "So when do you plan to leave, Mother?"

"Not until after Father gets the results from his exam. I want to be here to know what lies ahead, and I'll make regular trips out here to see you both once I'm back at Robyn's World and up to speed on everything."

"What about Roland?" Marcy asked. "When are you going to tell him what you are doing? Are you going to tell him how you feel about him?"

She hadn't thought the ramifications through on what she had been telling her father and daughter, and she still wasn't completely sure what she was going to tell Roland. She didn't want to hurt him, but then, neither of them had made any commitments or said anything at all about marriage.

"I'll tell him after we get the results of the exam. I'm sure he will understand that I have responsibilities. I need to be back with the business."

Marcy said dryly, "Yes, I'm sure he will understand."

That night, Sherry took the scrapbook and turned to the picture of the man who had brought her the check so many years before. "Look at this picture, Father. Who is this man?"

Her father chuckled, "That is a dear friend of mine, Dean Stevenson. I went to school with him, and I was the best man at his wedding. He was a professor for quite a few years at Nyack College. He had a flair for the dramatic in high school. He was in the drama club. When I needed someone you had never met to give you the check and be mysterious about it, I thought of him. He came and did a great job."

"And who was Consuelo? Was she another classmate?"

"No, that was just one of life's serendipities. Perhaps she was an answer to prayer. She was exactly who she said she was. She did come to our house looking for you. We really thought she just wanted some of your products, but she told us she had a long history of working in the cosmetics industry and wanted to talk with you about your product. We didn't know at the time that she wanted to help you get started, but we couldn't have planned it any better."

"Why didn't you just tell me that you and Mother wanted to give me the money to help build the business instead of going through all the charade? I would have paid it all back to you once Robyn's World was flourishing."

"If you remember, we had offered to work at your store and offered to give you some financial help, and you turned both of those offers down. We figured you would just continue refusing our help, so we came up with another way."

"Why didn't you tell me the truth once things were going well with Robyn's World?"

"We were afraid that you might become even more bitter or resent it if we did. We hoped that after some time and when you were successful, you would have a change of heart, and we could be a family again. Maybe we would have told you then. In any case, your mother made me agree not to tell you what we had done before things were better. She wanted to have you come back because you loved us, not because we gave you money."

"I hate to admit it, but you were probably right. I was so full of bitterness that all I could think about was showing you that I could make my own way and making you feel the pain I was feeling."

"Let's not talk about it anymore. Your mother and I never held anything against you. We never stopped loving you. We cheered you on, and we were so proud of what you accomplished. As far as I'm concerned, the bad is all behind us now, and the future looks bright. I have my daughter and my granddaughter back, and if I were to die tomorrow, I'd die a happy man."

"Let's not talk about dying either. I feel like we have all just started living again. I have to believe you are going to get a good report from the doctor, and then we will decide where we are going from there."

And so the rest of the day was spent talking about more pleasant things, but that evening after Jim went to bed, Marcy and Sherry sat on the deck and talked.

"Marcy, I am sorry, but I just can't remain out here indefinitely. I am really feeling pressure to get back to my office. If things turn out to be really bad for Father, I will either stay for a few more days, or I will come back out very soon."

"Mom, I can't stay here away from the office indefinitely either, but it would be a real plus for you to be here. He may need you more than ever if the disease is getting the best of him. I know you have had a wonderful effect on him just by being here. He needs someone to lean on."

Sherry replied, "I could hire a home health aide for him if you would feel comfortable with someone being here while you are at work, but that someone for him to lean on could just as well be you, Marcy. You were doing a pretty good job before I showed up. I would like to suggest something to you. I know that you like your job, but I would like you to consider resigning and spending your time with Father. I would pay you more than what you are making now, and I would cover all your household and other expenses while he is here. It would cost you nothing. What do you think?"

"I feel like you kind of have me in a corner. Let me think about it overnight. I'm not opposed to the idea, but I need to think it through. I certainly don't want it to mean you wouldn't be out here for him very often, but I think we can make a better decision once we find out how Grandpa is doing. I'll give you my answer once we know."

The receptionist from the doctor's office called Thursday morning and asked them to come in at three. The doctor wanted to talk with them all about the test results. They had been dreading this, but at the same time, they were hopeful that there would be a good treatment for the condition. The doctor had given them some encouragement when he had said that he thought the disease might be at a stage where it could be arrested or slowed down, but in each of their minds, because of how quickly he now wanted them to come in, there was a haunting uncertainty.

Once they were there, it became almost torture as they waited in the doctor's office. They were anxious to get in, while at the same time they were dreading the news they were preparing to hear. Marcy and Sherry fidgeted and leafed through magazines, but Mr. Miller sat quietly, staring, lost in thought.

When the receptionist called for Mr. Miller, they all stood up at the same time.

"Go down the hall to room number 3, and the doctor will be with you shortly," she said.

She was right. The doctor entered the room about five minutes behind them and sat down, shaking his head.

"Well, Mr. Miller, you are an interesting case. The latest tests show absolutely no sign of leukemia at all. We can't explain it because your earlier results were clearly correct, and you haven't received any treatment, but you seem to be in complete remission. You are a very lucky man."

The world suddenly seemed brighter. "That's wonderful, Doctor. Now what do we do?" asked Sherry.

"Just keep doing whatever you've been doing. It seems to be working just fine. I would like to follow him up in six months, but if he starts to feel overly tired before then, make an appointment, and we will get him right in."

"You're sure about this, Doctor?" it was Sherry's father. Having recovered from his surprise, he couldn't quite believe what he was hearing.

"The other physicians have gone over the results as well, Mr. Miller, and we all agree. You show no signs of the disease. We don't see a complete spontaneous remission like this very often, so it's always like a miracle when it happens.

"All you have to do now is stop and see the receptionist on the way out. She will make an appointment for you to come back in six months for me to check and confirm that you are still in remission. Be aware, the unfortunate fact is, some remissions are short-term, but yours is so fast and complete that I think you will still be clear then. Just the same, it's good to check, and if any problem should arise before the appointment, like I told you, just call the office, and we will get you right in."

It was hard for them to believe the good news, and as they headed home, they were giddy with relief and bubbling with emotion, but it was difficult for them to put their feelings into words. It was only when her father, out of nowhere, came out with a loud, "Praise the Lord!" that Sherry remembered her prayer, that God would heal her and the family.

She had to share what she had asked the Lord to do.

"I was just remembering what I prayed when I asked Christ to forgive me. I asked him to prove he was who he said he was by healing me and my family. I don't think he could have given me any better proof than healing Father. I really believe it is nothing less than a miracle. Marcy, have you given any thought to my suggestion for you and Father?" Sherry asked.

"Yes, but I haven't come to any decision yet. I'm thinking about it."

The ensuing silence was broken when Marcy said, "I think we should call Roland when we get home and tell him about Grandpa's test results. I'm pretty sure he would like to hear the news."

"Yes," she replied, "he will be excited. He has been praying for Father ever since I told him about his condition. It will give me a chance to tell him I am going back to Robyn's World too."

"Is that all you are going to tell him?"

"Yes. For now, that's all I need to tell him. He hasn't asked me to marry him, so I don't have to give him an answer or explain any more about why I'm not staying."

Marcy probed a little farther, "What if he does ask you before you leave? What are you going to tell him then?

"I guess I would have to tell him I need to think about it."

Sherry's father said, "I think you are making a mistake. I don't know why you can't see it. I hope you won't be sorry later on. He could end up marrying someone else, you know. It isn't like he would have a hard time finding someone that would be interested in him."

"I'll just have to cross that bridge when I come to it, Father, but it wouldn't be the end of the world."

That ended the conversation about Roland, but when they arrived back at home, calling him was the first thing she did.

"Roland, we got some very good news today about Father from the doctor. His tests showed absolutely no sign of the disease. He is in complete remission."

He was excited by the news. "That's excellent! It's the miracle that we have all been praying for. Faith is for things hoped for but not yet seen, but when it pleases the Lord, our faith becomes sight, even here and now. I am so happy for all of you."

"Thank you, Roland," she said. "Thanks to you and the Lord and all that has taken place here. I am happier than I have been for many, many years. Now that Father is well and he is so happy here with Marcy, I can feel comfortable leaving him. I have to go back to New York. This is a busy time of year at Robyn's World, and I need to be there."

There was silence at the other end. "Roland? Are you still there, Roland?"

"Yes, I'm here," he answered. "When will you be leaving?"

"Probably day after tomorrow. That will give me Sunday to unpack and get ready for Monday and work. I need to make arrangements and buy a plane ticket. Then all I have to do is pack, drop off my rental car, and head for home. I could probably do it all today, but I want to spend one more day with Father and Marcy before I head back East."

Roland noticed that she hadn't included him in the people she would like to spend one more day with.

He replied, "It seems like you just got here. I'd like to see you before you go. I have something I'd like to ask you."

She was pretty sure she knew what he wanted to ask her, but she also knew she couldn't avoid it.

"We will be here all day tomorrow," she said. "Why don't you come over for lunch?"

"That sounds good. Noon?"

"Yes. We'll see you then."

Roland set the phone down and picked up the decoy he had been holding when Sherry called. He turned it over, almost absentmindedly looking at its features, and then he got up and placed it on a shelf.

Sitting down again, his gaze swung around the room, but he wasn't thinking of decoys. Meaningful thought momentarily eluded him. In an instant, all the attraction of the decoys had dissolved. His mind was in stasis, his stare empty, as unease began to grip first his mind and then invaded his body. It was only with conscious effort that he shook his head and drew himself out of the pit, forcing himself to think. It required speaking out loud to himself and to the wooden audience that surrounded him.

"Okay, so now what do I do? I thought she was waiting for me to ask her to marry me. Have I been wrong? Is she leaving because I haven't asked her?"

No answer came from the silent painted wooden audience that stared back at him with a multitude of unblinking glass eyes.

"Maybe I've been fooling myself. Maybe she really hasn't been looking for anyone. Or maybe all my talk about not trusting myself alone with her in her room didn't sit well with her. That was stupid. Maybe she thought I meant she was the problem. Or maybe it's just simply because I haven't asked her.

"Maybe, maybe, maybe . . . it doesn't really matter, does it? She is planning to leave, and I haven't asked her to marry me. I don't know what she is thinking, but the only thing I can do now is ask her and see what she says."

"That's what I'll do!" he exclaimed to his motionless flock. "I'll ask her tomorrow. In the meantime, let's just be thankful for Mr. Miller's recovery."

It was late afternoon, and Roland's stomach growled at him. He hadn't been thinking about eating, but breakfast had been early. He thought about calling Sherry back to see if they would like to join him for dinner, but he decided against it. Today belonged to Mr. Miller and his family. Tomorrow would be soon enough.

I'm ready for one of Jak's burgers, he thought. *The wait shouldn't be too long, and besides, I've got nothing but time right now.*

When Roland arrived at Jak's Grill in Issaquah, it was rocking with a good crowd of happy people talking, laughing, and enjoying their meals. He left his first name with the hostess and sat down in a chair next to others waiting for their tables. His spirits rose as he relaxed and enjoyed the pleasant atmosphere. A low divider separated the waiting section from the bar, and soon a waiter stopped by and asked if he would like something to drink while he waited.

"Yes, I'll have a Corona with a slice of lime," he replied.

It was sort of plebeian, but he remembered the night when he and Sherry had shared a pizza and a beer after the reunion. It seemed so long ago; so much had happened since then.

While he waited for a table and sipped the cold brew, he thought about the events of the last few days. So much had been packed into such a short time. So many momentous things had taken place. Sherry was so beautiful, and her family so friendly and easy to get to know. His world felt so much larger.

He wondered, "Is it possible that this could all end? That Sherry will go back East and I'll be left behind to face my same, old world again?"

It wasn't really a thought he wanted to entertain.

His mind responded, *She may not have any idea what's been on my mind. She may be going simply because I haven't given her any reason to stay. It could all be my fault. It's possible that she will change her mind about leaving if I give her an alternative. I'll just leave it up to her and the Lord.*

Shortly after, he was wrapping himself around a Jak's Burger—a complex task, considering the dimensions of the culinary creation and the numerous toppings that continually attempted to escape from between the burger and bun.

There is no way to eat one of these burgers without getting a lot of it on you in the process, he thought as he alternated licking his fingers and wiping on his napkin between bites.

The signature burger had come with his favorite sweet potato fries. He renounced the use of a fork, opting instead to pick up each brown, flavorful strip with his fingers, feeling not the least uncouth or out of place in doing so.

"Some things are just meant to be," he told himself. "I'd really feel like a dufus trying to look refined eating this."

When he had finished, he felt so much better—true comfort food. While the fries were gone, a large third of the burger remained, and he decided to get a box and take it home to go with breakfast in the morning. It would not be the first time. Breakfast became something special to look forward to when such a generous tidbit shared the morning plate with a couple of eggs over easy.

Crawling in between the sheets that night, his mind once more settled on Sherry. It had been a long time since he had proposed to anyone, and he tried to decide on how he should ask her. There seemed to be no perfect way.

I guess I'll just have to play it by ear, he thought.

Then he confided, "Lord, I am going to ask Sherry to be my wife. It hardly seems possible that I could feel this way about her after such a short time, but I do. Lord, give me the words to say, and if it is your will, let her answer be yes. I will do my best to make her happy. Thank you, Lord, for her salvation and for Marcy's also, Lord. This has been a wonderful week, and no matter what, we are all better for it. You are unbelievably awesome, God. Please watch over Bryce wherever he is tonight, Lord, and keep him safe. Take care of Amanda also, Lord, and thank you for her. I'm going to conk out now, Lord. I'm counting on you. Amen."

He slept well, and awoke, not thinking of Sherry but of burger and eggs. He showered before he went to the kitchen. His next big decision was whether to put the burger in the microwave or not as he was cooking two jumbo eggs to perfection. Cold burger and hot eggs was the final product along with one slice of wheat toast for good measure.

He closed his eyes and asked the Lord to bless his food and added a postscript, reminding God about Sherry and his plans. His confidence was rising, and the great breakfast bolstered his spirit even as it pleased his palate.

I'm as ready as I'll ever be, he thought. *I can't think of anything else I can do.*

Suddenly, he was hit with a thought that panicked him.

Good grief. I don't have a ring for her. If she says yes, I'll be standing there with no ring to give her. That's not very good planning.

Putting the dishes in the sink, he left for the jewelers. He would find a beautiful ring for her. As he was driving, his mind started churning once more.

I don't know her ring size, but that will be okay. We can get it sized or get another one. But how big should it be? How many diamonds?

He didn't want to be ostentatious, but he certainly didn't want to say "I love you" with a less-than-impressive ring.

I love you? I have never said that to her, he thought. *Could it be that it has never occurred to her how I might feel?*

Finding a ring was not hard; finding just the right one was.

"I am looking for something two or three karats, and it has to be just perfect," he told the jeweler. "I want it to sparkle like a star from every angle. Show me the best you have, even if it happens to be larger."

Each one the jeweler put before him was brilliant, and each was somewhat different from the others, but eventually, he picked out the one that seemed to him to be just right. The three-and-a-half karat diamond winked, flamed, and sparkled with even the slightest movement. He hadn't even quibbled about the price. He knew, whatever it was, he could easily afford it.

Now I'm ready, he thought.

He had cut it a bit close, but still, he was on time and prepared when he arrived at the front door.

Marcy opened it, welcoming him.

"Come in, Roland, I'm glad you could join us for lunch. We've been sitting out on the deck, enjoying this beautiful day. Can you believe the weather we've been having? No rain for more than a week. I'm starting to get a tan."

"It looks good on you," he replied. "A few days of sunshine does wonders for all of us both inside and out."

"Well, come on out on the deck with us. Would you like something to drink?"

"No, thanks, I'm fine. Just lead the way."

Mr. Miller spoke first. "Hello, Roland. Good to see you again. You heard about my doctor's report, right?"

"Yes, I did, sir, and I am very, very happy for you. Now you can enjoy life without that cloud hanging over your head."

"Boy, that's the truth. I didn't realize how much just knowing I had cancer had affected me. No matter what I did, it was always in the back of my mind. It was like a cold, wet blanket on everything. No matter how I tried, I couldn't stop thinking about it. But now, I've started living again. It's fantastic!"

Roland smiled, nodding his head, "Yes, I'm sure it is." Then turning his head to look at Sherry, he said, "You must be on a high too. Your father's miracle must be the cherry on the sundae for you as well."

"It is, Roland. It really is. I can't even find the words to fully describe it, but I can feel it inside with an intensity that is almost unbearable. God is good."

"Well, amen to that. What are your plans now? You said you were going back to New York. Will you be back here again soon?"

"I don't know just when I will be back. I have a lot of things that require my attention back at Robyn's World. We have some new lines to introduce, and there are several shows I am going to have to attend. I've been handling some things online, but I can only do so much here. Right after I get back, I have a meeting with a company in France that I am considering acquiring. It's time for me to be back at the office."

"Don't you have a staff you can depend on, Sherry? It seems to me that someone like yourself could still be in control without having your hands on everything, personally supervising every move. Do you have to be at every show?"

"I do have some very dependable people, and they know what I want done and how to do it, but it's not the same as directing it all

192

in person, and besides, I love being part of everything, especially the shows. I thrive in that atmosphere."

He nodded his head and let the topic drop, turning back to her father, "So, Mr. Miller, do you feel up to getting out on the sound for some crabbing sometime this next week? The weather is predicted to be pretty good. Sherry said you might enjoy doing that."

"I'd love to go. I've never done any crabbing, but I'm sure I would have a good time. You just let me know when you are going, and I'll be ready."

"There's room for you too, Marcy, if you'd like to go," he offered. "I'll take the big boat, so it would be pretty comfortable. Have you ever been out on the sound?"

She smiled, pleased that he had asked her, and replied, "I've been on a lot of ferries, but I've never been out fishing or crabbing. I think I would enjoy giving it a try, though. Any chance we could have fresh crab for lunch on the boat? Mom told me it's the greatest."

"Could be. How does next Tuesday sound to both of you? It's supposed to be the best day of the week, at least as far as wind is concerned. The ocean should be fairly flat, so cooking a few crabs should not be any problem, providing we catch some."

"I can do Tuesday, and I'm pretty sure Grandpa doesn't have anything standing in his way. Let us know on Monday what we will need to bring and when we should be ready. It actually sounds like fun."

"We'll plan on it then," he said. "Sherry, are you sure you don't want to postpone your leaving and join us for the day?"

"It is tempting, it really is, but I need to get back to New York. You will have to give me a rain check."

Breaking the mood, Marcy said, "Okay, it's time we had lunch. It isn't anything fancy. We are having tuna fish sandwiches, chips, and a potato salad I whipped up and put in the fridge last night. Not quite like crab on the fantail, I guess, but it's filling. What would the rest of you like to do, eat in at the table or out here on the deck?"

The vote was unanimous for eating outside.

"I'll get us something to put our plates on," said Marcy, walking into the house and grabbing some folding TV tables, but before she was able to take them out onto the deck, Roland was there to give her a hand with them.

"Is there anything else I can help you with?" he asked.

"No. If you spread the tables around out there, Mom and I can round up the goodies."

She couldn't help thinking what a gentleman Roland was. He wasn't at all like she had at first expected a former CEO and successful businessman to be. He didn't wait around to be waited on but pitched right in to help. He was so pleasant, so easy to be around, and never seemed to put on any airs.

He's wonderful. What is wrong with Mom's head? she thought.

In no time at all, they had each filled their plates, and before they could get started with their meal, Roland asked if he could ask the Lord's blessing on the food.

Getting the nod, he began, "Lord, thank you for this day and for this family that you brought into my life. Thank you for touching Mr. Miller and restoring his health. Father, thank you for this food, and bless this time that we spend together. We thank you for it. Amen."

He tasted the small serving of potato salad he had taken.

"Mmmm," he said, "this is so good that I'm going to have to get a little more. I seldom eat potato salad because honestly, most of it just tastes like mayonnaise and celery salt, but this is like what my wife used to make. I love it with the olives and chopped onion. My wife was a great cook. I still miss her after all these years, and this salad reminds me of her."

"Thank you," Marcy said. "I appreciate the compliment. Maybe I will be able to tempt you to come over for lunch or dinner once in a while. Mom and I have sort of decided that I will quit my job and be a full-time housekeeper here with Grandpa. We have to work out the details, but I think it will work out best for all of us."

It was the first real indication that Marcy had given her mother that she was ready to take on the task they had discussed earlier.

"I'll probably have to tag along on some of your fishing and crabbing adventures with Grandpa. I'll even get a license. Maybe I could be your first mate," she said laughing.

"Well, he couldn't be in better hands, I'm sure," he said. "And you are more than welcome to make it a threesome whenever you would like. I'll have to make sure the boats are all spiffed up for inspection. Now, if you'll excuse me for a moment, I'm going to get that second serving of potato salad."

As they were finishing their lunch, Mr. Miller looked at Marcy and asked, "Why are you staying home with me? I can get along fine while you are at work. You don't have to give up a good job on my account."

"I know that, but I really want to be with you. We can travel around too. We don't have to stay in the house. There are lots of things to see and places to go. You haven't even scratched the surface. Lots of fresh air and exercise, that's what the doctor wants you to get."

"It sounds like a good plan to me," said Roland, "plus I'm only a short distance away if you should need me for anything." He looked at Sherry and said, "I'm sure there are lots of last-minute things you folks need to take care of, so I'm going to get out of your way and head for home. Would you walk me down to my car?"

She knew this was the moment she had been fearing. "Yes, I'll walk down with you."

As they strolled slowly toward his car, they both were filled with uncertainty. He knew the time had arrived to find out where he stood. When he reached the car, he could put it off no longer.

"Sherry, I have enjoyed having you here a great deal, and I really hate to see you leave, and I have to ask you something." Pulling the ring case out of his pocket, he opened it and held it out to her, asking, "Will you marry me?"

Reaching out, she took his hand in hers and gently closed the ring case as she replied, "I'm flattered that you would ask me, Roland. When I arrived in Washington, I thought I was ready to get married, and I admit, I was thinking only of you. But so much has happened since I got here. I have come to realize that I am not at all sure I really want to be married, and what's more important, even if I were, I don't think we are both looking for the same thing."

She saw the expression change on his face and quickly continued, "Roland, you are all a woman could possibly ask for, but I don't think

I can be what you would want or need in a wife. I am so tied to Robyn's World that I believe at some point, it would come between us, and we would both be miserable. This is about me, not you. I have enjoyed this time together with you immensely, but I am going to have to say no, at least for right now. I'm sorry if I've hurt you."

Freeing his hand, Roland slipped the case back into his pocket. He heard himself say, "I'm disappointed, but I'm not hurt. You may well be correct about us. We've made some mistakes in the past. There is no sense in making another."

They looked at each other as an awkward silence momentarily engulfed them until she moved to him and gave him a soft kiss on his cheek.

"Roland, you are the kindest, gentlest, most thoughtful man I have ever met. I know I may be a fool not to grab the gold ring, but I have come to care too much about you to do it. You deserve better than me."

He took her in his arms, giving her a long, gentle hug before releasing her.

"I understand, but I think you are being too hard on yourself. Still, you have to be who you are. Just be forewarned, I am not giving up on you. You may yet change your mind."

Turning and getting into his car, he gave her a wave, saying, "A bientôt," and backed slowly out of the driveway.

He had put on a bold front, but right then, he needed the comfort of his den. It had been a long time since he had felt so down.

She turned and started back to the house, feeling relieved yet somehow more miserable than she had been for a long time. A tear rolled down her cheek as she fought off second thoughts and turned her mind to other things.

Marcy met her when she walked through the door. "Well?"

"Well, what?" said Sherry.

"Well, what did he say?"

"Marcy, that's between him and me. I don't intend to discuss it with you, but I am not going to be staying on. I'll be leaving tomorrow as I planned. Roland and I are good friends. Let's just leave it that way."

"Mother! Just tell me. Did he ask you to marry him?"

Sherry paused. She could see this was important somehow to her daughter. "Yes," she said.

"And what did you tell him?"

She sighed and replied, "I told him I couldn't marry him."

"Why not?" Marcy continued.

"I have my reasons, and that's all there is to say. End of discussion."

Marcy could see that the conversation had come to a dead end. She felt bad for Roland, but she had already known that he was likely to be disappointed. She had hoped that her mother would have a change of heart, but the opportunity had come and gone, and there was no use in badgering her. She let it drop.

"When are you leaving?"

"I need to be at the airport by eight in the morning, so I'll have to be out of here by around seven. I'm almost all packed."

"Will you want breakfast before you go? I can get up and have something ready for you."

"No. If I'm hungry, I'll get something at the airport, but I've been eating all too well since I got out here. It's time for me to be a little more careful."

Then a dark, strained silence settled over them, neither knowing exactly what else to say or whether to say anything at all as they walked back to where Mr. Miller was sitting.

"Well?" he asked.

"You too, Father?" she felt a slight annoyance. "Didn't I tell you both that I was probably not going to marry Roland even if he asked me?"

"I was hoping, for your sake, that you would change your mind. You are not likely to find another man of his quality."

"Look, you two," she said, "I am not denying anything you have said about Roland. He is a wonderful man. I really think that any woman would be blessed to have him for a husband. When I came to Washington, I was not happy with the present, and I was fearful of the future, and I had the idea that getting married might change all that. I felt like I was being absorbed by Robyn's World, like I had no life of my own. I was fixated on him because I knew if he should want to marry me, it would not be for my money. Now, so much has happened. I am no longer sure what I want, but I have come to realize I am not yet ready to divorce myself from Robyn's World."

Closing her eyes and covering her mouth with her left hand as she tried to think, her thoughts were a jumble. Finally, opening her eyes and dropping her hand, she said, "The only thing I know is that I can't be what you two want me to be. I can't do what you want me to do. I have to be me. I have to do what I need to do, and right now, I need to be back at my office. Now let's talk about something else."

"Well, Mother, we may not be able to talk about it, but he may want to. I am not sure how I am going to feel around him. How am I supposed to respond if he asks about you? I don't want to see him discouraged, but I don't want to give him any false hope either if there is no hope."

"Marcy, you don't have to explain or defend me to him. I certainly don't want you to give him any false hope. This is all something that still needs to be resolved between Roland and me, and I am sure we can do it. Just be nice to him, but don't try to be an intercessor."

"Fine, but I don't think he is going to give up on you easily. I guess I will just have to play it by ear."

"Yes, Marcy, I think that is exactly what you will have to do," she agreed.

18

WORKING THINGS OUT

The following Monday, Marcy began sorting things out with her grandfather. Sitting at the breakfast table, she said, "I am going to talk with my boss this morning, but before I do that, I want to talk with you about how we should work out your care."

Smiling, he replied, "I don't think I require a lot of care, not yet anyway. I feel good, and I feel stronger every day. You know, I'd been living on my own for some time after your grandmother died, and I think I am also quite capable of getting around this house without you being with me every moment. I love the time we spend together, but as far as I'm concerned, I don't see why you should have to quit your job for me."

"I pretty much agree with you, but Mother would have a fit if I didn't make an effort to ride herd on you. So here's what I've been thinking. Instead of just quitting my job, I am fairly sure I can work from home most of the week, and when I do have to be in Seattle, I'm only an hour and a phone call away, so you should be fine on your own. Besides, Roland wants to take you crabbing, and who knows what all else he might want to do. I think he would like to impress Mother, but I believe he genuinely likes you as well. You will be in good hands with him."

"I think so too," he said. "Now, if you don't mind, as long as we are discussing what you and Roland are going to do, I'd like to put in my two cents. First of all, I'd like to do some of the cooking around here. Not that I don't like the cuisine, it's been great, but you won't have as much time once you go back to work. I'm a pretty good cook, you know."

Then he continued in a different vein, "You know, I have been thinking, I would like to have a car to use again, something to run to the store with or just to take some short drives around to get used to the neighborhood or go to the library. I'm a good driver."

She felt a moment of panic, but she knew he had a good point.

"I'll tell you what, Grandpa, I'm not going to say anything about that to Mother. What she doesn't know is not going to hurt her. I can take you down to the DMV, and we will see what has to be done."

"And the cooking?"

"I don't see any reason why we can't share the cooking. Let's try it and see just how it works out and what we are both comfortable with. I'm pretty sure we won't poison each other."

"Good," he said as he began picking up the dishes. "I'll do the dishes too. I need something besides TV and books to keep me busy. I think I'll feel even better being useful and active."

"Well, Grandpa, we can get started by letting you fix lunch today. I have to work things out with the office, and then comes the hard part, getting Mother onboard."

"Okay, I'm good with making lunch, but do you think we might be able to go to the DMV this afternoon?"

"Grandpa!" she rolled her eyes, and then looking at him, she winked and nodded her head. "This is going to be one interesting summer. We will see about this afternoon, but if we don't get to the DMV today, we will do it sometime this week, okay?"

"Fair enough."

"Now, I'm going to be in my office for a bit. Once I get an approval from my boss and know exactly what my schedule will look like, you and I will work out the details of our week, and then I'll call Mother. I am basically going to present her with a fait accompli. After all, there's really not much she can do about it, is there, Grandpa?"

"I like the way you think, young lady. Don't worry, when the dust settles, everything will be fine, just fine."

She found that working things out with the office was relatively easy. They were very happy that she was going to be back to work. After a working discussion, it was agreed that two days a week in the office would suffice most of the time, as long as she was willing to be there when extra time was required. They also felt it would be advantageous to all concerned if she were to come in on Wednesday and get back up to speed because a lot was on the burner right then. She could schedule her work at home however it worked out for her. As long as she was able to keep on top of things, the office would have no problem with her flexible schedule. Knowing her work was well respected in the office, she had expected there would be no problem, but she was very pleased and relieved just the same.

Taking down the kitchen calendar and rejoining her grandfather, she started writing, explaining, "I have to go into the office this Wednesday. My workdays may change once in a while, and sometimes I will be needed at the office on days that are not included, but for the most part, this is what we have to work around. You can see, Wednesdays and Fridays, I will be pretty much regularly in Seattle. Sometimes I might have to go in on Mondays, so anything we pencil in on that day should be things we can change."

"Well, Marcy, write in our crabbing trip with Roland for tomorrow. And Thursday, I think we should look around for a used car. I'm going to need a good car, but it doesn't have to be something too fancy."

"Grandpa, you have to have your license first."

"Sure, but that shouldn't stop us from looking for a good car, should it? Besides, I think it will be fun."

"Okay, penciled in. 'Look for car,' but we aren't going to be in any rush. Now I don't have anything else that I can think of that needs to be put on the calendar, but I'm sure we will add to it as time goes by. Is there anything you want to add?"

"No, but I do like the idea of a calendar."

"It will help us structure our time instead of just bouncing from one thing to another, Grandpa. We will have things to look forward to and things that we know we have to do."

"Are you going to call her now?"

"I guess there's no sense in putting it off." She sighed as she got up and started for her office.

"Good luck."

Once she was in her room, she decided to e-mail Sherry rather than call her.

"It will be much easier and faster to just e-mail her," she told herself. "With an e-mail, I can explain everything to her without her interrupting."

Opening her laptop, she wrote, "Mother, Grandfather is doing just great. As you know, we are going crabbing with Roland tomorrow, and he is really looking forward to it. As a matter of fact, so am I. We never really discussed the details of my taking care of Grandpa. You were in such a hurry to get out of here and back to work. So I wanted to let you know what Grandpa and I have worked out. First of all, I can't just flat quit my job, and you should understand this after what you said about Robyn's World. It wouldn't be fair to them, and it's not really necessary in order for me to take care of Grandpa. I can work from home most of the time and go in to the office one or two days a week, so he wouldn't be alone very much. I can pretty much schedule my own time. Grandpa is very comfortable with this. In fact, he prefers it to my being here all the time. He can always call me or Roland if he needs to, but I don't anticipate him having any problems. Because I will still have a job and an income, I don't see any reason for you to pay me to take care of him. We will be fine. I believe this is a very reasonable, workable solution, and we are working out all the nitty-gritty between the two of us. I trust everything is going well at Robyn's World. Love, Marcy."

After sending her message, she got up and returned to the living room where her grandfather was reading his Bible.

"Well, Grandpa, I'm done. I'm going to have another cup of coffee, and then we will think about the DMV."

"That went rather quickly," he said. "I didn't hear any shouting, so I assume your mother agreed with everything?"

"I didn't call her. I e-mailed her. She may stew a little bit, but she doesn't really have any say in the matter. It's what you and I like, and that's that."

"My, aren't you the brave one. You're right, though. We're the ones who have to live with our decisions, not her. Besides, she will be okay with it once she thinks about it."

"And by the way, Grandpa, I'd bet you haven't done anything about lunch."

"You'd lose, young lady. Why don't you just come on out and sit down at the table, and we will be ready to eat in a jiffy."

She noticed the table was already set as she entered the dining room. True to his word, soup, sandwiches, and iced tea arrived in quick order.

Before he sat down, he asked, "Should I put the leftover potato salad on as well? I'm sure it is still good."

"If you'd like some, certainly. I have been thinking about making another one for our crabbing trip. Roland seemed to really enjoy it the other day."

"That's a great idea. I'll put on some eggs to boil and get some potatoes going for you as soon as we finish lunch. That salad would definitely go great with fresh crab."

She thought, *Well this is working out pretty well already.* And she enjoyed the lunch.

As they were eating, she asked him, "Didn't you have a driver's license?"

"Sure, but I haven't driven in several years. My car needed some serious repairs, and the insurance and registration were another expense I didn't need or want. I discovered I could get around fine without a car, so I sold it. My driver's license has probably run out."

"Do you still have it?"

"I'm sure I do. I carried it for identification. Let me look."

He got up from the table and went into his room. In a few minutes, he came back out with his wallet in his hand. He sat down, took several cards out of his wallet, and sifted through them, coming up with his license.

"Here it is. Let's see. Why, it doesn't run out for another year and a half. Well, what do you know, I don't need to go to the DMV. I could drive on my old license."

"I'm sure you are right, but we will check with the DMV to see what you might need to do just the same. Now, let's get going on the eggs and potatoes. Since I sent the e-mail, I am not going to be calling Mother, so I can give you a hand."

19

GOING CRABBING

Roland called later in the afternoon.

"Hi, Marcy, are you both ready for our trip tomorrow? It's going to be a beautiful day. I was thinking I would pick you up at eight o'clock, and we would get breakfast on the way to the marina. We will get your licenses too. The tide will be going out, and the crabbing should be good. By the way, you might both want to bring a light jacket or a sweater because it can often get a bit cool out on the sound."

"Eight sounds fine. We will be ready when you get here. Is there anything else we should bring?"

"Not really. I'll have everything we will need on the boat. I'll pick you up at eight. Have a good night."

"That was Roland," she told her grandfather. "He is going to pick us up at eight. You won't need to think about breakfast. We are going to get something on the way. He said we should bring a jacket or sweater. I don't know about you, but I'm getting excited to be going crabbing."

"Did you tell him you were bringing potato salad?"

"Nope, that's going to be my surprise. I'm going to put it together as soon as the eggs and potatoes are ready so it can sit in the refrigerator as long as possible to flavor through."

In the morning, her alarm went off at six, and she hopped out of bed to get a shower and get dressed before she woke her grandfather.

When she stepped out of her bathroom, she knew she didn't have to wake him. The smell of fresh coffee wafted into her room.

Walking to the kitchen, she discovered him just taking the creamer out of the refrigerator. Completely dressed for the day, he turned and smiled at her and motioned to the table.

"I couldn't sleep this morning. I was so wound up with the idea of going crabbing that I decided it wouldn't hurt to have a cup of coffee before we left, so I got up and got dressed and made us a pot."

"It definitely got my attention," said Marcy. "I could smell it when I got out of the shower. You know, I have a feeling today is going to be a great day."

The sun was well up, and they were sipping their second cup when Roland pulled into the driveway. Marcy watched as he got out of the car and walked toward the house.

How handsome he looks, she thought to herself.

She opened the door when he knocked. "Come in. We are ready. I just need to get our jackets."

Mr. Miller joined them after putting the coffee cups in the sink.

"Hi, Roland, we had a cup of coffee before you came, but we are looking forward to a day of crabbing. Marcy and I are both probably more excited than you can imagine. Crabbing is going to be a new adventure for both of us. I sure hope we get some."

"You didn't have breakfast, did you?" he asked.

"No, Marcy said we would have breakfast on the way to the boat."

"That's right. I have a spot that I often stop at. Great breakfast and real nice people. Let's get your gear in the car, and we'll be on our way."

She said, "You two go ahead. I'll get our things and be right out in a jiffy."

Going back into the kitchen, she took the potato salad out of the refrigerator and put it in a cooler bag and then stuffed her sweater and Jim's jacket on top and zipped the bag shut. Roland had the trunk open as she got to the car, and she slipped the bag inside.

Starting down the road, Roland said, "We are going up to Oak Harbor and take out the big boat. I took it back up to the marina after your mother and I were out. I only take the small boat out when I'm going by myself or with a fishing buddy, and I don't need all the amenities. We are going for fun and comfort today, so it will be on the *Melissa*."

While the breakfast was every bit as good as Roland had said it would be, she couldn't help being impatient to get back on the road. When he asked if they would like another cup of coffee, she answered for both of them, "No, we are fine. If it's okay, we'd just like to get going and get out on the water."

Once they were on Whidbey Island, she gazed at the familiar countryside as they passed it by while Roland visited with her grandfather. She loved the island and had been on the ferry out of Mukilteo and up this road numerous times, but now it all seemed different. Today was special.

As they pulled into the parking lot at the harbor marina, she asked, "Doesn't your mother-in-law live here in Oak Harbor? Mother told me she had met her."

"Yes. Amanda lives here, and if we get some crabs today, we will drop two or three off for her. I had planned to stop by when we got back in any case. I called her yesterday and warned her we would probably be dropping in on her. You will like her, she's a wonderful person."

He loaded the bags into a cart and started down the ramp. Marcy and Jim followed, and she asked, "Wouldn't she like to go with us today?"

"I invited her. She likes to go fishing, but I can seldom interest her in going after crabs. She gets a little bored crabbing. We won't have any trouble getting her out on the boat later this year when the salmon are running."

Something told Marcy that she was going to like Amanda. "I'm looking forward to meeting her. She must have some interesting stories about you."

"Probably does, but be careful, she will talk your ear off if you let her."

"I won't mind. I'm a good listener."

He was pleased by her interest in Amanda, but he only said, "Well, don't say I didn't warn you."

Stopping alongside a large boat, he announced, "Here we are."

"Wow, some boat! Mother had said it was big, but let me tell you, this is impressive."

"Thanks. I've owned it for some time, but it's in A-1 condition, runs perfectly, and it's very, very comfortable." He stepped aboard and then held out his hand for her.

Climbing onto the boat, she asked, "How are we going to catch the crabs?"

"We use crab pots, traps that sit on the bottom and let the crabs come in through trap doors. Mostly what I brought with me today is bait and ice. I keep the pots stored onboard. It's too much bother to haul them back and forth. What's in your bag? It feels kinda heavy."

"I'll take it. I brought jackets for Grandpa and me." She didn't mention the potato salad.

"That's good, even though I'm thinking you probably will not need them today. Still, it's good insurance to have them. Why don't you two take a little look around the boat while I get everything settled and ready to go."

After she had explored some of the ins and outs of the craft, she heard Roland call her. When she found him, he asked her to hop back onto the dock and cast off the lines. The engines muttered smoothly as she accomplished the task and then took his hand again as she got back aboard.

She found it exhilarating to hear the muted throbbing of the engines and feel the almost-imperceptible motion as the boat cleared the slip and slowly turned. They crept by other boats large and small, rising and falling slightly in their slips on the small wake created by their passing. Not until they were clear of the marina and inner harbor did the engines crescendo, declaring their intent to climb upon the glassy surface and rapidly transport the passengers to their destination.

"We don't have far to go," he said as they cleared the outer harbor and swung past the channel marker. "We are going to drop our pots off Pennell Point. If we don't do much there, we will run partway down the shoreline of Camano Island. There are plenty of good spots, but some days, some spots are better than others. Besides, a nice boat ride is part of the fun."

It had looked like a long way across to the point as they sat in the cockpit, but they reached it more quickly than she had expected. Throttling back and coming to a drifting stop, he brought out three crab pots and showed her and her grandfather how they were baited before dropping the first pot over the side, then moving on to drop the others about a hundred yards apart—each tethered to its own red-and-white buoy by a long line. She noticed her name and address was written on the side of one of the buoys.

"Roland, I saw my name on one of the buoys."

"That's right. There are two pots apiece. Two have my name, two have yours, and two have your grandfather's. The laws are pretty stringent, and it doesn't pay to ignore them. We will have to fill out the catch information when we keep crabs too.

"Now we are going to take the other three pots and drop them off Camano. I changed my mind about putting in all the pots here. Once we get the other traps in, we can sit and chat for a while. We'll give the traps about an hour to soak before we go back to the first three and pull them up to see what we've got. For me, the wait is always the hardest part of the day. I have to force myself to let them be."

She learned what he meant as they drifted slowly back toward Pennell Point on the outgoing tide after dropping the other three pots. Roland took time to show her how to coil the bow and stern lines to make them neat and out of the way. In spite of the beautiful day and the relaxing lap of water on the hull, the hour oozed by, and she was aching to pull the first three traps long before the time was up. She could not force herself to stop checking the time on her cell phone every few minutes.

He noticed her watching the time and tried to take her mind off the wait by filling them in on what they would be looking for when they pulled the traps.

"We can only keep males, and they have to be six and a quarter inches across their shell. This little plastic tool is what we use to measure them. If it fits over the shell, the crab is too small. If the crab is so large, it doesn't fit. It's a legal crab as long as it isn't a soft shell."

Marcy was intrigued. She had never looked crabs over too closely, and the cooked ones in the market had all looked pretty much the same to her.

"How do you know the difference between a male and a female crab? They all look alike to me," she said.

"When we bring some crabs aboard, I'll show you. It's very easy to tell them apart. I had to show your mother too. Speaking of your mother, have you heard anything from her?" he asked.

"No, I sent her an e-mail yesterday, but I haven't heard back. She is getting ready for a trip to Europe, so I don't expect to hear from her right away. I believe she is going to be looking at a business that she has been considering acquiring."

"I see. So she wasn't just trying to get away from me. She really did have to get back to New York. I tried to talk her into staying for a while, but she wouldn't listen to it."

"I know you asked her to stay and go crabbing today with us."

"That's right," he said.

He didn't want to tell her that he had asked Sherry to marry him. The refusal to stay for a day of crabbing was a good cover for what he was feeling.

They continued visiting, making small talk about the beautiful weather and Camano Island.

Her grandfather announced, "We are going shopping for a car for me on Saturday. I want to be able to get out of the house and be on my own a bit. There're lots to see, and since I am going to be doing some of the cooking, I would like to be able to go to the store when I need something."

"That makes sense, but be careful. Traffic can be a bear around here when everyone is heading to work or coming home. Other than that, it shouldn't be any big deal. Do you know what kind of car you are looking for?"

"Not really. A used car will be fine. I just want something dependable, not too large and not too old."

"Well, there are plenty of them out there. Would you mind if I check with a couple of dealerships where I have some connections to see if they might have taken in any really good used vehicles? I might be able to help you narrow down your search."

"I don't mind at all."

He looked at his watch and said, "Okay, time's up. We'll go back to the point and pull the first trap."

The engines came to life as he turned the key, and in no time at all, they were nearing the buoy of the first pot they had dropped. He maneuvered alongside and Jim hooked the line. Roland cut the engine and joined him, taking the line.

Pulling the trap up from the bottom forty feet below, hand over hand, he commented, "It feels like we've got a bunch in this pot. Hopefully, one or two of them will be keepers."

Marcy let out a squeal as it broke the surface. The trap had a large number of crabs crawling about inside, and Roland brought it over the side and placed it on the deck.

"Most of these are a little on the small side, but it looks like we might have a couple of keepers," he said as he emptied the pot out into a plastic tub.

Using a set of tongs, he began tossing small crabs over the side until only five crabs remained in the tub. He picked up the largest one and turned it over.

"See this," he said pointing to the belly of the crab. "This is a male crab. His tail flap is folded up against his abdomen. You can see it is long and slim, sort of resembling the Washington Monument."

Placing the yellow plastic measuring device on the back of the crab, it was way too small to fit over his shell.

"This is a really nice crab," he said, reaching over and dropping it into the live well.

He picked up the next crab and, taking a quick look, said, "This one is legal sized also," and he dropped it in with the first. Picking up the next crab, he turned it over. "See how the tail flap is big and wide? It's a female and has to go back."

Picking up the next crab, he measured it, and the device just fit down over the shell.

"This one is too small, real close, but too small, so back he goes."

The last crab was another female.

"Okay, we've got two keepers. We are going to drop this pot back down to the bottom and go to the next trap. You grab the pot, Marcy, and when I tell you, drop it over the side with the rope and buoy on top."

She dropped the trap where he told her, and they moved on to the next, and by the time they had pulled and emptied the third trap, they had five keepers. Then they swung south toward the three traps off Camano.

As he pulled up alongside the buoy for the first of the second group of traps, Marcy asked, "Can I pull this one up?"

"Sure, if you want to. Just grab the line when he hooks it and lifts the buoy."

"Wow, this is heavier than I thought it would be," she said. She was sort of puffing when Roland got to her.

"Maybe you've got a starfish on it, or it's tangled in something. Let me help you."

He took the line in his hands and began pulling.

"I think we've got a big starfish hanging on the pot," he said. "Some of them can weigh twenty pounds." But as the trap finally broke the surface, it was his turn to say, "Wow!"

The pot was half full.

"That's one big bunch of crabs! We should get a few keepers here." He turned the crabs out into the tub and scratched his head in amazement.

"Can I sort them?" Marcy asked.

"Sure, you can. Just don't get your hand near the crabs. They will nail you in a heartbeat if you are careless, and it wouldn't be pretty."

She began dropping smaller crabs over the side, being careful to keep her hands well out of range of the angry claws reaching upward, and soon only larger crabs were left, an abundance of them.

He said, "Wait a minute before you go any farther," and he left.

Returning in a few minutes, he sat a 5-gallon pail down beside the tub.

"Take the crabs out, and check to see if they are females. Toss any of them over the side and put the males in this bucket. We will check them for size after the females are gone."

She found it easy to tell the females, and more than half of the larger crabs went back into the ocean, saved by their gender. Then she began tonging the crabs from the bucket.

"Can I measure them?" she asked.

"Sure, you can, but keep your hands back from the front of the crab when you measure. They can't reach back with their claws. You can usually see if the crab is big enough without getting the gauge actually on them. If they are so close you can't tell, put them back to get bigger."

Again, she accomplished the task without an encounter with a crab claw, dropping each legal crab into the live well and the sublegal ones overboard. She was just about to drop one large crab into the well when Roland said, "No, put that one back into the tub."

Putting it into the tub, she grabbed the last crab, measured it, and dropped it into the live well.

"How many did you put in the live well?"

"I put in four. Why shouldn't I put this one in as well? He's pretty big," she asked, pointing to the big crab in the tub.

"Yes, it's a really nice one, but I think it is a soft shell, and it needs to be put back. It wouldn't have much meat in it anyway."

"How can you tell it's a soft shell?" she asked, pushing on the back of the shell. "It feels hard to me."

"First of all, can you see how white the bottom of the crab is? His shell is new and hasn't gotten discolored by the ocean floor. That's a pretty good sign it's a soft shell. But let me show you another way to check. Pick him up with your tongs."

Taking the crab carefully from the tongs, he turned it over and pressed against the bottom shell just back from the big claws.

"See how this flexes?" he asked. "It really is a soft shell. You can't do that with a good crab." And he dropped him over the side.

"Now we have nine good crabs with two traps to go. We are only allowed six more crabs for our limit. If the next two traps have a catch like the last one, and I think they might, we are going to be putting back quite a few legal crabs by the time we are done, so we will keep just the really big ones." And he stowed away the pot.

His predictions were right on the money. Each pot was bulging with crabs, and the six largest went into the live well to join the others. The pots were piled on top of each other after the small amount of bait remaining inside was removed and tossed overboard.

"A free meal for the more fortunate ones," he said.

They went back and retrieved the first three traps, emptying their contents back into the ocean without any ceremony, and then stacked them like the others. The traps, when folded, took up very little space, and they left them piled on the deck.

"We will wash them off with fresh water before we finally put them away," he explained. "Now we will cook nine crabs. Six will be for our dinner here on the boat, and three we will leave with Amanda when we get back to Oak Harbor. I always cook and clean hers for her. She could do it, but it saves her a lot of mess, and even though she protests, I know she appreciates it."

"What are you going to do with the other crabs?" she asked.

"I'll take them back with us alive. I have a couple of friends who will appreciate them, and they can cook their own."

Soon the water was boiling, and in a short time the crabs were done. And he was cleaning them, both the ones they would eat and the ones for Amanda. He made it look easy as she watched him.

Finally, after he had finished cleaning the fourth crab, she asked, "May I try that?"

He looked at her. "You don't have to clean any, I don't mind doing it. It's sort of a messy job."

"Yes, I can see that," she replied, "but I'd like to give it a go anyway."

"Suit yourself. I'll watch and give you some guidance."

"Thanks, but I've been paying attention. I think I can do it."

He watched as she pulled the carapace off and then began rinsing out the gook on the inside of the crab. Then she cut the mouth parts from the front of the body and peeled away the gills.

"Bravo!" he cheered. "That's a great job!"

Her grandfather came to see what all the fuss was about.

"I've just cleaned my first crab, Grandpa," she explained, showing him the ready-to-eat crab.

"I wish you had hollered, I would have like to have seen that myself."

"Well, stick around, I'm about ready to do another."

Roland was impressed. Sherry had not wanted anything to do with the crabs until they were ready to eat. She didn't want to catch them. She didn't want to handle them, and she certainly didn't want to clean them, or even just watch.

How different she is from her mother, he thought. *She cleans crabs just like Betty used to, quick and easy.*

"It seemed like you enjoyed the crabbing, and you cleaned that crab just like someone else I once knew. I really was impressed," he said.

"Thanks. Let's get the rest of them done. I don't mind helping, and it will be faster together. I'm getting hungry."

When they had finished, he put six cleaned crabs into a large bowl and, pointing, said, "Okay, Marcy, You can open that cabinet and set the table while I'm warming some butter. I brought some bread, and I cooked a few ears of sweet corn, and I have a bottle of very good wine, so put on the good glasses."

"Aye, aye, Captain," she said smiling, giving him a little salute.

It seemed like the perfect thing to do at the moment, and feeling sort of girlish, she found she was enjoying herself immensely.

When she opened the cabinet, she was surprised to see that Roland hadn't been kidding about the good glasses. A set of beautiful crystal goblets was secured inside above the china. She had been expecting some sort of paper or plastic plates and cups and now felt a little foolish about it.

He must have had guests from time to time who would have looked for something better than paper and plastic, she thought.

Soon they were all sitting at the table, set with sterling silverware, wonderful china, and the "good" glasses.

Roland said, "Let's bow our heads and thank the Lord for a great day on the water and the bountiful food he has provided."

"Father, we thank you so much for your care for us, for this gorgeous day, and for this time that we can sit together enjoying each other's company. Thank you that Marcy was able to come. We thank you for this food that you have provided from your bounty and ask that you would bless this time we have together. Amen."

They were ready to begin eating after grace when she said, "Just a minute, I forgot to put something on." And she went to get her salad.

Placing it on the table, she saw his eyes light up, and he smiled. "Is that your fabulous potato salad? What a wonderful surprise! What a perfect day!"

Uncorking the bottle of wine, he poured a couple inches in each goblet. Picking his up, he said, "Before we begin eating, I'd like to propose a toast."

As they held their goblets, he said, "Here's to friendship, a great day on the ocean together, and Marcy's potato salad."

She smiled and protested that her salad wasn't all that special, but she felt a warm glow from the compliment, and for his part, he savored every mouthful of her salad. It went so well with the fresh crab and sweet corn.

Actually, he thought to himself, *Marcy's salad may be the best part of this whole meal.*

Sitting at the table after the veritable feast, Roland could not help but compliment her again on her potato salad.

"You know, I've had a fair number of meals on this boat, but none that will ever be more memorable than this one, thanks to you and your potato salad. It was delicious. I'm so glad you brought it, and I'm pleased that you enjoyed the crabbing. I must say, you really got into it."

"It's certainly going to be a memorable day for me too," her grandfather commented. "I've seen a lot, learned a lot, and eaten what I can only call gourmet food. That makes it one pretty darn good day in my book."

Marcy got up and began clearing the table.

"Hold on there, you don't need to do that," Roland said. "You are a guest on this boat. I'll take care of those."

"Nope," she replied saucily. "If I can clean crabs, I certainly don't mind clearing the table. Where should I put the dishes?"

"Put everything right on the counter by the sink in the galley. It will only take me a few minutes to wash them and put them away."

"Nope," she said again. "I will wash them for you."

"Very well. Then I will dry them and put them away."

"Deal," she said.

Jim sat back in his chair, listening and watching the two of them as they headed for the galley. He smiled and shook his head then finished the little bit of wine left in his glass, wondering if perhaps there might be just a little more in the bottle.

It was a happy crew that headed back for the marina after the dishes were done and the traps were rinsed and all stowed away.

On their way into the harbor, Roland asked, "Would you mind if we left the remainder of the potato salad with Amanda? I know she would love it."

"No, I don't mind at all. Heaven knows we ate enough of it for dinner."

"Yes, and I could probably eat all the rest with no trouble, but I know she will appreciate it just as much as I did."

The afternoon was well spent when they arrived at Amanda's with crabs and potato salad.

Stepping inside, Roland said, "You remember Sherry who was with me the last time I was here? This is her daughter, Marcy, and her father, Jim Miller. Folks, this is Amanda, my mother-in-law."

"I can see the family resemblance. The apple didn't fall far from the tree, young lady. You are just as beautiful as your mother. How is she anyways?"

"She is doing well. She is in Europe right now on business."

"Well, let's not just stand here. Come on into the living room and have a seat," said Amanda. "I know you don't make coffee on your boat, so I made a fresh pot for you and your guests."

"Sounds great. Marcy, Jim, would you like a cup?"

She brought the coffee and cups into the room, and they soon sat relaxing, enjoying the hot beverage.

"This really hits the spot," said Roland. "Thanks for having it ready for us. And speaking of having something ready, I've got three cleaned crabs for you," he said, "and a special treat. Marcy made her wonderful potato salad, and we have some leftover for you. You're going to love it. I'll put everything in the refrigerator."

"So you're a good cook, eh?" she asked, looking at Marcy.

"I can cook, but my grandfather does most of the cooking right now. I work at home and in Seattle, but I did make the potato salad."

"So what did you think of crabbing? Pretty boring, right? I always have to take a book."

"No, not at all. I got to do everything and then I enjoyed the fruits of our labor. Roland is a good teacher, a good cook, and a great captain. I would love to go with him again whenever the opportunity arises."

"Roland," she hooted, "it looks like you've got this poor girl hornswoggled. She thinks crabbing is fun."

"Not only that, Amanda," he replied, "she even cleaned some of those crabs I put in your refrigerator, and she did a first class job of it too."

"Well, doesn't that beat all! I went crabbing sometimes, because I loved being on the water, but I never cleaned crabs when I didn't have to. My daughter would wade right into them. My husband loved crabs and crabbing, and when he was off duty, he would take her right along with him if I begged off. She learned the trade from him."

"He taught her well," said Roland. "I didn't know that until we moved to Washington, right back into her old stomping grounds. She loved the ocean almost as much as she loved me, I think."

"The lure of the sea is strong in her family. They have served in the Navy in war and peace from the time our country was born. I was always a little surprised she didn't join the Navy herself."

"They still do, Mother. Bryce is carrying on the tradition. I suppose you heard that he was just promoted."

"Yes, I heard, and I'm proud of him, but I'd like to hear that he is getting married. I'd hate to think he is the end of the line."

"Give him time. He's just waiting for the right one to come along."

"Like you, I suppose?"

Roland looked at Amanda, but he didn't respond. Marcy could see he was uncomfortable, and she came to his rescue.

"He's working on my mother, but she is playing hard to get. It's not his fault at all."

Amanda's eyes narrowed as she looked at her, "Do you think she will change her mind?"

"I . . . I don't know . . . I hope so. If she doesn't, she is missing the greatest opportunity of her life. She will never find anyone else like Roland."

"Well, I guess we will just have to wait and see, won't we?"

Turning, she spoke to Roland, "The next time the three of you are going crabbing, give me a call. I might just go with you, but don't expect me to get too excited or clean crabs. It's just that I could stand a pleasant day on the ocean. She and I could have a good time visiting," indicating Marcy with the movement of her head. "I think we might have a lot in common. You and Jim could do the work, and we will get to know each other better."

"Well, that's a surprise! I had already told her that you seldom went crabbing but that we might get you out when the salmon are biting."

"Now, that I would enjoy! Fishing has always been my thing. We could see who catches the biggest fish."

Roland warned the others, "She does have a knack for catching the big ones. And don't make any side bets with her."

When they were leaving, Amanda gave Marcy a hug and said, "It was nice meeting you. I hope you go crabbing again soon."

"Me too," she replied.

20

BACK TO WORK

It seemed good and a bit strange at the same time to be back in the office, and there were three projects waiting on her desk. Most of her morning was spent in conference with her boss and two coworkers who were already working on the projects that she would have to review before Friday. By the time the day was over, she had the overall picture. But she knew digesting the details would take all day Thursday and maybe part of that night as well, in order to be ready Friday morning.

There wouldn't be any time for the DMV until Saturday, that was for sure. She thought about it on the way home. She knew her grandfather would be disappointed, but that couldn't be helped.

He met her at the door with a smile. "Come on in. How did the first day back go?"

"It wasn't pretty, but I thought it went okay. There has been a lot going on while I was away, and I'm going to have to work on the projects after dinner and probably all day tomorrow and most of tomorrow evening as well, and I'm going to have to go in on Friday. I'm going to get started right after dinner tonight, so I won't be able to help you with dishes, and I'm afraid I won't be able to get you to the DMV until Saturday."

"That's not a problem. I called them today, and they told me I could drive on my present Georgia license. If I am going to be staying here, I will need to get a Washington license in the future, but they can just use my old license to give me a new one. We could look for a car on Saturday instead."

"When we find a vehicle, we will have to get you insured before you can register it, so we are looking at next week before we could get you ready to go even if we found a car on Saturday. I am sure my agent would be happy to get you set up, but their office isn't open on Sunday, and I'm going to be just too busy to deal with any of it on Thursday or Friday."

"Okay, but we can go looking at cars on Saturday, right?"

"Yes, we will look on Saturday. Now what's for dinner? It smells really yummy."

"Well, there was some lamb in the freezer, so I made us a lamb stew. It sounded good to me."

"I thought that was what I smelled. When will it be done?"

"It's ready now, and the table is all set. I can have it on the table in just a few minutes."

"Sounds good. I want to wash up and put my papers in my room, then I'll be ready."

That night she dug into the information on the first two projects. They were relatively easy to digest, and she made some notes on her ideas to share with the others who would be working on them as well. She had left the third project for last because when they had discussed it in the office, it was obvious it would be more time-consuming than the others.

When she finally said good night to her grandfather and put herself to bed, she felt good about the last project. Confident that the next day would put that one well in hand, she let her mind take a break and thought about Roland and crabbing. The next thing she knew, there was a knocking on her door.

"Hey, sleepyhead, you going to sleep all morning?" she heard her grandfather's voice call.

"Not anymore," she replied, looking at her clock. She was startled to see it was seven thirty already.

"I'll be up and around. Give me a few minutes. Thanks for waking me up."

"The coffee is done, and I was thinking of making some French toast for a change of pace. How does that sound?"

"Sounds wonderful."

She got up, put on her robe, and pulled on her slippers.

I'll have breakfast before I take a shower, she thought as she brushed her teeth.

Walking out for breakfast, she found herself wondering what Roland was doing that morning instead of thinking about her project.

Breakfast looked and smelled great to her. "Sure looks good," she said. "You didn't mention the bacon."

"As long as I have it, I'm probably going to cook it. I hope you don't mind."

"You know I don't, although I have eaten a lot more of it since you came than I ever did before. Do you ever have sausage for breakfast?"

"Sometimes, but my favorite is bacon."

"I hope you won't mind, but I am going to have oatmeal once in a while. It's good for me, and I like it with milk and a little brown sugar. And I probably will cut back on the bacon a bit as well, but that doesn't mean you can't have your usual breakfast. I just want to keep my figure in shape as long as I can."

"No problem, I can even make you some right now if you'd like."

"That's not necessary, but I would go for it tomorrow morning before I go in to work."

"Is there someone special at work that you'd like to stay in shape for?" he asked.

"No, no one at work." Then she added, "I just believe in staying healthy."

As they ate breakfast, he said, "I'm going to check with Roland today and see if he has any information for us on cars we should look at yet. He said he knew some dealers he was going to check with."

She swallowed a mouthful of egg and replied, "I told you, I would take you out to look at cars Saturday."

"Yeah, I know, but it doesn't hurt to have a plan and get a line on a few cars before then, right?

"I guess it wouldn't hurt, but we don't need to be bothering him every day. First thing you know, he will get sick of hearing from us. He has a life of his own to live, and I'm sure there are things more important than us and cars on his mind. If it wasn't for Mother, we would probably see a lot less of him. It's not that he isn't a real friend, but I'm afraid that to some extent, we are just a way for him to get closer to her."

And then the phone rang.

Not too many people called her on her landline. In fact, she had thought about having it disconnected, but now that her grandfather was living with her, it had sort of become a necessity once more.

"Hello?" she answered. She heard Roland at the other end. "Roland, what a surprise. We were just talking about you."

"Oh? Something good, I hope," he said. "I apologize for calling so early and interrupting your morning, but I was wondering what you two are going to be doing today."

"Well, I am going to be working on a project all day today. Grandfather is pretty much free to do whatever he likes."

"I see. Well, the reason I called was to see if the two of you would like to look at a few cars today. I talked with a couple of salesmen I know, and they have some real beauties that they have just taken in on trade. They haven't even gone up for sale yet."

"That would be great, but really, I can't do it. If he wants to go with you, though, it's fine with me. I'll ask him, but I'm pretty sure what his answer will be. Hold on."

"It's Roland, he wants to know if you'd like to go look at some cars with him today."

"Wow! Sure, I would. Do you mind if I go?"

"Not at all. I'll tell him . . . Yes, he'd love to go. When are you thinking about going?"

"I am thinking about nine o'clock. I'd like to get an early start."

"That will be fine. He'll be ready for you. Thanks for calling. Bye."

She looked at him, shaking her head.

"He will be here about nine." She finished her breakfast and said, "Could you please take care of the dishes before Roland comes. I really do need to get to work. I'm going to be doing as much research on my company as I can online, and I need to spend some time digesting it and thinking. Don't bother to interrupt me when he gets here."

She resisted the temptation to get up when she heard the doorbell ring and then heard their muffled voices. She sighed and turned back to her computer, a little disappointed that her grandfather hadn't ignored her instructions and poked his head in to let her know Roland was there, giving her an excuse to say hello. When they were gone, she went to the kitchen for a cup of coffee and a muffin. She couldn't help wishing she had been available to go with them.

Returning to her office, she focused on the information she had been discovering and the questions she had jotted down. She was realizing she had more questions than she had answers. It was going to take more than the basic information she had on the project, but throughout the day, she was still able to put together a package of insightful thoughts and suggestions for Friday's meeting.

Other than a couple of breaks for coffee and a PB&J sandwich for lunch, she worked steadily on the project. It wasn't until about four o'clock that she began to wonder when grandfather would be back. Her timing was amazing, for just after the thought had come into her head, she heard a car pull into the driveway. She was ready to call it quits for a while anyway, so she took a quick look in her mirror; and when she heard the front door close, she walked out to greet the car hunters.

He wasn't there.

"Where's Roland?" she asked.

"I told him you were probably still tied up on your project. He didn't want to disturb you, so he went back home. He did say to tell you hello."

She could feel the disappointment well up inside once again.

"Do you have a few minutes to talk?" he asked. "I want to tell you about our day. We had a great time."

"Sure, I can sit down. I was ready for a break when you came in. I thought he would come in too, but that's okay. Now I'll be able to finish up what I was doing without having to interrupt my train of thought, but I would like to hear how you did."

"Well, we only went to three dealerships and a couple of used car lots, but boy, did we see some great cars. Roland said the best deals were at the dealerships, and he knows the owners personally, so if I decided on one of the cars we saw there, I could get a special deal. I even got to meet the owner of the Audi place."

"You looked at Audis?" she sort of gasped.

"Yes, we looked at Audis and BMWs and Mercedes."

"I guess I should have known where he would be taking you, but he should know better. I don't think you can afford one of those cars. He should have let you look at something like a Corolla or Camry, which would be more realistic. Did you look at something like a Toyota or Ford in the used car lots?"

"Yes, but mostly, we looked at the same kind we saw in the dealerships. Roland said it would give me some perspective on the kind of deal we could get from the dealers and what the going prices were."

She was nonplussed, but she didn't want him to see the concern she was feeling. She would just let him tell her about their day, what they had learned, and what else they did beside look at cars.

"So did you see any vehicles you really liked, and do you have any idea about what they would cost?"

"I saw several that would be wonderful to own, but I think I would like a Mercedes. I saw three of them at the dealership, and they were all beauties, but one was a bit older than the other two, and it was a lot less money, of course.

"I had looked at a couple of big luxury four-door sedans, and they really were luxurious, but I got to thinking, what do I need a big car for? I don't need anything like that to go to the store and buy groceries. So I got this idea in my head that I would like a smaller car."

"Well, a Corolla is a smaller car even if it has four doors," she said.

"Yes, I know, but I saw this one older car, and I was smitten. It was a silver Mercedes, SL500, two-door convertible, 322 horsepower, V-8, 5-speed automatic. I tell you, I felt like a millionaire just sitting behind the wheel. I asked Roland if he thought we could possibly take it out for a test-drive, and he said it was no problem, and we did. I really didn't know if I could afford to buy it, but after driving it, I knew I wanted that car. Even though it was ten years old, it looked like it was brand-new, and the mileage was really low, only 31,427 miles. It has leather, heated seats, and there was absolutely no rust on it. We were told it had always been parked inside when it was not being used, and it had always been serviced right there at the dealership. They said it was mechanically perfect, and it would come with a free three-year or 30,000-mile warranty on parts and labor."

"So what was the price on this marvelous vehicle?" she asked.

She was surprised when he said, "It was $15,495, but we saw some that were something like it at the used car lots that were a lot more expensive, with a lot higher mileage and only a ninety-day warranty."

"That actually sounds like a really great deal, Grandpa, and that's a great warranty. Maybe I should have him take me shopping the next time I need a car." She could hardly believe those words had come out of her own mouth.

"I'm so glad to hear you say that because I really fell in love with it. I have the weekend to think about it. They said they won't put it out for sale before next Tuesday. I don't know exactly what the payments would be, but at that price, I am sure I can manage them.

"You know, Marcy, I never owned anything but an old Chevy or Ford plain Jane. They were reliable transportation, but I always wondered what it would be like to own a sporty car. I'm not getting any younger. It may be crazy, but if I don't do it now, I'll always be sorry I didn't."

Yeah, I know just what you mean, she thought.

She had a suspicion that Roland might have had something to do with the price and the warranty, but she didn't voice her opinion to her grandfather.

Instead, she said, "Okay, let's think on it, and I would like to talk with Roland about it as well, if that's okay with you. And what else did you do? You were gone all day."

"Well, we had lunch around one o'clock in Mukilteo, and then we took the ferry and went to see his mother-in-law. We didn't have too long to spend there, but we did have a cup of coffee and visited for a while. Amanda is a very nice lady. She reminds me of your grandmother. She was sorry you hadn't come. She said to tell you she was still interested in going crabbing with you if we went again."

"I'd like that too, but I don't know when I might be able to go again. I'm going to be pretty busy for a while. I haven't even made anything for dinner. Are you hungry?"

"Ummm, not really, are you?"

"I could eat a bite, but no, I'm not very hungry either. How about fixing us a grilled cheese sandwich and some tomato soup?"

That evening, he told her more about the car and asked her to go with him on Saturday to see it for herself. He was winning her over, and she was beginning to think, *What real harm can it do for him to have a really nice car if it will make him happy?*

Before they went to bed, she said, "I will go with you on Saturday to look at your car. I have no idea how Mother will take your having a car, but since we haven't even told her you are getting one, I might just as well be hanged for a sheep as a lamb and go along with you."

The next morning found Marcy in Seattle engaged in a serious conference with her boss and coworkers. As they talked, it became apparent that she had, indeed, been plowing new ground with her concepts for the special client. As far as her boss was concerned, there was no question about it. She was to be the lead person on the project. There were a lot of unknowns that would need to be addressed, and she was already starting to prioritize them.

"Chose whomever you need to work with you on this project," her boss instructed. "We will be able to use many of your suggestions on the other two projects you reviewed, but you will not be working on them. I want you 100 percent on this one."

She knew this was the biggest opportunity that had ever come her way in her career, but she also knew it was going to require more time than she had thought she would be giving to her work when she was planning with her grandfather. It also meant less time for getting out on the ocean with him and Roland.

"Okay," she replied, "I'll get right on it. I believe I can give you a list Monday of the personnel I would like."

"Fine. Do it."

Returning to her office after the conference, she thought, *I'm going to have to put together a small team that can grab this and make it mesh once they see where I'm going. Who can handle that?*

She mentally began putting her fellow employees in three categories: those she felt couldn't or wouldn't fit in; then those she might want to include; and finally, some she definitely wanted onboard. She started jotting down names. One of them was already very involved in a project. She would be the hardest to pry loose, but Marcy had a second choice if it didn't work out.

She left work early. She needed some privacy as she thought about the project and how certain people might fit in. Home, without any distractions, was the obvious place to do it. She knew she could come up with a preliminary list for Monday and the rationale for each choice.

Heading home, time passed quickly, and almost before she realized it, she was pulling into the driveway. Getting out and grabbing her laptop bag, she heard her grandfather call her from the house as he stood in the doorway.

"Hey, you're home pretty early. Anything wrong?"

"No, I've just got something to do that will be easier here without distractions than in the office." When she got to the door, she asked, "What's for dinner?"

"Barbeque ribs, sweet potato, and tossed salad."

"Really? That sounds great. I think I'm getting hungry already."

"I hope you don't mind, but I invited Roland over to join us for dinner. He loves ribs. I had such a good time looking at cars with him yesterday I thought I could pay him back a little. Is that okay with you?"

"Sure, it's okay, Grandpa, but I can't help you get ready. I really need to get back to work. I've been named the manager for the Houston project, and I have to be up to speed by Monday morning. It's a little scary, but this is a wonderful opportunity for me. You will have to entertain Roland while he's here too. I just can't sit around and visit for very long."

"Well, congratulations on the job. What are you going to be working on here?"

"I'm trying to figure out what has to be done and who the best people are that we have for those jobs, but I've been struggling because I can't completely understand what the company is trying to do. I think I'm on the right track. I've done some research on them, and they are rock-solid, but it's hard to visualize how what they are asking us for fits in with their core business. I think I may end up having to fly down to Houston and have a firsthand look right at the home office and their facilities. I will probably need to talk with the CEO or the person he has in charge of the venture before I will feel really comfortable. I might have to leave you on your own for a couple of days."

He ignored the part about being left alone and replied, "You ought to have someone like Roland on your team."

"Oh, sure, like I can see that happening. By the way, give me a heads-up a few minutes before he is supposed to get here, would you?"

Once she was in her office, she became engrossed in her task, but the more she thought about it, the more she was convinced of her need to be more familiar with the workings of the Houston business and their goals for the project. It was much easier to come up with what she felt would be the best three additional people to fill out her team, but she knew she might have to adjust that once she had a chance to visit Houston. Calling the office, she told her supervisor that she would need to visit the Houston facilities as soon as possible and also that, if possible, she would really like to speak with the CEO.

"We were fairly sure you would want to do that," her supervisor said. "I would have been surprised if you had plunged ahead without anything more than the file we gave you. We already have a flight scheduled for you for Tuesday. Wednesday, you are scheduled to meet with the CEO. We have allowed you four days, but if you think you can't get all the information you need by Saturday, we will change the return flight."

Thinking of her grandfather, she wanted to protest that four days was more than she needed, but she knew he was right. She would just have to work it out.

"E-mail me the flight information and where I will be staying. I'll need a car as well. I'll stop by the office Monday afternoon to tie up the loose ends."

She was thinking about her grandfather and how he would react to being left alone for four days or even longer when he knocked at the door.

"Roland should be here in about five minutes. Are you able to leave what you are doing?"

"Yes, I'll be right out."

She took a look in her mirror and straightened up her hair. She didn't have time for a lot of freshening up.

They will just have to take me as I am, she thought and walked out to the kitchen.

"Grandpa, we are going to have to get the calendar out tonight and look at our schedule. I've got to be away for longer than a couple of days, and you would be on your own. I'm not completely comfortable with that. You could fly down with me, and we could take in the sights around Houston at night."

"When are you going, and how long will you be gone?"

"I have to leave on Tuesday, and I will be gone for at least four days, maybe as much as a week."

"What if I'd rather stay here?"

"Well, I could check in on you from Houston. I wouldn't even consider it at all if you were having any problems, but you are doing so well it could probably work out. Mother would have a fit if she found out, and she still hasn't said anything about our arrangement."

"Let's ask Roland what he thinks."

"No, we aren't going to saddle him with our concerns," she said as she took down the calendar.

She penciled in the Houston dates and the Monday afternoon in Seattle. She had barely replaced the calendar when the doorbell rang.

Her heart leaped at the sound, and she said, "It's Roland. I'll get it," as she headed for the door.

"Hello, it's me again. I hope you don't mind," he said as she opened the door.

"How could I mind seeing you? You are always welcome. Grandpa told me the two of you had a great time cruising for cars yesterday. Come right on in."

She was immediately very happy that he had been invited to dinner.

"Come on in and sit down. Grandfather has been bombarding me with facts and thoughts about one of the cars he saw yesterday. It sounded to me like quite a deal. I told him I would go with him to look at it tomorrow."

"Oh?" he answered.

"Yes, he wanted me to see it. He said he had been smitten by it, those were his words."

"I assume you are talking about the Mercedes sports coupe."

"Yes, the SL500. He said he was getting a great warranty if he bought it. Do those used cars usually come with a three-year warranty?"

He smiled as he said, "This one does."

"Did you have something to do with that?" she asked almost accusingly.

He looked surprised. "I hope you don't mind, but I pull some weight with the owner, and I let him know what I thought might be a good deal for Jim. It's a bit unusual, I admit, but I didn't have to twist his arm to get him to make the offer. Looks like I might be buying a new car not too far down the road, though," he smiled.

She wanted to tell him that he didn't have to do whatever he had done, but instead, she said, "Thank you for looking out for him. You are making him one very happy man. I guess going to look at the car is pretty much a formality, but I know he will love showing it to me."

"You know, if you would like to go on a test-drive with him in it, they are ready to let you take it for the day. I've already cleared it; just ask for the key. If he does buy it, they will take care of all the paperwork. You will just have to call your insurance agent and get it covered and have the information faxed to them. He could have the car registered by Tuesday afternoon."

"What's that about having a car registered on Tuesday?" her grandfather asked as he walked into the room.

"Roland was just saying that if you did buy the car, you could probably pick it up on Tuesday."

"But you won't be here to go with me."

"What's that?" Roland asked, "Are you going somewhere, Marcy?"

"Actually, I am. I have to go to Houston on Tuesday. I have an assignment that I am working on."

"When will you be back?" he asked.

"I'm not sure, but probably on Saturday morning."

"What about Jim? Is he going to be alone?"

She felt a little guilty as she answered, "Yes, but I'll be checking in on him every day. We've already discussed it, and he is very comfortable staying here on his own."

"That's right, we talked about my staying, and I don't have any problem with it. I lived alone for quite a few years and did very well. I have everything I need right here."

"Well, I'm sure you will be fine, but if you do need anything, just call me, okay?"

"Okay, now come on out, dinner is ready."

After dinner, she was torn between visiting with Roland and getting back to her work. She hadn't planned on spending very long with the two of them, but now it seemed hard to pull away.

She asked him about Amanda, "Grandfather told me the two of you stopped up to see Amanda. How is she?"

"She's fine, just as feisty as ever. It's really something, though. She still wants to go crabbing with you. If you are not back until next week, we will be getting closer to salmon fishing. Maybe we could do a combination of crabbing and fishing if the salmon show up and if you are interested and have the time."

"I can't give you an answer on that. I am not sure what my schedule will look like next week. It could be hectic."

She saw her chance to break away and continued, "In fact, I really need to get back to work. I'm getting ready for Monday, and I should finish up what I'm doing tonight so I have some free time this weekend. Please excuse me, but thanks for everything, Roland. Will we see you in church?"

"I hope so. By the way, before you leave, have you heard anything from your mother?"

"No, but I think she may still be in Europe. I'm sure she will be in touch as soon as she is back in New York. I will let you know if I hear anything. Now I really do have to get to work. Good night."

It was hard to get back on task. Her mind kept wandering back to Roland, and the fact that he was in the other room talking with her grandfather didn't make it easier. She knew she would rather be talking with them about crabbing, fishing, cars, Amanda, or almost anything instead of working.

She went over and over her short list of people to work on the project and gave up trying to go farther. She decided to go out to the kitchen for a cold drink, and maybe she would be asked to join them, but when she got to the living room, Roland had already left. She felt disappointed once again.

"I'm sort of worn out, Grandpa. I'm going to hit the hay early, and we will get out right after breakfast and go look at that Mercedes."

"That's a date," he said. "Sleep well, and I'll see you in the morning."

On Saturday morning, she got her oatmeal.

"You see, I remembered," he said. "We both can use a heart-healthy meal now and then, and I like oatmeal too."

She enjoyed the change of pace, and after the hot cereal, she finished with a slice of wheat toast with raspberry jam and a second cup of coffee.

She commented, "That was actually a treat. Sometimes I think we get into a rut. It was good to have something different."

"Well, everything seems to be different these days, and it just keeps getting better."

He started taking the breakfast dishes to the kitchen and casually announced, "I'm ready to go look at the car whenever you are."

She smiled. "Okay, just give me time to finish my coffee and get ready. Do you want to take the car out for the day, or do you just want me to see it?"

"Do you really think we can take it out for the day?"

"Roland said it would be okay, we just have to ask them."

"Well, sure, I'd like to take it out with you. That would be great, but where would we go with it?"

"I have no idea, but it might be nice to get out in the country, away from the heavy traffic. You never had traffic like what you see out here on 90, 405, and 5 when you were back East."

"Roland and I didn't go very far with it, but we were in some heavy traffic a couple of times, and I don't know as we were on any major highway. I think I did pretty well. I might drive a little slower than some drivers, but it's been awhile since I drove, and I want to be very careful about keeping safe distances between vehicles and changing lanes."

"Then give me a few minutes to brush my hair and grab a sweater, and we will go and see about taking your car out for a spin." She couldn't help feeling a little excited herself about the car.

She got an approving look from the sales representative as she told him who they were and that there was a car they were going to take out for the day. He knew exactly what she was talking about.

"Yes, Ms. Miller, the car is all gassed up and ready to go. Do you know how long you will have it out?"

"No. A few hours, I think." She gave a look at her grandfather and said, "We want to give it a good test and start getting used to it, don't we?"

"We sure do."

21
RETURN TO NYC

It had been on the Monday after Sherry had left Washington, and she was back at work when she received the e-mail from Marcy. At first she was flabbergasted and angry. After all, she had said she would stay home and look after Father. Her immediate thought was to write back with a blistering reply, but instead, she left the computer and took time to pray for wisdom, something she never would have done two weeks before. After praying at her desk in the privacy of her office, she sat in front of her computer and thought about what Marcy had written.

I guess it's not really a bad thing, she thought. *It probably will be best for both Marcy and Father. I might just as well give them my blessing and let it go at that, but by golly, she is going to have to accept some payment, or there's not going to be any deal.*

She was going to dash off her reply, informing Marcy that she was going to have to accept some payment, but thought better of it, deciding to wait until she had a little more time to think even that through. Her trip to Europe was more urgent now. She would write later. There was a lot of business information to review before she left.

Tuesday found her boarding a plane headed for France. She was going to inspect a business that she was considering for incorporation into Robyn's World. It would require her concentration. She needed to keep a clear head, and she couldn't be thinking about Washington and what she had left behind. She was back in her world, and she was excited by the possibilities the French firm offered, but she was also cautious. Everything she had seen indicated the business was sound, but things were not always as they appeared. Their product lines were finding acceptance, and there were two items that were especially appealing to her and Robyn's World, but she wasn't going to rush into anything. This would just be the jumping-off point.

While she was away, a large box arrived at her office addressed specifically to her from Roland. When the staff saw it, they each made guesses about what was inside. The consensus was that from the shape, it might be a painting.

The following Monday, she returned from France and when she walked into the office, Gwen greeted her.

"How did it, go Mrs. Williams?"

"Very well, actually. I will put all the information together, and I will discuss the possible acquisition at our staff meeting. I want everyone's input on it."

"A package came for you from Washington while you were away. It's in your office."

"Thank you, I'll take a look."

She checked the package Gwen had told her was in her office, guessing about what it might contain, until she opened it and discovered not a painting from Roland as she had expected it might be, but two original Roland Holtz oils.

"Oh my, Roland," she said to herself, "they are beautiful."

She called her secretary, "Gwen, will you have someone from maintenance come to my office please?"

"Is there a problem, Mrs. Williams?" she asked.

"No, but I need a couple of paintings hung. Please come in and help me decide where to hang them after you call maintenance."

She sat back in her chair and looked at the paintings. One was a seascape she thought she had seen in Roland's painting room, but the other was new to her. Prominent in the painted sky, a pair of A6s was descending toward a distant carrier. In the two paintings, she could feel the love that Roland felt for the sea and the respect he had for the Naval Air Service. She had no way of knowing that one of those aircraft carried the serial numbers of the plane Betty's father had been flying when he was lost over Vietnam, but it was a theme he had used a number of times.

She was having a difficult time deciding which one she wanted to keep for herself and which she would share with the rest of her world—a hard choice—when Gwen knocked and walked into the office.

As her gaze fell upon the paintings, she asked, "Did you purchase those while you were in Washington? They are extraordinary!"

"No, I didn't buy them, they are a gift from Roland Holtz. He is the artist. And you are right. They are magnificent. Which one should I hang in my office, and which one in yours?"

"Well, let me see. The one on the right with the aircraft is rather unusual, but it would go very well in here, either would look good in the main office."

"Where would you suggest we hang them?"

"I was thinking behind your desk, but maybe placing the one you like best across from you would be better so that you could see it whenever you looked up. And as much as I'd like to have one painting in the main office, I think you should put the other one up on the wall behind you, but over to the left where people will see it when they come in."

"Yes, that's a good idea. I'd like that, but maybe I could persuade him to send me one more for your office."

"I think one of his paintings would speak volumes for Robyn's World. The man is a very good painter."

"Yes, he is. I'll have to let him know how much they are appreciated. I'll do it after we get them up."

When maintenance arrived, she pointed out approximately where she wanted the two pictures hung and then guided him as he held them in place standing on his ladder. Once they were hanging, she sat down and admired them.

As she sat, she remembered that she needed to send a reply to her daughter. Turning to her computer, she began by writing to Roland instead of Marcy.

"Roland, thank you so much for the two paintings. They are wonderful, and I already have them hanging in my office. I especially like the one with the two airplanes. Also, and I feel a little awkward asking this since I just got two of your paintings, but would you have another one that I could hang in our outer office for everyone to enjoy? I was very selfish and kept both of the ones you sent for my own office. I hope the crabbing went well. Sherry."

Marcy was next.

"Hi, Marcy, I guess by now you and Father have started operating on your new schedule. It sounds like the two of you are happy with your arrangement. I give you my blessing, but I insist that you accept a monthly stipend from me, which you can use for whatever you wish. That is the only thing I ask. A check will arrive next week, and after that, I would like to make a direct deposit into your checking account the first of each month. So did you enjoy crabbing? How did Father like it? Let me know. Mom."

Once she had sent the e-mails, her mind turned back to the real task at hand, preparing for the discussion with the staff about the possible French acquisition. She knew they would give her their real thoughts and any concerns they might have. They were never yes-men, and that was why she appreciated them.

Meanwhile, back in Washington, Marcy and her grandfather had been settling into a comfortable routine, which had already started to become subject to frequent, but welcomed, interruptions by Roland. Their first trip on his boat had been an adventure, and they were both looking forward to more of them even though her time would be more limited now.

Marcy opened the e-mail and was relieved that her mother had sanctioned the living arrangements. She chuckled when she thought, *She doesn't know it yet, but she is going to be paying for grandfather's new car.*

She called Roland. "Hi, I just wanted you to know I heard from Mother today, and she told me to say hello."

"I got an e-mail from her too. She really liked the paintings I sent."

"That's it? She liked the paintings?"

"Well, she asked if I could send her one more, but that's about all. She seems to be ignoring me otherwise."

"I'm sorry about that."

"Don't be. It's fairly obvious that she is where she wants to be, doing what she wants to do, and I don't seem to fit into that. I can't say she didn't warn me."

"I'm sorry just the same. I have a favor to ask you."

"What is it? If I can help you, I will."

"Would you be willing to help my grandfather get the paperwork done on the car and help him get it registered and insured? I've already talked with my insurance company. I'll leave all the information I think he will need."

"I'd be happy to help. He should have the car home before you get back."

"Thanks. It's important to him that something is being done, even if it takes awhile. If you can get everything done, it would be great. I'm leaving in the morning. Just call him when you are ready to get into it."

"I'll do that, and you have a safe trip. Let me know when you get back."

"I will, and good luck."

She filled her grandfather in on the details and then got all her notes together for Houston.

"I'm getting to bed early tonight. I have to be off to the airport by eight. I'll call you to see how things are going, but I'm sure you'll be fine."

"You go ahead and get to bed. I'll have breakfast ready for you before you leave in the morning."

"Okay. Good night."

When she arrived home Friday night, the shiny new car was sitting in the driveway.

She thought, *Maybe I should think about a new car. Mine looks out of place next to his. I bet Roland could get me a sweet deal too.*

Walking into the house, she saw a "welcome back" balloon tethered to a vase of flowers on the dining room table.

"Hey, little girl, I missed you. Welcome back. Are you hungry?"

"A little. What do you have?"

"I've got a pizza ready to go in the oven. Twenty minutes, and it will be ready. I made a tossed salad to go with it."

"Sounds perfect. Boy, it seems good to be home. Thanks for the flowers and the balloon. It's a nice touch."

"Don't thank me, Roland sent them."

"Oh, how nice. I'll have to call and thank him for them."

"I've seen a lot of him this week. We finally got the car all taken care of this morning. It took a little longer than we thought it would. Did you see it out in the driveway?"

"How could I miss it? It makes my car stick out like a sore thumb."

"Yeah, I suppose so. I guess that was why Roland said you might need a new vehicle too."

"Did he really say that?"

"Scouts honor. And he wanted you to call him when you got home."

"Right. Well, I'll call him right after we have our pizza, but I'm going to take a minute right now to clean up from my trip."

About seven thirty, she called him.

He answered, "Hi, Marcy, welcome home."

"Thanks, and thank you for my flowers. They were beautiful. Grandfather said you wanted me to call."

"Yes, I know this week was hectic, and you've been eating every meal out, but I wanted to invite you out for one more. Do you feel like spending next Thursday evening with me?"

"Just me, or are you asking Grandfather too?"

"Actually, just you. I've spent a lot of time and shared a number of meals with your grandfather this week, and we had quite an adventure, but in the end, we got the car. So now I'd like to talk to the other half of the family for a change of pace. What do you say?"

"I say I'd love to. Where will we be going?"

"Let it be a surprise. I'll just tell you that it will be a quiet restaurant with wonderful food, where one can unwind from a stressful week."

"Well, I think I'm going to need that. I think the stress has barely started. You said Thursday evening. What time would you be coming for me?"

"I'll pick you up at four. You don't have to dress up for this restaurant. You can wear casual attire, and we will fit right in. Will that work for you?"

"Sounds like a plan to me. Thanks."

Riding to church on Sunday in the new car, she said, "I'm impressed. This is one fine vehicle. Maybe I will have to think about car hunting with Roland. I might be getting a raise or maybe a promotion, I could probably afford it."

He met them as they came through the door. "Well, how do you like the new car? You looked fine in it."

"It's really nice. I told Grandfather that I might have to start looking for another car now. Mine looks out of place next to his."

"Well, anytime you want to look, I'm available. I know some dealers," he smiled.

"You had better be careful, I might take you up on that one of these days."

"I'll be looking forward to it," he said. "Oh, and could you be ready at two on Thursday instead of four? I want to get an earlier start, if that's okay with you."

"I don't see any reason why not, but how far do we have to go for dinner?"

"You will just have to wait and see. By the way, I won't be around for the next three days," he said. "I'll be out of town on business, but I'll be back for Thursday."

"Business?"

"Yes, one of those things I do from time to time. That's all. I do keep busy, you know, busier than most people think. In fact, I'm going home to pack now. I'm leaving later today, so you'll have to excuse me, but I'll see you Thursday."

Watching him walking away, she said to her grandfather, "Mother is crazy, you know. I'd never let a catch like that go."

22

DINNER FOR TWO

"I'm so pleased that you came with me today. I would have invited Jim to come also, but I wanted some quality time just with you. Is he enjoying his car?"

"Well, I'm flattered. The car? Yes, I think so. It sure keeps him occupied. He washes it about every other day, and he is always looking for something that he can drive to the store to get. I'm so glad he has it. I have to admit, I was a little concerned at first, but now I think it was the very best thing that could have happened to him."

"Then I'm glad for him also, and for you. We haven't seen much of each other in the past couple of weeks. I've been busy, and certainly, you have too, but I've been thinking we should get back out on the sound one more time before Amanda decides she has lost interest in crabbing. Our schedules haven't lined up very well."

"I know, and I probably have about another week before my workload should start to taper off. I don't think I am going to have to be out of town again right away, at least not for more than a day or two, but I've got a lot of meetings and plenty of paperwork to do."

"Do you think you could work in a break for next Tuesday? I'm going to be free, and if the weather is good, we could pick up Amanda and get in that day of crabbing. The salmon aren't showing up yet, so we might just as well hit the crab one more time."

"I don't have my schedule with me, but they know I have planned to have Tuesdays off, and I've been leaving Grandfather alone a lot. So yes, I'd love to go, and I'm sure he would as well if he's invited."

"Sure, he's invited. I'll let Amanda know, and I'll have everything ready to go Tuesday morning. I have to confess something. I asked you to come earlier today because I wanted to show you some cars. I hope you don't mind. We'll be at the Audi dealership in about fifteen minutes."

"Roland! I can't buy a new car right now and certainly not an Audi, even a used one."

"It doesn't hurt to look, and besides, one never knows. We aren't buying anything, just looking."

"I feel a little weird about it, but if you want to look, I'm along for the ride."

After they did the Audis, they stopped to see the BMWs.

"Well, that was impressive, but I still can't see one of those in my future. Perhaps a good used one, but it would have to be reasonable."

"We can look at some used ones when you are ready. I just wanted you to get used to the idea of stepping up. You know, I heard from Sherry last week," he told her. "I had sent her two paintings while she was in Europe. She loved them and even asked if I might be willing to ship her one more for her outer office. I'm sending it tomorrow."

She felt an unexpected chill. "I got an e-mail from mother too. She was okay with the arrangements that my grandfather and I have worked out. My next hurdle will be telling her about the car."

"Did she happen to say anything about me?"

"No, I'm sorry."

"Don't be sorry. I guess we both have to realize that your mother wants to keep her distance from me. Did she tell you I proposed to her when she was here? I thought she came to Washington just as much for me as she did for you and your father, but I guess I was mistaken. She turned me down, and now I have begun to wonder if perhaps the Lord has someone else in mind for me. I think he might.

Do you think your mother will be upset about the car?" he asked, changing the topic.

"I don't know. I haven't told her about it yet, but at this point, it really doesn't make any difference. He has the car. We are happy with the situation, and we aren't going to change it, certainly not because someone three thousand miles away isn't pleased with it, even if it is my mother."

"Well, then leave well enough alone, let's go to dinner."

When they arrived, she commented, "It doesn't look like much, but there are plenty of cars in the parking lot. That's always a good sign."

"Good evening, Mr. Holtz," the greeter said as they walked in. "I have your table ready."

Sitting with the menus after the waiter left them, she said, "You are well known in a lot of the places we go to."

"Well, I do eat out a lot, and I leave a good tip. It's an unbeatable combination. Do you see something you would like?"

As she scanned the menu, she said, "I've been thinking about seafood. How is the fish here?"

"Excellent. Everything is very fresh. If you don't have a favorite, I would recommend the halibut in caper sauce. It is outstanding. That's what I'm having."

"If you recommend it, I'll join you. I was thinking salmon, but I do love good halibut."

"Would you like a glass of wine with your meal? There is a homegrown dry Riesling that I enjoy. It comes from the Columbia Valley, but it has won awards even in France. It goes particularly well with the halibut."

"Sure, I would like a glass, and I am all for supporting local companies."

Everything about the meal had been as good as Roland had indicated it would be. The dishes were taken away, and as they sat enjoying a cup of coffee, reflecting on the day and the meal, he said, "I have something special I want to ask you. It is part of the reason that I wanted just you to come and have dinner with me."

Her heart jumped unexpectedly for a moment before she asked, "What is it?"

"I don't know if I should call it a question or an offer. I guess it's kind of both rolled together. Would you consider coming to work for me?"

For some reason, she felt a twinge of disappointment but then was stunned, "Are you serious? What kind of job could you offer me? Have you gone back to work, taken a position somewhere, or what?"

"No, nothing like that, although one never knows when there may come a full-time opportunity that is too good even for me to ignore. No, I realize I give the impression that I really don't work, but the fact is, even though I no longer work as a CEO, I do consulting work, and I arrange financing for small businesses, especially foreign ones. I am also in the early stages of setting up a foundation to help with that financing. For much of what I do, I can work on my own schedule, but I have allowed the load to become more than I can handle alone—or at least, more than I want to handle alone. So I've been thinking for some time that I could use a personal administrative assistant. We used to call them a personal secretary, but what I really want will go way beyond that. Anyway, I was about ready to start advertising when it came to me that it isn't likely I could find anyone I would rather have to do the job or trust more than you."

She was speechless, but she knew she had to do something other than just stare at him. He was obviously waiting for a response.

All she could come up with was, "Are you seriously offering me a job, really?" And immediately, she felt foolish.

"I think that's what I did. I'm going to hire someone, and I thought I would go with my number one choice first."

"Well," she said, "again I'm flattered, and very surprised, but I don't know. I've never thought about leaving my present job. I'm good at it. And I don't want to sound doubtful or ungrateful, but you haven't known me all that long, and besides, it seems to me you have been getting along just fine without anyone."

"I've gotten along, that's true enough, but I'm at the point where I would appreciate some help in carrying the load. I've seen how you keep a calendar for you and your grandfather. You balance your work, caring for your grandfather, and your personal life. You do a great job. It's also true, I haven't known you very long, but I've been impressed with what I've observed."

"You see, I would like a buffer, someone I can trust to manage my appointments, handle my mail and correspondence, and be able to attend meetings with me to make sure I don't miss things, plus other tasks as they may arise. Right now it's mostly dealing with nonprofits and charities, but I have begun doing more consulting for companies that are having problems with their bottom line. I think your experience could be invaluable there. It's much like what you are already doing at your present position. I think you would be a great fit." The one thing he hadn't told her was that he had begun looking for a reason to spend more time near her.

Looking into his eyes, she took a deep breath and said, "Be completely honest with me. Does this all have anything to do with the relationship between you and my mother?"

It was his turn to be surprised. "No, nothing at all. Why would you think that?"

Marcy sighed. "Well, I asked you to be completely honest, so I will be candid as well. I thought maybe you might just want to use me and this new job as a way to get closer to my mother. Would you have made me this offer if she wasn't my mother?"

"Getting closer to your mother was never my intent. I asked you because I have witnessed your abilities and adaptability, and I know what kind of a job you do at your present position. I think you are capable of a lot more. You already do a type of consulting, and you are good at it. You ask the right questions. I've even gone so far as to have spoken with CEOs of some of the companies you have advised. I have been very impressed. Besides, you can be assured that if I couldn't persuade your mother to agree to become my wife, I am certainly not going to try to wheedle my way into her affections through her family, especially not now when I am having second thoughts. I'm sorry if anything I have said or done has given you that impression."

She felt guilty because it was exactly what she had been thinking all along about his interest in her and especially in her grandfather. Deep down inside, she had considered the possibility that they were pawns in his game with her mother, and it had seemed at least plausible. But now, was there someone else? Had she failed her mother?

On the flip side, she felt immensely relieved. Her appreciation for Roland was growing. He was genuinely being nice to them and concerned about them. At least, it didn't seem to be a ploy to gain influence with her mother, but this job offer was a whole different thing.

Marcy nearly told him no, but instead decided it would be prudent to at least find out more about the offer from him.

"Give me a little more detail about what you would require from your administrative assistant."

"Well, I am looking for someone who can be available when I need them, someone who could work from my office or their own depending on what needed to be done and when, someone who is free to travel with me or for me when necessary. As I said, they would act as a buffer for me, being my contact person and handling much of my correspondence. What I ultimately want is someone who can intuitively understand where I'm headed, who can anticipate my responses and can work hand in hand with me on my affairs. I realize it's a tall order, and it's not something someone could slip into right away, but I am confident we would make a great pair."

"Sounds like you are looking for a wife, not an administrative assistant."

He chuckled.

"Why are you laughing?"

"Because it's ironic. I married my last personal secretary, but don't let that put you off, it is not part of the bargain I am offering today."

"Roland, this is something I never expected, but you have to realize, I think I am finally hitting my stride at work. I've worked hard to get right where I am now. I'm not sure I want to give that up."

"You are starting to sound just like your mother," he said more pointedly than he meant to.

"Yes, well, I am not as successful yet as she is."

"If success is all that you are looking for, you could just as easily find it working for me, maybe even more quickly."

"I don't know if I could make such a transition. Besides, I've never been a secretary or an administrative assistant. But as long as it is on the table, may I ask what would the hours be?"

"I don't know yet, but I can tell you they would vary quite a bit from time to time. I know they won't be onerous. I suspect they will average maybe twenty to twenty-five hours a week, but I will be paying a salary, not an hourly rate."

"And if I should consider the position, may I also ask what might my salary be?"

"I would pay you double what you are getting right now, to start."

"You don't know what I'm getting right now."

"Yes, I do, and I believe you are being underpaid for a person of your talents."

"You are really serious, aren't you? This is pretty sudden, you know. I have to have time to think about it, and for another thing, I am in the process of fleshing out a project, and it could very well go south. It doesn't look good at all, and I would feel guilty if I quit before I had completed it, no matter how it ends up."

"That's not a problem. In fact, I would have been disappointed in you if you were willing to leave them in the lurch with a job half done. As you noted, I have been getting along okay, so even though it would be convenient for me to have someone, I don't have to hire anyone right now. Think about it, and take all the time you need, I'm not in any rush."

"I will, Roland, I promise I will. I'm sorry, it's just so out of the blue that my head is sort of spinning. I've been so absorbed by the project in Houston that there's no room for thinking of other things right now. Give me a few days, and we can talk about it again."

"Fair enough. By the way, could I impose on you to bring that potato salad you make on Tuesday?"

"That's no imposition, I was already planning to bring it. Any other requests?"

He hesitated for a moment before he said, "Since you asked, there is one other thing that I didn't have on my mind when I asked you to join me for dinner. Would you take a ride up on the island with me? It will mean we'll get home sort of late, but you can call Jim and let him know where we are and that he doesn't have to wait up for us. There is something I would like to show you."

"That is no imposition either. I love Whidbey. I'd live there if it wasn't such a long commute."

He looked at her and felt a lump come in his throat. "Someone else once told me that a long time ago," he said. And she could sense the emotion in his voice.

"What is it?"

"You will see. It will be another surprise."

Riding the ferry, he had her watching with him to see if they could see any salmon jumping.

"It won't be long before they start showing up," Roland explained, "and when they do, it's not unusual to see a jumper once in a while." There were none.

At first, it seemed like they were heading for Oak Harbor. She thought maybe there was something at Amanda's that they were going to see, or maybe something at the base or the marina. Could he possibly have a new boat? As they drove, it became obvious they were not going to Amanda's or the base. They didn't stop in Oak Harbor.

Finally, he pulled off the road, and getting out, he walked up to a locked gate guarding a gravel driveway. He unlocked and opened the gate. Getting back into the vehicle, he started up and pulled down onto the drive, stopping to lock the gate, and then they drove toward the ocean.

They arrived at a point where the gravel path made a wide loop. There was nothing there—only a few trees, tall, browning grass, brush, and Whidbey's omnipresent blackberry bushes. It felt a little strange to be off in the middle of nowhere.

As he opened her door and invited her to step out, she asked uncertainly, "Where are we?"

"It's my property," he answered. "I bought it years ago to build a house here. Betty and I had seen the property advertised, and we looked at it one afternoon as the sun was going down over the ocean. She fell in love with it. She said she would move right then if it wasn't such a long commute. So we decided to buy it and began planning.

We were going to build a house and retire here after the children were grown and bring Amanda here to live with us. I could have sold it a hundred times since then for a nice profit, but I've held on to it. I don't know why. Just the memories, I guess. I have a man come and mow and brush hog the area every so often, but other than that, it is just as it was. Doesn't look like my man has been here lately, though, I'll have to check on him."

As they slowly walked around the loop, Marcy looked at the trees, the ocean, and the sun dipping toward the horizon. She felt relieved. There was nothing ominous about their stop. Everything was so tranquil and so beautiful. She felt a bit ashamed that she had had any misgivings, even if they were only momentary.

"I think I can understand. This place is begging to have a beautiful home with people who love it and will take care of it. Thank you for showing it to me."

Nodding his head, he said nothing, but inside, the return of some of the old pains and regrets nearly brought him to tears. They walked silently back to the car. Opening her door, he let her get in. Closing the door, he slowly walked to his side of the vehicle and entered. He was conscious of the faint presence of her perfume.

"Would you mind if we stayed just a little longer and watch the sun go down?"

"No, of course, I wouldn't mind. It's so peaceful here. I think a person could be content here, never worrying about what the next day might bring."

They sat quietly as the sun slowly sank out of sight. He nearly reached over to take her hand but thought better of it. Afterward, driving back up to the gate in the gathering twilight, he wished he had.

It wasn't until the land and the gate had disappeared behind them that he said, "I know it's going to be late when we get home, but would you mind if we stopped for just a few minutes at Amanda's?"

"No, I don't mind. In fact, I was hoping we could stop and see her."

The lights were on in her home when they pulled into the driveway, and she met them at the door.

"Well, look who's here. Come in. You are out kind of late, aren't you? Were you out in the boat? You didn't call me."

"Whoa, hold on, we didn't call you because we only went out for dinner and then decided to take a drive, but we are planning to go out crabbing Tuesday if you are up to it."

"Sure, I'm up to it. I thought maybe you had forgotten me. You must have gotten a pretty late start this afternoon to be getting here so late."

"Not really. We took a drive after dinner. I wanted to show Marcy the lot. It's been awhile since I had checked on it."

"Really?" she gave him a strange look, and then turning to Marcy, she asked, "What did you think of the lot, young lady?"

"It's beautiful but very melancholy as well."

"He must have told you about the history of the lot, right?"

"Yes, he did."

"Mother, she knows about Betty, and I told her how it had been going to be our special place, and we stayed to watch the sun go down. That's all. That's why we are so late."

"Well, whatever, I'm glad you stopped by. Would you like a cup of coffee for the road?"

"No, I need to get Marcy back home before Jim starts thinking something has happened to us or that I ran off with her. We have to get going, but you be ready Tuesday morning unless the weather is bad. I'll call you."

As they walked out the door, Amanda laid her hand on Marcy's arm and whispered, "I'm looking forward to talking to you on Tuesday. Don't let him fall asleep going home."

As they pulled out of the driveway, he asked, "What did Amanda say to you when we were leaving?"

"She said not to let you fall asleep and that she was looking forward to Tuesday."

"Okay, you can keep me awake. Now, would you mind calling Jim and let him know we are going to be way late. We should have done it earlier."

Somewhere near Anacortes, her eyelids grew heavy, and she was asleep before they reached Route 5, but he didn't mind at all. It had been a wonderful afternoon. He hoped that she had taken his offer to heart. While it was true that he had been thinking about an assistant for some time, somehow it hadn't become a priority until he had thought about Marcy taking the position.

She awoke before they were home and felt a bit guilty because Amanda had asked her to keep him awake and she had fallen asleep on the job.

As they pulled into her driveway, she said, "Don't tell Amanda that I fell asleep on the way home."

"I won't mention it, and I had a very enjoyable evening. Perhaps we can do it again another night."

As she got out of the car, she said, "I'll think about the job. I'm not being negative about it, but I can't give you an answer, not yet. Give me a little while."

"Take all the time you need. Like I said, I'm in no hurry. You get a good night's rest."

His eyes followed her gently swaying hips until she was safely inside before he drove away. He was still thinking about her and how much he wanted her to accept his job offer when he slipped into bed a short time later. He also felt a bit guilty.

She threw herself back into the project the next day at the office. The culmination of her trip to Houston and the follow-up by the team wasn't the only thing on her mind, but she put Roland and his job offer way off in the corner. There was too much riding on what she had to do without being distracted by something more pleasant. The team had arrived at the same conclusion she had, and now she needed to draw all their thoughts together in a position paper for Houston. They would need to meet again on Monday to review it.

She didn't finish on Friday, so Saturday saw her putting the finishing touches to her work. When she finally read through the document, she was satisfied, and she put it aside to let it rest until Monday. Then she left her room to find her grandfather.

Walking into her office on Monday, Marcy looked around at her other world. She had never noticed before how really drab it was. She sat down behind her desk, put down some papers, and turned on the computer. Sipping a coffee she had picked up at the shop downstairs, she remembered what Roland's office had looked like. It had some personality. It was warm, not sterile, and she recalled how she had felt drawn into it when they had all been given a tour. There had been a couple of paintings, a few decoys, family photographs, and even a love seat.

Strange, she thought, *I can't remember the color of the walls.*

"Have you finished up on Houston?" she heard her boss ask.

Popping out of her reverie, she answered, "I'm just getting ready to review it, but like I warned you last week, I think this one is really a nonstarter. We spent all last week on this, and we can't find a way to make it work—not one we would recommend, at least. We came up with lots of reasons for them to drop it, but I'm going over it one more time. It doesn't seem to fit in with their core business, and in the back of my mind, I have this nagging suspicion that they weren't completely convinced themselves that they should be doing this. I'll have the final report on your desk before the end of the day."

"Will you be here tomorrow?" he asked.

"No, that's my day off, and I really need a break. This has been a surprisingly stressful assignment, but I'll be available the rest of the week."

"That's fine. I'll call Houston and send them the report tomorrow. It may be better that you aren't here when I do that anyway. Everything else under control?"

"Yes." She wondered what he was talking about since he had limited her to working on this one project. "That is, unless you are dropping something else on me that I'm not aware of. Why did you ask that? Have I forgotten something?"

"No, just force of habit, I guess. I'm always a step or two ahead of myself. Well, you are doing a great job. I'm looking forward to seeing the final analysis."

When he was gone, she pulled up the project. She remembered being really excited about it when they first began, but now the only thing she wanted was to have it completed. She knew that wouldn't really be the end of it. She would almost certainly have to meet again with company officials to make a presentation, but still the heavy lifting was nearly done, and the light at the end of the tunnel was coming into view.

Once again, she looked around the office.

Is this really what I want to be doing for the next twenty years of my life? she thought. *Do I really want this job to define who I am?*

Roland had been right. She was becoming like her mother. She had never thought about it that way before, but for now, she had to bring herself back to the moment and get on track. She had everything completed and on her boss's desk by three o'clock. It felt like the day had been twelve hours long.

The city traffic seemed to be heavier than usual when she finally headed for home. Once she was on Route 90, she felt more comfortable, but she was dying to get home and put her feet up. Tomorrow she would be crabbing. She could hardly wait, and who knew what the rest of the week might bring. Wednesday would probably find her with a new assignment.

As she neared home, she wondered what would be on the menu tonight. She knew her grandfather would have something delicious ready for her. It had turned out he wasn't just a competent cook; he was a great cook. And not only that, he enjoyed planning the meals and putting them together. In a few weeks, she had stopped feeling guilty about doing so little cooking herself and let him just go for it.

She could smell dinner when she walked through the door. She walked into the kitchen and found her grandfather busily finishing a wonderful-looking tossed salad.

"Hi, girl," he said.

"Hi, Grandpa, what's for dinner, spaghetti? It smells great."

"Lasagna. It hasn't been in too long. I got started on it a bit late, so I'm letting it finish up while I make the salad."

"Sounds good. I was just thinking today about what a good cook you are. I'm going to put on weight if I'm not careful. I'm one fortunate lady."

"I'll take all that as a compliment, but I don't know what I'd do with myself if I wasn't cooking and keeping things shipshape. It would be really tough for you if you had to take care of me and do all the cooking and cleaning in addition to your regular job, so I feel needed and appreciated."

"If you don't mind, I'm going to stretch out on the couch and put my feet up until dinner is ready. If I should doze off, make sure you get me up. I'd rather eat than sleep," she said.

"You've probably got about twenty-five minutes before everything is ready. You must have had a tough day today."

She was asleep almost as soon as she put her feet up. He came in to get her about a half hour later but decided dinner could wait a few more minutes and sat down and looked at her. He loved her so much that he often found himself mourning those lost years of her childhood.

"We can't change things and go back to do them over differently," he said to himself, "but how I wish we could, she's such a wonderful girl."

She woke with a start and saw him looking at her. "Dinner's ready?"

"Yes, it took a little longer than I expected. I was just going to wake you up."

"Well, let's eat. I'm starved. Work took a lot out of me today."

As she ate, she said, "I wonder where Roland is and what he's doing right now."

"He's probably having a steak and a glass of wine in a fancy restaurant, maybe even wondering what you're doing right now yourself," he said with a smile.

"He probably has enough on his mind to keep him occupied without thinking of us."

"I didn't say us."

"Grandpa! What do you mean by that?"

"Well, nothing really, but then again, he did take you out to dinner."

23

CRABBING WITH AMANDA

They picked Amanda up at ten Tuesday morning. She had seemed ready and raring to go, which was unusual when it came to crabbing. It was a short drive down to the marina. Roland and Jim saw to getting the bags and the bait down to the boat.

Amanda glanced sideways at Marcy when she asked, "Can I help with anything?"

Roland looked at the two of them and replied, "Why don't you and Mother just go on down and get onboard. We can get these things."

When everything was onboard and the engines were running, Marcy stepped off onto the dock, waiting for Roland to ask for the lines to be cast off. After the command was given, Amanda raised her eyebrows when he left the controls and took Marcy's hand, needlessly assisting her as she got back onto the boat. Then she had another surprise as Marcy picked up the lines and coiled them neatly on the deck.

He had watched her with the lines and then waited while she walked back to sit beside Amanda, before turning away and putting the boat into gear to move out of the slip. Once they were out, Jim pulled in the bumpers and joined Roland in the cabin.

As the *Melissa* slowly moved away from the marina, Amanda said, "So tell me a little about yourself. I know your mother owns Robyn's World. I met her while she was here. I know you appear to enjoy crabbing and being out on the ocean and that you can clean crabs and make great potato salad. I also know you share your home with your grandfather. That's about it. So tell me, what do you do? Does your mother take care of your expenses?"

Marcy was irritated momentarily but realized the question was probably a logical one.

"No, I work in Seattle and at home. I'm a business consultant and planner. I just got back a short time ago from working on a project in Houston. My mother has always wanted me to work for Robyn's World, but I wanted to make my own way and pay my own bills. She offered to buy me a house once, but I bought my own. I'm my own person."

She continued, "I'm a pretty good cook. I do more than potato salad. I attend the Snoqualmie Valley Alliance Church, and I just recently asked Jesus to be my Savior and Lord. Roland had a lot to do with that."

"Yes, I did know that. He was quite excited about both you and your mother coming to the Lord in such a short time."

"It was amazing, Amanda. I never understood what I needed before he explained it to me, and then suddenly, it all made sense."

He gazed in their direction momentarily from time to time. It appeared they were already having a good time, and he was pleased that they were hitting it off so well.

Amanda was aware he was watching.

"Do you have plans for the future? Do you have a boyfriend?" she asked.

Again, there was a slight bit of annoyance at the pointed personal question, but she said, "I want to move up in our business, and I am pretty sure I am going to get a promotion in the near future. And no, I don't have a boyfriend, but I haven't given up hope."

"What's the problem? I can't imagine that no man has found you attractive?"

"There's no problem. I just haven't found the right one. I want a man that respects me and that I can respect in turn, and now that I've become a Christian, I want a man that is a Christian also. Most of the men that I have dated were more interested in what they could get out of a relationship rather than what they could put into one. I've never hopped into bed with any man, and I'm not about to start now. That's what way too many men think is going to happen. Well, not with me. When I find the right man who truly loves me and wants to marry me, not hop into bed with me, I'll know it. That's the man I'm looking for." Then she turned the tables. "So how about you, Amanda? How come you've never remarried?"

"Oh, my dear, I had a wonderful marriage. We were so happy, and we thought we would grow old together. When my husband was lost over Vietnam, a huge part of me died with him. There were men who were interested in me, even a couple of his fellow pilots, but I just had no interest in another man. As I have grown older, I have come to realize that I might have been better off, perhaps even happier, if I had been willing to start again, but a broken heart is a tough thing to mend."

"I'm so sorry, Amanda."

"Thank you, but God sent another special person into my life when Roland married my daughter. They were as happy as her father and I had been, and just as much in love. I was ecstatic. I won't go into it, but he had rescued her from a pit of despair and made her life worth living again. I loved him for that. But then just like me, he lost the love of his life and had a tough time dealing with it. Now I believe after all these years, he has finally come to the point where he is ready to live again, and he seems to have placed all his chips on your mother. But with all due respect, I'm not at all sure that's a good bet." Looking straight into Marcy's eyes, she asked, "Honestly, what do you think?"

Staring back at Amanda, she felt a strange panic begin to seize her, and she had to look away as she answered, "I don't know, Amanda." Looking back at her, she said, "I know he cared for her, but my mother seems to be conflicted between her business and getting married again. However, when she came out here, she was actually thinking about marrying him if he asked. I thought it would be a done deal. I thought she would jump at the chance, but then suddenly, things changed, and I'm not sure exactly why."

"Do you think she will change her mind?"

"I don't know. Perhaps, but somehow I don't think so. Maybe it doesn't even matter."

"Well, if it isn't to be, he will get over it. There are plenty of women that would, as you say, jump at the chance to marry him, but that has always been true. I think he is still looking for someone special, just as you are. I hope you both find what you are looking for."

The boat was now moving up on plane as it headed out of the harbor toward Camano Island in the distance. The air felt refreshing and clean.

Amanda took a deep breath and then asked her, "Do you know what I love about the ocean?"

"No, what?"

"Everything, but most of all, I like just being out here in a boat with friends and family. There is no place quite like it anywhere else in the world. I especially like the fishing, crabbing not so much."

"I believe I have to agree with you about everything being so great out here, but I do like crabbing, so I'm glad that he likes to have me come along with my grandfather when they go. There is something special about it. I'm always a bit sad when the day comes to an end. I'd almost like it to go on forever. Amanda, what do you do with your time in Oak Harbor? Why don't you live with Roland or at least near him?"

"It's not his fault. He has asked me many times to come and live with him, but my home is here on Whidbey. Sometimes I still drive over near the base and watch the A6s land and take off. I used to do that when my husband was based here. I'd watch for his plane. He knew I'd be there watching, and he would waggle his wings just a bit as he passed over. I know I will never see him again on this earth, but I feel closer to him when I watch those aircraft drop in from the sky. I can't bring myself to leave that behind.

"As for the rest of my time, I do a lot of reading, and I help out at church. I make meals for those who need them, for some reason beyond their control. I love to fish, and when the salmon are running, Roland sees to it that I get out a few times. The other thing I do is go fishing by myself. I just go down to the marina or drive up to Coronet Bay and fish for smelt in one of those places. It's not hard to catch enough for a dinner. I don't need many. I like jigging for them. In the spring, we go out a few times for halibut. It can be a bit boring, you don't get a lot of bites, but when you catch one, you've got some great eating. It seems like there is always something to do."

"I thought I saw in the paper that the Navy was going to retire the A6s," Marcy said.

"It's true, and I will miss them when they are gone," Amanda said. "But they are still flying them for now. I love the roar they make when they are coming in to land. No other jet sounds quite like them." Then she added, "Tell me, what do you think of my son-in-law?"

The question came right out of the blue and caught her off guard, but she had a fairly safe answer.

"He's a real gentleman. He's thoughtful, cares about people, and I love the way he has sort of taken Grandfather under his wing. Did you know he took him car shopping?"

"No, I didn't know that. Jim is buying a car?"

"Actually, he has already purchased it, but I'll let him tell you about it. I don't want to steal his thunder."

They were still talking as they felt the engines throttling back and the boat slowed in preparation for dropping the pots. In a few minutes, the men came walking to the stern, each carrying two traps.

"We are in about forty feet of water. We should continue to drift a little bit closer while I bait the traps, and then we will get to crabbing," Roland said.

"We're only going to put out four traps?" Marcy asked.

"Well, four spread out here and then a couple more down the island a ways, but that's all, just six. We have lots of time, so we will let them soak real well before we check them. Have you ever played hearts? It's Amanda's favorite card game."

"No, I don't play cards very much, but I'm willing to learn."

"Great, we'll get the traps out, and then we will teach you and Jim how it's played. It's pretty simple, really, and it helps pass the time while we are waiting for the crabs to find the bait."

As soon as the four traps were down about one hundred feet apart, the boat moved a quarter of a mile before the last two traps were sent to the bottom, and Roland pulled the boat away far enough to anchor without bothering the traps or hungry crabs.

"Let's move into the cabin," he said. "The breeze isn't much, but it might blow the cards around. We will have time for about three or four games before we have to head back down for the first traps."

Roland and Amanda spent about five minutes giving Marcy and her grandfather a basic introduction to the game and some suggestions about strategy, and then the game was on. Everyone was having such a good time that the hour passed quickly. Amanda won three out of the four games they played.

Roland gathered up the cards and said, "I should have warned you. She is just as good at playing cards as she is at catching big salmon. Let's go see how our traps are doing."

While he guided the boat back to the first traps, Marcy got the tub and the bucket and brought them back to the stern.

"Now we are ready," she said to Amanda.

"They could have gotten those. Did he ask you to do that?"

"No, but he's busy, and I don't want my grandfather to work too much while he is out here. I want him to relax and have fun. Besides, I like to help out and be useful."

"Well, why don't you sit down and relax for a few minutes more yourself. I have a few more questions."

She sat down next to her and said, "Okay, what do you want to talk about?"

"Well, I was wondering what you thought about the lot that he showed you the other day."

"Oh, it was a lovely location. I can understand why he bought it. I could picture myself just sitting on a porch in a place like that, watching the sun slip into the ocean."

"You liked it that much?"

"Yes, we sat in the car and watched as the sun set before we left. It was so peaceful, so . . . so perfect."

"He bought it for Betty, for a place where they would be able get away from everything from time to time. They said they would retire there someday and take me there to live with them. He even had an architect draw up the plans, but then she was gone, both her and our wonderful Melissa."

"Yes, I know, he told me," she replied softly.

"I don't think he has ever taken anyone else there besides me and Bryce over all these years. He let you into a part of his world that he has kept locked away for way too long."

"I could tell that it was very special to him." Marcy thought for a moment and then asked, "By the way, Amanda, did he ever tell you he was thinking about hiring a personal administrative assistant?"

"Yes, he has mentioned it two or three times in the past, but nothing ever came of it. Why?"

"Well, he asked me the other day if I would be interested."

Amanda sat up straight and said, "Really? What did you tell him?"

"I didn't give him a real answer. I told him I would have to think about it."

"Well, Marcy, I realize it's none of my business, but you know there probably wouldn't be a better person in the whole world to work for."

"I think you are probably right, but I'm just not sure I want to make that change right now."

Amanda shrugged her shoulders as the boat started to slow down with the first buoy ahead, bobbing off the starboard bow.

Jim came back with the boat hook and reached out, snagging the buoy as it neared the stern and pulling it back to the side of the boat just in time for Marcy to grab the rope and start pulling the trap toward the surface.

"It feels like we've got a good catch," she said.

Roland arrived in time to hoist the first trap over the rail, and indeed, it was stuffed with crab.

"We'll surely get a few keepers from this bunch. It looks like it is going to be a banner day," he said as he began emptying the trap into the tub.

Marcy grabbed the tongs and began the process of sorting the catch. The good-looking males were dropped in the bucket to be measured after the rest were released. Then she began checking them for legal size.

Roland said, "Don't keep anything that isn't at least six and a half inches. We should get plenty without having to keep the ones that are just over legal, and watch for soft shells."

"Aye, aye, Captain," she replied.

The end result was five fine crabs in the cooler; it was a great start. "At this rate, we might have our limit even before we pull all the traps. The crabs are really plentiful this year."

He was right, and when the last trap was onboard, they had a limit of large crabs—some close to seven inches and a couple that looked huge.

"It's time to prepare dinner," he said.

"What are we going to do with so many?" Marcy asked.

"I told the pastor that we would bring him enough for his family if we had good luck, and Mother can always use a couple. And I have a few other people that won't be offended with a free crab or two. I have never found it to be any problem to get rid of extra crabs."

Amanda and Jim sat together and visited while they watched as the pair cooked and cleaned crabs for dinner plus several others that would be put on ice. It was apparent that they were enjoying the task that she had always tried to avoid. It wasn't that she couldn't do it or hadn't done it when necessary, but she was happy to let others do the honors.

She remembered having watched Betty and Roland happily engaged in the same role so many times. Nothing that they had done together ever seemed to be distasteful or beneath them. She was thinking that now, here was someone he obviously enjoyed being around, and she seemed to have no problem helping him with menial tasks. Why shouldn't she be his assistant, and who knows? It would probably be a very good move for both of them.

"This meal is superb," Jim said. "I think Dungeness crab is the best seafood I've ever had, and I love the venue. I never thought before Marcy brought me to Washington that I would be drinking fine wine and eating crab on a big luxurious boat in the middle of the ocean."

"Well, this isn't a really big boat, Jim, and the sound isn't quite the middle of the ocean."

"It's closer than I ever dreamed I would get. And speaking of dreams, Amanda, did you know that I have a new car? Well, not a new car actually, but a really nice used one, thanks to Roland."

"Really? What did you buy?" she asked smiling, glancing at Marcy.

"It's a Mercedes," and he went on to describe it in great detail.

When he had finished, Amanda said, "Maybe I'll get a chance to see it one of these days."

"I'll make sure you do. It's a beauty."

While Jim and Amanda visited, Marcy and Roland picked up the leftovers and the dishes and took them to the galley.

"Well, wash or dry?" he asked.

"I think I'll dry," she answered with a smile.

As they were finishing up the dishes, he asked, "Have you come to any decision on my offer?"

"Not yet. You said you weren't in any rush, and I've been really busy. But honestly, I have been thinking about it. You put away the pots and pans, and I'll put up the stemware."

When they had finished, he said, "You know, I don't know what is wrong with my head. Here I've been, talking about people who would like some crabs, and I forgot about you guys. Would you and Jim like a couple of the crabs to take home? They keep real well in the fridge."

"I'm sure he won't turn them down," said Marcy. "Of course, it won't be quite the same as eating out here on the *Melissa,* but we can rough it."

"Done then, you've got two crabs. I'll wash down the crab pots, and then we'll head in. I don't know when I'll be able to get out again, but I'll try and make it when you can go, and it shouldn't be too long before the silvers show up either."

That afternoon, when they got back to Amanda's, she invited them in for coffee, as usual, and it was ready shortly after she had put her crabs away in the fridge.

Coming back into the living room, she said, "You know, I actually enjoyed crabbing today. Maybe it was the company that made the difference."

"Well, that doesn't say much for me, Mother."

"Oh, shaw. You know I always enjoy being with you even if it is crabbing, no matter how much I complain, but having guests made it a special day."

"Apology accepted, I think," he smiled.

Later, on the way back to Snoqualmie, Jim could hardly stop talking about the crabbing, about the *Melissa*, how beautiful the ocean had been, and how much he enjoyed just sitting and talking with Amanda.

"We have a lot in common in some ways. You know, Roland, she gets lonely in Oak Harbor even with all the friends she has. I know what that's like. I felt it before Marcy brought me out here. She didn't say so, but I know she would be hurting a lot if it wasn't for you visiting her so often. I really like Amanda. She told me the salmon should be in anytime now, and she said to make sure I come with you when you go."

"I don't know just when they'll show up, but it won't be long. And certainly, you are both invited when we go."

Marcy hated to see the day end when he took them home. She told him, "I'm going to be busy during the next few days, but I know I'll be thinking about today. Thanks so much."

That night, lying in bed, she spent some time thinking about Roland and his job offer. It seemed from Amanda's comments that it was legit. But the idea that it might still be tied to her mother, in spite of what he said, was haunting her. It was the one thing that was holding her back from accepting the offer. On the other hand, it was exciting to think about having the chance to work closely with him, and it was more about that than the money the job would bring.

She wondered if it would be possible to take the job without her mother knowing anything about it. If she didn't know, at least it couldn't possibly be used to draw her closer to Roland. It seemed either so complicated or so easy, but she couldn't make up her mind which one.

She decided to try one other thing. She prayed, "Lord, I need your help. I need to make a decision, and I'm having a hard time with it. Please help me to know what I should do. I don't know if you are willing to help me out with this sort of thing, but if you are, I'd like to know what I should do when I wake up tomorrow morning. Thank you. Amen." In a few moments, she was asleep.

There was no answer in the morning.

Wednesday was sort of a letdown after the last assignment. On her desk were a couple of folders, the next jobs in her future. But as she looked at them, she wondered if maybe there really was something better. She couldn't help thinking about Roland's offer, even if she had gotten no help from on high. As she looked at the material from the office in the first envelope, all she could think was, *Why not?*

She was not very effective that day, but she did force herself to go through the two folders and start making some notes. Between thinking about Houston and Roland's offer, she found it impossible to get her head into the new materials, and finally, she had to leave a little early taking the folders with her.

Wednesday was a different experience for Roland. He called Amanda.

"Hi, Mother, I hope you really did have a good time yesterday, it sure looked like you did."

"I had a great time. Marcy and her grandfather are very nice people. I enjoyed visiting with both of them. I learned you offered her a job working for you."

"I did. What else did you talk about?"

"Oh my, we talked about a lot of things, about Robyn's World, her mother, her grandfather, and her job and where she saw herself going with it if she didn't take your offer. We also talked about church and boyfriends."

"Boyfriends?" She couldn't see him raising his eyebrows. "She has boyfriends?"

"A young lady as attractive and intelligent as she is will always have her admirers, but surprisingly, she doesn't seem to have a boyfriend. She actually wanted to talk about me and what I did living by myself and why I never remarried. She also wondered why I didn't come and live with you."

"I've wondered that myself. You know you are welcome to come and live with me. I would love to have you. The invitation is always good."

"You just want someone to cook for you and do your laundry," she said. When he started to protest, she stopped him, "No, I'm just yanking your chain. You have been a wonderful, considerate son-in-law, and I know I would enjoy living with you, but I am so tied to Oak Harbor and all my friends I don't think I could leave all that."

"Well, it's good enough for me that you know I'd take you in a heartbeat."

24

JIM TAKES A DRIVE

Thursday morning at breakfast, Jim announced, "Marcy, I'm going to take a little drive today. I thought I might even hop on a ferry and poke around a bit. Are you okay with that?"

She knew it would be coming, but she hadn't thought it would be quite so soon. She wasn't 100 percent comfortable with the idea yet, but on the other hand, he had been fine navigating around the local areas.

She swallowed hard and said, "Well, you have your GPS, and you can call me if you need to, so I don't see any reason why you shouldn't spread your wings a bit. Do you have a ferry schedule? Where do you think you will go? Do you have any idea?"

"I don't need a schedule. I thought I might drive up to Mukilteo and take the ferry over to Whidbey. I think the traffic will be pretty light once I get on the island."

"Grandpa, are you going up to Oak Harbor?"

He smiled, "Yes, I am. I promised Amanda on the boat the other day that she would get to see my new car sometime, and I called her yesterday while you were at work to make sure she would be home. I just need to let her know I'm actually coming today, if you're okay with it."

"You have Amanda's number? Sometimes I'm amazed at you, Grandpa, but you know what you want to do, and I'm just crazy enough to let you go do it. Besides, you don't really need my permission, but I do appreciate your asking and letting me know where you're going. When do you think you will be getting back?"

"I am leaving as soon as I have the meat in the crock pot. Then up on the island, I'm taking Amanda out to lunch. I don't have a plan beyond that, but I expect I'll be back here in time for dinner. If I'm not, you can start without me if you want to."

"That's fine. I'm working here today, so we can probably just eat when you get home. I suggest you get an early start back, or you will get into some pretty heavy traffic, okay?"

"Okay, I can do that. Would you like me to call you when I get to Oak Harbor so you won't have to worry about me?"

"I'm not going to worry about you, Grandpa."

"Now, you know that's a lie. You will be worrying about me all day until you see me here tonight. But I'll be fine, and I'll stay in touch."

He had been right, of course. She thought about his big adventure all morning, wondering just where he was and how he was doing. It was a little hard to stay on track once she was working, but she finally let it go and zeroed in on what she was being paid for.

He found the traffic a little heavy until he had gotten past Everett, but then he breathed a little easier and the rest of the way to the ferry was a piece of cake. He paid his fare and got in line to board.

Wanting to stretch his legs after the drive, he got out and walked down toward the pier where he could watch the ferry in the distance as it plowed its way toward the dock. Once it was getting close, he returned to his car, where he waited until the load of vehicles getting off the ferry had moved by up the hill. Then as the vehicles in his lane boarded the ship, he drove on cautiously but found that there really was nothing to it. Of course, he had been on the ferry in Roland's car, but it was a little different doing it oneself, even if it wasn't hard.

He got out of his car and went to the upper deck for a better view as the ferry began its trip back across the channel toward Whidbey. It wouldn't be long before he would be in Oak Harbor. He felt like a teenager with his first car. He was so eager to show off his Mercedes to Amanda.

He had an easy drive up the island, and the first thing he did when he arrived at his destination was call Marcy to let her know he had arrived safely. As he was talking with her, Amanda had come out of the house and was walking down the drive toward him. He said a quick good-bye and got out of the car to meet her.

She spoke first, "Well, that's one nifty car, all right. Have any problem getting here?"

"No, it was a piece of cake. I loved every minute of it. Come on over, and get a closer look."

He was beaming as she inspected the car inside and out. He even opened the hood so she could take a peek.

"I told you it was a beauty. I feel like a king when I'm riding in it. I never owned anything even close to it before. It's still almost like a dream to me, and my granddaughter is okay with my driving pretty much wherever I want to go. It's like I've started a second life these days."

"Good for you. There's nothing quite like getting a second lease on life, and it looks like you are doing it in spades in a number of ways. You are a very fortunate man. I'm very happy for you."

"You're right. I got the chance to come and live with Marcy, to meet Roland, to get my daughter back, to find out my cancer had disappeared, and I got a great car. And I got the chance to meet you."

"Well, lucky you," she said smiling.

"Lucky or not, I'm enjoying life again. I thought my life was over when I was lying in the hospital before Marcy came to see me. I didn't care if I lived or died. It's been like a whirlwind ever since then. So many things have happened so quickly it makes my head spin. The Lord has been so good to me, I can't thank him enough."

"Well, amen to that."

"So where would you like to go for lunch?"

"There is a Chinese restaurant that I like. If you like Chinese, they have an excellent buffet."

"Chinese it is then. If you're ready, hop into my car, and tell me how to get there," and he held the door open for her.

That afternoon, over portions of Gen Tso's chicken and pork egg foo young, they shared many more things about their earlier lives. It was cathartic for both of them to reminisce and put things into perspective with their current situation, and when he took her back home, they both had a new picture and appreciation for each other.

Before he left, he told her, "We'll have to do this again sometime."

"I'll look forward to it," she answered. "Maybe we could pack a lunch and go watch the planes come in at the base, or maybe go up to Coronet Bay and do a bit of fishing."

It had been such an enjoyable day that he felt almost like he was floating on air as he drove back down to the ferry. Once he was back at Mukilteo, he called Marcy and let her know that he was on his way back and should be home in time for dinner. Even the traffic back to Snoqualmie didn't dampen his spirit.

She heard him come in. She took a few minutes to straighten up her papers before she came out of her office. She found him humming to himself and setting the table.

"Well, you sound happy. I take it you had a good day."

"You bet! I didn't have a bit of trouble driving, and Amanda and I had a really good time at lunch. She is a super person, you know. I enjoyed talking with her. I'd visited a little with her on the boat, but this was a lot more relaxed. I'm going to go back sometime, and she is going to take me to watch the A6s and other planes coming into the base. She said we could pack a picnic lunch and make a day of it, maybe even run up and do a little fishing at Coronet Bay. You know, she is just fun to be around. I like her."

"Well, sounds like Roland has some competition. I wonder what he will think of you squiring his mother-in-law around."

"You are picking on me, but I think he will be fine with it. He wants her to enjoy herself, and he has encouraged her to make new friends. I'd say I sort of fill that bill in both ways."

She changed the topic, "Is that pot roast I've been smelling? I'm famished for some reason tonight. Is it all ready?"

"I'll put it on the table in about fifteen minutes. The meat will be tender. It's been cooking on low all day. I put the vegetables in with it to warm up when I came in. I cooked them yesterday. I'm not all that hungry. I made a pig out of myself at the restaurant, but I will have a little bit. The leftovers will be good for your lunch tomorrow. You know, Amanda asked me if you had made any decision about taking the job that Roland offered you. What job is that anyway?"

"Well, he wants to hire me as his personal administrative assistant."

"What does that mean?"

"That's what I asked him. At first, it seemed to me like he wanted someone to work as a glorified secretary, but it's a lot more than that from what he told me. I would handle a lot of items that he has been dealing with himself, and in some ways, I'd be doing a job sort of similar to what I'm doing now. Actually, the more I think about it, the more challenging I think it could be."

"So have you made any decision?"

"I think so, but I'm not positive yet. He said I didn't need to be in any rush to decide. I would still have some loose ends to take care of at work if I do accept his offer. He understands that too, and Amanda thinks I would be crazy not to take the offer, she told me so."

"So are you saying you might be going to go for it? Because, you know, for what it's worth, I agree with Amanda, I think you would be missing a good thing too if you didn't take it."

"Yes, I believe I'm going to accept the offer, but don't you dare tell anyone yet, especially Amanda. I'll tell Roland I am leaning that way, but I'm going to ask him to walk me through the things he actually wants me to deal with before I make a commitment. I want to be sure I can handle the job, but more than that, I want to make sure it isn't some sort of a make-work job. He has assured me that it isn't just a way to get to my mother, but getting the job offer is such a coincidence that I need to be sure."

"I understand, but I think he can be trusted. I don't think he would lie to you."

"I think so too, but I've got to be sure. You can see that, can't you?"

"Yes, I can, and I know you will make the right decision when everything is said and done. I won't say anything to anyone until you know for sure what you are going to do."

"Thanks, Grandfather. I promise I won't keep you waiting too long. In fact, I'm going to call him after dinner and set up a time to look at what I would be working with. Now let's eat. I can't wait any longer."

That evening she called him. He wasn't in, but she left a message, telling him she wanted to discuss his job offer. It wasn't until about eight thirty that he called back.

"Hi, Marcy, I got your message. How would you like to do this?"

"What I'd like to do is come over and look at what you are doing and get a better idea of just what my part would be. I am thinking about accepting, but I want to be sure I can handle the job before I make that decision."

"That makes sense. It's a little late to do that now, but anytime tomorrow would be fine if you could do it. I expect to be home all day, so just give me a call to let me know when you will be coming."

"I can tell you now. I will be there at three o'clock. If I run into a snag, I'll let you know."

"Three o'clock it is. I look forward to seeing you."

25

WHAT'S BEHIND THE MAN

The next day was a mixed bag at work. Before noon, she was already thinking about her meeting with Roland. She realized she didn't have any questions to ask him other than what she would actually be doing. She had already been given some information when he asked her to work for him, but she wanted more detail. At eleven, her boss informed her that she and the team would be headed for Houston Monday afternoon for a Tuesday meeting. They would be returning Wednesday morning.

She pulled the team together and informed them about the meeting. She advised them to bring everything they would need to back up their conclusions.

She ended by cautioning, "When each of us explains our reasons for not recommending they go ahead, we will have to be as careful as we can to avoid stepping on any toes. You know from experience, it's always easier to give a project a boost than to throw up red flags or put up a stop sign. We don't want to make anyone look bad, but this is probably somebody's pet project we will be tearing down. We don't want to make any enemies, but we don't want to put our business in a bad light. At the end of the day, I want everyone to have a good taste in their mouth. We will meet at ten Monday morning to go over any last-minute details."

She really wasn't worried about Tuesday when she left Friday afternoon. She knew their work was sound, and this wasn't the first time any of them were involved in delivering a message that the client didn't want to hear. Her mind turned to her meeting with Roland instead. She could have just told him yes, but she couldn't visualize why he would need an assistant. That's what he was going to have to show in order to convince her.

She rang his bell at precisely two fifty-five, and a few moments later, he opened the door. And immediately, she had the foolish feeling she was going to be his assistant no matter what transpired. He walked her to his office and offered her a seat.

"Now, what can I show you or tell you?"

"I want you to show me why you need an assistant and convince me I am the one for the job."

"Well, that's cutting to the chase. Turn around, and look behind you. See those three-file cabinets? They hold hundreds of reasons, and that small stack of folders on my desk, a few more reasons."

She looked around as he had directed and said, "It's green."

"What?"

"The office walls, they're green. I couldn't remember the color from our tour of your home. I like it." She got up and went to the first file, opened the second drawer from the top, and took out three folders. "May I look at these?"

"Certainly. Look at as many as you wish. Would you like a cup of coffee?"

"That sounds good."

"Regular or decaf?" he asked as he walked across the room.

She turned to look and saw one of the one-cup coffeemakers that were becoming so popular.

"I'll have a regular, it's been a tough day."

"How so, because you had to come here?"

"No, that's a good part, but I learned today I have to fly to Houston on Monday for a Tuesday meeting."

"Do you know when you will be getting back?"

"I should be back on Wednesday. I don't know what time. Roland, these files are about African businesses. Not very large ones, it looks like."

"Yes, that's right, you took them out of the Africa file."

"The Africa file?"

"Yes, everything in there is African. The second file is Asia and South America."

"What's the third file?"

"That's the one where I make the money to help fund the other two, mostly the United States. Here's your coffee. I put two creams in it and no sugar. I hope that's okay, it's the way I've seen you take it right along."

"Perfect. So tell me about your African businesses."

"I do extensive work with small start-ups in Africa as well as Asia and South America. I am trying to encourage any person who has the desire and potential to be an entrepreneur to go for it, and I fund their start-up. Not many of those businesses become very large, but they do provide an income for a family. I look for ideas that come from the people for businesses that will be managed by the people and provide rewards for the people. My own 'of the people, by the people, for the people' type of thing."

"What's in it for you?"

"Nothing really, other than satisfaction. The businesses that actually thrive create employment for other people, and those successful businesses contribute a small amount to a fund to help create more start-ups in the same area, but I make nothing from them, if that's what you mean."

She thought for a minute before getting up and replacing the files. Then she opened each drawer in the three files and scanned the contents before closing them.

"You have quite a diverse clientele, how do you keep track of all of them?"

"Now you see why I need an administrative assistant. Only a small portion of these may be active or require attention at any one time, like those on my desk, but it's still daunting at times. I am currently in the process of setting up a nonprofit foundation partly for tax purposes. The foundation will then manage the actual operation once it has been approved and is up and running. That will actually take some of the pressure off.

"Africa is the biggest challenge. We will travel there two or three times a year. In all cases, I am especially interested in having a second pair of eyes, a second pair of ears, and a second brain. You will have an active part in every venture, but your main duty will be to catch anything I miss.

"So that's the gist of it. You will be our contact person, and you will be a buffer between myself and some of the clients. When it comes to my consulting work in the States, your experience at your present job will be a perfect fit for ours. Once we have a large-enough collection of requests for assistance, we will visit them firsthand."

"You sound like I have already agreed to take the job."

"You said you were leaning that way last night, but let me do a little more convincing. The work will be interesting and challenging, the pay will be double what you are making now, and you will be working closer to your grandfather. Are you still interested?"

"Grandfather, yes, that is a consideration. I don't know if I will feel comfortable about going on extended trips, leaving him alone. I'll have to talk with him about that."

"Do you think he would like to see the world? He could travel with us at company expense. In fact, it just occurred to me that he might make a very good part-time employee as well. I assure you, if you agree to work for me, neither you nor Jim will ever regret it. So have I convinced you to leave your Seattle office and spread your wings across the globe?"

She was mesmerized. Never in her wildest dreams had she ever imagined anything like this.

"Yes, I'll take the job, and I think Grandfather will too if you really do want him."

"Of course, I do. I've already started thinking of ways he would fit in."

"I'll have to give my notice, but I won't do that until I'm back from Houston. I have a couple of weeks of vacation time I can take, and then I should be done."

"Then it's settled. You're hired. You can start as soon as you are free and ready. Now it's up to you to convince Jim he needs to be part of this arrangement. I can feel the weight lifting off my shoulders already. Oh, yes, another thing I didn't mention. The job will mean you and your grandfather will be expected to attend a couple of decoy shows with me each year. I hope that's not going to be a problem."

"You're the boss, how can it be a problem? I'll go home and let Grandfather know about everything. I think he will be excited."

"One more thing, I think we all should go out and celebrate with dinner."

"He probably already has something on for dinner."

"No, he hasn't. I called him this morning and told him we were all going out for dinner, either to celebrate or for the two of us to convince you to take the job."

26

SHIFTING GEARS

It was early Monday morning when her phone rang. It was Roland.

"Hi, I'm glad I caught you before you left for work. I just learned that the salmon are showing up. A big slug of silvers has moved in, and it's time we thought about that fishing trip with Amanda. I'm going to be tied up most of the week, and so are you for a few days, so even though I would like to get right out, it looks like a weekend trip. Would you and Jim be able to go on Saturday?"

"I think so. I know we don't have anything on our calendar, and I'm sure Grandfather will love to go. I know I would."

"Okay, I'll call Amanda. I expect she will be overjoyed to have the chance to go fishing again, but I do need to check with her and make sure. I'll get back to you with the details."

The next call went to Oak Harbor.

"Hey, the salmon have started running, would you like to go on Saturday?"

"I had heard that too, and I've been expecting your call," said Amanda. "Are you bringing Marcy and her grandfather?"

"Yes, they are both coming."

"Are you taking the *Que Sera Sera*?"

"I plan to. It's all set up for fishing. We could use the *Melissa*, but it would be a bit of a pain getting her ready for salmon fishing. It's been awhile since I've used her for that."

"Well, I'm ready for a half-day trip anyway. Are you going in the morning?"

"I plan to. The tide will be right, and I'd like to get an early start."

"Well then, why don't you bring them up Friday and spend the night here? The rooms are ready. They've been lonely for company, you don't stay over often enough."

"Thanks for asking. Actually, I was hoping we could do that. I'd like it very much. I'll let them know what we will be doing, and I'll call you Thursday and let you know when we will be getting there."

He called Marcy back.

"Hey, it's me again. Would you and Jim be okay with going up to Whidbey Friday afternoon? We will stay with Amanda overnight and get out early Saturday morning if you can get away."

"That's no problem. I expect to be at home, so I'll be able to leave pretty much whatever time you want to go. Do we have to bring anything?"

"No. We will go out for dinner when we get to Amanda's. Then the next morning, we'll either have breakfast at Amanda's or stop at a diner, and I'll have everything we need for fishing on the boat. Just remember to dress warm. It can be cool out there first thing in the morning even this time of year."

"Okay, I'll let Grandfather know. And thanks, I'm really looking forward to this."

Humming happily to herself, she went to tell him the news.

"Roland called, he's going salmon fishing this coming Saturday. I don't suppose you would like to go."

"All right! I've been just waiting for this. He's told me all about the fishing, and I've been ready ever since I heard about it. Amanda is going, right?"

"Yes, we are actually going to Amanda's Friday afternoon, and we will stay overnight there so we can get an early start Saturday. I'm sure it will be fun. I was about ready to leave for work when he called, so I'll get on my way, but I'll be home all day Friday, so we can leave when he's ready. You have a good day now."

The chores in Houston on Tuesday went even better than she had expected. The figures and information that she and her team had put together was chewed on a bit by the board, but eventually, the logic of what they were presenting won the day. The best part was that they were thanked profusely for saving the company from going forward with what, for all intents and purposes, promised to be a costly misadventure.

Marcy was relieved because the fact that the board deep-sixed the project instead of shelving it, or trying to save it, meant there would almost certainly not be any follow-up meetings to tie her up. She felt free to turn in her resignation and get ready for what looked like the job of a lifetime.

Her boss was sorry to see her go, and he told her that if she ever wanted to come back, they would be glad to have her.

When Friday rolled around, she had begun to use the paid vacation time she had coming. She was surprised that it was a hard time for her because she had poured herself into what she had been doing and she had some good friends in the office. But when she had cleaned out her desk, she never looked back.

Her grandfather had not been a hard sell on working for Roland, and he was looking forward to whatever the future had to offer him. When she told him that he would be doing quite a bit of traveling with them and where they would be going, he said, "I'll have to take the job just to be your chaperone if for nothing else."

"You know you might be closer to the truth than you think on that."

"What do you mean?"

"Well, I have a confession. I didn't intend for it to happen, I didn't want it to happen, and I know it's foolish and could never work out, but in the short time I've known him, I've fallen in love with Roland."

"Listen, little girl, that's not news. I have known that for a while now, it has been pretty obvious to me every time we're around him. In fact, I don't know for the life of me why he hasn't seen it. I know Amanda has."

"Oh, no! What does she think of me? Is she upset with me?"

"Not at all. We talked about it a little bit on the boat. And we talked a lot more about it when I went to see her. She thinks you already make a great couple, he just doesn't know it yet. Don't worry about her, she's in your corner."

"Grandfather, I think I would do just about anything for him, but I am feeling so guilty that I can hardly stand it. Here I am thinking about what it would be like to have him as a husband while he's interested in my mother. How can I even think about trying to take him away from her? How could I ever look my mother in the eye?"

"It seems to me that your mother has more or less removed herself from the running. I can't see any reason for you to feel guilty. Don't let your concern for her stop you from pursuing what you want. You have every right to be in love with him."

"Well, it's not just that. He hasn't done anything to indicate he has ever thought of me in any way other than my mother's daughter. Treating me nice doesn't mean he has any interest in me."

"I'm not so sure that's true. Maybe you've been missing some signals."

"What about our ages? I'm young enough to be his daughter."

"Baby, you are talking about a normal man, a man who is looking for a wife. I don't think he would be put off by a younger woman, especially one he seems to like so much."

"But what would people say? They would probably accuse me of being a gold digger."

"I suspect most women would envy you, and yes, some might call you a gold digger, but just about any single woman would trade places with you right now. Are you interested in his money?"

"No, you know better than that, but what should I do?"

"My advice to you is to keep doing what you've been doing. Let him make the first move, if there's any move to be made. But by all means, don't try to push your mother out of his mind. I think he is already letting go of her, but trying to speed that up could be a mistake."

"You know, thinking about spending the night at Amanda's, I wish I was his wife already. I've never felt this way before, and it sort of scares me. Maybe I shouldn't have been so quick to go to work for him. I'll be with him so much."

"You'll be fine. Just keep your mind on the fishing and on being just your normal sweet self at work."

"I can do that. Thanks, Grandpa, I'm glad I had this talk with you.

"I am too, baby."

Looking at the clock, she said, "He could be here almost anytime now. Are you all packed?"

They were both ready and excited when he drove into the driveway. He walked to the door and took their bags.

"I know I don't have to ask this, but you both brought jackets, right? It can be chilly first thing in the morning even this time of year."

They assured him they had each packed one, and soon they were headed north to catch the ferry. She sat in front with him, and as he drove, she described her recent experience in Houston. He listened intently.

"That's exactly why I wanted you to work for me," he said. "We won't run into too many things where there's a problem like that, but we need to make sure projects we accept get a proper evaluation, not just look at them for face value. Just wait until you are dealing with African entrepreneurs. It can be exhilarating and challenging. I can't explain it. You will have to see it for yourself."

They also visited a little about the fishing. "You know, Roland," said Marcy, "I've never been fishing before for anything. Is there much I have to learn?"

"Well, yes and no. I'll do most of the work getting the lines set and running the boat. Once we actually start fishing, the rest of you can watch for a hit. It's a good idea for you all to decide ahead of time who will take the first fish and who will be second. Then after you have each had a turn, you can start the cycle again.

"Since you've never been fishing before, there are some basics you will need to know, but we can talk about them once we are on the boat. The rods and reels will handle the fish. All you have to do is know how handle the rods and reels. It's not hard to learn. Amanda is an old hand at this. She will see to it that you do what you are supposed to do."

The drive up went quickly, and they were in Oak Harbor just about four o'clock. That afternoon they visited and relaxed before going out for dinner, but after they got back, he took Marcy down to the marina to see the *Que Sera Sera*. It seemed much smaller to her than the *Melissa*.

"What are those things on the back of the boat?" she asked.

He looked to see where she was pointing. "Oh, those are downriggers. They allow us to get some of our lines deeper when the fish are too far below the surface for our lures to reach them by just trolling." Taking her hand, he said, "Come on the boat, and I'll show you how they work."

She was intrigued by the large lead downrigger weights and picked one up.

"Wow, they are heavy. Just how heavy are they anyway?" she asked.

"They weigh eight pounds. They clip onto the cables on the downriggers," and he fastened the one she had held onto the clip and let it hang.

"Once they are on the cables, our fishing lines can be fastened just above them with release clips. Sometimes we put more than one line on a cable at different depths. Many of the fish we catch tomorrow will come from the lines we fasten to them."

"It sounds complicated," she said after hearing the description.

"I guess it would to someone who has never used them, let alone never fished before, but I'll take care of the downriggers tomorrow. All you will have to do is catch fish."

"What will we use for bait?"

"I use spoons and a hootchie-flasher combination. When we find out what's working best, we will change some of the rigs."

"I see," she said. She really didn't know what he was talking about, but she didn't want to tell him. "I'll wait until tomorrow, and then everything will make more sense to me."

When they got back to the house, Amanda asked if anyone would like a dish of ice cream. They all agreed that ice cream sounded good.

As they were enjoying the treat, she asked, "What time do you want to get up?"

"I think five thirty will be early enough. I'd like to be out on the water early, but the tide doesn't really start moving until seven thirty, so that should give us enough time to be set up and trolling by the early bite."

"Okay, I'll be up at five and have breakfast ready for you when you get up."

"Can I help you?" Marcy asked.

"There's no need, but thanks for asking. We will need to get to bed soon, or at least, I will, if I'm going to be up at five."

Marcy woke up before five and slipped into her "fishing clothes" that she had laid out before she hit the hay. She got up and found Amanda in the kitchen with coffee already made.

"I told you that you didn't have to get up to help, but as long as you are up, why don't you set the table. There's some half-and-half in the refrigerator that you can put on. Just leave it right in the carton, there's nothing fancy this morning. There's orange juice too, pour four glasses."

"Do you mind if I get myself a cup of coffee, Amanda?"

"No, of course not, and pour one for me too. I've got the bacon going. When it's done, I'll do the eggs, and you can make the toast."

"You're making my grandfather's favorite breakfast. He will love it," she said as they sat down together."

'He's quite a man, your grandfather. He told me you will be working for Roland and that he might be too. I'm so pleased. I told him that I would like him to come up and go fishing with me next week if he's not working, and we will have a picnic. He's perfectly capable of driving up here, you know."

"Yes, I know. He always reminds me about that when he plans to go somewhere. If he wants to come up here, I don't have any problem with it at all, it makes him so happy."

Amanda smiled and got up to check the bacon. "Marcy, you better check on the men and make sure they are getting up. Tell them breakfast will be ready in just a few minutes."

They were both awake, and when they came out to the dining room, the eggs and toast were on the way to the table. As soon as breakfast was finished, Jim helped Amanda carry the dishes out to the kitchen where they stacked them in the sink to be washed.

A short time later, they were walking down the ramp to the marina to board the *Que Sera Sera*. Roland and Marcy tossed the lines onto the deck, and then he helped her into the boat, and Jim followed suit with Amanda.

The twin engines roared into life, then Roland throttled them back and put the boat in gear. A couple of other boats were being prepared for the day, and as they passed one of them, a man called out, "We hit them really good yesterday, Roland. You should have been here."

"Thanks, Carl, I was busy all week. I hope you left a few for us."

"Shouldn't be any problem, like I told you, the fish are all over the place. Have been for three or four days now." He waved and said, "I'll see you out there in a bit."

"That's Carl Smith, a good friend. He's the one who called to let me know the run was on. I'm sure we will see him out near us before too long. He called me again yesterday shortly before I picked you up and told me where the fishing had been the best. That's where we will both be starting this morning."

It was a longer run than they had ever made for crabbing, but after a while, he slowed to a crawl and watched the screen in the cockpit. Finally, after a few minutes, he shut the engines down and brought out the rods they would be fishing with.

"I was marking quite a few fish on the depth finder, and there are a couple of bait balls here as well," he explained. "We will get the lines ready and start right here. I'm sure there are some fish up near the top, but I saw quite a few down about thirty-five feet. Amanda, you know the drill. I want the two rigs with the flashers on the downriggers. Put them down thirty feet and back about thirty feet, and fasten them on just above the ball. Once they're down, run the flat lines back about a 150 feet. We will start with the spoons that are on them and see how they do. Are you ready?"

"Ready as I'll ever be. Go ahead and get us moving."

"Marcy, you stay back here with Amanda, and Jim, you come with me. You may have to run the boat a little today, and I want to show you around the cockpit."

When Roland had the boat moving, Amanda fastened the clip just above the lead ball and then began letting line out in back of the boat.

As Marcy watched the dodger and lure disappear, she asked, "How do you know how far behind the boat the lure is?"

Amanda showed her the reel. "This is a counter. It tells you how much line has been run off the reel. When we see we've let off thirty feet, which is just about . . . now, we will use the clip to hold the line like this, and then we will let the ball down with the line. This is an electric downrigger, which makes it easy to bring the ball back up when a fish has grabbed the lure, and it also had a counter that tells us how far down the ball is. Watch this." And she let the ball go straight down, stopping as the counter quickly came to thirty feet.

"Now we tighten this line up until the rod is bent right over. When a fish hits, the rod will pop up, and then we grab it. Notice the reel is on top of the rod, and this is how you have to hold it. Reel with your right hand, and keep your rod tip up."

She repeated the procedure with the second rod, letting it down with the rigger on the opposite corner of the stern.

"Now we will let the spoons back on the other two lines. Look here, notice with these reels, you put your thumb on the spool before releasing the line with this lever. If you don't, you will have a giant tangled mess of line that we call a bird's nest. We don't want to let that happen."

Marcy watched closely as Amanda continued, "See how I do it? I hold the spool and flip this lever up. Then I slowly ease up the pressure of my thumb and let the line run back like this until the counter reads 150 feet. Then we put on the thumb pressure again and flip the lever back down, locking the spool. Okay, now you try it with this rod," she said, handing it to her.

Marcy held the rod like it was a bomb ready to explode. She let the spoon down into the water, keeping thumb pressure on and then raised the lever and slowly let up on the pressure of her thumb, and the line began to run off the reel. She was so pleased with herself that she forgot to keep track of the counter. When she remembered to look, she had two hundred feet out, and she quickly clicked the lever down.

"That was pretty good," Amanda said.

"Well, I got out more line than I should have. It is out two hundred feet instead of 150."

"Don't worry about that. We could reel it in a bit, but let's leave it out and see what happens. Who knows, it may work better than being closer. Just put the rod in the rod holder like I did, and we are fishing. If a fish hits one of the flat lines, the rod will bend down, not pop up like a downrigger. You take the first fish, Jim the next one, and then it's my turn. Okay, Roland, the lines are out," Amanda reported. "Come on back here and sit down," she said to Marcy as she moved to the two seats behind the cockpit. "We don't have to stand by the rods. We can get to them quick enough if we get a hit."

Roland insisted that he would let them do the fishing, and he would be the guide. Turning around to them, he said, "They should be turning on. I'm surprised that we haven't had a hit yet, but we aren't going to change baits or tactics for a while yet. I'll make a turn and run back the way we came. I marked fish all the way. Maybe I'm figuring the current wrong."

She was becoming almost mesmerized watching the rods, willing a bite to happen, when suddenly, the rod that she had let out began to buck and dance.

"That's a fish. Get that rod, Marcy, and give it a yank."

She jumped up and went back to the rod. Amanda was right behind her, giving advice as she took it out of the holder and yanked back on it. She could feel the pull and the power of the salmon as the line peeled off her reel.

"Roland!" she squealed. "Help me, it's getting away."

Leaving Jim at the helm, he came back to her. "You don't need help. It looks like you are doing just fine," he said.

"But it's taking line off my reel even if I turn the handle."

"That's normal, Marcy, the drag on the reel lets the fish take off some line when it pulls hard, which keeps the line from breaking. Don't try to crank him in while he is taking line off the reel. All you have to do is keep the rod tip up and let the rod and the reel fight the fish for you at first. When he starts to slow down, you will be able to start reeling in some line. Just keep the pressure on him. If you don't, the hook might come out."

He stood there, watching her play the fish. He couldn't help but think how Betty had loved doing exactly the same thing.

Then he could see the rod tip was slowly dipping lower and lower. Standing closely behind her, he reached around her, putting his hands over hers on the rod and lifting the tip higher.

"Keep it up like this," he said. "If you don't, the fish has a better chance of tearing off the hook. The rod plays the fish by bending, so keep it up where it can do its job."

As he stood there with his arms around her, he was suddenly aware of the smell of her hair and the feel of her body. Just for a moment, he had the urge to give her hands a squeeze and hold her closer. He recoiled, releasing her hands.

"There, I think you've got it," he said. "I think you can start reeling him in now, but don't be in any hurry. He will come when he's ready."

"Are you okay, Jim?" he asked, turning to look at the cockpit.

"I think so. Do you want me to stay on the same course?"

"Yes, I don't see any boats we need to avoid, so just hold her steady. We're going slow enough, there shouldn't be any problems."

He could see the fish come to the top out behind the boat, and he said, "Okay, Marcy, start reeling a little faster. He's up on top. If you reel fast, he won't be able to pull against you on his way in, and we don't want to give him any slack. I'll get the net."

Then things started picking up. As he went for the net, one of the downriggers popped. "Grab that rod, Amanda. Jim can get his turn later, he's busy."

Marcy had the salmon close to the boat, and Roland moved to the stern with the net. "Lift your rod, and just step back a bit."

As she followed his instructions, he slipped the net underneath the fish and lifted it onto the deck.

"There you are, your very first salmon. He's a beauty, maybe Amanda won't get the biggest fish today. Let me take care of him, and then I'll get my camera, and we'll get a picture."

When the salmon had been stunned and bled, he brought it back to her. Amanda was still fighting her fish, so he took a couple of shots of Marcy holding her first fish before taking it back and putting it on ice.

Then he turned to Amanda, "How are you doing? Is he starting to come in?"

"He's coming. He feels like a big one too, so don't be too sure that I'm beaten already. Get the net over here, and I'll have him ready in just a couple of minutes."

When she slid her salmon to the back of the boat, Roland deftly scooped it up and deposited it on the deck in one move.

"He's a nice one, but I think Marcy still has you beat."

"The day is young. I'm just getting started."

He smiled, and after taking care of the fish, he put the two lines back out and then relieved Jim.

"It's your turn to catch one, Amanda had to take that last fish, so the next one is yours."

"Marcy, why don't you come up here with me, and the two of them can watch the rods."

When she joined him, he had her sit in the captain's seat.

"You should learn how to run the boat. It's fairly easy. You have twin throttles, which you shouldn't need to touch while we are fishing. That's them right there. We are only running one engine right now, but if we wanted to head out from here, we would start the other motor and move both the throttles together. If I have to go back to help out with a fish, all you have to do is steer the same course on the compass that's right in front of you. Now it's all yours."

"You said something about a bait ball. What's that?"

"Watch this screen, see those marks? Those are fish, probably salmon. Bait shows up as a big cloud. Watch for a few minutes, and you will probably see what I'm talking about."

She was curious and she paid close attention. Then she saw a dark mass come onto the screen. "Is that a bait ball?" she asked.

"Yep, that's it. Now there should be fish below them, maybe we will get a strike."

They had trolled and visited for another couple of minutes before they heard Amanda call out, "Get that rod, Jim."

Turning around, they saw him grabbing the rod, with her right beside him.

"Are you going back with them?" Marcy asked.

"Nope. He will be fine. She can give him all the coaching he will need, and she can net the fish as well as I can. Let's just stay out of their way and let them enjoy it together."

While they were watching the fight, he leaned a little closer and said to her, "You know, she has taken a real liking to Jim. I'm pretty sure she looks forward to seeing him."

"He thinks a lot of her too. I know he phones her and has come up to Oak Harbor a couple of times to see her, and they have been talking about going on a picnic and maybe doing some fishing. She took him over to watch the planes come in, but Grandpa told me she had tears in her eyes when the A6s came over."

"I don't know as she will ever get over the loss of her husband. I don't know if she wants to. Those planes are a connection to the past for her."

They listened to the two of them talking as he brought the fish up alongside and she netted it. Another nice fish was in the boat.

Jim called to Roland, "Hey, get your camera and take a picture of my fish."

Walking back, he saw that she had clubbed the salmon already, and Jim was holding it in front of the two of them. He also had his arm around Amanda, and she didn't seem to mind at all. It was a great picture.

They finished out the morning with five fish in the cooler, and several more had been released. Marcy ran the boat as they headed back in all the way to the marina where he showed her how to use the two engines to back it into the slip.

As it turned out, Marcy's fish was the biggest one they had caught, and Amanda told her they would have to have a rematch soon. They all agreed that another salmon trip should be planned for the next weekend if the weather looked reasonable. That afternoon, they put Marcy's salmon on the grill.

"There's nothing better than a salmon fresh out of the water," Roland said, looking at Marcy as he brought the fish to the table. "The only thing that would have made it better would be if I had remembered to order the potato salad."

Amanda looked at Marcy, and they both smiled. Going to the kitchen, Amanda came back with a big yellow bowl.

"She didn't tell you she was bringing this with her. She snuck it by you, and we stored it in the refrigerator for today."

As they started eating after asking the Lord's blessing and giving thanks for the day, Amanda said, "Save room for dessert. I made a raspberry pie yesterday, and I don't want a lot left to tempt me. And yes, Roland, I have some French vanilla ice cream to go on it."

"Talk about being blessed," Roland said. "Marcy's potato salad and your raspberry pie are two of my favorite things. I won't forget this day for some time."

When it came time to leave, Amanda said, "I've got something to tell you. Jim and I have been talking, and I've invited him up to go fishing with me and have a picnic on Thursday, and since we are planning on going fishing next Saturday, if you aren't scandalized by it, I've asked him to stay up until you come. I would like to show him around the area properly."

"I don't know if that's up to us," Marcy said, looking at Roland. "If he wants to come and you're willing to put up with him for a couple of days, why not." He just nodded in agreement.

On the way home, Jim confided in them, "If you are not happy with me going up on Thursday, just say so, and I can get out of it. I know it was kind of sudden, but I don't want anyone getting bent out of shape over it."

"I can't see any reason why you shouldn't go if you want to. I doubt if the neighbors will talk about you, and we certainly won't find fault with you. I think the two of you will have a great time, and while you are running around, have her take you over to my lot."

When he dropped them off, he said, "I'll see you in church tomorrow, but if you are up to it, plan on coming to work on Monday at nine o'clock."

Monday morning, she rang the doorbell at five minutes of nine, and she was surprised how quickly he came to the door to let her in a few moments later. She followed him to the office, but somehow, she felt a little weird.

"You seem to have recovered from our fishing trip," he said.

"That didn't take much. I had a great time."

"Are you ready to go to work?"

"Yes, but I have to tell you, it seems a little strange. My first day on my new job, and I'm not even sure how I should address you here, let alone know what I'm doing."

"That's all easy enough. In most cases, just call me Roland. I think an administrative assistant should be on a first-name footing. However, if you are speaking with someone on the phone or a visitor whom you haven't met before in the office, refer to me as Mr. Holtz. I think you can figure out which one to use depending on the particular situation, but if in doubt, use Mr. Holtz. On the plus side, I seldom meet with anyone in my office. Almost all my meetings take place off-site. As far as knowing what you are doing, we will start working on that today. Any other things that seem strange to you?"

"Well, it all seems a bit strange, but I guess any new job would be like that. I may be a bit of a pest until I have had a few days to adjust, but I'll be fine. I hope I will be what you are looking for."

He smiled, "I'm sure you are, and don't be at all hesitant about asking for any help you need. As for today, just begin to familiarize yourself with the files. You might start with the red ones on my desk as they are the ones we will be working with first, and look over the information in the e-mails for the past few months. That should give you a better picture of what I've been into and what you will be dealing with. For the time being, if anyone calls, just take a message and get a callback number. Before long, I think you will be able to field a big percentage of the calls for me, and that will become part of your responsibilities. Oh, and if anyone comes to the front door, there is a camera and an intercom so you can find out who they are and what they want. You can unlock the door right from your desk. Let me show you how it works.

"You should be very comfortable with some things because they are much like what you've been doing for some time. I have been a consultant to a number of American firms, and I'm actively working with three. I think your years of dealing with companies and their CEOs will be a plus for both of us. You see things on a different slant than I do, so we should complement each other. That's one of the reasons why I thought you'd be perfect for the job.

"Now, I am not fixed on any particular arrangement of this office, and I'm not going to have a separate room. My desk will remain where it is. You will just have to get used to my being around. I purposely started with your desk near the door for obvious reasons, but if you want to rearrange anything else, let me know. Any questions?"

"Not right now. I'll start with the files."

"Good. Oh, by the way, I think you probably noticed last week, but there is a coffee bar over there. It's a one-cup job, so feel free to fix yourself a cup anytime you want one. Creamers are in the small refrigerator on the counter, and you can use it if you have anything you want to keep cold. I guess that's about it.

"Oh, yes, one more thing. I won't always be in the office, but if I'm not, most days I'll be somewhere in the house unless I tell you I'm leaving. If you need me, just press the red button on the phone to get me. Settle in, and I'll be back in a little while," he said and then walked out.

This sure is going to be different, she thought. *But on the other hand, it's not all that different from my working at home.* Picking up a couple of files from his desk, she laid them on her own and sat down to read.

It wasn't long before she was intrigued and engrossed by what she was reading. The more files she perused, the more fascinated she became. It seemed like only a short time before the door opened and he walked back in.

"Well, how is it going so far? Are you ready for lunch?"

"Lunch?" she asked.

"Yes, it's almost one, and we are going to go out for lunch. After today, though, you can decide if you want to bring in a lunch or if you would prefer to go home, unless I think we should go out. We will get that all figured out fairly soon. But today we are eating out."

While they enjoyed a leisurely lunch, he said, "I hope you didn't mind my sort of encouraging Jim to go up to Amanda's this week. I really couldn't see any harm in it."

"No, not at all. It isn't like we were turning two teenagers loose in a house together. I'm good with a 'don't ask, don't tell' policy, but we may have to keep a close eye on them in the future," she said with a wink.

"Great. They aren't going to do anything we would disapprove of, and it seems they really do enjoy each other's company."

"Roland, why did you want Amanda to show Grandfather your lot?"

"I am rather proud of it, and I was telling him about it while we were fishing. He said he would like to see it. I'm planning on building there soon. I just wanted him to get the chance to see it and know what it looked like."

"I would like to see it again myself. It was so new to me when you took me there that I couldn't take it all in, but it was a wonderful location."

"Well, how about we go Saturday after we are done fishing? In fact, if you are up to it, we could plan on staying up Saturday night and going to church with Amanda Sunday morning."

"Oh, I'm for that. Maybe we could even go up on Friday night again after work?"

"It's a possibility. I'm going to be busy most of Friday, so you can have the day off, but I will talk to Amanda in the meantime. If she's okay with it, we should be able to leave at least by six, and we could grab a bite to eat on the way up. We will work out the details during the week."

And such was her introduction to working for Roland. During that first week, she vacillated between wading through one file after another and daydreaming about the fishing trip coming up on the weekend. Tuesday through Thursday had been same old, same old; but anytime she tired of reading through folders, she could take a break, have a cup of coffee, or even grab a cold drink and sit for a while on the deck. That was when she did her best daydreaming.

Arriving home after work on Thursday, she found a note her grandfather had left her.

"Hi, I don't have anything going in the Crock-Pot for dinner. Sorry, but there are some good leftovers in the fridge. Take your pick. See you Saturday."

It felt lonely in the quiet house as she warmed something to eat without her grandfather. It was something she had never experienced to any noticeable degree before he had come. Now her life had become so different. She was intertwined with several people, and this loneliness was an unexpected side effect. She didn't like it.

After taking care of the few dinner dishes, she thought about watching the news but decided instead to e-mail her mother. She went to her room and checked her own e-mail. Nothing too exciting there, nothing from her mother, and she realized she hadn't heard from her in a while.

It was time she brought her up to date about her father's car and the job change. She tried to picture her mother's face when she read the news.

"Mother, haven't heard from you in a while. Hope you are doing well. Thought you might like to know about us. Grandfather has a new car—a used one, that is. That's right, he wanted some freedom, and now he has it. He is doing just great, no problems with our traffic, and he is very happy and content. We have become really close. I have a new job. I've gone to work for Roland. Isn't that a hoot? It keeps me closer to Grandfather, and it pays much better. He is a great boss, and I enjoy him and the work. We have been crabbing a few times, and last Saturday we went salmon fishing for the first time. Grandfather and I each caught our first salmon. I just love both of Roland's boats, and it is always a special treat to be out on the water. Amanda went with us. I have grown to appreciate her so much, and so has Grandfather."

She decided not to tell her that he seemed to be becoming more than just Amanda's friend, which had surprised her, but *Lucky him*, she thought. Then she added a couple of pictures of him with his new car and the picture of grandfather and Amanda with his fish. In the car pictures, he was wearing the new cap he had bought just to wear when he was driving.

She finished the e-mail, "I know you are busy these days, but I would like to hear from you. I miss you."

Once she had sent it, she knew she would have a hard time waiting for a reply. It was late in New York, but she would probably get a reply in the morning. She didn't know what her mother's response would be, but a lot of thoughts were running through her mind. On top of it all, she knew that, for better or worse, there was nothing Sherry could do to change things with her and her grandfather, and she didn't care.

She was up early the next morning. The first thing she did was check for an e-mail from her mother. She drew a blank. After showering and getting dressed, she checked again, still nothing. The house was so quiet, and she had gotten used to the smell of coffee when she got up. She started to the kitchen to make her own but decided instead to go out for breakfast.

I need some comfort food and some people, she thought.

Pancakes with fresh strawberries topped by whipped cream filled the bill on the first, and the restaurant was busy. There were plenty of people around, but she still felt like she was alone as she finished as much of the order of delicious pancakes as she could and sipped a third cup of coffee. The only conversation she had was with the waitress, and though she was courteous, she was also quite busy, so even that was fleeting. The rest of the day dragged by, and she checked her e-mail about every hour until four o'clock when she found an answer from her mother.

"Marcy, it was good to hear from you. It sounds like you and your grandfather have been kicking up your heels. I was surprised about his car, but he has driven for a lot of years, and if he is feeling well, I guess there is no reason for him not to have a car. The pictures of him were very nice. Thank you for them. I was surprised even more about your job with Roland than I was about Father's car. After all, I could never persuade you to come and work for me. I miss you both also, and I am very happy that things are going so well for you. Keep in touch."

She didn't know exactly what she had been expecting, but her mother's response was not it. No objections to his car and no questions about Roland. It was like she was on cruise control.

Roland came for her at six o'clock on the dot and carried her bags to the car. "Do you have any potato salad hidden away in these?" he asked.

"Not this time. I don't want it to become too commonplace. There are other things to eat."

"I think you are right. Keep it special. That's true with a lot of things, like crab and salmon. As much as I like both, I would probably tire of them if they were all I had."

Getting into his car, she wanted to ask, "Is that true of people too?" But she didn't. She hoped he would never grow tired of her.

At the ferry, he asked, "Would you like some Ivar's chowder?"

"Is that going to be our dinner?"

"No, think of it as an appetizer. We will get dinner on the island."

"You know, I'd just as soon have a cup of chowder and a fried fish sandwich here and pass on stopping somewhere else for dinner, if that's okay with you."

"Sure, it will get us to Amanda's sooner too, and I know that will be fine with her."

They pulled in behind Jim's car, and he got their bags out of the trunk. There was plenty of light left in the day. No one came out to greet them, so he rang the bell. Soon Amanda came to the door.

"Hey, we didn't expect you quite so soon. We are out in back. Put your bags down, and come and join us."

Once they were all together, Jim started telling them what he and Amanda had been doing.

"We spent a lot of time just driving around the island. It's a neat place. We drove by the base and on a bunch of roads, just going wherever they took us. She said we couldn't get lost. We went up to Deception Pass and parked by the bridge for a while. I really like to just stand on it and watch the water run through the pass. It's quite a sight, all that water moving so fast. Then we had a picnic in the park near the pass, and afterward we sat down by the water for a while and took it easy just visiting."

"I really like that area too," Marcy commented, "and that park is so peaceful. It's a good place to go when you want to just sit and think."

"I'd never been there before, but I wouldn't mind going again. Do you go there much?"

"Not really. I have never come up on the island a lot during the time I have been out here, but when I have, I would usually stop there. It was like saying hello to an old friend you don't see often enough. Mother always insisted we come up when she was out."

"Well, when we left there, we drove up to Anacortes. She calls it a big little town. Then we went to La Conner. We got a milk shake there, and we picked up a couple of cinnamon buns from the Calico Kitchen. Amanda says we will have to go there for breakfast sometime, that the eggs Benedict with smoked salmon are outstanding. We were bringing the buns home for our breakfast this morning. They were great, and they were huge."

"Oh, I love their cinnamon buns, but I've never had breakfast there. That's the place Mother always wants to go just for her sweet tooth," Marcy said. "So what else did you do? It sounds like you had a pretty full day."

"We got back down on the island, and we stopped where we could get off the road and watch the planes coming in. She knows what most of them are. We saw a couple of Orions. They are long-range reconnaissance planes. We saw a number of A6s and a couple of AE6Bs. The A6 is called an intruder. It's what her husband flew. There were some fighters and a transport too. Then we went back to Oak Harbor and got a pizza. Man, was it good."

"And then you came back here?"

"No, not yet. After the pizza, we drove out of town, and she took me to see Roland's lot. You were right. It is a beautiful location. She said you had watched the sun go down there with him, and we ended up doing the same thing. I like the mountains, but boy, that afternoon ocean view is something."

"I know just what you mean. It is a beautiful spot."

"And then we came home. We had a cup of coffee and ate one of the cinnamon buns for a snack, and she suggested we play a game of Yahtzee. I had never played the game before, but it was simple enough, and she whomped me, but it was fun anyway. Boy, did I sleep last night!"

"I imagine so. And what did you do today besides rest up?"

"There wasn't any time to rest up. I made breakfast for her. She didn't want me to, but I told her it was the least I could do for the good time I was having, so she sat and talked with me until it was ready. We split our cinnamon bun to go with it."

"He does a great job with breakfast," Amanda said. "My eggs were perfect, and the bacon was crisp but not overdone. He could make breakfast for me anytime. I don't object to being pampered once in a while."

"He is a great cook. He has been doing his best to fatten me up, and it hasn't been easy to resist. Between him and Roland, it's a wonder I can fit into my clothes," Marcy said.

"After breakfast," he continued, "we went to the marina and fished for smelt. Now that's something else I've never done before. We only caught about fifteen, and they are tiny things. They are in the fridge if you want to see them. I think I caught the biggest, but that isn't saying much.

"I cleaned the smelt, and then she took me to Coupeville, and we ate at the Knead and Feed. It's a cute little place, and they have great soup and sandwiches. I almost didn't have room enough for the homemade pie. Then we came back and sat in the backyard. We've been having a wonderful time, and I'm looking forward to fishing tomorrow."

"Wow, you certainly packed a lot into a couple of days. I hope you saved something for the next time you are here."

"I believe there will be more things to see and do, but if there wasn't, I could handle another dose just like I've had. Amanda said we would have to take the ferry some day from Anacortes and sail up through the San Juan's and over to Victoria."

"That's a trip I have always thought I would like to take," said Marcy, "but I just have never taken the time to do it. Everyone I know who has done it says it is the best."

Roland hadn't said anything during Jim's description of his time with Amanda, but he jumped in now, "I think that would be a great idea. Maybe we could spend a day and night at Friday Harbor too. I could make some reservations for us if you would like to go."

They spent some time talking about a possible trip and where they might stop. Finally, they came to the unsurprising conclusion that they would all love to go. It was left up to Roland to make all the reservations and set up their itinerary.

Before they settled in for the night, he said, "Why don't we get breakfast in town tomorrow. We don't have to get out on the water at first light, so we will have plenty of time. There's no sense in someone getting up too early."

He didn't get any argument.

They were heading out of the harbor the next morning at eight thirty, and Marcy had the helm. Roland was acting as the first mate, but there was little for him to do in the cockpit. So once they cleared the harbor, he put on his guide's hat and went back to ready the rods for the day's fishing. It didn't take very long, and soon he was back beside her.

"We are going to fish the same area we did last week, but if that's slow, we will head for the southern end of the island. For now, just follow the course on the plotter. I put in yesterday's location, and it will take you right where we have to go."

When they got to where they wanted to fish, she brought the boat down to a crawl, and he went back to help Amanda put the lines in.

Jim said, "You know, Roland, I think Amanda and I could do that."

"Give it a shot then. I'll just stand back and watch. In fact, I think I'll catch a few fish myself today, and one of you can run the boat while I do."

"Do you want the first crack at it?" Amanda asked.

"Why not? I have a long way to go to catch up with the rest of you."

The lines were not even all out when she said, "You might want to grab that rod, Roland. There's a fish waiting to be caught."

He hadn't seen the rod pop. He had been looking at Marcy piloting the boat instead of at the rods, but he picked it up and checked the hook set.

"He's on there, feels like a good one too. We've got one back here, Marcy. Just keep the boat on the same heading while I play him."

She turned around and looked at him and the bending rod. "All right! That was quick. I'm not seeing much on the fish finder, but there must be some here."

Jim netted his fish a short time later and dropped him out on the deck.

"That is a really nice fish," said Amanda, "looks like I've got my work cut out for me."

Forty minutes later, they were still looking for their second fish.

"That's enough," said Roland. "There isn't any bait here, and not any salmon either from the looks of things. We are going to run south for a ways, and then we will do some prospecting. Pull them in, Amanda, we are going to go and see if we can find some fish."

"I'll second that move. I was beginning to think we were going to troll here forever. Jim, you reel in the two flat lines, and I'll get the ones on the downriggers."

Soon they were on their way.

Later, after having found a good school of salmon, they were on their way back with four nice cohos in the box.

Roland suggested, "I think one of those fish will make a great dinner tomorrow after church, and I plan to have one smoked. Why don't you take one, Amanda, and Jim can take the other."

"That sounds good to me," she said. "I'm going to freeze mine whole, and the next time you are all going to be up, I'll have a salmon chowder ready that will knock your socks off."

He said, "She's not kidding about that. Amanda makes a chowder that is out-of-this-world fantastic. I like salmon a lot of different ways, but her chowder is one of my favorites."

That afternoon, they had pizza in the backyard and relaxed.

"So, Jim, you liked the lot where I am going to build?"

"Yes, very much. Do have any idea when you might build?"

"I haven't told anyone, but yes, I've got a builder coming this week to put in the footers. They have the blueprints, and the lumber is already on order and should be arriving around the end of the week. I'm going to take Marcy over for another look at it a little later today."

Marcy was surprised to hear about the building project, but now she wanted to see the place again even more. She could almost see herself living there, but there had been nothing to indicate she might be in his plans, even though she wished she were.

"When do you think it will be done?" she asked.

"It should be finished and ready to move into in less than two months."

She had several more questions she would have liked to ask but didn't. She wondered if he was planning on moving or just staying on the island at times. Would he run the business from up here, and where would she work? The fact that he was building his dream house should have made her happy for him, but it filled her with foreboding. Would this affect her and the job she had just started? It didn't make sense that he would hire her and then put her in jeopardy. It was disconcerting.

Leaving Jim and Amanda at the house late that afternoon to visit the site, Marcy and Roland strolled around on the gravel circular driveway. There were two white birch trees growing close together outside it.

"You aren't going to take down those white birch trees, are you?" she asked.

"No, they stay. Do you like them?"

'They are very attractive. As long as you don't build too close to them, they should add to the charm of the property."

"I wouldn't take them out. Betty planted them as saplings. There were originally four of them. When she planted them, she said there was one for each of us. Now there are only two. It's rather ironic, isn't it?"

"I'm sorry, Roland, I didn't want to call up sad memories."

"No, that's okay. The memories aren't sad, although they are bittersweet. I still feel the loss of Betty and Melissa, but my memories of them are a treasure for me. I can't live in the past, and I don't, but those memories live in me. Probably, they always will."

She wanted to change the subject. "Tell me about the house. What is it going to be like?"

"Two stories, with a three-car garage. There will be a sliding door in the master bedroom opening onto a good-sized balcony. There will be a kitchen, three baths—two upstairs and one down—a living room with a fireplace, a painting room, an office, a large den big enough for my decoys, three bedrooms, walk-in closets, a laundry room, and a large deck."

"Not exactly a cottage. How will it be oriented on the lot? Will the front face the ocean or the east?"

"I wrestled with that, but the front of the house is what you will see driving in, and the driveway will be paved for the whole length. There will be an ample paved parking area in front. The birch trees will be off to the right. The rear of the house faces the ocean, so in the evening, I can walk out of the bedroom and watch the sun set."

"It sounds delightful."

He was pleased that she liked it. "I think it's going to be. They will have earth-moving equipment in here on Monday. The footers will be poured before the lumber arrives, and they will be putting in the septic system too. I'm going to leave the paving until after the heavy trucks are gone. The gravel is good enough for now.

"The builder asked about water and if I needed a drilling permit, but that's not going to be a problem. I had a well drilled years ago, and it is still just fine, but all the same, I'm having them put in a water collection system to save rain water from the roof. I'm not worried about cost, but water is a precious commodity in Washington, especially on the island, and it doesn't hurt to have a supply for the garden that doesn't come from the aquifer."

"A garden? Sounds like you have thought of everything."

"I hope so, but there will probably still be some things that come up before it's all done."

"I suppose that could well be. Say, do you think we can stay long enough to sit in the car and watch the sun go down again?" she asked. "It won't be too long."

"I'd love to," he said. "But it's pretty warm. We don't have to sit in the car, there's a bench under the white birches. It's been a long time since I sat on it with anyone else. Would you like to try it?"

So before heading back to Oak Harbor, they sat quietly together in his special spot, waiting to bid adieu to the sun. She had no idea just what he was thinking right then, but she realized she was having thoughts about him she should not have. How she wanted to throw herself in his arms and tell him how she felt.

Later, when they walked into the house, Amanda winked at Marcy and said, "You were gone so long we were wondering if there was more going on than just checking out the property."

She was just kidding, of course, but to Marcy, it was like she was fully aware of what she had been thinking. As she felt heat suddenly warming her body, she was glad only Amanda could see her face because she knew she must be blushing.

"Mother," Roland said from behind her, "we were just sitting on my bench, watching the sun go down before we left."

"I know, I know," she said, but she wondered why Marcy had seemed so flustered by her remark.

She hadn't known her very long or spent a lot of time with her, but everything seemed to point in just one direction, and if she was right, she would be very pleased.

27

THE LADY IN THE RED BMW

The following week, Marcy spent most of her time continuing to familiarize herself with the files. Most were just informational, requiring no work, but he wanted her to look through them just the same. Even though the files were in order, they were each in either a green folder, yellow folder, or a red folder—depending on what was happening with them at the time.

Green folders required no attention at all. The enterprises they contained were on an even keel, doing just fine. The yellow were ones that were doing well but still required some monitoring or help. The red ones contained either new enterprises or older ones that were struggling and needed attention. They were the files they worked on most often.

All the information was also in their computers, but he liked printouts for the paper files, a holdover from earlier days. She actual liked working with the folders. It was easier on the eyes than staring into a computer screen all day.

It had not taken her long to become comfortable in her new job, and she and Roland had begun taking part of each day to work together, zeroing in on specific red-file enterprises. She listened to him, and then she shared her thoughts. She could see that he was quickly processing what she was saying.

While she was on her own, she had worked her way through the first two file cabinets, looking at just the red folders before she went to the US files. That was a whole new ball of wax. There were only a few folders in the top drawer and a larger number in the second drawer. All the folders were fatter than most of the ones in the other two cabinets. The top drawer contained information about companies he was currently involved with. The second drawer contained information about completed jobs.

On Thursday morning of her second week, she let herself in and went to the office. He was not at his desk yet, which happened once in a while, but she took a red folder off his desk and checked the name. Opening up the file on her computer, she made herself a quick cup of coffee and settled down in front of the screen. She was just nicely getting into it when he came in.

"Hi, Marcy, I see you are right on the job, early as usual. There will be a Ms. Carol Whitley coming to see me this afternoon. She isn't on your calendar, so just write her in. When she gets here, bring her in and call me if I don't happen to be in the office. I don't have time for coffee right now. I have a couple of things to attend to this morning, but I should be back by eleven or so. While I'm gone, pull out the Burstein file and take a look at it. We'll talk about it when I get back."

Checking the files, she didn't find the folder he asked for. She took the one she had been working on back over to his desk and checked the other folders there and found the one he had wanted to discuss. She closed the file cabinet and started reading the material in the folder.

She had discovered as the days went by that he had meant what he said about wanting her point of view and her input on his work, and she was pleased that she had been able to justify the confidence he had placed in her. She enjoyed working side by side with him.

Every morning she looked forward to getting to the office and having a cup of coffee with him before she dug into her paperwork. Morning coffee was a time to discuss the strategy for the day, as well as other things that had no connection with work. It had quickly become the favorite part of her day. She was a little disappointed that he had to leave so early this morning.

Sometimes as she was working, she would look up and find him looking at her, smiling, before he went back to what he had been doing. It didn't bother her or seem strange because she found herself guilty of the same thing at times.

I could look at him forever, she thought.

She was amazed at how quickly they had developed a real working relationship. The ease with which that developed indicated to her that there was a high degree of compatibility between them, and it only increased her admiration of him. Leaving her in charge while he left the house was just another indication of a growing trust.

She was thinking on those things as she dove into the Burstein file.

He didn't arrive back in the office until just before noon.

"I'm sorry, I'm late, it took me a little longer than I thought it would. Why don't you go ahead and get your lunch, and we will talk about Burstein after. You know, it's a beautiful day, why don't you take your lunch outside, and I'll join you in a few minutes."

Boy, this beats working in Seattle by a long shot, she thought.

Since she had started working for him, they had eaten lunch on the deck together several times and gone out to a restaurant a couple of times. He never mentioned work while they were eating.

No business lunch here, she thought. *I'm good with that.*

This day was a little different.

When he sat down with her for lunch, he said, "I've been thinking about your grandfather. It's been awhile since Jim said he would be willing to work part-time for me, and I haven't done anything about that yet. Has he asked you about it?

"Well, he has been wondering what you were going to want him to do, but he has been busy at home, so it isn't like he had nothing to do."

"I'm going to have him come in with you next Tuesday morning, and we will talk about some things he might be interested in doing. I shared a few ideas with him while we are fishing to give him time to think about them before he comes in."

"I'm sure he will be pleased."

After they had finished their lunch, she went back to the office. He came in a few minutes later, and she said, "I have the Burstein file here, but I've also got it up on my screen," she handed him the folder.

"Great. What did you think?"

"Well, I'm not through reading the information yet. Mostly, what I've gotten through is information about the company and their products and the financials. I'm not sure what they want you to do, but so far, it looks interesting."

Handing it back, he said, "Okay, finish reading, and we will talk about it. I haven't actually agreed to work with them yet. I'm just considering it, just so you know."

While she continued reading, someone came to the door. She checked to see who it was. It was an attractive woman she didn't recognize.

"Can I help you?" she asked over the intercom.

"Yes, my name is Carol, I have an appointment to see Roland."

"I'll let you right in."

Getting up, he said, "Wait, Marcy, don't buzz her in, I'll go and let her in personally."

A few minutes later, he walked into the office with his visitor.

"Carol, this is my new administrative assistant, Marcy Williamson. Marcy, this is Carol Whitley. We have some things to discuss, and while she is here, I am going to show her around the house. I'm not going to have time to discuss that project today, so why don't you take the file home with you and take your time looking through it. You won't need to come in tomorrow. I'm going to be away, but we'll get our heads together on Monday, and I'll fill you in on what they want from us."

And with that, he and Ms. Whitley were on their way out of the office.

She wondered why he was showing the woman around the house, but it wasn't any of her concern, and she had the rest of the week off other than finishing the file. Everything she needed was in it. As she was leaving the house, she could hear Roland and the woman talking somewhere. When she closed the door, she wondered again what they might be doing. Driving out, she noticed a new red BMW.

Impressive, she thought, *must be hers.*

She was still wondering about the woman in the red BMW when she went to sleep that night.

Before breakfast Friday morning, she continued looking through the file she had brought home the day before. And after another of her grandfather's scrumptious breakfasts, she was in the process of finishing up.

Her grandfather looked in on her and said, "I'm going to the farmers' market, do you want to go?"

"No, you go ahead without me."

After he had left, she poured another cup of coffee.

I should have gone with him, she thought as she sat on the deck. Finally, she got up and went out to her car with the file.

I'll just stop over and leave this and pick up a couple more, I can't just sit around, she thought as she left for the office at his home.

As she started up his driveway, she came to a quick stop. There, ahead of her, was the red BMW she had seen the day before. She must be there again. Didn't he say he was going to be away?

Marcy paused and then pulled back out of the driveway. She didn't want to disturb them. Perhaps his visitor was the reason he told her she didn't have to come in today. Maybe he will be going somewhere with her.

When she arrived back home, she checked her e-mail again. Still no response from her mother. She wondered if she had read her message yet. She vainly checked several more times that morning.

Her grandfather still wasn't back by noon, so she decided to go out for lunch, and she headed for one of Roland's favorite spots that she especially liked as well.

When she got to the restaurant, she saw his car out front. A warm feeling was creeping into her body even as she entered the restaurant, but just after coming through the door, she saw them. Roland's back was to her, and Ms. Whitley was not looking her way, but there they were.

I should have known, she thought.

She ducked back out the door, wondering if she should go in and say hello or leave and say nothing. Not knowing what was going on, the latter seemed to be the best course. She was disappointed, not because she would have to find another place to have lunch, but because it was another woman having lunch with him instead of her.

Who was she? Was she a new client? It didn't seem likely because he would almost certainly have told her. Maybe she is one of the people who will be part of the foundation or are supporting it. That was probably it. It was a bit confusing, but once more, she decided if it was any of her business, he would tell her. However, she had lost interest in lunch.

Back home she had time to think a little more about the woman. She looked to be about forty-five, maybe a little younger. She was attractive, to say the least, and she certainly had kept her figure in good shape. She had a nice smile, and she looked sharp. It was hard to believe that her clothes could possibly have come off the rack. Maybe she did have something to do with the foundation Roland was setting up. Maybe she was someone from the government. She gave up trying to figure it out, knowing that he would tell her when she needed to know.

Her grandfather came in with a couple of bags. "The vegetables were great today. Come and see what I've got."

She went to check them out. "You were gone a long time today," she said as she went through the bags. "What took you so long?"

"Oh, I just got to talking with some of the vendors, and before I knew it, it was time for lunch. You should have come with me. I had a great pulled pork sandwich."

"You are right. I should have gone with you. My day has been sort of a bust, and I haven't had any lunch. I was just thinking about a tuna fish sandwich."

"I'll make one right up for you. Tomato and lettuce?"

"Sounds perfect. Then I'm going to curl up in the easy chair and watch a movie."

She couldn't really enjoy the movie because her mind kept going back to Roland and the woman with the red BMW. The more she tried not to think about them, the more she thought about them.

Her grandfather came into the living room and sat down.

"I'm looking forward to getting together with Roland next week. He said he had some things for me to do that would have me up on Whidbey every once in a while. I think it might have something to do with the house he's building."

"That's a lot of driving."

"Yep, but I don't mind it, and he said he would pay me for my mileage. Besides, I'll get to see Amanda more often."

"Well, we will all know next Tuesday. Maybe he will even have more information for you Sunday."

Sunday took forever to come, but when they got to church, Roland wasn't there, and he didn't show up. He had not said anything about being away. It wasn't like him.

"I don't know what happened to him, Grandpa. He didn't tell me he wasn't going to be here. Maybe that woman had something to do with it."

"What woman is that?" he asked.

"It's all kind of crazy. There was a woman who came to the office Thursday afternoon. Her name is Carol. I have no idea who she is other than her name, but Roland gave me the rest of the day off when she came and told me he was going to be away Friday, and I didn't have to come in. I went over to the office Friday morning to return a file I had brought home, and I thought I'd pick up a couple more to work with. When I got there, her car was in the driveway, so I came back home. Then later, I went out for lunch, and guess who was in the restaurant, Carol and Roland. They didn't see me, and I came home. It would have been better if I had gone to the market with you."

"So maybe he has a new client, who happens to be a woman. What's the big deal with that?"

"Well, he showed her through his home, and he had lunch with her the next day when he said he would be away. She's beautiful, and I hate to admit it, but I feel threatened by her. What if she has designs on him?"

"I think you might be overreacting. Better wait and see what she is there for. If it's business, you will know soon enough."

She tried to convince herself that he might be right, but she had a bad feeling about the woman. She was just too perfect. When she went to bed, she spent a long time asking the Lord to get that woman away from Roland and that he might come to love her instead.

Monday morning, as Marcy was arriving, she saw a candy apple–red vehicle disappearing around the corner beyond Roland's home. She started to pull into the driveway before changing her mind and pulling back out on the highway. A car horn jarred her, and she slammed on her brakes just in time to avoid a collision. Checking to be sure the way was clear, she drove away to the corner where she had seen the red car, but it had disappeared, and she made a U-turn and drove back to Roland's.

In spite of the near miss at the end of the driveway, she was in the office before nine, and he came in a few minutes later.

"Coffee?" he asked.

She nodded, and he made two cups for them. She came over, put cream and sugar into her cup, and sampled it.

He picked up his cup when it finished filling and said, "Let's go out on the deck, I've got something I want to talk to you about."

She was apprehensive, and when they were settled on the deck, he looked uncertain and reluctant to begin, so she asked, "Okay, what's up?"

"Marcy, I don't know any other way to tell you this. I called your mother last night and had a long talk with her. I told her I was withdrawing my proposal. I wanted to tell you myself before you heard it from someone else, especially from her. I hope you are not too disappointed or angry with me."

"I'm not disappointed, and I don't blame you. I didn't think you would wait forever. How did she take it?"

"She said she understood, and she apologized for keeping me hanging. She felt it was probably for the best. That pretty much confirmed what I'd been thinking."

Marcy asked, "How do you feel now, if you don't mind my asking?"

"I don't mind. You know, for a while I was hoping she would call and say she would marry me, but before too long, I actually started dreading that because I was no longer sure that's what I wanted. I was miserable. Now I feel free, and not only that, but I think I've found the right woman for me."

She felt like she had been kicked in the stomach, and she wanted to ask who that might be but thought better of it because it had already dawned on her. Carol, Carol Whitley! Of course! She seemed to have dropped in out of the blue. She was young, but not too young, beautiful, obviously well off, and she certainly had been spending a lot of time with him recently even though it didn't appear she was a client. That was probably her car that must have left from Roland's driveway. And he had dropped her mother. It had to be her! What other explanation could there be?

She was crushed. The world she had begun to hope for, even dared to tenuously imagine, was collapsing. She had started to believe, after talking with her grandfather, that it wasn't such an impossible dream that he would notice her, that he might return her love, but now there was Carol.

She was at a loss for words, but she was thinking, *Why couldn't it have been me? It isn't fair. Why did he show me his lot? Why did he invite me to sit on his special bench with him? Was he just leading me on?*

Then she had another horrible thought, *Maybe he thinks of me as his daughter. Maybe he is just treating me as his little girl.*

He was watching her with concern. She did not appear to be taking it well, and he felt bad about that.

She asked, "How long have you known Carol?"

"Carol?" he said. "About five or six years. Why?"

"I was just curious, I thought I saw her car leaving here this morning," she said, but she was thinking spitefully, *So now you are free to take up with her. Why didn't you do that before you met Mother? Why not before you met me?*

He said, "You could have, she was here earlier."

She said nothing. She had been right. It had been her car, and she couldn't help wondering, was she just there in the morning, or had she been there all night? Scenarios began to play themselves out. They were all ugly.

Observing the tortured look on her face, he said, "I can see the news about your mother and me has upset you, and I'm sorry. I just wanted to clear the air before someone else told you, not to hurt you, but I guess it is what it is. It's done. Now, as much as it may have hurt, we all need to put that behind us and move on. Let's go back into the office. I would like to go over some things with you on the progress of the foundation, and then we will discuss the Burstein file."

The morning did not go well. As much as she tried to concentrate on the foundation and the people who would very likely become part of it, she found her mind wandering and constantly slipping back to all the things that had happened in the past couple of months, to Carol, and to her own feelings about Roland. She found herself becoming more and more frustrated with moments of anger. It was a losing battle.

"Roland, I'm not feeling well. I'm sorry, but I'm going to have to go home. Can we work on this tomorrow?"

He was beginning to feel as bad as she seemed to.

"I can understand how you must feel. We can get back into the work on the foundation tomorrow, no problem, and Burstein can wait. I hope you feel better, but when you get home, would you please remind your grandfather to come in about ten tomorrow morning. I want to get him started on some things."

"I'll tell him. Now, I'm sorry, but I have to go."

He watched her leave. He hadn't expected quite such an emotional effect on her from his actions. But telling her about his decision had turned out to be harder than telling her mother had been. Now it was his turn to feel blue. Marcy was the last person in the world he had wanted to hurt. He tried to work but found he was not up to it any more than she had been. He went to his den to consult with his wooden friends, but even they failed to overcome the deepening gloom.

Finally, he turned to the only person he knew that might have some insight and advice, Amanda. He called her, even though he didn't know exactly what he wanted to say.

"Hello, Mother. How are you this afternoon?"

"I'm fine. What's up? Are we going fishing?"

"No, nothing like that. It's something more complicated. I want your advice, or at least, I need someone to listen."

"What is it? I can listen, but I don't know what I could possibly give you advice on?"

"You asked me what was happening with Sherry the last time we were out, and I didn't give you much of an answer. I don't know why you asked, but I have been thinking about it since then, and Sunday evening I called her and told her I was withdrawing my proposal."

"Why did you do that?"

"Well, even though at first I thought I was in love with her, I realized I wasn't and that it wouldn't have worked out anyway. She is too much in love with her business. She turned down my proposal because even though she wanted me, she wanted Robyn's World more. There didn't seem to be any real room for me. That's the main reason I backed out."

"Then you aren't in love with her? You don't want to marry her?"

"No, I don't."

"No matter what?"

"Yes, no matter what."

"What did she say? Was she upset? Is that why you are calling?"

"No, she wasn't upset. She said she understood, and basically, she told me she was okay with it. We had a good talk, but that is the gist of it all."

"I see. Have you told Marcy?"

"Yes, I told her today, and I don't think she took it very well. That's why I'm calling."

"But you really had to do that. It was best that it came firsthand from you."

"I know that. That's why I told her. At first she seemed to understand, but then she became ill and had to leave the office. She went home."

"I'm sorry to hear that, but I'm sure she will get over it."

"I know you are right. She will get over it in time, but it sure has put a crimp in our relationship for now."

"What relationship are you talking about? With your business? With her family?"

"I mean, our relationship as friends. The relationship between all of us—you, Jim, Marcy, and myself, and her mother, I guess. I don't want Marcy upset with me."

"So what do you want from me?

"I don't really know. I guess I just needed to hear a friendly voice and have someone I could share my problem with."

"Son," she said, "you asked for advice, and I think I can give you some, or at least, I can tell you something you should know."

"Go ahead."

"Marcy isn't going to be on the outs with you for very long. Haven't you realized yet that she is in love with you? I don't think your breakup with her mother is the problem. It has to be something else."

He was stunned. "You say she's in love with me? Why would you say that? I haven't done anything to encourage her."

"I'm saying it because of the way she looks at you and the way she speaks to you, the way she talks to me about you. Everything fairly shouts that she is in love with you. I think I can recognize the signs even as old as I am. And if that isn't enough, Jim told me she is. And I'm pretty sure that just being who you are and how you act has encouraged her, whether you meant anything by it or not."

"Amanda, stop and think about what you are saying. There is about twenty years difference in our ages. I think she probably sees me more as a father figure, that's what she must be in love with."

"I don't think so, but tell me something, are you in love with Marcy?"

He had a strange feeling, like he was being boxed into a corner. He thought for a minute, but he couldn't bring himself to admit his feelings.

He replied, "I like her very much."

"That's not what I asked you. Do you just like her, or do you love her?"

Again he took a moment to think. Could it really be true about Marcy? Was he wrong to feel the way he did? His heart was thumping as he answered, "Yes, I do love her. I love her so much I can hardly stand it. Whenever I am near her, I want to be closer. I want to hold her. I would love to be her husband, but I don't know if it could work. I'm just too old. She should have someone young like herself, and then what about Sherry?"

"Son, you need to give love a chance instead of looking for reasons why you shouldn't. What about Sherry? It seems to me she passed up her chance to have you."

"But she's Marcy's mother. What is she going to think about me if I ask Marcy to marry me?"

"What does it matter what she thinks?"

"What would her grandfather think of me?"

"I think he would be elated. He thinks the world of you."

"What about you, Mother, how would you feel about it?"

"I would be so happy for you. I know the years have been tough for you since Betty died, but it's time you moved on with your life. I think my daughter would agree."

"Do you know what's really strange? Now that I've talked with you, I am starting to be afraid that if I did tell her I love her or ask her to marry me, she might turn me down. Maybe she would even walk out of my life. And I don't even know how to ask her."

"Son, it's not as hard as you are trying to make it. You will find the right way. I'll be praying for you, both of you."

"Thanks, I feel better, I think. I'll consider everything you've said. Thank you so much. I love you. Bye."

After his phone call, he was actually feeling better. He certainly had plenty to think about. That night he was looking forward to the next day when he went to bed, but in the morning, he was badgered by indecision and doubt, and it lasted until Marcy came in. Then it got worse.

"Good morning, Roland, I'm ready to get started on the foundation, and Grandfather will be here at ten," she said matter-of-factly, without smiling as she walked into the office, sat down at her desk, and opened her computer.

He made himself a cup of coffee and asked, "Are you having coffee this morning?"

He received a curt, "No, thank you."

He was at a loss where to go from there. She certainly didn't sound very loving in spite of what Amanda had told him.

"Would you like to go out on the deck and talk?"

"Not really, I think we should get started on the Burstein project."

Taking his coffee to his desk, he opened his computer, wishing they could sit on the deck and talk instead.

"Let's catch up on the foundation first and then Burstein. I don't think that is going anywhere anyway."

They spent the first hour completing paperwork for the IRS and discussing aspects of what he wanted to accomplish. She was careful not to let her feelings interfere with the essence of their work, but he was acutely aware her answers and comments came bare-bones without her usual demeanor. The passion she had already developed for the work in just a few weeks seemed missing, and it created a soulless atmosphere.

Jim arrived exactly at ten, and Roland was relieved to see him.

"Come in, would you like a cup of coffee?"

"Sure. I can always use another cup of coffee. Amanda says I should own stock in a coffee business."

"It's a beautiful day outside," Roland said. "Let's take our coffee out on the deck and talk about what I'd like you to do for me."

Turning to Marcy, he said, "Why don't I get you get a cup of coffee, and you can join us. This concerns you as well since it will take Jim away from your home at times, and I'd like you to know what I'm asking of him."

She had been hoping he would ask and give her a reason for sitting in on their discussion. It would be awkward not to do as he was asking, so it wasn't like she was indicating she was okay with anything else.

"You go ahead, I'll get my own coffee, and I'll be right out," she said.

When she joined them, they were talking about Africa.

"Marcy, I was just telling your grandfather that it won't be too long before we will need to schedule our semiannual trip to Africa. You will be going, and I want him to come with us. There will be plenty of details that he can help us with. It won't be an onerous task, but it will make things a lot easier for us, letting us pay more attention to business."

"I'm not sure you really want to drag me along. Maybe it would be better for me to stay here and work," she replied.

Without thinking, he said, "Wait a minute. I hired you to work for me and with me. Part of the job is to accompany me when I am out in the field. I told you we would be traveling when I hired you. I thought you understood that when you took the job."

She was surprised at his sharp response and not at all sure that she liked it, but he was right.

"I was only trying to say that you don't have to take me if you don't want to. Of course, I'll go if that's what you want. After all, you are the boss."

Boss. He didn't like that term.

"It's not what I want from you, it's what I need from you. You are a very valuable asset here, and you will be even more so in Africa. I hope we don't have a problem with that."

Jim watched and listened in amazement. He wondered what in the world was going on. This wasn't what he had imagined it was like for her working for Roland.

"No, I don't have a problem with that," she said, but she was thinking, *So now I'm an asset. Maybe everything he has said and done is more about protecting an asset than being an indication he might care for me.* The thought did nothing to raise her spirits.

Jim broke the spell, "Maybe I should come back later. I can come back this afternoon."

"No, you're fine. For right now, what I'd like you to do for me is act sort of like a clerk of the works for the house I'm building. I have full confidence in the builders, but it doesn't hurt to have an overseer, and it will keep them on their toes. They are working on the inside now, so try to stay out of their way, but make sure they know you are around. I know the owners of the company, but I don't know the men who work for them."

"I can do that. It sounds like an easy job."

"It should be. I'd like you to run up this afternoon and introduce yourself to the workers. Tell them you work for me and that you will be there often. They already know someone is coming. Ms. Whitley was up there yesterday to look at the progress, and I asked her to let them know."

Marcy winced as she heard that.

"Take as much time as you need to for lunch," he said, "and if you want to run up to Oak Harbor for lunch, that's okay too. You know how to get to the site, right?"

"Yes, I won't have any problem with that."

"Fine, when you are finished with your coffee, you can get whatever you need and head on up if you are okay with starting today."

"Yes, I'll probably have a late lunch with Amanda and then go to the site. I'll let her know I'm coming and take her with me if she wants to go. Is that okay?"

"That will be just fine. Why don't you call me this evening and let me know how it went."

"I'll do that. I'm done with my coffee, so I'll get right on it. See you later, Marcy," he said as he left.

The rest of the day was painful, but they accomplished quite a bit while she was very focused on what had to be done, trying to shut everything else out. He wanted in the worst way to ask her what was wrong but continued to believe it was his breakup with her mother that was the cause.

Wednesday was a little better. She avoided their early morning time and conversation on the deck. She didn't want to talk. Marcy was still stewing, but throwing herself into the work was a good temporary antidote. There was no mention of Carol and no mention of the house he was building for her. That helped, but thoughts of her were seldom far from surfacing in her mind.

In the afternoon, they started to work on the itinerary for their trip to Africa. It was ambitious, but Roland assured her that they should not have any problems meeting the schedule. Much of the groundwork had already been done at the office, and the on-site visits would be of a more personal nature.

He told her, "I'll be counting on you to evaluate the people we talk to, plus hopefully, you can talk to other people in the communities and get a feel for what our prospective entrepreneur is really like underneath what we are able to see. I think you will be able to do really well at that. You see things other people might not."

By the end of the day, they had accomplished setting up the schedule for each visit with the only thing missing being the exact dates, because it hadn't been decided when the trip would actually start. That was a bit frustrating to Marcy, but he said there were several things that still needed to be put into place before they could make that decision.

When she was ready to leave, he told her, "Have Jim call me when he gets home tonight. I want to see how it is going for him, and work on his schedule. We will get back on the itinerary tomorrow morning."

On her way home, she thought about the job. She enjoyed what she was doing and was confident that she would like it even more as time went by. She told herself she was going to have to get used to the fact that he was only going to be her boss, nothing else. She had begun the difficult task (for her) of untangling the job from her personal feelings. When she got home, she didn't feel like eating. She didn't feel like doing anything. She turned on the news and kicked back, waiting for her grandfather to get home.

It was after eight when he came in. "Hi, welcome home. How did it go?"

"A piece of cake. That place is going to be a palace. They are putting premium-grade materials into it, and the guys building it are good. He doesn't need me up there, but I don't mind going."

"Well, speaking of that, he wants to talk with you. He wants you to call him."

"I can do that. Did you have anything for dinner?"

"No, I wasn't hungry."

"Would you like some pizza? I thought I would order one."

"I guess I would eat a piece or two."

"I'll order it, and then I'll call Roland."

When the pizza came, she was glad he had ordered it because she had begun to feel hungry and the pizza smelled so good.

When she and Jim sat down, she asked, "What did he have you call him for?"

"A couple of things. He wanted to get my impression of the job they were doing, and he told me I didn't have to go up tomorrow but plan on Friday. Is this a great job, or what? I'd do it for free, but I'm getting paid."

By the time Marcy got to work on Thursday, she had persuaded herself that she could at least be civil, but her feelings kept creeping into their conversation.

They had worked on the itinerary until ten o'clock when Roland said, "We will come back to this tomorrow. Let's take the afternoon off. I'm picking up a new car today, and I would like you to go with me," he said. "I am not trading this one in, and I'd like you to drive it back for me."

She sucked it up. "Well, hey, it's your time and your money, I get paid either way. But talking about pay, I have a question. Will I still have a job after you are married?"

He was aware of the sarcasm in her voice. It puzzled him.

"Certainly, I'll be needing you even more then." He smiled, "I may well give you a raise."

She didn't answer.

"Are you okay?" he asked. "You haven't seemed like yourself lately. Are you upset with the things I've been having Jim do? Is it too much for him?"

"No, he is doing fine," she said crisply, "and he likes being busy. Besides, when he goes up to the island, it gives him a chance to have lunch with Amanda. He enjoys what he is doing. He told me that he would be more than happy to do it all for free."

"Then what is bothering you? Are you still feeling bad because I told Sherry I was no longer interested in her? I hoped we had gotten past that, but you have seemed different ever since then, more quiet and distant."

"I don't hold that against you. I actually think it was the right thing for you to do. She wasn't being fair to you. I know I don't like it when people are not fair with me."

There it was again, that tone of resentment in her voice. What had he done?

"Well, I know that something is bothering you. Whatever it is, we can work it out. We can talk about it when you are ready. I don't intend to pressure you."

"It's nothing," she lied. "I'm just trying to figure out where I'm at and where I'm going. There have been so many changes. I guess they have all caught up with me at once."

"If you need time to deal with anything, you know you can have it. I won't mind. I'm very pleased with what we have been able to do in just a few weeks. Maybe I've been pushing you."

"No, I don't need any time off. I will be fine, everything will be fine. There is nothing to talk about. Can we just drop it, please?"

"I have upset you. I apologize. If you are willing to go, let's get out of here and pick up that car. Maybe I can make your day better."

It was a quiet drive to the dealership. Several times he wanted to say something, but he noticed she was always looking away from him out the window. When they got there, she let him go into the office by himself.

When he came back, he said, "They will have it right out here in just a few minutes."

When the new car pulled up alongside, he said, "Come on, get out and take a look at it with me."

"It's very nice," she said as they walked around the vehicle.

He opened the driver's side door.

"Why don't you try driving this a little ways. Tell me what you think."

"I don't want to drive your new car."

"It's not my car," he replied. "It's a company car, and you will most likely be driving it a lot more than I will. In fact, you can drive it back and forth to work on company gas. So do you want to try it?"

"Sure, I'll try it out if you want me to," again that tone of voice.

"I do. Let me get in the other side, and we will do a test run."

"Where do you want to go?" she asked.

"Drive up to Mukilteo, and we will take the ferry."

"Are we taking it up for Amanda to see?"

"Maybe, but I want to take a look at how the house is coming along. Jim has been keeping track of it for me, and he thinks they are doing a bang-up great job. They'd better be, that's what I'm paying for. I want everything just right."

"He's not up there today, is he?"

"No, he was at the site yesterday. I told him last night that he didn't have to go back up until Friday. The roof is done, and the outside walls are on. They have been working inside because they are waiting for a final decision on the siding, so we are going to take a look and make the choice."

"I don't think you need me for that. Why don't you ask Carol?"

"I already did that. She thought a light gray might be the way to go, and I was thinking just white, but I'd like to know what you think."

"Okay. I'll look at it. Grandfather has told me about it. He says he thinks it is going to be a beautiful place when it's done."

"I certainly hope so. Has he mentioned anything else?"

"Well, he said the material they were using was first class and the workers were quick but competent, not slapdash."

"Yes, he has told me that too. He took some pictures, but now I'd like to see it myself."

"He told me Ms. Whitley had been there Wednesday."

"That doesn't surprise me. She has a vested interest in it."

She bit her tongue. "I think I'd better pay attention to my driving. I don't want to be distracted thinking about something else and wreck your new car."

"Our new car," he corrected.

The drive the rest of the way to the ferry was a quiet one, and even though the August afternoon was sunny and hot, he could feel a chill that had nothing to do with the air-conditioning.

He spent the time rethinking his plans. Maybe this wasn't such a good idea. They could just turn around and go back. Another day might be better. Today it seemed like she would rather be at the office than on her way to Whidbey. That feeling of closeness and friendship was clearly missing. Could Amanda have been completely wrong about her?

It wasn't too late to change his plans, but when they arrived at the ferry, he had made up his mind to see it through and hope for the best, and when the ferry docked on Whidbey, he forced a smile and said, "I'll drive the rest of the way. You never know, I might use the car once in a while myself."

"Yes, I think you should—use it once in a while, I mean—plus I haven't learned the route to the house anyway."

"You will soon enough, I hope," he said.

She was miserable as she rode. Here she was alone with him, but it was obvious to her that there was no future for her other than being his administrative assistant. She wanted to tell him that he had picked the wrong woman and that she loved him, but she couldn't bring herself to do that.

It would have been easier if he had married Mother, she thought. *At least then I wouldn't have dreamed what life with him would be like. Grandfather had been wrong. Roland wasn't thinking of me. All this time he had his eye on someone else, and it hurts.*

There was no joy in going to see the new house, and she became more depressed when they left the highway and drove down the gravel lane. The whole world she had begun to dream about was crumbling. She wished she had not come.

But unexplainably, her heart jumped when she caught sight of the raw wood-covered structure. It looked magnificent even in its unfinished condition. And somehow—she didn't know how or why—her attitude began to change. She wanted Roland to be happy, and if this new house and Carol could do that for him, then so be it. It was selfish and foolish of her to be angry or upset over it. It still hurt, but she knew she could deal with it for his sake.

In the short time before they stepped out of the car in front of the building, she had completely let go of her anger.

"It is going to be lovely, Roland. It's going to be just like I imagined it would be."

He was struck by the change in the tone of her voice. "I'm glad you like it. Now what do you think about the siding? White or gray or something else?"

"I think you should go with what Ms. Whitley suggested, light gray."

"Okay, light gray it is. Walk around back with me."

At the rear of the house, he pointed to a double sliding door.

"Carol suggested a patio outside the door would be nice. It wasn't on the original plans, but we could do that or build a deck or a lanai. What do you think?"

"I like the idea of a lanai, but if Carol prefers a patio, you'd better go with it."

She was surprised how quickly she was getting adjusted to referring to her as Carol instead of Ms. Whitley.

"What do you think of the balcony off the master bedroom?"

"I think it is a great idea. It will be another wonderful spot to watch the sunset from or get some cool morning air when you get up."

"I agree," he said. "That was exactly what I was thinking. I only have the deck back at my place, but I like to use that. This will be even better, and I think the lanai is a good idea too. It's a good thing we decided on that now before they put the siding on."

As they finished their walk around the building and back to the car, he said, "I'm going to have Jim do the gardening here, putting in the shrubs and flowers. He will have professional help, of course, but he can oversee the job, just like the house. If you have any preferences on flowers, you can let him know."

Before they got into the car, she asked him, "Why are you so interested in what I think? You should have Carol here with you instead of me. Why don't you just go with what your future wife has to say?"

"Well, I'm trying to do that, but I haven't asked her to marry me yet."

"Why not, for heaven's sake?"

"To be completely honest, it's because I'm afraid she might turn me down."

"You have to be kidding me. Carol would never turn you down. Take my word for it."

"Carol? She's not the woman I want to marry. She and her brother own the construction company that is building my new home. Is that what's been bothering you? You thought I was involved with Carol?"

She was blindsided. "Yes, I'm sorry, but I had taken it for granted that she was the one. I have been so jealous, but it explains why you have been spending so much time with her. But if it is not her, then who is it? Do I know her? Have I met her?"

His heart had soared when she said she had been jealous, and he knew this was the time.

"Don't you know, Marcy? It's you I'm building this house for. I'd like to spend the rest of my life with you. I realize I'm a lot older than you, but I think we could make it work." He held out a ring. "Will you marry me and make me the happiest man in the whole world?"

Tears began running down her cheeks as she took the ring and said, "Yes. Oh, yes, I will. I never really believed this would happen even though I've been praying for it. I love you so much. Of course, I'll marry you."

There, in front of their new home, they shared their first hug and kiss, and all was right with Marcy's world once more.

Taking her hand, they walked to the bench, their bench now, and they began sharing their joy and their planning for the future.

Epilogue

It was late after he and Marcy had watched the sun set from the bench beneath the white birches as they discussed the future holding hands as she snuggled up against him, ignoring the heat. It was a delicious treat they had been denying each other. They drove to Oak Harbor and rang the bell at Amanda's.

When the door opened, she smiled at them and said, "Come on in. I didn't know you were both on the Island. Jim only said you were coming, Roland."

"I didn't tell him Marcy was coming with me," he said.

As they walked into the living room, she saw a sparkle coming from Marcy's hand. She was suddenly excited, but she said nothing about what she had noticed.

"We have something to tell you, Mother," he said. Marcy held out her hand, as he said, "Marcy has agreed to marry me, and you are the first person we have told."

"Congratulations. I am so happy for you both. My only question is, what took you so long? Jim and I have known you were falling in love for some time. It was so much fun watching it, but we were beginning to wonder if either of you were going to make a move."

"I don't know how long it would have taken if you hadn't helped me. I told Marcy what you had said, and she told me Jim had encouraged her as well."

"I can't get over it. My heart is just bursting for you two. When I watched you on the boat, I just knew you were made for each other. You are soul mates.

"I have a suggestion. If you don't have to be back in your office tomorrow, why don't you stay overnight—separate rooms, of course, nothing has changed there yet—and I'll call Jim and tell him you are here and ask him to come here in the morning instead of waiting until noon. The job can get by without him for a few hours. That way, you and Marcy can make the announcement to him in person. I won't tell him why I want him to come. What do you think?"

He looked at Marcy, and she nodded.

"We would love to stay. We won't be staying here much once the house is done, and we were talking about that this afternoon. We would like you to consider coming to live with us after we have moved in."

"Thank you for asking, but I'm not sure newlyweds would want a mother-in-law hanging around. We can discuss that later maybe after Jim gets here in the morning. I'll call him right now and let him know you are staying here tonight because it's so late, so he won't be worried. I won't say a thing about your engagement, so you can surprise him. Then we can all go over to the site after breakfast."

After she had called him, she came back into the living room.

"He will be here by nine. I asked him to bring up a fresh outfit for you, Marcy. We ladies like to stay fresh. Men always seem to be able to get by a second day when they have to."

"Thank you. I've been so excited I hadn't even thought of that. By the way, after we are married, what should I call you? Just Amanda? Would you mind if I called you Mother, like Roland does?"

"Either would be fine, and I would be honored if you decided to call me Mother."

Marcy had to tell her all about what she had been thinking and how she had been so jealous of Carol and upset with Roland until she learned she was not a rival but a contractor. She told her how he had proposed. She had to tell her all about what the house looked like and the big bedroom that was hers if she wanted it.

"I've been over a couple of times with Jim. I agree it is going to be beautiful. I can hardly wait to see it finished. So tell me, have you thought of a date?"

He said, "We talked about it, and we both agreed that we would like to get married sooner rather than later. We would like a traditional wedding, but we aren't interested in a huge one. There just aren't that many people we would invite. There are a few of her coworkers and her mother, and I have a handful of people I would like to have come. However, I am going to give an open invitation to our church family, so we might have as many as 250. Also, I am hoping Bryce might be able to get home for the occasion, but you never know."

"So that's a small wedding? Do you have an actual date in mind?"

"We are thinking about three weeks from this coming Saturday. I am going to see if the church is available for that date, and if it is, we will go from there. If not, we will take the first open Saturday or maybe go to a Sunday afternoon. I know I can find a caterer and a place for the reception without any problem. We might even be able to have it at the church."

"What are you going to do about a dress, Marcy?"

"I'm going to see if I can't get one right off the rack or have a seamstress adapt one for me."

"Okay, a September wedding would be wonderful, and you and I are going to sit down tomorrow afternoon and do some planning and get things lined up. He can check on the church tomorrow morning, and once we have that date confirmed, we can build everything else from there. And, Roland, don't expect this poor girl to be in for work for a few days. She will have her hands full. I'll come down and stay with you, and we will go shopping for a dress and flowers. I might want a new dress for myself."

"Who's going to give you away?"

"I was thinking I would ask grandfather to do that."

"Sounds good, but I think we should stop now and wait until tomorrow afternoon, and we will get all this on paper.

Amanda looked at the clock. "My goodness, this has been quite an evening. I don't know where the time has gone. What say we hit the hay. Tomorrow is going to be a big day."

When Marcy told Jim the news the next morning and showed him the ring, he was almost surprised.

He gave her a big hug and said, "I told you so, didn't I, baby? I told you so."

Turning to Roland, he shook his hand and said, "Congratulations. I suspect you already know you are getting one very special lady. You are one lucky man, and I'm so happy for both of you."

Roland thanked him and said, "No one is cooking this morning. We will catch breakfast on the way to the house. We want to show Amanda where she might be staying with us."

Jim glanced at Amanda with a quizzical look. She smiled back and winked.

Breakfast talk was filled mostly with replaying the day before and all that had led up to it. Jim and Amanda both said how much fun it had been to watch the two of them falling in love. The morning had been so enjoyable that they didn't arrive at the work site until close to noon.

Getting to the house when they did turned out to be good timing even though they hadn't planned it. The workers were all getting ready to quit for lunch, so they were able to go inside the building and look around. It was just a skeleton, and the pipes and wiring were all exposed but pretty much completed. The stairs were in, and the subflooring was in. Roland checked with the men, and they assured him it was safe to go upstairs, so they went up.

"This will be the master bedroom. The bathroom will be over there with a walk-in linen closet, and there will be a big walk in closet over there for our clothes," he explained.

Then walking to the far end, there were two other rooms. "One is a bedroom, and the other is an art room and gallery with plenty of light," he explained. "And the bedroom has a whole bath, and the art room, a half bath. Now let's go back downstairs."

On the first floor, they saw where the kitchen was going, and he told Marcy, "You will have a chance to go over the kitchen plans with Carol and make some decisions on appliances. I want you to have the kitchen you would like. And the two of you can decide on wall colors. Carol looked around my home and got an idea of what I like, but the only thing I really planned was my new den."

Moving to the north end, he said, "Amanda, this would be your room if you come to live with us. You would have your own bath, plenty of closet space, and the room is actually bigger than the master bedroom upstairs."

They walked out to where the lanai would be, and he explained that there would be a balcony opening from the master bedroom. After looking at everything, they walked back to the car.

"Well, Mother, what do you think?" he asked.

"I love it. It is going to be gorgeous. I appreciate that you are thinking of me, but honestly, I don't want to live in your house. I have grown used to my privacy, and I hate to give it up."

"Well, what if we built you a cottage right over there?" he said, pointing to an area beyond the white birches. You would be close by, but you could have your privacy as well."

"That might work. Let me walk over there for a minute. Jim, would you come with me please?"

They walked past the birches onto the area Roland had pointed to and then looked in every direction from there. They talked for a few minutes while he held her hand.

Suddenly, as Marcy watched them talking, she realized that in all the excitement and planning, she had completely forgotten about what her grandfather would do. He would be all alone in her house. Maybe he would like the room that Amanda was turning down, and he would be close to Amanda too. That might work out just fine.

When the two of them returned, she asked him, "Grandpa, would you like to live in this house with us?"

"Thanks for thinking of me, Marcy, but I can't do that."

"Why not? There's no sense in your living in Snoqualmie when there is plenty of room here, and we would love to have you."

"I can't because I would rather live with my wife in that cottage that Roland is talking about," he said, raising Amanda's hand to show off her engagement ring. "I asked her to marry me last week, and she accepted. I gave her a ring today. I had forgotten to get one before I asked her. If Roland is serious about building that cottage, we would be pleased to live there. We couldn't ask for better neighbors."

Three and a half weeks later, there was a lovely double wedding, and the four of them spent their honeymoons in Africa.

ABOUT THE AUTHOR

Leon Archer had a library science minor at SUNY–Albany. He worked thirty-two years as a high school librarian at G. Ray Bodley High School in Fulton, New York. He has written a weekly outdoor column for *The Valley News*, for thirty-one years, starting in 1985. He has also been published in a number of outdoor magazines. As a member of the New York State Outdoor Writers Association (NYSOWA), he has been named the winner of their prestigious Excellence in Craft Award six times. He has been a committed Christian, actively involved in his church since 1968. He presently lives in Fulton, New York, with Geraldine, his wife of fifty-five years.

CPSIA information can be obtained
at www.ICGtesting.com
Printed in the USA
LVOW11s1957290517
536192LV00001B/259/P